LOVE AT *Second* SIGHT

Also by F.T. Lukens

In Deeper Waters
So This Is Ever After
Spell Bound
Otherworldly

LOVE AT Second SIGHT

F.T. LUKENS

Margaret K. McElderry Books
New York   Amsterdam/Antwerp   London
Toronto   Sydney/Melbourne   New Delhi

MARGARET K. McELDERRY BOOKS

An imprint of Simon & Schuster Children's Publishing Division
1230 Avenue of the Americas, New York, New York 10020

Text © 2025 by F.T. Lukens
Jacket illustration © 2025 by Sam Schechter
Jacket design by Rebecca Syracuse

MARGARET K. McELDERRY BOOKS is a trademark of Simon & Schuster, LLC.
For information about special discounts for bulk purchases, please contact Simon &
Schuster Special Sales at 1-866-506-1949 or business@simonandschuster.com.
The Simon & Schuster Speakers Bureau can bring authors to your live event. For more
information or to book an event, contact the Simon & Schuster Speakers Bureau at
1-866-248-3049 or visit our website at www.simonspeakers.com.
Interior design by Rebecca Syracuse
The text for this book was set in Embury Text.
Manufactured in the United States of America
First Edition
2 4 6 8 10 9 7 5 3 1
CIP data for this book is available from the Library of Congress.
ISBN 9781665950947
ISBN 9781665950961 (ebook)

FOR MY FRIENDS

1

A RAVEN PERCHED ON MY WINDOWSILL, AND SHE WANTED to talk.

For most people, this might be an uncommon, and perhaps unsettling, occurrence. Especially since said raven hopped along the ledge of beveled wood, swiveling her head so she could peer into my room with her glossy black eyes. She rapped her beak against the windowpane, the tap-tap-tap an eerie sound in the otherwise still and gloomy dark hours of the morning.

However, given that my best friend was a witch, this wasn't uncommon or unsettling, merely really freaking annoying, especially since it was before six a.m.

"No," I said from my tangled nest of blankets and my soft pillow, eyes still heavy with sleep. "Go away. If Al wants to talk to me, they can use their perfectly good phone." I fished mine out from the sheets and held it up as an example, waving it lazily in the direction of the window to convey my drowsy displeasure.

The raven—named Lenore, since Al could never resist a fun allusion—glared at me and ruffled her midnight-blue feathers. She cawed in irritation and lifted her leg to show the small cylinder attached.

"No. I refuse." I rolled over and pulled the blankets over my head.

My phone screen glowed 5:49. Eleven whole minutes still existed before my alarm would sound. And I was determined to relish every last second before my day was scheduled to begin. I closed my eyes, tucked my hands beneath my chin, and steadfastly ignored the messenger on my windowsill.

Lenore tapped again, the sound sharp and aggressive.

I didn't move.

She cawed.

I didn't answer.

She struck her beak against the glass in short rapid-fire bursts, acting more like a woodpecker than a raven, taking her attention-seeking efforts up a level.

I refused to budge.

Lenore let loose a series of high-pitched, indignant squawks, because how dare I snub her. Well, she could continue rapping at my chamber door—er, window. I was an expert at avoidance.

I managed to slip back toward a blissful, dreamless sleep. But then she raked her talons across the glass. I cringed at the awful nails-on-a-chalkboard sound, and the hair on my arms stood on end. Clapping my hands over my ears, I curled into a tight ball. She made a cawing noise akin to a cackle, then did it again.

Any semblance of my resolve instantly shattered.

Before she decided that a third wince-inducing scratch was required, I sat up and dramatically threw off the blankets. "Ugh. Fine, you win, you demented bird. Keep it down."

Lenore quieted immediately. Her attempts to deliver her message in a timely manner had been loud enough to wake the dead, which meant she also could have potentially woken my parents, and I was certain they wouldn't appreciate being roused by a loud, irritating bird, much less a magic one.

"You're a menace," I whispered harshly as I stalked over to the window.

She didn't flinch when I pushed it open. She simply lifted her head and held out her leg as if she hadn't just been throwing a tantrum. Typical magical-bird behavior.

Removing the small piece of parchment from the tube attached to her leg was something I'd done a thousand times. Back when neither Al nor I had had phones to contact each other, back when we were younger and thought using a bird for messages was the epitome of magic, we'd send each other notes constantly. It was a miracle Lenore had survived the number of trips she had flown between our houses.

But then we grew up and the childhood wonder around magic dimmed for both of us, in different ways.

And, well, now we could text.

I grumbled a thank-you to Lenore and unrolled the missive.

Today we embark on our journey to fully embrace our future and our true selves. Are you ready? See you in an hour!

Ugh. I couldn't be too mad at that. I grabbed a pen from my desk, flipped the paper over, and wrote a note in return.

Ready. Let's do this. Text me next time, though. Your bird is a bully.

I added a heart at the end to soften my words. Al would appreciate that. And it would add to the sincerity since I wasn't all that enthusiastic about Al's plan of a themed sophomore year. They were adamant that we approach our new school year with a guiding purpose and a slogan, as if we were middle-aged suburban adults on New Year's Eve rather than teenagers embarking on yet another year of high school. My suggestion of the theme "unremarkable school year" was overruled despite my objection that it was unfair to allow Lenore to cast the deciding vote.

I rolled the paper and slid it into the cylinder on Lenore's leg. She bobbed her head, nipped lightly at my finger—as was her way of showing affection—then flew off.

Stretching my arms over my head, I yawned, then shut off my

alarm since I was up anyway. I padded to my dresser, where I had laid out my clothes the night before. My phone beeped with a text alert.

Did you get my message?

I shook my head, my honey-blond hair falling across my brow.

Yes. Why are you so dramatic?

The reply came quickly. One of us has to be.

Sure. But not at 6 in the morning.

Al's response was the thumbs-up emoji. I narrowed my eyes. That basically meant they had read my text and acknowledged it but would more than likely send Lenore even earlier tomorrow. Al had a passive-aggressive streak a mile long and could be petty with the best of them when they wanted. And now I would have to endure it every day.

A delighted thrill ran through my middle. Despite their antagonistic emoji usage, I couldn't help but be excited at the prospect of seeing Al at school.

Al and I had been best friends since first grade. We had been inseparable all through elementary school and the beginning of middle school. But when their mothers had relocated their house to be closer to their coven headquarters, Al was suddenly in a different school district. And they had been forced to change schools. We'd stayed friends, of course, though we were only able to see each other on weekends or over breaks, and only if my older brother, Aiden, was able to drive me.

We'd used Lenore to keep in touch until we were deemed old enough to have phones. But cute notes paled in comparison to hanging out with Al in person.

This year would be different, though. The school system had built and opened a new high school, and the district lines had been redrawn. We would be attending the same school for the first time since sixth grade. It was the miracle I hadn't known I needed.

Especially since Aiden was no longer around.

I scrolled through the messages on my phone and stopped when I found the last one I had sent him. It was undeliverable, presumably because he had changed his number or blocked mine. The text before that had been from him telling me to "follow my own path," whatever that meant. And to "trust myself," and that "everything would be okay." Those were dated from May. It was now August, and I hadn't heard from my older brother since.

The last time I had seen him was in January over his winter break from his second year at college. I wished I could go back in time. I'd prod him more about school, about his studies, about his life, about anything, and maybe I'd find out why he'd chosen to abandon our family. Abandon *me*. But I didn't have access to anyone who could change the past. And I had to live in the present.

My backup alarm went off, reminding me I needed to get a move on, or I would be late to my first day of sophomore year. I shucked off my pajamas and changed into the outfit I had specifically chosen for the day. A pair of jeans ripped at the knees and a concert tour T-shirt of the Hexes—Al's favorite all-witch rock band; we'd managed to score tickets to one of their shows over the summer.

I zipped to the bathroom, ignoring the closed door at the end of the hall that had been Aiden's. I scrubbed my face, my cheeks turning pink against my fair skin. I dabbed a little concealer over the pimple I had on my chin and the few that clustered just above my dark eyebrows. Then I styled my hair with a side part that exposed my forehead, just not the side with the zits. I added a leather bracelet on my left wrist and a thin silver necklace. And perfect. I wasn't normally this vain, but it was the first day of school, and I'd been the quiet, odd artistic kid last year. This year I wanted to blend.

I tilted my head to the side and squinted. I should've gotten my ears pierced like Al had suggested over the summer, but I hadn't wanted to push my parents' boundaries too far. Maybe another time.

Anyway, I couldn't keep Al waiting. I ran back to my room and grabbed my backpack, ensuring my sketchbook was safe inside along with all my other supplies. I'd picked up my schedule at orientation the other night, so I knew that Al and I had English Lit together, our first class of the day. Then we parted ways until lunch, where we had the same block. I slung my bag over my shoulder and breathed deeply, centering myself.

Now, to get past the parents who were hopefully asleep despite Lenore's earlier theatrics. I descended the stairs, my socked feet not making a sound on the carpet. Success! I only had to slip on my shoes and slide out the door.

"Cam!" My mother's voice rang out from the kitchen. "I hope you're not trying to leave for the first day of school without saying goodbye."

Damn. My plan had been foiled. My shoulders sagged. "No. I'll be right there."

I squeezed my eyes shut and steeled myself. *Okay. I've got this. I'm an unaffected king.* I gripped the straps of my backpack and walked down the hallway into the bright kitchen.

My mom sat at the kitchen table, a cup of coffee in her hands. She appeared impeccable and unapproachable, the same as she'd been my whole life. She must have been up for a while, if she was already dressed for the day. She'd probably been anticipating my attempt at an escape. Her makeup was on point, her hair immaculately styled, the same brown shade as my natural color, though highlighted with a few strands of gray.

I stood a few feet away and waited as her gaze roved from my feet up to my reddening face. Her eyebrows lifted at the holes in my jeans and went even higher at the shirt featuring the Hexes. The side of her mouth dipped into a slight frown as her stare reached my hair. She hadn't said anything when I originally dyed it, but I bet she'd assumed I'd color it back once my roots had started to show at the end of the summer. I hadn't. I had merely dyed it again.

"You're up early," I said, forcing a grin. "Was it Lenore? She was in rare form this morning."

She tapped her manicured nails against her coffee cup. "That's what you're wearing?" she asked, her tone even. Her disapproval was reflected in the purse of her lips.

I looked down at myself and tried not to fidget. "Yes?"

"Are you sure?"

My spirit sank, but I smiled through it. My second go-to coping mechanism was humor. I knew exactly which article of clothing created the problem—the T-shirt for a popular witch band—but I could be flippant. "Is it the bracelet? Or the necklace? Are they too much?"

She sighed into her coffee. "They're fine," she said simply, and left it at that.

"Okay. So I'm going to head out."

She hummed. "It's early still. Why don't you have breakfast before you leave?"

"Oh. I don't have time. Sorry."

"Really?" She made a show of craning her neck and looking at the clock. "Is there something that you need to do before school? Is that why you were in such a hurry that you weren't going to say goodbye?"

And that was the sticky part. My mom had never outright voiced her displeasure at the friendship I had with Al, but she had been visibly relieved when Al had changed schools. She hadn't said that while I was sobbing my eyes out about it when I was younger— she wasn't cruel—but she did try hard to guide me toward friend- ships with other kids. Other non-paranormal kids. Because while my mom and dad were well aware that there were witches, werewolves, faeries, sprites, and a whole host of supernatural entities living all around us, shopping at the same grocery stores and attending the same schools, that didn't mean they were stoked for me to be friends with them. We were only human, after all.

There had been a handful of paranormal kids in my classes in middle school and at the high school I'd attended the previous year, but I wasn't close to any of them. Or close to anyone, for that matter. I wasn't the most outgoing, and once best-friend-forever friendships weren't based on forced proximity but actual social acuity, I tended to melt into the background.

But when the new high school was built and the school lines redrawn, it wasn't lost on many parents that the majority of the known paranormal groups were in the boundaries for Central Shady Hallow High. Though my parents would never admit it, they weren't happy that our neighborhood was also included. I'd overheard them discussing a few different options like pulling me from public school, or moving to another neighborhood or, even more drastically, out of Shady Hallow altogether. In the end, they hadn't, but I knew better than to flaunt my friendship with a witch *or* my crush on a werewolf.

I cleared my throat. "I'm meeting Al. We're going to walk to school together."

The corners of her lips twitched downward. "Do you think that's a good idea?"

"Why wouldn't it be?"

"This is a new school with new opportunities. You should try to make other friends."

"I can make other friends and still be friends with Al."

My mom sipped her coffee and then placed the cup on the saucer with slightly more force than necessary. "And what happens when Al makes friends with other witches? Will you be invited along? Or will they leave you behind? It's already happened once before."

I clenched my jaw. "That was out of their control, and we stayed friends."

"They're a witch, Cam."

"Oh, and humans can't abandon people?"

My mom's frown deepened, as did the worry lines around her mouth and the creases in her forehead. She leveled an intense glare in my direction, and I had to look away, because that expression meant I was in trouble. Bringing up Aiden was a bad move on my part. I had to smooth this over, or else I would have to suffer through a few awkward family dinners until her anger faded.

I rocked back on my heels. "Al and I have one class together. I'll . . . try to talk to other students and make friends." Before she could push further, I added, "Human friends."

"Just make an effort. That's all I ask."

I shrugged. "I will."

"Good. Now, how are you getting to school?"

"I'm riding my bike to the corner, then meeting Al and walking from there."

She huffed. "I assume Al is taking their broom?"

I bristled but didn't rise to the bait. "I think one of their moms is driving them. Anyway, I have to go. If I don't leave now, I'm going to be late."

"Fine. Have a good day, Cam."

I left the kitchen and made a beeline for the exit. Once I was on the front stoop, I leaned against the door and allowed my head to rest against the thick wood. I closed my eyes and swallowed back my frustrated tears. Wow, this day was off to a great start. I had been woken up early by a belligerent fowl, and then my mom had basically unearthed one of my biggest fears and brought it right to the forefront of my mind.

I had wanted to retort that Al and I would be best friends forever. But she wasn't wrong: Al was a witch, and I was human. I couldn't tell the future, unless the occasional weirdly specific dream counted, but as Al's message had said this morning, I could still embrace it.

Possibly.

Or I could ignore it until it became an actual problem.

Either way, I still had to go, or I really was going to be late.

2

SHADY HALLOW WAS AN IDYLLIC TOWN. IT WASN'T A BIG CITY by any means—especially in comparison to New Amsterdam, our closest neighbor—but it wasn't small either, in area or population. That said, the council had made it a point for Shady Hallow to continue to exude the quintessential picturesque small-town atmosphere, with sidewalks in residential areas to increase walkability and trees planted in beds all over to provide shade and aesthetics. They employed sprites to keep the flora healthy and witches to spell the streets clean. There were bike and broom lanes on all the major thoroughfares, full-moon parks for werewolves, night shopping for vampires, and robust support for paranormal-owned small businesses.

I wasn't so naive as to think that Shady Hallow didn't have its problems. But on the surface it was seemingly perfect—a place that anyone would want to live in, human or otherwise. So it bothered me that my parents had even contemplated moving us from my childhood home over something as silly as a new school.

Other than being able to attend with Al, one of the best aspects of Central Shady Hallow High was that it was in biking distance, and it was a fairly easy route through a few neighborhoods to get there. Within fifteen minutes I was skidding my bike to a stop at the corner of Maple and Fourth, where Al was already waiting for me. They had their arms crossed over their chest and were tapping the toe of their chunky black boots against the concrete sidewalk, their backpack and two large iced coffees at their feet. They were annoyed, but even in their irritation they were strikingly gorgeous. Their beautiful brown skin gleamed with warm bronze undertones in the morning sun. Their curly black hair was braided close over one ear and tumbled down to their shoulder on the other side, the loose coils framing their angular face. A beauty mark sat underneath their full bottom lip, which was currently pushed into a frustrated pout. They somehow were intimidatingly stunning while also exuding a cottagecore witchy vibe that was comforting and cozy.

Well, most of the time.

Right then they were angry.

"Where have you been?" they said, dropping their arms. The sleeves of their flowy purple blouse fluttered in the slight breeze. "I've been waiting forever."

"Sorry," I muttered as I hopped off my bike. My shirt was stuck to my skin with sweat, especially the area beneath my backpack. My carefully styled hair hung limp across my forehead, and my fingers ached from where I had clutched the handlebars. "I biked as fast as I could."

"Ma dropped me off, like, fifteen minutes ago. Which, convincing her to drop me off here instead of at the actual school building was a feat in and of itself, but it was even more difficult when you weren't here yet." They pulled their phone from their pocket, and their fingers flew over the screen. "Okay. I've sent a text to tell her that you've finally arrived. You know, I've been waiting here on the street corner like some kind of illegal traveling potion-peddler." They threw up their hands in apparent frustration. "And it's so embarrassing since Ma had to drive me, while Amy used a teleportation charm to zap to the front door of her school. Mom went with her but didn't even have to bolster it. I can't even ride a broom."

I winced. Al's younger sister, Amy, was a superiorly gifted witch and was four years younger. Amy was capable of spells and charms and other witchery way beyond her age level, surpassing what Al was able to do. Despite Al being supportive of their sister, it was still a deep sore spot.

"And to make matters even worse," Al continued, "the Lopez brothers drove by and offered me a ride. And I said no, because I was waiting on your slow self. The Lopez brothers! The hottest werewolf trio in the entire school. No, in the entire *town*. And lowly sophomore me *turned them down*."

I snapped my head up from where I'd been studying the cracks in the pavement. The sun shone through the branches of a large tree nearby, dappling the ground in splotches of shade that did little to dispel the rising heat of late summer. "You talked to Mateo?"

"Of course that's what you're worried about. And no, I talked to Danny, and maybe if you'd been here, we could've said yes, and then you could've squeezed into the back seat with Mateo. Sparks might have flown, Cam! But no, you—" They cut themself off as they finally looked at me—*really* looked at me.

They narrowed their eyes. "Okay. What happened?"

I shrugged and kept my expression as impassive as possible. "My mom caught me leaving."

Their gaze zeroed in on my Hexes shirt, and they winced. "Oh."

"Yeah."

"It looks cute, though." They waved their hand over me. "Your whole outfit is working."

"Thanks. There was effort involved. You look great too."

Al swished their ruffled black skirt, the hem bouncing right above their knees. Purple-and-black-striped tights covered their legs, and their ankle boots completed the ensemble. "Thank you. There was effort here as well. But *I* made it on time."

I rolled my eyes. "I would've been here, but my mom wanted to talk to me. It's fine. I'm here now. Let's go so we're not late."

On the bike ride over, what my mom had said about Al's and my friendship had percolated in my brain. I shouldn't have let my mom get into my head, but I was on edge. And I couldn't help but think about the possibility that the new school could end up splitting Al and me apart.

I shouldn't dwell on it. Al was my best friend. And if they did decide to ditch me at some point in the future for new witch friends, well, I'd resign myself to being the lonely, weird kid for the rest of my high school career. Maybe things would change once I went to college. I would've loved to talk with Aiden about that, but . . .

"No."

Al's voice brought me back to the present and out of my spiraling thoughts.

"No? What do you mean, no? We're not skipping the first day, Al."

"I mean *no*." They picked up one of the coffees and shoved it into my hand. "You're not brushing this off. You agreed to a themed school year about embracing our futures and ourselves. You pinky swore."

"And?"

"And that means being truthful about our feelings! I know you have perfected your impressive resting bitch face, but I can tell how much whatever she said bothers you. Okay? You don't have to pretend. Especially not with me."

Puffing my cheeks, I blew out a breath. I pushed my bike forward with one hand, balancing the coffee with the other. We took a right at the corner, and the entrance to the new high school gleamed in the distance. It was only a block away, which meant I didn't have to be introspective for long. Al fell in step beside me.

"Fine. She doesn't like that we're friends, and she wants me to find new ones this year."

Al squinted. "Is that all? She's been like that for as long as I can remember."

"Well, it was particularly pointed this morning." I didn't mention the other piece about Al leaving me behind. That wasn't first-day-of-school conversation.

"Ugh. Well. I'm sorry. That sucks." Al kicked a pinecone out of our path. It rolled, bits of the scales spinning off, until it settled on the grass. "But I'll be your friend until we're both in the ground."

I pulled my gaze from the uneven concrete and met their warm brown eyes. "I know."

"Good."

Of course, the moment was ruined when the tire of my bike jarred into a raised section of the sidewalk. The handlebar slipped from my sweaty grip and fell to the side, the pedals jamming into my leg. I yelped, dropped my coffee, and barely kept myself from tripping. The coffee hit the ground, the plastic lid doing nothing to stop the explosion of ice and liquid from splattering across my shoes and the legs of my jeans.

I stared down in horror.

Al winced in sympathy. After a pause in which I contemplated turning around and heading home, Al stooped down and inspected the mess. They stood. "I have a spell for that," they said, gesturing to my stained jeans.

"Um . . . it's okay," I said, trying to brush off the mess.

"No, really. I can do it. I'm sure."

I hedged. Al's magic wasn't . . . the most stable. But it wasn't powerful, either, so it wasn't like they could make things much worse. "Okay. Sure."

They smiled as they rubbed their hands together. "Okay, hold still." They held their spread fingers over the splashes of coffee on the fabric and narrowed their eyes. Al muttered a string of words, and the air shimmered. And that was all.

After a moment Al dropped their arms.

"Damn it!"

Secretly relieved, I patted their shoulder as they straightened. "Thanks for trying."

"Ugh. I should be able to do that. I just—"

"Hey, it's okay. Maybe I'll start a new fashion trend. We'll call it the splatter look."

Al raised an eyebrow, then laughed, the tension breaking. "Dork."

"What?" I said as we continued toward the school. "I'm serious. It will be all the rage." I nudged them with my elbow.

They returned the gesture, knocking into me with their shoulder. "Glad you've cheered up, buttercup. It *is* the first day of our sophomore year, which is going to be epic."

"I think our definitions of epic are wildly different," I said as we approached the front entrance. But they were right; the small moment of levity had brightened my mood.

They snorted in amusement. "Let's plan to hang out together after school one day this week."

I was immediately on board. "Sure. How about tonight?"

"Oh, I can't tonight. Monthly coven meeting."

"Tomorrow?"

"I really should practice my spells. Especially if we're going to start having homework this week. Thursday?"

I grimaced. "Since Aiden left, Dad has mandated family movie night on Thursdays."

Al made a face. "Really?"

"I know. Mom doesn't even pretend to watch—just scrolls on her phone. And it's always some movie from the late '80s or early '90s. Most of them are cringe."

"At least he's trying?" they said, voice going high at the end.

"I guess."

"Wednesday, then."

"Wednesday sounds good. Not only is it pizza day, but it is also the name of my favorite *Addams Family* character."

Al rolled their eyes playfully and then proceeded to launch into a diatribe about the theater department at their last school and how certain students were always favored for different parts and how they hoped to at least have a line in the school play if the school put one on. I half listened as they rambled. Despite our friend-date plans, my mom's words ran in an anxious loop.

"Cam," Al said, grabbing my shoulder. "We're here."

Oh. We were.

The district had spared no expense in the construction of the new high school. The front entrance was massive, and it looked more like the museum downtown than it did a school. The concrete gleamed in the morning sun. Two sets of wide stairs led up to tempered glass doors, reinforced of course to handle unexpected bursts of strength from pubescent werewolves, sprites, witches, and the random telekinetic psychic. There was a ramp to the side, near the sign that proclaimed CENTRAL SHADY HALLOW HIGH SCHOOL, HOME OF THE SAINTS. In the morning sun, with the white façade and the huge windows, the whole building was blindingly bright— the only shade offered by a single towering tree thriving off to the right. That was probably why I initially missed the two large aluminum signs that sat on the staircase, sporting a list of rules.

NO GUM

NO SKATEBOARDS

NO HORSEPLAY

NO LOITERING

NO POWERS

The signs weren't doing a great job, since a kid had just sped by on a skateboard and a girl was sitting on the stairway, blowing a huge pink gum bubble. Another girl stood nearby with an umbrella while a conjured gray cloud hovered over her sprinkling rain. A pair of boys floated past us, the heels of their new sneakers several inches above the ground, and Al sighed wistfully at the display of a strong hovering spell.

I found a metal rack, jammed my bike into one of the slots, and then wound the chain and lock through the spokes of my front tire. A handful of brooms sat upright in the broom spaces, but my bike was the only form of wheeled transportation. Comparatively it would be easy pickings for anyone who chose mayhem that day, as the brooms were undoubtedly protected by anti-theft spells. Best to at least secure it well.

"Are you ready?" Al asked, tossing their hair over their shoulder.

"No. But I also don't want to be truant. So I guess we have to go in."

"That's the spirit!"

As I hitched my bag higher on my shoulders, we dodged the dozens of students who milled about the steps. They were packed into clusters, most of them talking and laughing, while others peered over their shoulders at the rest of the groups. It was an odd mix of students. Some of them I knew from my last year as a freshman at West Shady Hallow High, but there were students I didn't recognize at all. I guess that's what happened when the lines were redrawn for the opening of the third high school in the county. Everyone was reassigned and jumbled up, and the cliques had to be reestablished.

The school building itself had been constructed to house a bigger student population. More kids equaled more chaos. The school ecosystem would need to recalibrate and hopefully find equilibrium over the next week while a large number of werewolves, witches, sprites, psychics, and humans figured out how to function within the new, fuller class sizes.

I spied the Lopez brothers off to the side. Danny, the senior; Javi, the junior; and Mateo, the sophomore. They were with a group of kids, presumably other werewolves. Mateo brushed his dark brown hair from his forehead. His muscles flexed beneath his flawless brown skin, and when he smiled at something one of his brothers said, his eyes crinkled. Hanging off Mateo's arm was a willowy girl with long strawberry-blond hair and a smattering of freckles across her pale cheeks, and she leaned into Mateo's side as she laughed.

And ugh. This day had started off badly enough. Why did it have to get worse?

I had harbored a crush on Mateo since I'd literally bumped into him in the hallway last year. We had both apologized—his voice had been low and gruff—and then he'd brushed past . . . and that had been the entirety of the interaction. That was really the sum of *all* our interactions, except my pathetic mooning whenever we were in the same room, which wasn't often since he was in all advanced classes. I didn't really *do* crushes, but there was just something about him that made my middle squirm in that first-drop-of-a-roller-coaster way.

I didn't realize I had been staring until the girl caught my eye and nudged Mateo. Mateo whipped around and glared. I startled, tripped on the stairs, and barely caught myself. The girl laughed. Mortified, I kept my head down, not wanting to see Mateo's expression.

I quickened my pace, and Al grabbed on to my backpack to keep up.

"What the hell was that?" they asked, grinning as we pushed through the front doors. "Did the force of Mateo's beauty cause you to lose your balance?"

"Shut up," I groaned. "Let's just go."

Al wrapped their arm around my shoulders and jostled me. "Come on, grumpy. Our future awaits."

Of course it did. The only problem was that the excitement I'd had that morning had dimmed. But that was the thing: no one could stop the future from coming, even if they wanted to—even if they chose to ignore it.

3

MY FIRST-BLOCK LITERATURE CLASS WAS UNEVENTFUL. Before the teacher started her lecture, the intercom buzzed on, and the overhead announcements reminded us all of the various rules and responsibilities of being in a brand-new building (no vandalism of any kind, including graffiti and latrinalia; no gum; and no tape on freshly painted walls) as well as guidelines about class time, including that, per a new school board edict, any special ability used for credit had to be preapproved by not only the instructor but the administration and the board as well.

The girl next to Al swore under her breath. "There goes my gym grade," she muttered, snapping her book shut hard enough that the papers on her desk ruffled in the burst of wind.

Afterward our teacher passed out the syllabus, followed by the first book we would read and discuss for the year. Then she promptly told us we'd have a quiz on Friday on the first four chapters. She gave us the rest of the period to read. When the bell rang, Al and I parted ways. I fumbled through the packed maze of hallways to my second block, which was Algebra II.

The girl who had been cuddling with Mateo sat behind me, much to my annoyance. During roll call I learned her name was Kaci. She kept to herself when the teacher gave us free time toward the end of the class, choosing to write in a journal rather than interact with our classmates. I made reluctant small talk with the guy next to me, who I vaguely recognized from the previous year.

Third block was World History, and class was much of the same, except that halfway through, the bell rang for our lunch period. I grabbed my wallet and booked it out of the room toward the cafeteria, hoping to get a good spot in the underclassman lunch line so I wouldn't spend the short thirty minutes waiting for soggy fries. Also, I was starving since I hadn't grabbed breakfast. Luckily, Al was already there and let me cut in line with them.

Food acquired, we eyed the tables arranged in parallel sets, trying to find an empty spot that wasn't already saved. The cafeteria was loud, buzzing with conversation and raucous bursts of laughter. The telltale hum of witch magic hung in the air, as did the heavy, cloying scent of fresh, fragrant flowers and the humidity caused by water droplets of spring rain, which came from a shimmer of sprites crowded around the table near the window.

A girl with a floating tray of food in front of her waved at Al. "Hey, Al!"

I stiffened.

Al nodded their head toward her since their hands were full. "Hi, Lex!"

"Who's that?" I whispered as we maneuvered through the crowd.

"She's a member of our coven. Her dad is great with plants and potions and tells the worst dad jokes. She's pretty cool too."

"Oh . . . cool." I couldn't have been less enthusiastic. Al shot me a side-eye as my worries pinged around in my head, but they didn't comment.

"I've been thinking about what your mom said," they said, settling across from me at our table in the corner next to the wall. My stomach soured as they scanned the lunchroom. "It's not a bad idea, honestly."

If I had been standing, my knees would have buckled. "What?"

"Well, it makes sense. I'll have more responsibilities with the coven soon, and I really need to put more effort toward casting my spells and learning potions and being involved in coven life. It would be good for you to have people to hang out with when I'm unavailable."

A lump lodged in my throat. "Oh."

"It wouldn't be an awful thing for you to make more friends. And it's not like I won't still be your BFF. But like we said this morning, we're embracing our true selves, right?"

No. Yes. Maybe? I didn't know. I didn't even know what "true self" meant for me. Cam, the best friend? Cam, the son to disappointed and disapproving parents? Cam, the brother to a missing sibling? Cam, the teenager besotted with a werewolf boy who smiled at him once? And new friends? I didn't want to find new friends. Socializing was exhausting and really flew in the face of my plan to blend into the wallpaper for the entirety of the school year.

Al continued, unaware of my internal crisis. "And for me, that's being a witch. I need to concentrate on that a little bit more than in the past."

Al's plan seemed logical for them. It was just . . . my mom's words from the morning had gotten stuck in my brain, and the sting of Aiden disappearing was an ever-present ache. I didn't think I could bear losing Al, too. It all put me on edge. But it was a *me* problem, not an Al problem.

"I get it," I said, forcing a smile and slotting back into my best friend role. "It's cool."

Al huffed and shook their head, smiling indulgently. "Don't sound so worried. I'll help you. We'll scope out some candidates, and it'll be great."

"Great," I said.

"Or I could walk up to Mateo and tell him about the huge crush you had on him last year and all the pining you did from afar."

My face burned. I kicked their ankle under the table. "You wouldn't dare."

Al cackled. "No. I wouldn't." They pulled out a small notebook from their bag and clicked a pen. "Okay. Mission Find Cam a New Friend has commenced."

"What? *Now?*"

"No time like the present. What about him?" Al nodded toward a guy eating alone. He was hunched over his tray, scrolling through his phone.

"No," I said, struggling with my small packet of ketchup. This was happening too fast. I was ill prepared to have to interact with new people. While Al surveyed the lunchroom, I took out my ire on the unsuspecting plastic rectangle. My sweaty fingers slipped along the edges.

"Why not? He's kind of cute. He looks lonely. I think he's human too, so your parents would approve. And who knows—maybe he'll help you forget all about your crush on Mateo."

The top of the packet finally ripped, and ketchup squirted out in a long sinuous line onto my plate. "No thanks."

"Why not?"

"Because I'm not going to randomly approach a person you picked from the cafeteria on a whim." Irritation prickled along the back of my neck. I squirmed in my seat, careful not to slide around too much on the new cafeteria stools. They were hard molded plastic—uncomfortable in every way, terrible for posture, and tiny enough that even my admittedly small butt was in danger of slipping off if I moved too enthusiastically in any direction. "Just no."

"Okay. Fine. What about that girl? She's drawing. You like drawing. You can be friends."

I twirled a fry in the small puddle of ketchup I'd created. My appetite had fled. "No."

"Okay. How about—"

"Al," I said, grimacing. "I don't like this game. Can you stop? Please?"

They frowned. "I'm just trying to help."

"And I appreciate it. But I'm not going to suddenly make friends because you say I should."

They huffed and crossed their arms. "Cam—"

I understood what Al needed. They were a witch. They needed to have witch friends and be able to do witchy things that didn't involve me. I got that, though it didn't feel great. But why were they so hung up on this *right now*? "Why are you harping on this? What are you trying to accomplish?"

Al frowned, and they threw down a chicken nugget. They looked away, shoulders tensed. Their grip was tight around their can of soda. "Like I said, I'm going to have more responsibilities with the coven this year once I turn sixteen. I don't want you to be lonely when—"

"So you *are* leaving me behind," I blurted out.

Al snapped their head around. "What? No. Just—things are changing. I have a duty to the coven, and I need to do better. I need to *be* better."

"You're amazing the way you are."

"Thank you. But that's not enough."

"What's not enough? Al, what's really going on with you?"

Al flashed a brittle smile. "You know what? Never mind. You're right. We don't need to do this now. Don't worry about it."

Don't worry about it? Al had spent our walk here lecturing me about being honest with myself and with them, and they now had the nerve to blow me off? To not follow their own advice?

Unless they didn't want me to know. My heart sank. It was just like my mom had said. Al was just trying to soften the blow before they pulled away. Okay. All right. I could deal with this. I swallowed and gathered myself, easing back into the exterior that I used around everyone but Al.

"Ah," I said.

"What does that mean?"

"Nothing." I shook my head. "I've got to go. I'll see you tomorrow."

"Cam," they groaned. "Wait. Don't be upset."

"I'm not," I lied as I gathered my things. "We'll talk later."

I left the table and, on the way out of the cafeteria, dumped my whole tray in the trash. We weren't exactly allowed to leave if it was our lunchtime, but the cafeteria staff couldn't keep me from going to the bathroom.

I walked out the doors and tried to remember exactly where the restrooms were around this labyrinth of a place. I barely knew how to get back to the classroom I was supposed to be in once lunch was over. I guessed and turned to the right, and met a dead end. Then I backtracked, barely paying attention to where I was going, because the only thing running in my head was *This was not how things were supposed to work out.* I felt stupid for having been so excited that morning. My stomach hurt, and tears gathered in my throat, because Al was all I had left. And now they might abandon me too. I couldn't handle it.

I walked faster and faster as if I could outrun my spinning thoughts. When I finally stopped and took a shuddering breath, I found myself in the senior hall. There was a banner hanging by strings from the ceiling tiles, welcoming the seniors to the first day of their last year of high school. It was already torn in half and fluttering in the breeze from the air-conditioning. A few choice phrases were emblazoned in red marker along its edges. The hall sported small splashes of color that the other hallways didn't. The floor was a checkerboard mix of white and blue tiles, and tall lockers alternating in blue and yellow lined the walls. At my size and height, these were definitely spaces I could be stuffed into if someone chose to do so.

Crap.

I grabbed my phone from my back pocket. Maybe there was a map of this place on the school website that I could use to find my way back. Otherwise I was going to be at the mercy of the upperclassmen.

The bell rang overhead, and I tensed as not twenty seconds later the hall flooded with students. I was caught in the stream of people, with no idea how to find my way back to my history class. Oh well—I would just be late, I guess. The teacher really couldn't hold it against me. It was a new school, and—

"Hey, howler boy!" A loud voice echoed down the hall.

A kid who happened to be next to me suddenly halted. He turned on his heel, his sneakers squeaking on the pristine floor. "You talking to me?" he called back.

"Yeah. Who else? I said 'howler boy.' That's what you are, right?"

"Yeah. I am. What do you want, slimer?"

"Slimer"? That was a new one. I'd never heard that insult before, and I wasn't quite sure what it meant. But the other boy, who was pushing his way through the crowd, obviously did, if his absolutely furious expression was any indication. He was flanked by a girl and another boy. The girl had bright electric-blue eyes and matching hair, while the two boys' eyes glowed green. Oh. Sprites. The girl was a water sprite, while the boys were earth, maybe? I wasn't quite sure how sprite classification worked.

I tried to maneuver away from the impending altercation, but the whole crowd had stilled to watch whatever was about to happen. A few folks had their phones out, vying to record the next viral social media moment. And as the trio approached, a low murmur rose among the student body, and the crowd shuffled, parting like a school of fish trying to get away from a shark. I was stuck, squeezed between the offended werewolf and a mob at my back.

The werewolf kid stood his ground, feet spread, chest puffed out as he faced the three sprites. His pale face was flushed red in anger.

It was like watching a Wild West showdown in the middle of the hallway.

"I think you owe my friend here an apology," the boy in the middle of the trio said, gesturing to the sprite at his right. "For kicking his bag when you were leaving class."

The werewolf narrowed his eyes. "I don't owe him shit."

And oh my gods. *Why?*

The trio chuckled humorlessly. I had to get out of there before things got worse.

"What's going on here?" A new voice joined in, the tone jovial but with the hint of an edge.

The crowd shifted again, and I was swept along with it but still unnervingly close to the combatants. Javi Lopez had appeared, and I didn't know whether to be relieved or tense up even more. He was the middle of the Lopez brothers, not quiet like Mateo and not mellow like Danny. He was loud, talkative, dramatic, basically every middle-kid cliché. And it was a crapshoot whether he would calm everyone down or instigate things further.

He rested his hand on the other werewolf's shoulder. "Everything okay, Nate?"

"Stay out of this, Lopez. This doesn't concern you," one of the sprites spat.

Javi raised an eyebrow. "As you well know, Reese," he said, addressing the tall one in the center with the auburn hair, pale skin, and shocking green eyes, "if a werewolf is involved, then it does concern me." He clucked his tongue. "And three against one? You know I have to intervene just to balance the odds."

"We don't want a fight," the girl said. "But we are prepared to defend ourselves if necessary." Droplets of water flicked from her fingertips.

"Yeah," the third sprite taunted him. "We have to protect ourselves from that famous werewolf aggression."

Javi's jaw clenched. "I don't want to fight either," he said, and then broke into a wide smile as he opened his arms, posturing for the crowd. "Let's just all go on our way and forget this even happened."

Reese crossed his arms, a smug grin blossoming across his face. "When he apologizes."

Javi sighed. He shook his head and slung his arm around Nate, tugging him close. "And here I was hoping *not* to get suspended on the first day of school."

And okay. This was happening. I didn't particularly want to be a witness to a fight between a pair of werewolves and a shimmer of sprites in the hallway, so I attempted to squeeze my way out of there. The two sides continued to banter, and the insults rose in pitch and viciousness as I searched for an escape route. I turned my back on the scene and had my shoulder wedged between someone's backpack and the wall, trying to slide out, when the physical part of the fight erupted.

I didn't see who had charged whom, but the *ooh*s of the crowd went up instantaneously. I was jostled along as everyone moved to make room for the fight. The impact of someone against the lockers on the other side of the hallway clanged loudly amid the rumble of the student body. The squeaks of shoes as the crowd ebbed and flowed like a current, the grunts and growls of the fighters, and the flash-bang of magic all tumbled together as the altercation intensified. I was craning my neck to see what was happening when the crowd suddenly surged. I was pushed hard from behind. I stumbled forward, my shoe slipping on a patch of water, and landed on my knees with a painful jolt.

Oh, that *hurt*. I braced myself with my hands to push upward, but someone stepped on my fingers. My phone skittered out of my grip and slid across the brand-new linoleum. I reached for it, but someone else's bag whacked into my ribs, knocking the wind from my lungs. I wrapped an arm around my torso and resisted the urge to curl up on the ground. I had to get upright or risk being trampled.

I did my best to scramble out of the way, but there were feet and legs blocking my sight and my path, and every time I tried to gain my footing, the crowd would push in another direction. A girl tripped over my ankle and landed on her butt. Another person slipped on the growing puddles of water and smacked their chin against the floor. I crawled toward the side of the hallway, making little progress amid the screams, groans, and cheers of the fight happening around me.

Puddles of water and bunches of leaves were scattered everywhere. The knees of my jeans were soaked, and wayward bracken stuck to the fabric of my clothes and tangled in my hair. My hands were damp from both sweat and sprite magic. This was easily the worst day of my life, and I would go home and cry over it as soon as I could stand up and get away from this mess.

A strong hand gripped my upper arm over the sleeve of my shirt and tugged hard, helping me lurch to my feet. Finally! Before I could turn and thank my savior, a yell split the air way too close for comfort. I looked up in time to see three bodies locked in a fighting embrace hurtling toward me.

They rammed into me, throwing me into the lockers. All my breath left me in a whoosh. The back of my head smacked into the metal, and stars burst behind my eyes. My knees went weak as blackness encroached in the periphery of my vision, and I slid to the floor in a heap. A body landed on top of me, crushing me between the lockers and the floor. There were shouts in my ears. Pain radiated from my ribs and the back of my head, and panic seized my chest. I couldn't breathe. I couldn't move. I couldn't *see*.

Someone grabbed my wrist, their skin hot and clammy against my own. I couldn't make out who it was as my eyes glazed over, my vision tunneled, and the chaos around me disappeared, the sound of voices muting until they were gone altogether.

And suddenly I wasn't in the hallway at all.

4

I **STOOD IN A FIELD.**

It was dark, save for ripples of soft moonlight. Trees lined the perimeter in the far distance, but a weird shimmery fog blurred and softened the edges of my sight, so I couldn't make out any other details. Clouds rolled overhead, obscuring the moon and bathing the scene in blue gray. Short grass tickled my ankles, and when I took a step, my bare feet sank into the damp soil. The wind blew softly, and I shivered in the cold. The air smelled like a mixture of rain and fresh mud, with a hint of rotten eggs. Somehow it tasted metallic.

I had the awareness to realize that those smells and that taste were oddly specific, something that I shouldn't be able to sense, but the thought was shoved to the back of my mind.

Because there was something in front of me . . . no, not something. *Someone.*

Fear shuddered through me.

Despite it, I shuffled forward.

The person . . . the girl . . . raised her head. Her golden-brown hair fell around her in wild tangles. Her eyes were wide and scared. The scant light illuminated the red paint spattered across her face.

"Please," she said, her voice weak. She pushed herself up. Her arms trembled.

"Please," she begged again, raising her hand. Her palm was streaked with bright white and crimson. She hoisted herself to her knees but then flopped sideways with a gasp after only a moment, like a puppet with her strings cut.

And that was when I realized it wasn't red paint. She was covered in blood. Her blouse was stained dark red. Her jeans were soaked. It seeped from deep wounds in her torso and slashes across her arms.

There were voices in the distance. Yelling. Screaming? A bush rustled off to the side. Twigs snapped in the forest nearby.

I hesitantly stepped closer. Stone-cold dread weighed down my every movement.

"Please," she whimpered again, but it was barely a whisper.

I didn't reassure her. I *couldn't*. I was mute, trapped by whatever magic this was. Because it had to be magic. I was sure of it. I could sense the tendrils of it wrapped around me.

The girl had stilled. Her body lost all tension, and her eyes slid half-closed, staring unblinkingly through the grass . . . at me.

My heart lodged in my throat. I wanted to help her. I wanted to scream. I wanted to run, but my feet were stuck fast, sinking into the mud. I wanted to do *anything*, but all I could do was stare as her breath stuttered to a halt.

My gaze dropped. Then I noticed that I held an object at my side. My fingers were curled around the handle of a large knife. Wait, not my fingers . . . someone else's.

The blade gleamed in the moonlight, the sharp edge tinged red.

5

I WAS SUCKED THROUGH A DARK TUNNEL. AT LEAST THAT WAS how it sounded—as if large amounts of water had suddenly spiraled down a recently unclogged drain.

I rocketed awake with a gasp.

I sat upright, my gaze flickering about wildly. My heart pounded. A scream caught in my throat, which I managed to wrangle down to a strangled yelp.

I wasn't in the field.

I was in a bed. In the nurse's office. My hands clutched the bedding beneath me so tightly that the sheets were in danger of ripping. My chest heaved, my breaths stuttering in panic.

What had happened? Was that a dream? How had I gotten here?

"Camden?"

I snapped my head to the side, thinking for a moment I'd see the girl from the field, but it was only the nurse at her desk. She stared at me with a concerned expression, her body held stiff on the edge of her chair like she wanted to bolt from the room. Same, lady. Absolute same.

"Do you know where you are, Camden?"

I took that as permission to look around some more. The nurse's office was an open floor plan. There were two beds separated by a curtain, though it was currently drawn aside, exposing me to the whole area. I was in the one on the farthest side of the room. The other one was empty, though the sheets were rumpled as if someone else had been there. There was a closet door that was propped open, and it looked to be full of first aid supplies and linens.

"Camden?" she prompted again.

Oh. Yes. I should respond. Like a normal functioning human. Not one who had been a casualty in a hallway fight between werewolves and sprites and then had been transported to a hellish midnight meadow.

"Cam," I corrected, voice a croaky squeak.

She nodded, then stood and crossed the room slowly, as if I were a skittish woodland creature that might dart away at any second. And maybe I was, because I could not get my fists to loosen or my spine to relax. "How are you feeling?" she asked.

She reached out to take my wrist, and I flinched. I didn't know why, only that I didn't want to be touched. She hesitated and then backed away.

I blinked. My head was killing me. It pounded in time with my elevated pulse. And I was so tired. If I could calm down, I definitely wouldn't mind curling up in this bed and sleeping for approximately a week. But to be honest, I was a little freaked out, and I didn't foresee the ability to unclench occurring anytime soon.

That girl . . . she'd been attacked. She'd *died*. What the fuck was that? Had I actually been there? Or had it been some weird hallucination brought on by my head being knocked into the lockers?

I shuddered as the picture swam across my mind's eye. I could still see the blood and hear her helpless cries, and I really needed to stop thinking about it.

I needed Al.

"My head hurts."

"I can give you a painkiller," she offered, gesturing to my file on her desk. "Your parents signed off on that with your paperwork."

"Okay." I swallowed. My throat was dry. Had I been screaming?

How long had I been there, anyway? Where was my phone?

She shook two pills from a bottle into a small paper cup and fished some water out of a mini fridge next to the closet. She placed them on the table next to me and stepped away, watching me as I choked the pain reliever down with a swig of water. She went back to sit at her desk and scribbled something in a log.

"How did I get here?" I asked.

"Danny Lopez brought you."

My body went hot with embarrassment. I groaned and slumped onto the pillow. Danny must have been at the fight as well. Or the aftermath. "Really?"

She clicked her pen and made another note. "Have you . . ." She trailed off. "Has that ever happened to you before?"

"Accidentally getting flattened in a fight in the hallway? No. That's a new one for me." I sighed and picked at the blanket that had been tossed over my legs. I still had my shoes on. I wiggled my toes and then shifted in the bed, my damp jeans slithering unpleasantly across my skin. "Wait, I'm not in trouble, am I? I didn't start anything. I just got caught up in it. I was an innocent bystander. I swear."

She waved away my concern, a slight smile pulling at her lips. "You're not in trouble. The Lopez brothers and the other kids involved all stated you were not part of the altercation."

I blew out my breath and relaxed further onto the bed. Exhaustion had caught up with me despite my mortification at the thought of Danny carrying me through the halls like a damsel in distress. And despite the horror of . . . whatever it was I had seen. But thank goodness the eyewittnesses had vouched for me. I'd hate to get a detention on the first day. My parents would kill me.

"I meant—" She paused. "The other kids . . . they said you—"

"I passed out, right? From hitting my head?" I reached up and gingerly felt the knot on the back of my skull. It hurt. But at least it didn't look like it had bled. "Are you going to call my parents?"

The nurse frowned. "Yes. I will be calling your parents to come get you."

"Oh. Can you not?"

Her eyebrows shot up. "Why? Do you not feel safe at home?"

"Oh! Nothing like that. Just . . . they're going to be upset. And I don't want to disturb them at work. Can I just hang out in here until the end of the school day and then go home?"

She shook her head. Her blond hair swished behind her in a high ponytail. "Sorry. Any time there is an incident, we must call the parents. It's school policy. Especially if it involves the manifestation of abilities."

What had I done in a past life to warrant such bad karma on the first day of my sophomore year? And why didn't painkillers work instantly, because my brain felt too big for my skull and—

I propped myself on my elbow. "Wait, what? Abilities? What are you talking about?"

The nurse picked up my slim file and flipped through the few pages. "There's nothing denoted in your paperwork that you're a psychic. So I assume this is the first time it's happened?"

I scrunched my nose. "What?"

She set down the folder and tapped her pen several times against the desk in rapid succession. She looked away and licked her lips. And—oh, she was nervous. For me? *Of* me?

"The other students reported that when you hit the lockers, you fell to the ground."

Okay. Made sense. I remembered that part. Not my finest moment, but there wasn't much I could do about it, since three huge upperclassmen had barreled into me.

"And?"

"And while you were on the ground, your eyes remained open, and you were murmuring. But it was too low for anyone to hear. Based on the description of events and eyewitness accounts, your passing out was not the result of the head injury but of a clairvoyant vision." She ran her finger over a page in a huge book next to her elbow. "I'm not very familiar with visions. I don't even know if that's the modern term for it. Damn, I need to read up on current literature, because this book is practically ancient, but—"

"What?" I said weakly.

She answered, but my hearing fuzzed out.

Clairvoyant vision? That girl . . . that was her future? My stomach roiled. The meager amount of lunch I'd eaten burned up my throat. "I'm going to be sick."

The nurse grabbed the wastebasket by her desk and ran across the room, shoving it into my hands.

I vomited up fries and bile and the water I'd just drunk and the two painkillers. I squeezed my eyes shut. My head felt like it was going to explode. I heaved again, my mouth burning, and clutched the wastebasket closer to my chest, needing something tangible to hold on to as my worldview completely and utterly shattered.

"I'm . . . going to call your parents. Be right back."

The nurse's shoes slapped on the floor as she darted away.

It gave me a moment to think, to process. As much as I wanted to deny the fact that I'd fallen into some kind of vision during that fight . . . I couldn't. I didn't know anything about seers or psychics or prophets or whatever term the paranormal folks used these days, but I did know that whatever I'd seen, whatever had happened in that field . . . felt *real*. I'd touched the ground under my feet and shivered at the breeze on my skin. I'd smelled the mud and the rotten eggs. I'd heard her desperate cries. I'd seen the blood. I'd held that knife.

I couldn't ignore *this*.

I couldn't pretend that it hadn't happened.

And there was no humor to be found here. No jokes to be made.

I threw up again.

6

WHILE THE NURSE WAS OCCUPIED, I SCRAMBLED OFF THE bed, setting the gross wastebasket on the floor. My backpack was on a chair by the door, with my books and supplies stuffed inside. Thankfully someone had brought it, along with my books from my third-block class. But that didn't tell me where my phone was. I patted down my pockets just to make sure it hadn't miraculously zapped into my jeans, but nope.

It was probably still in the hallway. I'd have to go back to the scene of the fight.

I checked the clock on the wall. It was close to the last hour of the school day, which meant I really needed to talk to Al, preferably before one of my parents showed up. Unfortunately, I couldn't contact Al without my phone because I had no idea where their fourth-block class was. I would kill to have access to Lenore right about now.

Okay. Step one. Calm down.

Step two. Find phone.

Step three. Text Al and hope they could tell me what the hell had happened to me.

Step four . . . never return to school and go live my life as a hermit in a hut in the woods? I mean, not a bad plan for someone who had been humiliated at least twice in one day.

My hands shook as I slung my backpack over my shoulder. My head still felt like someone was ramming ice picks into my ears. And I couldn't be sure that I wouldn't throw up again. The rational thing to do would be to stay in the nurse's office and wait for my parents. But rational had taken a hike the moment I slipped on sprite water. I took a deep breath, willing my heart rate to chill. I wasn't successful.

I heard the nurse end her call with my mom. Okay. Step one would just have to be "in progress," because I needed to dip if I was going to have a chance at step two.

I carefully pressed down on the metal door handle and then slowly pulled the door open, just enough for me to slide out as quietly as possible. Success.

I took one step down the hallway, then promptly had a heart attack.

Because Mateo Lopez stood in front of me in all his athletic, five-foot-eleven, ridiculously attractive glory, dark eyebrows raised, brown eyes staring at me with a curious glint. His hair curled in soft waves around his face and caressed the sharp jut of his jawline. It was as if I'd stepped right into one of my daydreams. Him—eyeing me up and down, full lips in a pout, body language expectant, like he was waiting for an opening to talk to me. All the details were perfect, except I was probably concussed, damp in unpleasant ways, breathing erratically while clutching my chest, and on the verge of losing my mind. Running into Mateo while I was definitely not firing on all cylinders really was the icing on top of my already catastrophically bad-day cake.

The nurse called my name in the room behind me.

I winced. Then, without really thinking about it, I grabbed the crook of Mateo's arm and made a wobble for it. It wasn't a run. My head was swimming too much for that, but it was enough to get us down the hallway and into the small alcove by the restrooms. And huh. *There* the bathrooms were.

To his credit, Mateo didn't resist or even blink, though his expression had morphed from curiously amused to downright confused.

"Sorry," I breathed, leaning against the wall nearest the water fountains. "She called my parents, and I just don't want to deal with it, you know?"

Mateo frowned.

And oh. Maybe he didn't know.

"Anyway," I plowed on, "I really hope you were planning to talk to me, or I just basically yanked you down the hall to the bathrooms for no reason."

Mateo's lips twitched. "Here," he said, and held out my phone.

My phone!

"Fantastic!" I said, sounding completely awkward. I reached out to take my phone from Mateo's hand, but for some reason I paused halfway, my fingers hanging limply in the space between us. Mateo tilted his head and waited. "Sorry," I breathed, suddenly and acutely wary of touching him. "Sorry. Um, let me just . . ." I gingerly lifted the phone and made sure not to graze his fingers. Great, now I also *looked* incredibly awkward, as evidenced by the incredulous expression on Mateo's face.

Today really was just not my day. My phone sported a new large, jagged crack running from the top right corner to the opposite bottom. Awesome. I tapped the screen, and thankfully it still worked. I had a ton of messages from Al. But . . . they could wait. I looked back to Mateo and smiled.

"I was just going to go look for it. Thank you, really. And thank Danny for me. I heard he carried me to the nurse's office? Is that true?"

Mateo put his hands back in his hoodie pocket and shrugged. "Yeah. He did."

My face lit on fire. Seriously. I could roast marshmallows near it. "Well. Thanks."

Mateo's brow furrowed. "Are you . . . okay?"

"I'm fine," I said, lying through my teeth. "I have a headache, but otherwise I'm good."

"You look . . ." He trailed off.

Looked what? Cute? Amazing? Like boyfriend material?

He finally settled on, "Pale."

"Ah," I said, my hopes deflating like a sad balloon. "Yeah." I gestured to my head. "Unfortunate side effect of being launched into the lockers."

His expression didn't ease, but he didn't speak further.

And this was embarrassing. Really embarrassing. I didn't know what to say, and my eyes throbbed like they were going to pop out of my skull, and I wasn't certain that I was going to make it through this interaction without vomiting again.

My phone's screen lit up with a text. And then another. And oh— saved by intrusive technology.

"I should probably get to these," I said, holding it up.

He nodded. "I should go back to class."

"Yeah? What class are you in right now?"

"Art block."

"Oh! Me too. I mean, I should be there. I don't think I'm going, though. Actually, pretty sure my parents are on their way here as we speak, so . . ."

"I'll take notes." He coughed. "To share."

My middle fluttered. "Thanks. That would be really helpful."

"Okay." He rocked back on his heels. "See you." And then he was gone, striding quickly away. I watched him until he disappeared.

And what the hell was that? I'd have to unpack that later. Right then I had more pressing issues.

I slid my thumb along my screen and opened my texts. There was a string of them from Al.

Come on, Cam. Don't be mad.

Fine. Be mad.

Where are you?

Did you hear about the fight?

Wait. You were IN THE FIGHT?

Are you okay?

You're freaking me out.

Text me ASAP.

Cam?

And one from my mom:

I'm on my way to the school.

Ugh. That was not going to be fun.
I texted Al.

I'm fine. Can you get out of class and meet me on the front steps?

The reply was instant.

Yes.

I bolted. I found my way to the front of the building, past the main office, and out the door. The sun gleamed off the bleached white façade and sent a spiking ache behind my eyes. A fragrant breeze ruffled the manicured flower beds, but when I inhaled, the smell of rotten eggs and blood clung to the inside of my nose.

There were a few kids ditching, sitting under the receptionist's window where no one could spot them from inside. They glanced in my direction and then went back to batting different brightly colored balls of light back and forth, in some kind of game that I didn't understand and that seared my eyeballs when I stared too long.

I found a place in the shade, under the large oak tree near the HOME OF THE SAINTS sign, and waited. I closed my eyes and leaned on the trunk. I was so tired. Just drained. I wanted to go home and curl up in my bed. I wanted to talk to Aiden. I wanted to forget the image of the girl in the field. I wanted to rewind the whole day and start over.

The sound of footsteps filtered in, and I opened my eyes to find Al jogging over.

"What the hell happened?" they asked as they joined me by the tree. "The rumors are all over the place."

Ugh. Great. Rumors could make or break a reputation. Mine was certainly going to take a dive after everyone found out about Danny swooping in to save me.

"There was a fight. I was collateral damage. I'm fine."

"You look really pale. Are you going to pass out?"

"I already did once. I think. Anyway, my head is killing me, and I've thrown up. So I'm not at my best. And my mom is on her way here."

Al shuddered.

"My feelings exactly," I said. "But anyway—"

"Don't you think you should see a doctor?"

"I don't know. Maybe?"

"If you passed out, you definitely should. You could have a concussion. Why did the nurse allow you to wander away?"

"I wandered away of my own volition."

"Cam! That's dangerous. What were you thinking?"

"Al," I said a little forcefully. "The fight and the aftermath aren't a big deal. Okay? Something else happened, and I need your help."

Their eyes widened. "What?"

I sucked in a breath. "When I fell, I saw . . . something. The nurse said that the other kids in the hall saw me have a vision. But I'm not sure. I really don't know."

"A vision? What do you mean?"

"You know. Like a clairvoyant vision. That's what she said, at least." I held the heel of my hand to my aching head as the world spun nauseatingly around me. "I don't know about that, but I did see . . ." I trailed off, swallowing down the fear and the bile bubbling in my throat.

Al dropped their voice. "Like a seer-type vision? A glimpse?"

"I . . . guess? Maybe? But whatever it was . . . it was *real*."

"Are you certain?"

"Yeah. I could feel it and smell it and . . . and taste it." I shivered. "It was like I was there, but not fully. It was weird."

"Wow," they breathed. "That's really cool."

"It was terrifying!" I snapped. "Not cool at all."

"Sorry."

I shook my head, which was a bad idea. My sight went blurry, and I stumbled to the side. Al reached out to steady me, but I jerked away from their touch. They froze, then took a step back, observing me in much the same way the nurse had. I didn't like it.

"Cam—"

"I'm fine," I said, way too quickly for that to be true. "Just . . . I need you to find out everything you can about visions, or glimpses, whatever they're called. The real stuff. Not like internet shit. The stuff paranormal folk know."

Al readily agreed. Their curls bounced as they nodded. "Yeah. Sure. No problem."

"But don't mention it to your moms. Can you keep it between us? Just for now."

"Cam, if you are—"

"I'm *not*."

Al pursed their lips.

"I mean, it may have been just the head injury. Actually, I'm pretty certain that's what it was. A hallucination or something. But please don't say anything, not until we know for sure."

They crossed their arms and tapped the toe of their boot. "Fine. I won't tell my moms for now. But what did you see that's made you so . . . fidgety?"

My throat tightened. "Something I don't want to revisit. Not right now." Or ever again, honestly. But I had a sinking feeling that I would have to.

"Okay. I can respect that."

"Good. Look, my mom is going to be here any second. And it's already been a catastrophe of a day."

Al held up their hands. "Say no more. I need to head back to class anyway and grab my stuff before the bell."

"Thank you."

They gave me one last concerned look and then fled up the stairs and into the building, ducking through the front doors.

And just as they did, my mom whipped her black SUV into a parking space right in front of the school. My whole body tensed when the driver's side door opened and she stomped out, her rigid posture and long strides indicating just how absolutely livid she was.

I sighed and rubbed my brow.

Time for damage control. I plastered on my best fake smile, which was more like a pained grimace at this point, and met my mom on the stairs, ready to lie through my teeth.

7

AFTER MY MOM SAVAGELY CHEWED OUT THE ADMINISTRA-tion, we shared a strained car ride, punctuated by cloying silence, to the urgent care center. A physician assistant con-cluded that I did not have a concussion but told me to catalog any new or lingering symptoms. When my mom stepped out to take a phone call from work, I took my chances.

"Could hitting my head on the lockers have caused a hallucination?"

The PA frowned and looked at the information from the school nurse. "Are you confirming that you experienced an extrasensory phenomenon? Because if so, I should refer you to—"

"Nope!" I said as my mom stepped back in. "I'm not confirming that."

He sighed, stamped a form, and sent me home with instructions to rest and stay home from school for at least the following day.

We went home, and I endured an uncomfortable dinner with both parents, dodged all questions about the "incident," and claimed I'd seen nothing when the topic of psychic visions was brought up in a very roundabout and reluctant way. My parents, especially my mom, grumbled all through dinner about assumptions the nurse had made based on "conjectures" from "students," and how she'd be speaking to that woman's supervisor the next day. And then any and all talk of visions and clairvoyants ended with a final stab of my mom's fork to the pot roast, much to my relief.

Once excused from the table, I went upstairs with a plan to text Al or search the internet or even mull over the syllabi I'd collected that day, but instead I collapsed into bed and fell asleep immediately.

After a few hours of absolute dead sleep, the nightmares filtered into my subconscious. My dreams were horrible, filled with a barrage of screams and blood and rain and the sight of my fingers wrapped around a knife. I woke up with a wet gasp that was more sob than air. After a trip to the bathroom and a glass of water, I attempted to sleep again. But the images burned behind my eyelids every time I closed them, no matter how hard I tried to block them out.

At four a.m., I gave up and threw off my sweat-soaked covers. I padded across the room to my desk, flipped on my reading lamp, and pulled out my sketchbook and graphite pencil.

I drew the girl.

I wasn't the greatest at figure drawing, but by dawn I had the scene in black and white in front of me, with all the details I could remember. The edges of my sight had been blurred in the vision, and with the lack of light and the clouds, nuance and small elements had been distorted. But I drew the best I could, adding color once I had the basics completed. I hoped I hadn't forgotten anything, but also I would have gladly forgotten the blood and the fear in her voice, if I'd had a choice in these things. However, those aspects seemed to have stuck fast.

On the back I wrote down my other sense memories—the breeze on my skin, the smells, the sounds. All of it. After a moment of consideration, I added the date in the corner.

I wasn't convinced it was a vision of the future—I still couldn't wrap my brain around that—but it had been *something*, and as much as that scared me, I needed to document all the specifics.

I don't know how long I stared at the sketch, but I was certain it was an unhealthy amount of time to ruminate over watching someone die in a hallucination or a glimpse or whatever it was, so finally, with shaking hands, I closed the sketchbook and tucked it away in my backpack.

I slept on and off for the rest of the day, my head aching, my body sore from the impact with the lockers and then the floor, and my brain filled with the same image over and over. I felt feverish and bone-tired and not up for social interaction beyond scrolling through my personal social media feeds.

The next day I was mildly better but by no means ready to return to school. My parents gave me side-eye but didn't push, which I was grateful for.

When I finally did emerge from my blanket cocoon, there was a raven on my windowsill. Backlit by the late morning sun, Lenore's feathers shone purple black as she lightly tapped her beak against the glass. She was subdued, not at all like the tantrum-throwing fowl she had been on the first day of school.

"Lenore?" I whispered.

I crossed the room and opened my window. Lenore stuck out her spindly leg. My fingers trembled as I took out the missive.

Meet me after school. Our place at the old pool park. No texts. No response.

That was probably the most terror-inducing letter I'd ever received from Al. My whole body went cold. Crumpling the paper in my fist, I thanked Lenore with a small pat to the head, and she flew off.

No texts. No response. No paper trail.

What had Al found?

I was jittery the rest of the day. I tried to read the chapters for lit class, but I found my thoughts wandering so much that I ended up starting over three times just to figure out what the characters were doing. I glanced at the math syllabus and started on the practice problems we had for homework that night, but without instruction from the teacher, I quickly gave up.

I couldn't sleep. I didn't eat lunch. I couldn't even watch TV without my brain replaying that scene over and over, shrouding the stupid reality show competition on the screen with blood and desperate pleas and gore. I scrolled through ClickClack, the latest must-have social media app, and half-heartedly watched videos of people living their daily lives—a vampire's list of best treatments for sunburn, a werewolf playing with their new puppy, a sprite child using a leafy vine as a jump rope, a witch showing off the best way to care for a travel broom. It was entertaining, but it didn't quell my anxiety at all. When it was finally time to go meet Al, I had bitten the nails on my left hand down to the quick, smearing blood across my ravaged cuticles.

I pulled on my shoes, grabbed my keys and wallet, and left the house.

My parents worked in the city about thirty minutes away. My mom always drove, but my dad rode the train in, claiming it was better than battling the New Amsterdam traffic. We lived in the suburbs, in a house with a fenced-in postage stamp for a lawn, where we could easily look into our neighbors' windows if we wanted. We had a small driveway, but most folks parked their cars on the street. The sidewalks were cracked by the roots of the trees planted along the curb strip. At least they were shady, and they offered a reprieve from the sun as I biked to the nearby park.

The park had once been a complex with an outdoor pool and a playground. The playground remained, but the pool had been filled in once a newer one had been built a few blocks over with more amenities and an indoor section. Now there was a field next to the playground that the little kids played soccer on in the spring and fall. A buffer of tall trees separated the park from a busy road on the other side. The complex's outbuildings remained, and they were a great place for Al and me to hang out when we didn't want to be at either of our houses but didn't have money to go anywhere else. Normally there would be a few other kids around as well during the summer, but since school had started, the playground and the surrounding area were empty.

I hopped off my bike and leaned it against the wall of the old clubhouse. Then I sat in a spot of shade, the wild clover tickling my ankles, and waited for Al.

I was lightly dozing when they finally arrived, striding across the field with a purpose. The sunlight illuminated their curly hair like a halo, and their thick-heeled boots left deep impressions, flattening the uncut blades of grass. Al appeared uncharacteristically serious, and my body thrummed with unpleasant anxiety.

"Hey," they said, casting a glance over their shoulder. "You okay?"

"Yes," I lied.

They settled next to me in the clover. Their gaze dropped to my hands, and they raised an eyebrow. "Liar."

"Well, my best friend sent me a really cryptic message by raven this morning, so I've been a little keyed up."

They pulled up a lump of grass with their hand. "Yeah. I just . . . I didn't want texts on my phone about this. My moms could see, and they might accuse me of keeping you a secret from them."

I furrowed my brow. "I don't understand that at all."

"Yeah. Figured you wouldn't." They took a breath and pulled at more grass. "Are you okay? Physically? Did you go to a doctor?"

"Yeah. I did. I'm fine."

"No concussion?"

I shook my head. "No."

They worried the leaves and stalks of the grass with the tips of their fingers. "I just wanted to rule out anything medical, you know? Like head trauma."

I didn't like the sound of that. I cleared my throat. "I'm really fine, Al. I have a bump and I'm bruised, but nothing that would've caused . . . *that*."

They nodded. "Okay. Here's the deal. I looked through some of my moms' scrolls, and well, visions aren't rare."

I blinked. "They're not?"

They shook their head. "No. People supposedly have them all the time."

Relief flooded my body. The stress and anxiety from the last two days melted away from my bones, and my joints went lax. My head thumped against the wall of the building; the painted wooden slats scratched against my T-shirt. The exhaustion crept in around my eyes, and I could totally take a nap right then. "That's amazing. So it's not out of the ordinary?"

Al bit their lip. "No. It's surprisingly normal for people to have visions, especially in dreams. That's where the whole déjà vu phenomenon comes from."

"Okay. That's so great." I smiled shakily, feeling a little loopy. "So why the weirdness? Were you just being mysteriously witchy today?"

"Because you didn't just have a vision, Cam. You had a psychic interlude, otherwise known as a glimpse."

I stiffened. "What?"

"I asked Danny what happened."

My body twitched. "You talked to Danny?"

"Yeah. Be proud of me. It was a whole *moment*."

I was impressed. Danny was the most laid-back of the three brothers, but that didn't mean he was easy to approach. They all possessed an untouchable aura of importance, which was a combination of their high school social standing, paranormal status, and the fact that all three of them were unfairly gorgeous. "What did he say?"

Al took a breath. "He said you were slammed into the lockers during the fight, and when you hit the floor, your eyes were open, and you were muttering. The fight stopped immediately once people realized you were hurt or were . . . something, but you wouldn't respond to anyone. Danny and a few other people tried to wake you out of it, but you were in a full clairvoyant state. And then you went limp and passed out. That's when he took you to the nurse."

I buried my face in my hands. My skin was hot against my palms as I flushed in both embarrassment and despair. All my fears about the incident flooded back in; my shoulders tensed, and my muscles bunched. "Oh my gods."

"Cam, while psychics have the ability to do a lot of amazing things, like read auras and sense things beyond the physical, not many of them can go into a clairvoyant trance like you did. That's an extraordinary skill."

I gulped. "It is?"

"Yeah. The ability to see a glimpse of the future is really uncommon. And what Danny described to me is exactly how the scrolls described it too."

"Did he know . . ." I trailed off.

Al winced. "Oh yeah. He literally asked me if I wanted to know about the fight or your glimpse when I walked up to him. And that's not all."

I groaned. Pulling my knees to my chest, I rested my forehead on the ripped fabric of my jeans. What could be worse? Everyone had seen me in some weird psychic state. Not to mention that I had witnessed a girl gruesomely dying.

"Cam," they said, tugging on my sleeve. "Are you listening?"

"I don't want to know."

"Yes, you do. Seers are extremely rare. Divination is one of the hardest and most difficult talents in the witch community.

And according to the Psychic Guild website, most psychics aren't clairvoyant."

"Kind of like how all pineapples are fruit, but not all fruit is pineapple."

They snapped their fingers. "Exactly. All clairvoyants are psychics, but not all psychics are clairvoyant. Divination as a discipline takes years of study and work. And most people use an instrument to offer insight into a possible future, like tarot cards or palms or even tea leaves. Then they counsel the people who seek them out. It's an important function in their respective communities. The Psychic Guild has a whole class specifically designed for non-psychics to understand the intricacies of foresight."

"That's nice of them, I guess."

"Part of their educational outreach. Anyway, people who have actual psychic interludes, like the one you had, are one in several million. The last verified seer in this area died a *century* ago."

"Verified?"

"Someone who has accurate glimpses."

"Wait. They can be inaccurate? They can be wrong?"

Al sighed. "Yes."

I shot up from my slump. "What? So there's a chance the glimpse I had was incorrect."

Al shrugged. "I mean, there's a greater chance it's false than true. That's what the scrolls said."

That was great. If what I saw wasn't accurate, then . . . that'd be awesome. The best outcome, even.

"There's also, like, so much more," Al continued. "Like what triggered your glimpse, and how can you control it, and how to know if what you saw will come true."

I shuddered and covered it by running a hand through my hair, gingerly touching the knot on the back of my head. It was still swollen and tender. "I hope it's not via head injury," I said. "That would suck."

Al gave me a wry glance. "I read that it could be through touch, though." At my confused look, they sighed. "You flinched away from me after school."

"So?"

"So maybe that's what triggered it, and your body reacted via sense memory. Did someone touch you in that fight?"

"Yeah, about a dozen people. The people who hit me, the people who tripped over me, the person who helped me up the first time . . . I couldn't see any of them, though. Everything was a blur."

And the girl in the vision . . . I didn't recognize her at all. Was she a classmate? Holy shit, had she been part of the fight yesterday? Had she touched my hand, leading me to see her horrible end? Bile gurgled into my throat.

Al nudged my shoe with the toe of their boot. "Cam, what did you see?"

I swallowed. And with my eyes squeezed shut, I told Al everything. Exactly what I'd witnessed. All of it. How it felt. How it smelled. What I'd heard. Every little detail.

I didn't realize I was crying until I stopped and took a stuttering breath, a sob caught in my throat. I opened my eyes and wiped away the stream of tears that had slid down my cheeks.

Al stared at me in silent shock. They reached out to touch my hand but paused before their skin touched mine. They clenched their jaw, placed a comforting hand on my clothed shoulder instead, and squeezed.

"I'm sorry. That sounds so disturbing."

I chuckled humorlessly. "Yeah," I said, my voice flat. "It was. So what do I do now?"

Al gave one last squeeze to my arm and released me. "Well, it depends. What do you want to do?"

Run. Ignore it. Crack a joke. Go back in time and not flee from a tough conversation in the lunchroom and get lost and end up in that hallway and subsequently get swept up into a fight. But I couldn't go back in time. And I couldn't ignore it. That was someone's possible future, and . . . and . . . I had to know if it was inaccurate or, gods forbid, *true*.

"I don't want *this*," I said, waving my hands, indicating the possibility of being clairvoyant. "But I can't ignore what I saw."

"I agree."

I bit my lip. "Maybe we figure out who the girl is and warn her? And tell her not to go wandering around at night near a forest. Just until we can figure out what's going on with me."

"Okay. We can do that." Al tapped their chin, lost in thought. "The school library probably has old yearbooks from the other high schools. We can look through them and see if we can find her. If she's from the area, she'll be in there."

"That's not a bad idea."

"Well, I only have good ones."

I rolled my eyes. "Okay. Do you think the library is open now?"

Al shook their head. "Oh, no, friend. You look like hell. You're going home to rest. We'll go tomorrow after school."

"But what if it happens tonight?" I threw up my hands. "What if—"

"You said the breeze was cold, right?"

I paused. "Yeah."

Al spread their arms, palms up, and tipped their head back, their face upturned to the sun. "Does it feel cold to you right now?"

No. It was hot. And the air was muggy and dead. Not a ruffle of a breeze in sight.

"Good point." But just in case, I checked the weather on my phone. The next few days were supposed to be hot and stale, with very little chance of rain. Not at all like the weather in my vision. That was a welcome relief. "Okay," I said.

"Get some rest." They gave me a reassuring smile. "It'll be okay, Cam. We'll talk more tomorrow."

Okay. We had a plan. That was better than what I'd had that morning. And even though I still felt awful and guilt sat heavily in my gut, at least I could look forward to a brand-new day and a fresh start at school.

8

WHY IS EVERYONE STARING AT ME?" I WHISPERED TO AL as we walked to our first class. At first I thought I was imagining the low murmur that followed us, but when the first freshman we passed whipped her head around so fast that her braided pigtails became projectile weapons, I knew something was up.

I'd done my best to get some rest. And by that I meant I'd laid in bed all night and stared at the ceiling and counted the little glow-in-the-dark plastic stars I'd stuck up there as a kid that had lost all their glow several years ago. There were thirty-seven of them, and there was no rhyme or reason to the pattern—no constellations or galaxies, no order except the whim of an eight-year-old—though my actively anxious brain tried to conjure one the entire night so that I wouldn't focus on the horror of the glimpse.

Since the whole "resting" thing had not gone as planned, I'd watched a few video tutorials on how to hide under-eye circles with makeup. I may have been humiliated the first day of school and absent the second and third, but this fourth day was my do-over, and I wasn't going to look like walking death. Even though I felt like it.

"Hate to break this to you, bestie," Al said out the side of their mouth, "but you're the tornado spinning the rumor mill."

"Oh my gods."

"That fight will basically be the talk of the school until it's replaced by something bigger, so just be your normal, nonchalant self."

"Just the fight?"

Al's jaw clenched. "There've been murmurs about the other stuff. I mean, psychic interludes don't happen in school hallways often."

Right. I should've known the account of my glimpse would be just as interesting as the fight, if not more. Especially among the paranormal kids, if what Al had said about the rarity of interludes was true.

"But it'll fade, Cam. Just don't freak out, and no one will make it a big deal."

Okay. I could do that. RBF engaged. Hopefully something juicier would come along shortly, and I'd be knocked off the list of the top five people talked about in hushed whispers by the lockers and water fountains. I needed some power couple to break up or someone to cheat on a test. *Oh, please let a student make a morally dubious decision before lunch so I can eat my square pizza in peace.*

Unfortunately, none of that had happened by the time I walked into my second block. I ducked my head and slid into my seat, tucking my backpack beneath my desk. I hooked my feet in the basket beneath the chair in front of me and pulled out my notebook and a pen. I was early—keeping my head down and engaging in a celebrity-in-an-airport walk through the hall had allowed me to arrive before everyone else. Al's don't-bother-us glare had been impressive and scared anyone from approaching us in first-block lit class, but they weren't with me now.

As a few other students entered, I curled around my book and hoped I exuded enough of a standoffish vibe to ward off questions and classmates. That hope lasted five seconds.

Someone tapped my shoulder from behind.

I closed my eyes and pinched the bridge of my nose. I could ignore it, but that might seem weirder than just finding out what the person wanted. I mentally shook off my nervousness and put my cool exterior in place. Slowly I turned and met the wide-eyed gaze of Kaci, Mateo's touch-happy girlfriend. Great. Was she going to ask me about the conversation I'd had with him three days ago? The one I had neglected even telling Al about? I'd hoarded the moments of that endearingly graceless interaction we'd had and kept it close to my chest as the rest of that day became public knowledge.

She regarded me with a blank expression, her green eyes flicking to the side every so often like she was distracted. I glanced that way as well and only caught the last of our classmates filing into the room. When she didn't speak for a moment, I raised an eyebrow.

"Yes?"

"Let me know if you need help," she said simply. She brushed her long strawberry-blond hair over her shoulder and tapped her pencil against her book.

"Oh. Thanks." That was surprisingly friendly and not at all what I thought she'd say. "I wouldn't mind your notes from yesterday if you can share."

"Oh," she said in return. Her voice had a quiet, dreamy quality to it—ethereal in an unfocused way. She lightly touched her throat with her fingertips. She had long, manicured nails; I unconsciously clenched my fists and tucked them into my lap to hide my own nails, which I had bitten jagged. A faraway smile stole across her face, her freckled cheeks bunching into pink apples. "That's not what I meant."

I gulped. "What did you mean?"

"You're spirited. Like me."

I wrinkled my nose. "Spirited? Like a cheerleader?" She slowly tilted her head in confusion. I added, "'Rah-rah, go Saints!' school spirit-like stuff?"

She laughed. "No, silly. 'Spirited' as in 'psychic.' I can help you with your psychic abilities."

I blanched. I could literally feel all the color leaching from my face as my mouth flapped open. "What?" I asked weakly.

"I'm a psychic too." She leaned in closer as if imparting a secret. "Among us psychics, we use the term 'spirited' because we believe souls are the source of our powers."

"Whose souls?" I asked, parroting her conspiratorial tone.

"Ours. And sometimes *others'*."

I floundered. My thoughts flopped around like a dying fish on land. What? She was a psychic? Um . . . "spirited"? Not a werewolf? Could she be both? Was that possible? I snapped my mouth shut and tried to gather myself. So much for remaining cool. I took a steadying breath. "Look, I don't know what you heard. But I'm not—"

"I'm a medium," she said, cutting me off with a delicate wave of her hand. "I see ghosts."

"You see ghosts." I said the sentence slowly, punctuating each word with wild incredulity. Because this string bean of a girl with a cute smile and shy demeanor saw ghosts.

"Yes. I see ghosts. Spirits. Souls." Her focus flittered away again, then settled back on me after only a moment. "There's one right over there in the corner," she whispered, her hand cupped around her mouth.

My whole body went cold and rigid. I craned my neck, but of course I didn't see anything other than a poster about polynomials.

"You should think about joining the Psychic Guild," she continued, as if she hadn't just tilted my worldview. "We're a great network, though we haven't had a clairvoyant in our ranks in quite a while. Clairvoyants are rare, you know."

I gripped the back of my seat. Kaci saw ghosts. There was one in the room with us. She was a member of the Psychic Guild. She was "spirited," whatever that meant. That was totally fine and normal.

"I'd really just like the notes," I said.

She shrugged. "Sure." She pulled out her phone and snapped pictures of her pages of notes from the previous day. "Can I text them to you?"

"Uh . . . okay."

Her smile sharpened. "I need your number."

"Right."

There was no harm in giving Kaci my number. Right? Maybe?

"I'm Cam, by the way," I said as I wrote my number on the top of her notebook.

"I know who you are." Her smile grew, and then she winked. "I'm Kaci."

My throat was dry. "I know."

"Your best friend is a witch. And everyone thought you were a regular human. So if you do need help with your psychic powers, my offer stands. Even if it's only to point you in the right direction for information."

"Um . . . I'll keep that in mind."

"Oh, he's coming over."

"The teacher?" I asked, looking around.

Kaci shook her head, smiling wide. "No, silly. The ghost." Her voice dropped into a whisper. "He's sitting in Mr. Smith's chair."

And okay! This interaction had dipped into certifiably strange territory. When my phone pinged with the notes, that was my cue to end the conversation.

"Thanks," I said, before flinging my body back around in my seat.

Her tinkling voice came a moment later. "You're welcome!"

The bell rang, and our teacher entered the room, throwing his bag onto his desk and plopping into the chair.

I shuddered.

--

The good news was that I was able to dodge any other interaction with the student body until the bell rang, signaling it was time for lunch. The bad news was that there had been no other incident to incite raging gossip, so by the time I'd made it through the lunch line and secured my square pizza, the whispers that had followed me all day reached a crescendo.

I slid into the seat at the table I shared with Al. They sat across from me.

"So," they said, drawing out the vowel before plucking a chicken nugget from their teetering stack. "How's your day going?"

I shot them a glare. "Kaci sees ghosts, and my algebra teacher sat on one during class. How's your day?"

Al's mouth dropped open. "Are you serious?"

"As a heart attack."

"Who is Kaci?"

"The girl who hangs out with Mateo. She sits behind me in class."

"Wow." Al shook their head. "Just, wow."

"Right?" I sipped my soda, the edge of the aluminum can cool against my lips. "She's a psychic medium, and she called us both 'spirited,' which is a psychic thing. I don't know. What about you?" I asked while tearing off a hunk of pizza. A cube of pepperoni rolled onto my tray, leaving a trail of grease in its wake. I picked it up and popped it into my mouth, much to Al's disgust.

"Well," they said, ticking off their fingers, "I've learned that you only swooned during the fight to get Danny's attention because he is objectively the hottest guy in school."

I rolled my eyes. "No, he's not."

"He is."

"Debatable."

"Yes, we know you only have eyes for the youngest Lopez brother. But that does not negate the fact that two-thirds of the student population would gladly die to have Danny scoop them into his muscular arms."

"Not so loud," I hissed, leaning over. "There are ears everywhere. And some of them hear way better than others. Or so the internet tells me."

They huffed. "Fine. Anyway. I also learned that you're not clairvoyant and it's all a ploy. That you *are* clairvoyant and have been hiding it your whole life. That you are completely inaccurate. That you have one-hundred-percent accuracy. That you predicted the end of the world, et cetera. And so on and so forth."

Huh. Those rumors weren't so bad. And technically they weren't wrong since I didn't know anything myself. And the more outrageous ones would only be believed by a handful of people. And Al was right. As long as I didn't give credence to anything, they would eventually fade away.

"Hey."

I startled so badly, I almost slid off my seat. Engrossed in my conversation with Al and subsequently my own thoughts, I did not clock the person who had sidled up. I recognized him as the potential friend Al had pointed out a couple of days before. When not hunched over his phone, the guy towered over the pair of us as he stood next to our table. I craned my neck to look upward; the fluorescent lights above cast a halo around his head. He had shaggy brown hair with bangs that flopped across his freckled forehead, wide shoulders, and an athletic build, and he wore a T-shirt with a professional sports team emblazoned across the chest.

He didn't give either of us a chance to respond in greeting before he continued.

"You the psychic?"

He didn't say it loudly, but all the air was sucked out of the lunchroom. It went so quiet that I swore I could hear the pen scratches of people still in class down the hallway. And I suddenly felt like the lead in a school play, where the heat and brightness of the spotlight were shining down on me, highlighting me only, while all eyes were glued to my every move.

So this was fine, in a room-on-fire-meme way. "Uh . . . I don't see ghosts," I said quickly.

He rolled his eyes. "But you're clairvoyant, right? You can see the future?"

"Um . . ."

He didn't give me a chance to gather my thoughts before he continued. "I have a basketball game tonight, and I need to know if we win."

I exchanged a glance with Al. I know we had talked about embracing our futures and ourselves, but this was too main character for me. I frowned at them. They shook their head. I kicked them under the table. They shrugged. Which was no help at all.

"Is it basketball season?" I finally asked, my voice cracking. "I thought football was *the* fall sport."

"It's AAU. Not school."

"Oh."

"It's an important game against the best team in the league, and"—he licked his lips, hesitating a beat before continuing—"there's a lot of pressure to perform well."

Ah, and wasn't that the universal constant of being a teenager? The pressure to achieve. I wonder if he recognized the irony in saying that and then asking me to basically go into a clairvoyant state on command in front of dozens of people. If I could even do that. Could I do that? I had no clue. Despite my best judgment, I had done a brief internet search the previous night, but all it had done was confirm a few aspects of what Al had relayed, which then proceeded to freak me out.

I stood from my seat to at least be eye level with the guy's chest, because crap, he was tall. "I hear you," I said. I knotted my fingers. "But I'm not what you think I am. Seriously, it was a fluke. Okay?"

He clenched his jaw. A red flush crept into his pale cheeks. "That's not what the rumors say. You had a psychic interlude in the hall the other day."

I glanced helplessly at Al. They grimaced.

I cleared my throat. "Look, friend—"

"Dennis," he interrupted, introducing himself and offering his hand.

Without thinking, I took it to shake.

His grip was a little sweaty but firm, which was great because in an instant, it was the only thing holding me up.

The lunchroom went dark. The lights cut out, as if that play I was the lead in had gone into intermission, and everyone and everything around me diminished into the background, muted until there was only me standing in the blue gloom. When the lights flickered back on, I wasn't in the cafeteria at all.

I stood on a basketball court.

The crowd roared in my ears. Sweat dripped down my body. My uniform stuck to my back, and my chest heaved with breaths. Excitement and adrenaline coursed through me. The ball was a comforting and familiar weight in my hands. My teammates' shoes squeaked on the glossy parquet floor as they darted and moved in an intricate pattern that must have been some kind of strategy. I glanced above at the clock winding down. Thirty seconds left in the game. I didn't know how to play basketball, other than what I'd learned in middle school gym class. But I dribbled down the court, around an opposing team member who had a hand in my face. Well, *I* didn't. *Dennis* did.

Dennis passed it to a shorter guy, who had put distance between him and his defender. The small guard stood just inside the three-point line. The clock ticked down. He faked a pass, stepped back on a dribble, and took the shot.

The ball arced in the air. It rattled around on the rim, then fell into the hoop.

The crowd erupted. The bleachers shook. The numbers on the scoreboard increased for our team. We'd won by one point! Pure elation swept over me. But wait—the referee had gone over to the scoring table, beckoning the other ref over. An anticipatory buzz swept over the gym as they conferred with the scorekeepers. I jogged over to the bench and stood with the team and the coach, confusion and dread swirling within my tired body. The referee blew a whistle; I glanced up at the display, and the score changed. The buzzer sounded for the end of the half. It was tied. Overtime. Exhausted and distraught, I collapsed into a chair on the sidelines.

And I woke up on the floor.

I blinked to find Dennis and Al hovering over me. At least I was upright: my knees bent in crisscross applesauce, my elbows resting on them, sitting in the thin crevice between two of the long tables. My head hung forward, my view more of Al's boots and Dennis's expensive sneakers than their actual faces, and I could tell from the pain spiking up from my tailbone that I'd fallen on the floor.

"Hey," I said, my voice a rusty creak, squinting against the humming lights above as I lifted my gaze to the room at large.

Al muttered a relieved curse.

Dennis's hands clenched at his side. "Do we win?"

Al cast him an incredulous look. "Really?" they shouted, gesturing toward where I limply sat. "That's your only concern? You can't even ask if he's okay?"

Dennis's thick brown eyebrows drew together. "Are you okay?" he asked me.

I nodded despite my pounding head. Nausea churned in my stomach, but I didn't think the few bites of pizza I'd had were going to reappear.

He pointed at Al. "See, he's fine. Do we win?"

Al rolled their eyes. They reached out to help me stand but paused and waited before touching my skin. Oh gods. I couldn't do another one of whatever that was, so I waved them away, not wanting their touch to accidentally trigger another glimpse. I heaved myself to my feet, using the stools and table for leverage. I wobbled, but it wasn't as bad as the other day. And as I stood, my headache eased from a painful throb to a dull ache.

"So do we win?"

I squinted. "I don't know."

Dennis threw up his hands. The crowd murmured. I startled, my body jerking. In my dazed state, I'd forgotten we were in the lunchroom, and I was surrounded by nosy observers. Someone had their phone out, filming. Great. My palms were clammy, and my head spun, and I wanted to ease back to the floor and take a nap with the abandoned floor fries and the gum stuck under the new tables.

Dennis fumed. "All those theatrics for nothing? What a waste!"

"Theatrics?" I asked, squinting at Al.

They wrinkled their nose. "Muttering." They gestured at their eyes. "You went a little glazed too. And you did fall over."

Well, yeah—I'd gathered the falling piece. I'd probably have a bruise. I wished I'd brought a hoodie to hide under, because I was unexpectedly freezing. I wrapped my arms around my body and shivered, goosebumps blooming all over.

"Sorry," I said, despite not really knowing why I was apologizing.

Dennis ran an agitated hand through his hair. "Whatever. Should've known you were a fake." He turned and walked away.

I wasn't known for bouts of anger. I wasn't known for overt emotions at all. But his dismissal pissed me off. How dare he? He'd bothered *me* during the one break we got during the day. And I didn't understand all this myself, but I for damn sure wasn't fucking faking.

"Hey, asshole!" I yelled, stalking forward, albeit with wobbly knees. "You approached me. I would've liked not to have a whatever-that-was in the middle of my lunch. And now my pizza is cold, so you're going to hear what I have to say."

Dennis stiffened, then slowly turned to face me. His eyebrows were raised. I walked right up to him, toe to toe, and wow, he was muscular and broad. This was a bad idea. Oh well. Too late now.

"And what's that?"

"Overtime," I spat. "It's tied at sixty-seven at the end of the fourth quarter."

Dennis stiffened. "What?"

"You heard me. That's what I saw. Take it or leave it. I don't care."

"You didn't see the end of the game?"

"No."

He rubbed his chin. "Huh," he said. Then he tried to grab my arm.

I skittered away, shoes slipping along the floor, until I knocked into the edge of the table. "What the hell?"

Al was in front of me in an instant, blocking Dennis's path.

"Okay, that's enough, Dennis," Javi Lopez said loudly from the other side of the large room. He strolled across the distance purposefully, but he was smiling, like he didn't have a care in the world. He tossed an arm around Dennis's shoulders. Javi was shorter than Dennis, but he possessed an aura of confidence and charisma that made him seem like the largest and most important person in the room. His presence dwarfed everyone else's, and he instantly defused the situation with a quip and a grin.

Javi gave Dennis a friendly but rough shake, and then turned to the cafeteria at large. "Let's all leave Cam alone. Go back to your lunches, kids. Nothing left to see here."

Javi winked at me. My cheeks went hot.

"I thought he was suspended," I said to Al.

Al shrugged. "For one day. Everyone said he tried to stop the fight. So the administration thought it was only fair to give him one day instead of three."

I hummed. That wasn't quite how I remembered it, but Javi was coming to my rescue now, so I couldn't complain.

Miraculously, the entire student body listened to him. They went back to their lunches, and the general hum of conversation returned to normal.

I sat back in front of my pizza. It was cold and floppy, the grease having soaked into the crust completely. Oh well—I had lost my appetite anyway.

"Touch is the trigger, then," Al said.

I sighed. "Looks like."

"And you saw the basketball game? How did you control it?"

"I didn't. That's just what I saw." I rubbed my hands over my face. "This is all so exhausting and strange."

Al frowned in sympathy. They offered me a chicken nugget, and when I shook my head, they bit off the end of it.

"When it happens, what does it look like?"

"It's weird. I saw the game through Dennis." I frowned at my lunch. "Like I was him on the court. Because I for sure can't dribble and pass, so it wasn't *me*. And I felt what he felt—the excitement, and the worry, and . . ."

Wait. I had seen this glimpse because it was what Dennis's future self would experience. But the other glimpse . . . that hadn't been from the girl's point of view. It was the experience of someone who had been there, who was seeing her in that field. Someone who frightened her, someone she'd begged to . . . stay away? Leave her alone? Someone who held a knife.

Al snapped their fingers. "Earth to Cam. What's wrong?"

"The girl," I breathed.

"Yeah?"

"She couldn't have been the person who touched me in the hallway."

Al cocked their head to the side. "Why not?"

"Because I didn't see the vision from her point of view. It was from someone else's."

"Who could it have been, then?"

My blood went cold. I couldn't believe what I was about to say. It sounded like something out of one of those teen drama shows that I secretly watched, but . . . it was true. It had to be true. All signs pointed to this conclusion.

"Cam?" Al prodded. "Who?"

I gulped. "Her murderer."

9

I SURVIVED FOURTH BLOCK BY THE SKIN OF MY TEETH. DESPITE art being my favorite subject, and one that I was actually proficient at, it was my first time attending class for the year and meeting the teacher. She was an artist and a stickler, and she informed me that I was already three days behind my classmates on our first project. That was not a good start to my tenure in her class. My heart nearly gave out when she dropped a thin stack of paper topped with the syllabus on my desk.

"Your classmate Mateo was kind enough to share his notes. I copied them for you," she said.

My cheeks heated instantly, and I glanced toward Mateo. He didn't look up from his book, but the tips of his ears turned red, then twitched and lengthened into points. He grabbed his bag and yanked out a beanie. Quickly pulling it on, he squashed the dark curls of his hair and tugged the edge down to cover his shifting ears.

The teacher cleared her throat. "Cam," she said.

I swiveled my attention back to her. "Yes?"

She sighed, then pointed to a stack of art books and instructed me to get to work on the essay due at the beginning of next week.

After that, I didn't have time to worry about visions or

basketball games or the fact that Mateo didn't look in my direction once during the whole period.

The library was deserted this early in the semester. Only the student assistant sat at the checkout desk, their head in their hand as they poked at keys on the ancient desktop computer. They didn't acknowledge Al or me when we walked in after the bell rang for the end of the day; they were too absorbed in whatever was on the screen. Which meant they didn't question it when Al and I lumbered around the study cubicles, group tables, and tall motorized bookshelves, until we found the stack of old yearbooks tucked away on a freestanding unit in a corner. We contemplated how to haul them all over to one of the rounded tables near the windows without garnering too much attention.

"I have a spell for this," Al said with a sharp nod, already spreading their fingers over where the books were at our eye level.

I bit my tongue. It would be easier to grab a wheeled cart, but I didn't have the wherewithal to argue after my spectacularly long day.

Al said a few words under their breath, and the yearbooks trembled. With a flick of Al's wrist, the thin hardbacks launched themselves into different variations of a swan dive, pages rustling and covers flapping as they hurtled toward the floor. I preemptively winced, but much to my surprise—and to Al's, based on their expression—the books banged to a halt right at ankle level.

Al grinned triumphantly. "It's not pretty," they said, beckoning the books to follow us as we weaved toward the back table. "But it works."

"It's great."

Al shot me an assessing look, but finding only sincerity, they nodded. We reached the table, and after a few futile tries to coax the books into ascending, we were forced to retrieve them from the floor. I didn't say a word as I dropped a stack, the thin covers slapping against the wood.

"Let's hope she's in one of these," Al said, tossing their backpack onto the table as well.

I slid into a seat across from them and shoved my own bag on the chair next to me. "Or let's hope that these visions I keep having are fake."

Al pointed a finger gun at me and made a clicking nose with their mouth. "I like the way you think, friend. I'm not all that enthused about sharing classes with a potential murderer."

"Me neither."

I pulled my sketchbook out of my bag and flipped it to the drawing of the girl. I slid it between us.

"Is this her?" Al asked, trailing a finger over the edge of the page.

I nodded. "Yeah. To the best of my ability. I mean, the coloring is not great because the whole atmosphere was weird, but she had light brown skin and golden-brown hair." I squinted at the page. "I don't think that comes across well. And the lines aren't great, and you know that figure drawing is not my strongest skill, and—"

"Stop," Al said. "It's good. It's very good. You know," they added, cracking open the first book, "if you aren't psychic, you could have a great career as a sketch artist."

I huffed. "More like a caricature artist on a beach boardwalk."

Al tilted their head. "Both are valid career paths."

"Shut up," I said with a laugh. I took the book from the year before and opened it to the senior section. I scanned the faces on the glossy pages, and when I didn't find her, I thumbed to the juniors.

"Seriously, though, you've gotten better over the summer."

I frowned down at the page. "Well, I didn't have much else to do."

Al pursed their lips. "Yeah. Well." They went quiet, and I realized we'd never addressed the not-fight we'd had in the cafeteria on the first day. I'd been so wrapped up in the events that had happened afterward that I'd never revisited why I'd run out of the lunchroom in the first place.

I wanted to broach the subject because I didn't want that hanging between us as we dealt with . . . whatever was happening to me. But it was a tender topic, an unsettling ache that permeated my being when my thoughts even edged in that direction. I gathered what little courage I had, my fingers trembling on the glossy sheets of the yearbook.

"So," I said as we both leafed through the books, "that was a pretty cool levitation spell. How is the rest of your magic going?"

Al shrugged. "Okay." Then they rolled their eyes and slid their yearbook aside, grabbing the next one in the stack. "Well, not as okay as I'd like. Amy is so far ahead of me, it's ridiculous. And I can't even . . ." They inhaled a shuddering breath. "I can't even brew a potion correctly. I finally got my package of water-sprite hair clippings—"

I gagged.

They shot me a look. "All our ingredients are ethically sourced. You *know* that. You've known that since you encountered Ma's vial of extremely rare dragon toenails."

"Yes. Regulations, paperwork, contracts with other factions. I know."

They nodded sharply. "Anyway, I screwed the potion up. And now I have to put in a request for another package." Their shoulders heaved with a sigh. "Amy is already using magic in her daily life, you know? Casting spells to help with her chores and with transportation, brewing potions, charming objects, and I *can't*."

The frustration in their speech mirrored how Aiden had sounded sometimes when he talked with our parents. A voice thick and on the verge of tears, shaky with screams held in the back of their throat. For Al, it was magic that caused that tone. I didn't know what it had been for Aiden, only that the arguments he'd had with my mom and dad always ended with that sound, like he was angry and tired all at once. If I knew why, maybe I'd know where he was.

"I'm sorry," I said sincerely, even as I shoved a book toward the growing pile of nos. "You'll get there. I know you will."

Al frowned. "Maybe. I mean, I hope so. That's . . . well . . . that's kind of why I wanted to help you find a different friend. I should be reaching out and socializing with the other teens in our coven, to help bond, and maybe that will bolster my magic ability. Instead I'm "

And there it was, the crux behind their push for a new friend. "Friends with me," I said, heart sinking. "A magicless weirdo."

They lifted their head and met my gaze. "Well, you may not be magicless anymore." They turned the book and pointed toward a girl on the page. "Is this her? She has a similar face shape."

I leaned in. "No."

"Shucks."

We sat in heavy silence as we pored over the yearbooks for an hour, looking through all the grades from the past several years from the other two local schools, and—nothing.

I snapped the last book shut, and a satisfying whack echoed in the space. With my hopes dashed, I slumped in my seat. "She's not here," I said, rubbing my fingers along my brow. I was equal parts relieved and stressed. Relieved, because at least I didn't have to go knock on some girl's door and tell her she might, maybe, possibly die in a field because I'd had a weird glimpse of the future. And stressed—well, we weren't anywhere closer to figuring anything out.

"Well, then she's not a resident of Shady Hallow."

"Or she was absent for each picture day for her entire high school career."

"Or she goes to private school."

"Or was homeschooled."

"Or," Al said, fingers tapping their chin, "she's not real."

I perked up at that. That would solve *everything*. "Oh my gods, maybe she's a figment of my imagination or a composite of a bunch of different people. That would be awesome."

Al rolled their eyes. "Anyway, Ma can't pick us up for another hour, so I'm going to start on homework. You might want to do the same, since you're already behind. And don't you have movie night with your dad tonight?"

I groaned and crossed my arms on the table. I laid my head in the crook of my elbow. My cheek squished against my overheated skin. "Or maybe I'll take a nap."

"That is also a course of action you could take."

The judgment in their voice was loud and clear, but I was tired. A short nap, and then I could stay up later that night and work on schoolwork after enduring whatever dated movie my dad wanted to inflict on me.

My phone vibrated by my outstretched fingers.

I didn't get texts often. Al was right across from me. And my parents were probably commuting home. Maybe it was Aiden!

I snatched it up and held it close to my face.

It was from an unsaved number, but just above the current text were the pictures of math notes.

Kaci?

You should see this.

Followed by a link to a video on ClickClack.

"You suddenly look worried."

I *was* worried.

When I didn't respond, Al leaned across the tabletop, brow creasing. "Who's that?"

"Kaci."

Al's eyebrows shot up. They clambered to my side. "Ghost girl from your math class?"

Reluctantly I sat up, my skin leaving sweaty streaks on the wood. I nodded. "Yeah."

"Are you going to click on it?"

"I don't know." My heart hammered. What did Kaci, who saw ghosts, think I should see? "What if it's a virus or malware? It could be spam—I mean, that is a pretty generic message."

"True." Al said it in a way that very much meant *false*. "Except it's literally a link to ClickClack."

My phone pinged again.

Seriously.

"Click on it," Al said, with a nudge to my arm.

"If this results in a jump scare, I'm going to scream in your ear."

"Noted."

I pressed my thumb to the screen. The ClickClack interface popped up, and a video began playing.

It was me.

A cold, shivery sweat broke over my skin.

Video-me marched after Dennis in the cafeteria, my honey-blond hair disheveled, my T-shirt rumpled, my cheeks flushed pink. With my jaw clenched and my eyes a little wild, I exuded quintessential teen main character energy—the person of the group who always bit off more than they could chew, caused some drama, and then needed the other characters to come rescue them.

"Hey, asshole!" My voice was tinny over my subpar phone speaker.

I cringed so hard, I could've turned myself inside out.

"You approached me. I would've liked not to have a whatever-that-was in the middle of my lunch. And now my pizza is cold, so you're going to hear what I have to say."

Dennis turned. It was very much a predator-stalking-prey

movement, and I was the prey. Wow. His shoulders were broad. I couldn't believe I'd actually done this, because in comparison he could've snapped my short, slight frame in half without breaking a sweat.

"And what's that?"

"Overtime. It's tied at sixty-seven at the end of the fourth quarter."

"What?"

"You heard me. That's what I saw. Take it or leave it. I don't care."

The video paused and then cut to a gymnasium. And oh shit. It was *the* gymnasium from the basketball game in my glimpse. The camera focused on the scoreboard overhead. I shot to my feet; all my muscles tensed.

"This is Gem-Jam from Situation Paranormal," came a high-pitched voiceover, "and I'm at the AAU basketball game featuring the Panthers versus the Wolverines. The reason? Camden Reynolds, the new resident seer, has predicted that the Panthers will tie this game at the end of the fourth quarter, sixty-seven to sixty-seven. As you saw in the video clip, student Dennis Smith, junior at Central Shady Hallow High, asked Cam to foresee the outcome of the game. Thus far it's been close, with several lead changes. Right now there are thirty seconds left, and the Panthers are down by two. They need a three to win it. Let's see if Cam's prediction comes true."

The camera panned down to the players on the court and zoomed out jerkily to show the crowd and the clock ticking down. My breath caught in my mouth, a distressed sound jammed behind my teeth, as Dennis passed the ball to the kid on the three-point line. He shot as the glaring red numbers of the clock ticked to zero and the buzzer sounded. The ball fell in.

"Smith passed the ball. And the shot goes in! Final score is sixty-eight to sixty-seven! Looks like Camden Reynolds was incorrect," the voice of Gem-Jam said with utmost finality. No room for argument. "Cam may have glimpses, but this one appears to be inaccurate."

And what a *relief.*

"There you have it, folks. Shady Hallow's paranormal community will not be upended by the emergence of a . . ." Gem-Jam trailed off. "Wait. There appears to be a conference between the referees by the scoring table. And oh! Asan's foot was over the line. The basket will only count for two points, not three."

The scoreboard changed.

67–67 flashed green.

"Oh wow! The score *is* sixty-seven to sixty-seven at the end of the fourth quarter. The game is going into overtime!"

My stomach dropped to my feet. I went lightheaded and plopped into the cushioned library chair like a wet rag. My whole body went limp except for my arm, my fingers white-knuckled around my phone.

The video continued.

"And Camden Reynolds has the makings of a verified seer. He needs three documented correct predictions to make it official, and we've just witnessed the first. The community will have to wait and see. Pun intended. Well, this was Gem-Jam for Situation Paranormal. Signing off."

The vid cut out.

"Cam?" Al's voice was muted, as if they were in a different room or underwater, not right next to me, watching me with concerned creases between their brows. "Cam?" This time it was a little sharper, more urgent, and the sound broke through the white noise that had taken up residence in my brain.

My vision of the basketball game had been *real*. It hadn't been a hallucination but a real glimpse. Not only real but *correct*.

The video began to play again, and Al took the phone from my hand, careful not to touch my skin. She paused the loop as my arm flopped uselessly to the table, my knuckles smacking the surface with a solid whack.

"Was that live?" I croaked.

Al glanced at the phone. They shook their head. "No. Recorded. It was posted about fifteen minutes ago."

"Okay." I was on autopilot. Basic systems only. No other functions active. Heart pumping? Check. Brain braining? Check. Everything else had crashed. Cam.exe was not responding.

"We'll find whoever Gem-Jam is and ask them to delete it," Al said.

"Okay."

"I'm reporting it. For . . . targeted harassment and misinformation. That might get it taken down before we even have to approach them."

"Okay."

"I texted Kaci from your phone, and I asked her to do the same."

"Okay."

"It's not that big of a deal." They grimaced as they said it.

Because that was a lie. It was a big deal. A very huge fucking deal.

I was a . . . seer. Prophet. Clairvoyant. Psychic. There was no way to deny it now, no way to pretend that the visions I saw weren't glimpses, no way to avoid the fact that they were accurate some of the time. Well, at least I'd showed them I wasn't a *fake*.

Oh shit. This meant I wasn't quite human.

A whine fell from my parted lips. My parents were going to *kill* me. I was going to be grounded forever if they found out.

And my problems were the least of my worries.

My gaze fell to the sketch of the girl on the table.

A cold shiver slid down my spine.

A girl who might be murdered at the hands of one of my classmates.

And I was no closer to finding out who she was.

10

WHEN I WOKE UP THE NEXT MORNING, TWO THINGS IMME-diately grabbed my attention.

Lenore was on my windowsill.

And I had a text from Kaci.

The text was the easiest to address in my rumpled, half-awake state. But of course, because my life had taken a turn into main-character-in-a-TV-show territory, the message was one that no teenager ever wanted to hear about an embarrassing video featuring them. Three words that struck fear into the hearts of every social-media-obsessed person on the planet.

It went viral.

Huh. Well, if there was ever a moment for an expletive, it was this one. *Fuck.*

How viral? I texted back.

Very viral.

Well, shit.

I slid out of my sheets and crossed the room. Better see what Lenore wanted, or else I would have an irritated raven on my hands. She stuck out her leg as soon as I opened the window. The scroll was more smashed together than rolled, as if Al had rushed to send Lenore, as if they hadn't wanted to be caught. Lenore flew away in a flurry of black plumage as soon as I had the scroll in my fingers.

Huh.

I carefully unfolded the message.

Mothers are pissed I didn't tell them about your glimpses. Grounded for reasons.

Ah, that was why the paper had been squashed, and why Lenore had left in such a hurry. It was a clandestine mission. But why was Al grounded? They hadn't lied. Just omitted telling their mothers a secret that wasn't even theirs. Weird.

FYI: the paranormal community knows. Be prepared.

Be prepared for what? For more jerks like Dennis who felt entitled to their futures at the cost of my free time? Or worse, the loss of my bodily autonomy? Great. More reason to find this Gem-Jam and . . . well . . . yell at them, I guess. It would be like closing the barn door after the horse had already escaped, but it might make me feel better.

I sighed.

Well, at least I knew more than I had when it'd first happened. I had psychic interludes. The two I'd experienced had been triggered by touch. And of the two, one had come to fruition as I'd seen it. Other than that, I had no clue how anything worked. Maybe I should take Kaci up on her offer and talk to someone at the Psychic Guild. Except . . . if Al's scrolls were correct, there hadn't been a verified seer in a century. Would anyone at the Guild even know how to help me?

Ugh. Why was this happening? I had wanted to coast through my sophomore year at the new school with my head down, unnoticed, while helplessly pining away for a cute werewolf boy. It was Al who had wanted a dynamic, self-embracing school year. I'd only agreed because of the very serious BFF code. So of the two of us, why was I the one who had suddenly developed psychic abilities? Al would've been way more suited for this. They would've loved it. But going viral? Being a seer? This wasn't what I wanted.

This wasn't *me*. Or at least not the version of me I'd known for the last fifteen years.

Was it? I'd experienced two glimpses, and one had come true. So was I really . . . clairvoyant? Was that who, or what, I was supposed to be now?

I put my head in my hands and gripped my hair in my fists. The pull and sting in my scalp grounded me, yanking me from my swirling thoughts. Okay. First things first. Get ready for school. Meet with Al. Find this Gem-Jam and tell them to take the video down.

I flew through my morning routine, opting for long sleeves when I thought about how Dennis had tried to grab my arm the previous day, and jeans with minimal rips. Trying to balance "fashionable" with "sudden psychic ability" was difficult, but at least hoodies were always in style. I paused at my dresser and, after an internal debate, yanked open the top drawer. I didn't want to stand out—that was absolutely the last thing I wanted. But "viral video" pinged around in my brain, as did the knowledge that my glimpses were activated via touch. And no matter what I did, I wasn't going to be able to traipse around school unnoticed, at least for today, and maybe even next week. I grabbed a pair of gamer gloves that a well-meaning relative had gifted me one birthday, even though Aiden was the one who actually played video games.

Aiden. Had he seen the ClickClack video? Would he contact me if he had? It *had* gone viral, so maybe he'd reach out? For the thousandth time since he'd left for college, I wished he was there, or at least accessible. But he wasn't. I had to rely on myself. I shoved the gloves into my pocket.

Okay. Now to move on to the next task of getting to school and tracking down this Gem-Jam person. I slipped down the stairs and into the kitchen for a quick breakfast before heading out. After that first day, my mom hadn't confronted me again, which was great but also unnerving, especially after her quarrel with the administration.

Anyway, her absence in my morning routine meant that when she popped up from behind a huge vase of flowers and a fruit basket, I let out a strangled yell.

"Mom!"

"Cam," she replied evenly.

I stumbled to a halt, one hand wrapped around a water bottle, the other reaching for a banana on the counter.

"What is that?" I asked, gesturing toward the massive bouquet and pile of fruit. "Are those from one of your clients?" My mom was a commercial real estate agent in New Amsterdam and sometimes received gifts from her happy clientele. It wasn't out of the ordinary for flowers or gift baskets to appear at our house—just not ones so . . . vibrant.

She raised an eyebrow. "They're addressed to you."

"To me?"

She held up a card pinched between her thumb and forefinger. On the front of the envelope was my name in beautiful, glittering calligraphy.

I frowned. "Where did they come from?"

"They were on the front porch this morning. Your dad brought them in. What have you done, Cam?"

"Me?" I squeaked. "I haven't done anything. I have no idea what they are." If this were a normal day, I'd have been affronted at her tone and the assumption that I'd done something ridiculous enough to warrant a giant package of nature showing up on our doorstep, but normal? I didn't know her.

I carefully approached the basket. The fruit gleamed. Not a brown spot to be seen. And the flowers . . . they were so fragrant, it was as if someone had aggressively sprayed air freshener throughout the kitchen and dining room. I sneezed and rubbed my nose with my sleeve.

My mother thrust the message at me impatiently.

Sliding my finger beneath the flap, I popped open the envelope and removed the card. A sparkling apple adorned its front. I raised an eyebrow and flipped the note open.

Please enjoy this small portion
of our bounty.

The Sprite Alliance

What the fuck?

"Well?" my mother demanded.

"It's from Al's family." I crumpled the note in my hand and shoved it into the kangaroo pocket of my hoodie. "In celebration of our friendship."

My mother's mouth turned down in the barest of frowns. "Really?" She eyed the fruit and the flowers. Then she leaned in and delicately sniffed. "Are they safe?"

"Why wouldn't they be?"

She raised an eyebrow.

"I'm sure they ordered them from somewhere," I said, my voice flat, shoulders drooped in weary annoyance. "I highly doubt they've been spelled. Besides, Al has been my friend for years. They wouldn't send something you'd consider dangerous." That was probably true. Unfortunately, the rest of my statements were outright lies. I hid my shaking hands in my pockets.

My mom tented her fingers. "It's . . . interesting that they would send anything at all."

"What can I say? They're witches. They do interesting things. Anyway, see you after school."

"Cam!"

I ran to the front door and hopped into my shoes. "Sorry. Gotta run. Going to be late! Thanks!"

And, holding my banana and water bottle, I slammed the door behind me. I grabbed my bike from beside the brick front stairs and rode to school. At least this morning was a little cooler than the days before, and I wasn't baking in my extra layers.

Once there, I jammed my bike next to a pair of humming brooms in the rack and locked it. I waited for Al outside on the school steps, under the "No Gum, No Skateboards, et cetera" signs. The area was abuzz in conversation, and I wasn't vain enough to think it was *all* about me, but there were definitely a few choice phrases that couldn't be anything but. If I thought the attention had been grating yesterday, this day was shaping up to be far worse. I did my best to ignore everyone, and despite my aversion to seeing myself on video, I opened the ClickClack app.

I navigated to the Situation Paranormal account, and my stomach ached at the number of views and likes on the video. Thousands upon thousands of residents of Shady Hallow and the greater New Amsterdam area, not to mention places far beyond, had seen that video. Despite my better judgment, I scrolled through the comments.

I know that kid! He's in my math class and hangs out with Spacey Kaci. She's such a weirdo.

Well, that was rude, user CentralShadyHallowSux.

Deepfake for sure.

Okay, well. Obviously not fake, because that had all happened literally yesterday. Jerk.

Gemma James is the most annoying kid in Shady Hallow. I hope Cam predicts a horrible accident for her.

Well, again. Rude. And also murderous. Maybe user TiffaniWithAnI was the killer I was looking for. I doubted it, but at least she'd given me the name of the infamous Gem-Jam.

Cam is cute.

Aw, thanks. That was nice.

This kid is so ugly.

Less nice.

All methods of divination are black magic. Do not be led astray! The end is nigh!

Gross.

And that was enough of the comments. I violently exited out of the posts and scrolled through the Situation Paranormal account. The video of my vision predicting the basketball game outcome was by far the most viewed. But the others were . . . all about the paranormal. Like where and when ghosts were most active. And basic lore about werewolves. A history of the Sprite Alliance, and why the different elemental sprites had banded together. The best way to repel a vampire if needed, and how some of the myths weren't true, along with a statement that vampires often don't need to be repelled because they are nice beings and deserve respect. Well, at least Gem-Jam wasn't overtly prejudiced.

I clicked on the one about the Sprite Alliance, since they'd sent me an enormous gift basket that morning and it wouldn't hurt to figure out *why*.

I was so engrossed, I didn't hear when someone approached, and I only looked up when a shadow passed over my screen.

Al stood there with their arms crossed.

"Oh, hey," I said, standing. I grabbed my backpack from the step next to me and slung it over my shoulder.

Behind Al idled their ma's minivan. Purple and pink puffs of smoke trailed out of the exhaust pipe from the magic alternative-fuel source. Amy hung out of the passenger window, her mouth gaping open, her expression one of awe, even though she'd known me for most of her life. She'd even seen me drool on their couch and had been there when I'd once shot soda out of my nose. She'd always regarded me with a cool distance, like she was better than me (she was) and I was just Al's weird non-magical friend. I guess she'd seen the video. I waved and called out a greeting to her. She squeaked, clapping a hand over her mouth, and then ducked back into the car.

"What was that about?"

Al rolled their eyes. "She's suddenly a Cam fan. Don't ask."

"Okay. So how grounded are you? And why?"

Al sighed. "Severely. And because I didn't tell them that you were a potential seer before the word got out to the whole para-normal community."

I shrugged in forced nonchalance. "They know now. Along with the rest of the world. What's the big deal?"

Al shook their head. Strands of their dark brown curls caressed their cheeks. "Because I should've put the coven first, before our friendship."

Ugh. Of course. And just like that, the relief I'd felt when Al had walked up vanished completely, leaving me hollow. "I'm sorry? Is it because we stayed late in the library last night?"

Al squinted. "No. They . . . wanted the advantage. They wanted to be able to approach you before anyone else."

"Approach me? Your moms have known me since I was six. They can approach me whenever."

"Not like that."

I furrowed my brow. "I don't understand."

"I know. You will, though."

"What does *that* mean?"

"Just," they said, their lips pinched in annoyance, "can we go to class?" They turned and climbed the stairs with brisk, irritated stomps.

"We still have, like, twenty minutes before the bell," I said, jogging after them to keep up.

"Well, maybe I want to get there early today."

"And I had another idea." I flashed them my phone screen. "I want to find Gemma James, aka Gem-Jam, and talk to her. And see if she'll take the video down."

"A whole lotta good that will do. It's no longer only on ClickClack. It's everywhere."

"Well, fine. Maybe I want to talk to her about the invasion of my privacy. Or maybe she can delete all the gross comments."

Al's amber eyes went wide. "You read the comments?"

"Well, yeah."

"Don't you know that the first rule of the internet is to never read the comments? Oh my gods. How bad was it?"

"'The end is nigh'?"

Al huffed. "Fine. We'll find this Gem-Jam."

"I have a spell for this," Al said, following me to the main office. "A tracking spell. I'm sure I could at least find what hall she's in."

I didn't have the patience or the time to indulge Al in a wonky use of magic that morning. But I also didn't want to hurt their feelings, and I surely didn't want to die. "It's okay. I have a plan."

Finding Gemma James was actually ridiculously easy. I went to the main office and asked for her locker number, and the secretary handed it over with no questions asked. The irony about invasions of privacy was not lost on me as I took the slip of paper and a copy of the school map from the top of the desk.

Al and I traversed the maze of corridors to the freshman hall in search of Gemma's locker. And the more the tension grew between us, the more I blamed it on Gemma James. It wasn't all her fault, but a deep righteous anger percolated beneath my skin the more I thought about how she'd blasted my unwitting glimpse and its consequences across a very public, worldwide platform. How she'd taken away my chance to reveal my ability on my own terms, to whom I wanted, when I wanted, or whether I wanted to at all. And I wholeheartedly knew the "whom" was *not* the entirety of the ClickClack userbase. With each step toward the freshman lockers, I became angrier and angrier. My face was hot. My hands balled into fists at my sides. And I was going to give this Gemma James a piece of my mind.

We turned one last corner, my sneakers squeaking to a stop at the mouth of the freshman hall. It looked the same as the sophomores'— white sparkling floors, freshly painted white walls, white ceilings with no pencil holes or blobby brown water marks as of yet. Blue lockers lined both sides of the hallway. At the end were huge double doors, which led to the inner courtyard and the detached gym.

Even though the incoming class was larger than ours, the area was sparsely populated for the time right before the first bell.

"What if she doesn't even use her locker?" Al asked.

"We'll burn that bridge when we cross it."

"That's not the idiom," Al said with a roll of their eyes, though a smile ventured to break through their otherwise sour expression.

At least I could still make them laugh.

There was a cluster of girls toward the end of the row, all surrounding one locker. One of them must know Gemma, or heck, even *be* Gemma, so I gathered my annoyance around me like armor and approached. The girls had their backs toward me and Al, and they giggled like only mean girls knew how. High-pitched, acid-laced titters filled the air as they did something.

"Hey!" I called, crossing my arms.

The group—three of them—startled. They whirled around, eyes wide. They had glitter pens and paint markers in their hands, which they shoved quickly behind their backs as they regarded us.

"What do you want?" one of them said with a plastic smile.

"Do any of you know Gemma James?" Al asked. They wore a bored expression that matched their tone.

The girls laughed. "You mean Situation Abnormal?" They glanced over their shoulders and giggled again. "Yeah. We know her."

Al yawned, then admired their sparkly purple fingernails as if these girls were worthy of only the barest attention. "And is that her locker you're vandalizing?"

"So what if it is? Are you going to tell on us?"

I inwardly groaned. I neither had the time nor the patience to deal with bullies. I pointed over my shoulder to the corner near the ceiling. "We won't," I said. "But that video camera probably will."

The girls paled.

"Also, the administration is going to be pissed at this first act of vandalism of their precious brand-new school building. I imagine they'll want to make an example of the perpetrators."

One of the girls dropped her pen, glitter exploding over the floor and her shoes. "Did you . . ." She pitched her voice low. "Did you see that in a vision?"

"No!" I said, dropping my crossed arms. "It's common sense."

Al sighed. "The bell is about to ring. You three should go and think about your life choices."

They didn't need to be told twice. They ran, tiny particles of glitter winking silver and pink in a trail behind them.

Once they'd fled, the artwork—and I used that term lightly—on the front of Gemma's locker was revealed. It wasn't too horrible. Scrawled across the metal door were the words "wannabe" and "abnormal" and "know-it-all," written in paint marker and accentuated with glitter. The whole situation wasn't great, and my heart sank.

But there was no Gemma. At least I didn't think there was.

"I hope she's not stuffed in there," I said to Al.

"I'm not."

We both spun around.

The girl who stood a few feet away from us didn't match the picture I'd painted in my head, based on the voice in the video. This wasn't some brash and confident teen investigative reporter. This girl was *tiny*, barely scraping five feet. Her hair was shaved on the sides over her ears, then spiked at the top. It was also alarmingly pink. She blinked her big blue eyes through her coke-bottle glasses and pursed her thin lips. Her pale skin glowed in the light streaming in from the window—almost as if she were a sprite herself, but based on the "wannabe" written on her locker, I didn't think she was. She held a large history book clasped to her chest in the cross of her arms, bearing it like a shield in front of her overalls and rainbow-colored sneakers.

"You're here about the video." She said it as a statement.

"Well, I was," I said. "But then I saw this mess." I gestured to her locker, feeling awful that Al and I hadn't stopped the girls, even if they'd been mostly finished when we arrived. "So now I don't know what I'm doing."

"Oh, that," she said, taking it in. She shrugged. "It happens all the time."

All the ire I'd stoked drained right out of me. "Oh."

Gemma pushed her glasses up her nose and peered at me, drawing her shoulders back. "You're in over your head," she said simply. "I did some research, and your family tree is mostly human."

Mostly? *Mostly?* What did she mean by "mostly"? "I . . . *What?* You researched my *family*?"

"It was all fairly easy. Public records. Only slight digging required. But believe me, I was not the only one who was doing it. I think you've already received a gift from the Sprite Alliance."

Al's posture stiffened at my side, any amusement they'd had at the mile-a-minute information from Gemma evaporating in an instant. "You didn't mention that." They said it to me like an accusation.

My stomach dropped. This was not what I'd been expecting when I had decided to confront content creator Gem-Jam. I really wished I could stir up some feelings of anger again. But all I had within easy reach was astonishment and a little guilt and a lot of incredulity, and something that felt an awful lot like dread.

"I didn't know it was important," I said to Al. "It was just a basket of fruit and some flowers. And . . . how did you know that? Are you stalking me?"

Gemma looked at me as one would look at a clumsy puppy. "No. I'm not. I just knew you wouldn't understand most of the customs around the emergence of a seer in the paranormal community. Oh, wait. Are you going with 'oracle'? Perhaps 'prophet'? 'Soothsayer' if you want to go old-school." She snapped her fingers. "I've always liked 'clairvoyant,' you know. It gives a certain je ne sais quoi to the role."

I exchanged a glance with Al. "What is happening?" I asked.

"I'm here to offer my services." Gemma stepped forward and thrust out her hand. I skittered back before I even realized it, not wanting a repeat of the incident with Dennis. She raised an eyebrow but didn't move. A rectangle of cardstock was wedged between her fingers.

I removed it carefully. It was a business card for Situation Paranormal, offering research on all different areas, including genealogy, history, hauntings, general paranormal phenomena, and the emergence of powers. She even had a podcast among her impressive list of social media accounts.

"Um . . . thanks. But my best friend is a witch, so . . ." I drew out the last vowel.

Gemma squinted at Al. "You haven't told him." It was another statement, this time directed at them.

Al grimaced. "No."

I could now add confusion to the list of feelings clogging up my insides. "Told me what?"

Al narrowed their eyes but didn't elaborate.

"Wait, is this about the 'be prepared' from the note this morning?"

Sighing, Gemma rubbed a hand down her face. "You need me, Cam. You need an impartial human on your team. And I can be that person."

"What?"

"The bell is about to ring. I look forward to speaking with you at a later time."

Gemma did an about-face on her rainbow heel and walked off, her massive backpack banging against her lower back as she disappeared around the corner.

The bell rang overhead, signaling that it was time to get to class.

Al and I walked to English Lit. We didn't talk, an unfamiliar discomfort growing between us. And I realized I'd forgotten to tell Gemma to take the video down.

11

GEMMA'S CARD BURNED A HOLE IN MY POCKET ALL THROUGH lit class. Meanwhile Al kept their head down, their curls hiding their face, and didn't talk to me after we both handed in our quizzes. For the record, I didn't initiate conversation either, because I didn't know what to say or how to broach the distance that had been escalating between us since the first day of school. What had started off as a crack in our friendship had suddenly become a crevasse as of a few minutes ago, when Gemma had revealed there was some kind of secret surrounding my newfound abilities that Al knew and had neglected to let me in on.

And I didn't know how to handle that at all. There wasn't a chapter in the best friend handbook that involved the unexpected emergence of clairvoyant talent in one of the parties when the other was already thoroughly rooted in paranormal society.

We parted ways without so much as a "see ya at lunch" or even a wave.

My heart hurt when I slipped into math.

Kaci was not present, and I was secretly glad. I hadn't texted her back after the viral video conversation. I'm sure she would've had something to say to me about the vid, or a ghost, or my apparent spiritedness. And I just didn't want to think about it anymore.

Yes, I'd had a glimpse come true on camera. Yes, the Sprite Alliance had sent a gift basket to my house. Yes, my best friend had kept a secret from me. Yes, a strange freshman wanted to be my advisor. Yes, a terrifying glimpse was hanging over my head, and I had no clue who the girl killed in it was, nor the person who'd touched me in the hallway to trigger it.

And no. I didn't want to talk about any of it. Okay. Thanks.

I pulled my hood over my head in the hallways, and when the bell finally rang for lunch, I decided not to head to the cafeteria. I couldn't stay in the classroom because it was the teacher's break, so I headed to the vending machines near the gym. Luckily, I had enough cash on my debit card and was able to secure a bottle of soda and a bag of chips.

I didn't want to go to the library because there would certainly be people there. So I wandered the halls, like one of the ghosts Kaci saw, until I found an empty room. It was the honors science lab, and it was the perfect place for me to disappear for a little while.

I eased open the door a crack and wiggled in. The lights hummed overhead, and someone's backpack was lying on one of the thick block tables, but they were probably at lunch. I slid onto one of the stools, hooking my feet in the rungs, and dropped my vending machine spoils on the table.

I pushed back my hood and sighed as I took my phone from my pocket, allowing my body to melt onto the cool surface.

"You shouldn't be in here."

Oh crap. I raised my head and bit back a sigh. The owner of the backpack *was* there. He'd just been in the supply closet at the back of the classroom. And it was none other than Mateo.

Heat rushed to my cheeks. "I know. I should be at lunch, but I'm a little tired of being gawked at, and I really don't want another Dennis scenario."

Mateo raised his eyebrows. He set a thick textbook on the table near his backpack and reached into his bag. "Al's glare seems to be enough to keep people away," he said, taking out his own lunch. The corner of his mouth quirked.

In any other universe, I'd be beside myself in the presence of Mateo alone, and over the moon hearing him joke. But I was exhausted and felt like crap.

"Yeah, well, Al and I aren't exactly on the same page at the moment." I winced as I said it. I pulled my hand into my sleeve and rubbed the fabric over my face. "Just give me a minute and I'll leave."

"You can stay," Mateo said quietly.

"I can?"

He shrugged. "When Kaci has a bad day and doesn't come to school, I come in here to study and eat lunch. Ms. Downs doesn't mind."

"Ah." Right. Kaci. His girlfriend. I hadn't seen them during my lunch block, but I hadn't really looked for them to be honest. Too much had been going on, and I didn't think my heart could take seeing them cuddle each other in the cafeteria.

"I'm going to study," Mateo said.

I mimed zipping my lips, taking the hint.

Mateo stared, then sat on a stool. Two lab tables were between us, but Mateo faced me as he took out his lunch. He flipped open a textbook, settling in, and that was my cue to focus on my bag of chips and my bottle of soda. Except they didn't seem as appealing as they had a few moments ago. I pushed them away and buried my face in the crook of my arm. The soft fuzzy fabric of my hoodie brushed my cheeks, and the familiar smell of faded detergent and fabric softener was weirdly comforting. I pulled up my hood, blocking out the sight of Mateo and the brightness of the overhead lights. Then I allowed myself to shed the pressures that had plagued me and just relax for a moment.

The swish of Mateo turning the pages of his book became background noise as my eyes slid closed. I wasn't fully asleep, just drifting, but it was . . . nice to exist in silence. No need to talk about anything. No expectations to address all the big changes happening in my life. Just the quiet rustle of pages and the occasional scratch of a pencil.

I didn't remember falling asleep. But Mateo woke me up with his large hand on my shoulder, gently squeezing it.

"Cam?" he said, his voice soft.

"Yeah?" I mumbled.

"The bell's going to ring."

The weight of his touch lifted. I pushed up to my elbows, blinking slowly. "It is?"

Mateo stood next to me, his backpack slung over one shoulder. "In two minutes."

I groaned and rubbed the sleep from my eyes. "Then why didn't you let me have two more minutes?" I grumbled.

"I didn't think you'd want the sound to jar you awake."

And shit. Mateo was considerate as well as breathtakingly handsome. Kaci was a really lucky psychic. "Oh. Thank you. Sorry, I'm grumpy when I wake up."

I swept my hair out of my eyes. The blond ends stuck out from the edge of my hood.

"No worries." His lips twitched into a small grin. "You should hear Danny in the morning. He cusses so much, my mom bought him his own personal swear jar."

"Danny?" I asked. "Your really composed and mature older brother?"

Mateo snorted. "The same."

"Huh."

The bell rang, signaling an end to our conversation.

"Well, this has been fun," I said, grabbing my things and shoving them into the front pocket of my hoodie. "We should do this again sometime."

"Which part? Hiding, studying, or napping?"

I blushed. "Who says we can't do all three?"

Mateo chuckled. It was a low, breathy sound, and it was a punch to my gut. For as much as I had spent the last year staring at Mateo whenever I was in his general vicinity, I'd only heard him laugh a scant few times.

Mateo walked toward the door, leaving me having a crisis on the lab stool.

"Sure," he tossed over his shoulder nonchalantly as he left the room.

My brain short-circuited. Was that flirting? No. It couldn't have been. Mateo was just being politely playful. But I sat staring at the classroom door for way longer than appropriate as I replayed the conversation.

I was late to class.

12

I MADE IT TO THE WEEKEND.

Friday night I spent streaming the newest superhero TV show that had just dropped, intent on not thinking about visions or Al or the paranormal community or *any* of it. Since I was sequestered in my room, my parents didn't even bother me for dinner. I just heated up a frozen pizza and sat on my bed while I watched flashy fight scenes and listened to expositional dialogue.

I slept through the morning on Saturday. My parents had already left for their weekly trip to the farmer's market.

But at around noon, the doorbell rang.

A small spark of hope lit in my chest as I thundered down the stairs, hoping that Al was on the other side. We'd been noncommunicative since early Friday. I didn't know what either of us was doing, honestly, but every time I unlocked my phone to text them, I just didn't. Maybe because, deep down, I knew that the conversation that might follow was going to hurt. And I wanted to avoid that as much as I could.

But maybe it was Al.

Or Aiden! What I wouldn't give for it to be Aiden. I *needed* a hug.

But when I wrenched open the door, it was neither of them.

A brand-new bike sat on the porch. The paint a sparkling

green. It was far nicer than the current bike I owned, since that one had been a birthday gift back in middle school. A tag hung from the handlebars. I yanked it off to read the message in thick black lettering.

We look forward to meeting you.

The Psychic Guild

Okay. A gift basket was one thing. But a bike? One that easily cost several hundred dollars?

I looked around the front porch, but there was no sign of who-ever had rung the bell. Shoving the message into the pocket of my sweats, I eased the bike under the awning where my old bike also currently sat. Hopefully my parents wouldn't notice it when they came home.

But this did mean that Gemma was right—I was in over my head.

Trudging back upstairs, I picked the jeans from Friday off the floor and rummaged through the pocket. The edge of Gemma's business card bit into my palm as I yanked it out.

The embossed lettering gleamed in the afternoon light coming in from my window.

Well, it couldn't hurt to reach out. I tapped a text and hit send.

This is Cam. Can you talk?

The response was immediate.

Meet me in an hour at Drip.

Don't ride the new bike.

That was creepy. How did she know already? Well, at least it proved she had connections and a much wider knowledge of the paranormal factions than I did.

I texted her back.

Okay.

I freshened up, changed my clothes, and headed out on my old bike to the coffee shop. It wasn't that far of a ride, and the day was nice. My flannel shirt flapped behind me in a breeze that signaled summer was finally breaking toward fall.

Drip was housed on the bottom floor of an old brick building in Shady Hallow's downtown area. It was hipster trendy, not a location I thought Gemma would use for a meeting, but at least it had a bike-and-broom rack outside. I locked my bike and pushed through the entrance, grateful for the blast of cool air that greeted me as I stepped over the threshold.

The interior was comprised of exposed brick walls and low hanging lights that emitted a soft glow compared to the bright afternoon sunlight outside. I wandered to the counter and ordered a large iced mocha and a muffin from the bored college student minding the register, then moved to the side and waited for my drink. Small round, wooden tables with chairs littered most of the area, and there was a stage at the back with a single stool that was, thankfully, unoccupied. Low chatter from customers filled the air, and as I glanced around, I noted a few students I recognized from school among the smattering of people.

I tucked the sleeves of my flannel down to my knuckles and curled my fingers over my palms, suddenly nervous. Had any of these people seen the video?

"Iced mocha."

I took the plastic cup from the counter. "Thanks."

"I'll bring the muffin out in a minute."

"Okay."

I chose a table wedged by a corner, my back to the brick so I could observe the shop, and drummed the tips of my fingers on the glossy surface. I didn't have to wait long before Gemma entered in a whirlwind of pink-haired rainbow glory. She didn't say so much as "hello" before she plopped in the seat across from me, her stuffed unicorn backpack thudding on the hardwood floor at her feet.

She rested her chin on her tented fingers and peered at me, her blue eyes huge behind her glasses.

"So," she said.

"So," I replied.

"You need help," Gemma said. She seemed to prefer to make blunt statements rather than ask questions, like she'd misplaced her allotment of question marks.

"I need help?" I asked.

"Yes."

The girl from the counter came over and dropped a small plate with my muffin in front of me. She put her hands on her hips.

"The usual?" she asked in a flat voice.

Gemma squinted at her and gave a sharp nod. "Yes. Extra caramel drizzle, please."

The girl rolled her eyes. "Coming right up."

"Come here often?" I asked.

Gemma waved her hand at the departing employee. "My sister. She works here."

"Your sister?" I whipped my head around, taking in Gemma's sister as she worked behind the counter, making whatever concoction was Gemma's usual. She was tall with long brown hair, dark red lipstick, and black winged eyeliner. While Gemma exuded a chaotic, unbound energy, her sister decidedly did not.

"Yes. My sister. Val. She's from my mom's first marriage. I'm from the second. Thus the age gap. But anyway, she doesn't mind me hanging out here, and she makes good enough coffee that I can forgive the vibe."

I snorted. "Yeah. Didn't think this was your kind of place."

"It's not so bad. Just avoid open mic night."

I shivered. "Noted."

"Anyway." She leaned in and blinked. "The gifts have started appearing. Right?"

I peeled away the wrapper from the edge of my muffin. My appetite disappeared in a flash. "Yeah."

"And Al . . ." She trailed off.

The weight of the distance that had grown between me and Al settled like a stone in my middle. "We're not talking about Al."

"Fair enough." Gemma puffed her cheeks and blew out a breath. "Okay. So. Here's the thing. You're not a verified seer. Not yet. You need two more confirmed accurate glimpses."

"I gathered that from your video. Which, by the way, I meant to ask you to take down."

Gemma blinked. "Take down? Why?"

"Because it's embarrassing. And I didn't want people to know."

"Why not?" She cocked her head to the side, genuinely confused. Her blond, glittered eyebrows were raised, and her nose was scrunched in thought.

"Because I don't even know what's happening to me, and suddenly this new ability, which I had no idea I even had, is blasted across a worldwide social media platform. Do you not see how that would suck?"

Gemma sat up straight, her fingers clutching the edge of the table. She frowned. "No."

"No?"

"No. You have an amazing gift. You're destined to be the center of the local paranormal community. You have main character energy. Why would you hide it?"

"I'm what?"

"The center."

"I don't even know what that means, but it doesn't matter. I wasn't ready to share it, Gemma. You kind of revealed my psychic abilities against my will." And ah, there was the anger I'd been searching for on Friday morning. It flared to life, sending heat into my face. "It really sucked and has quite frankly made the last few days of my life incredibly stressful." My grip tightened on my plastic cup, and beads of coffee bubbled up from beneath the lid.

Gemma's shoulders drooped. She tucked her hands in her lap, and her cheeks flushed. "I'm sorry. I didn't think about it like that. I just thought that if I had an amazing gift like yours, I'd want everyone to know." She pulled out her phone. "I can take it down."

Ugh. That was too endearing. I should be mad at this kid, but all I could muster was a slight annoyance, and that was outweighed by a protective instinct. Like Gemma was an energetic kitten that had clawed the furniture, but you could only stare at her and coo despite your couch being ruined.

"No," I said on a sigh. "It's too late. Just . . . can you block the comments?"

"Yes. I'll do it right now." She opened her ClickClack account and tapped a few settings. "Comments are frozen, and I'll go through and delete the mean ones later."

"Thanks. And next time, for someone else, could you just . . . think before you post?"

"Yes. I will. I'm sorry, Cam." She ducked her head, sheepish. "For that I'll offer my services free of charge."

It was my turn to blink. I hadn't even considered that Gemma might charge me a fee. I mean, I guess I should've? She had actual business cards, after all. "Okay. Sounds like a deal."

"I'd suggest we shake on it, but your glimpses are triggered by touch."

Right. Glimpses. "Yeah. I guess so."

"You're lucky. I read about a clairvoyant from the 1700s who had glimpses triggered by *smells*. I mean, smell is the sense most connected to memory, but could you imagine?"

My lips twisted into a wry smile. "Yeah. I can. Pretty clearly, in fact."

"Oh. Right."

Val appeared with Gemma's "usual," which consisted of a drink with entirely too much whipped cream and caramel drizzle, along with a massive piece of pie. "We're even, you little ghoul."

"Agreed," Gemma said. "For now."

Val pursed her lips and stalked off, muttering under her breath.

"I caught her sneaking in after curfew," Gemma said as explanation. "I didn't say anything to our mom because Val is technically an adult, and I don't care what she does. But don't tell her that. Because I don't want my access to this shop's pie cut off."

"You blackmail your sister?"

"Yes. That's what siblings are for."

"Okay." Apparently I'd been doing sibling relationships wrong for my entire life. Well, maybe I had, since Aiden wasn't talking to me, and at least Val and Gemma were on speaking terms. I pulled off a piece of muffin. It crumbled unappetizingly onto my plate, leaving a blueberry smear on the porcelain. "So are you going to tell me why the Sprite Alliance and the Psychic Guild have sent me gifts?"

"Oh!" Gemma said around a mouthful of strawberry and cream. "Right. So seers are extremely rare."

"Yes. I know."

"Okay. Great." She leaned in, her elbows on the table. "And they are *powerful* allies. Think about it—you're a member of the Shady Hallow Coven of Witches & Warlocks, and you need an uninterrupted supply of specific ingredients to brew your bestselling potion. If you have a seer on your side, you'll know if a sudden drought is going to affect your supply chain. It's the same concept if you are part of the Shady Hallow and Sunny Peak Combined Werewolf Family or the New Amsterdam Suburb chapter of the Sprite Alliance. Seers can tell you any number of things that can assist your members. Also, they are great alarm systems—you know, in case tensions between the groups escalate."

My stomach dropped. My unease must've been apparent in my expression, because Gemma quickly continued.

"What? Don't act so surprised. It happens. Usually it's instigated by humans, but as you experienced in the hallway, other groups have their centuries-old beefs. And if a seer is allied with someone other than your faction, then they—well, know more than you do and have an advantage."

I froze. *That* was why Al's mothers were mad. They'd lost whatever perceived advantage they'd had from Al and I being BFFs once the knowledge of my existence was out to the whole paranormal community. In their eyes, Al had prioritized me and my life-changing revelation over their own coven. No wonder Al had been conflicted, especially if their mothers had grounded them for it. But Al hadn't spoken to me since Friday morning. Did that mean they'd chosen not to be my friend now? Or did that mean I'd have to choose to ally with the coven in order to continue my friendship with them? Would that mean I couldn't be friends with anyone else who was a member of a paranormal faction?

I took a large gulp of my coffee to soothe my suddenly parched throat. "But what if I don't want to ally with any of the factions?"

"You'll want to. For the perks and the protection."

My eyebrows shot up. "Protection?"

"Yeah," Gemma said, shoveling in another bite of pie. "Why do you think all the different paranormal entities have coalesced into groups?"

"For the group health insurance?"

"Safety in numbers. It's not wise to be on your own."

A cold blanket of fear settled over my shoulders like a shroud. "Can I ally with more than one group?"

Gemma squinted at me. "That's a good question, but that's not the way it's done. Werewolves don't ally with faeries, and faeries aren't interested in allying with sprites, and so on and so forth. They might be friendly with one another, but when push comes to shove, they're not friends. I guess you'd fit best with the Psychic Guild, but the last verified seer in this community wanted nothing to do with them. She allied with the witches."

"I don't understand."

Gemma heaved a sigh and set down her fork. "Look, Cam. I get it. You were on the outside looking in for your entire life. So I'm not going to fault you for not knowing *basic* information. But you have to at least try to follow along."

I bit down on every unkind word I wanted to say and let Gemma continue.

"If you are a verified seer, you will need to pick a faction and ally with them. There will be a contract where you get cool stuff or, like, money for your services, and then you use your ability for the profit or protection or prestige of that group *only*. You ally with the witches, you only work *for* the witches. No one else. It's tradition."

"Okay. Why and how did this tradition come about?"

Gemma rolled her eyes. "Like I said, *protection*. You'll learn this if you take Paranormal History and Society I and II as electives, which I highly suggest you do, but back in the day, seers were often . . . you know? Um . . ."

And this worried me. Gemma had been blunt to a fault up until that point. Why would she hedge now? "What? Seers were what?"

"Kidnapped. Or killed. Depending on the circumstances."

"Are you *serious*?"

"Deadly," she said, perking up with a bright smile. "But that was a long time ago."

My stomach churned. "But what if I'm *not* a verified seer? That changes things, right? Like, if I don't document two more accurate glimpses..."

"That doesn't mean you're not a seer at all. Just that your psychic ability isn't as valuable as if you did. The factions will probably back off. But you'll still want to consider joining the Psychic Guild just for the training and, like I said, the perks. I think the Guild offers tuition assistance and can even help you run your own small business if you want. Like, it's not a bad deal."

"What if I don't want to do *any* of it?"

Gemma's mouth dropped open. "What do you mean?" she asked with absolute incredulity.

"I mean, what if I want to be normal Cam instead of paranormal Cam? Is there a way to opt out of all this?"

"Um...I guess...if you want to? Well, just don't have any more glimpses. And if you do, don't document them, so no one will ever know if you are a seer or not."

I gave her a pointed look. "Like if someone hadn't uploaded a video of me to ClickClack?"

Gemma had the grace to look contrite. "Yeah. Something like that. Anyway, whichever decision you make, you need to do it quickly. Or the gifts will keep coming, and then the requests for meetings will follow. Think of it as, like, you're a super big athletic talent, and all the colleges want you on their team."

"Um...that seems like a lot."

Gemma continued, "Well, it's not like *all* the different paranormal organizations will want to meet with you. Only the regional ones, most likely. The vampires and the cryptids don't have chapters here because their members have congregated elsewhere. And they already have clairvoyants on their staff in the big cities. The local faery grove probably won't want to either, since they usually stay out of all the faction drama. Pretty smart, if you ask me. We're talking the groups like I mentioned before. The sprites, the witches, and the werewolves. And the Shady Hallow chapter of the Psychic Guild."

"Faeries?" My brain was overloaded. All I could manage was to repeat the word that had stuck out the most from what Gemma had said in her information vomit.

"Yeah." She opened a large notebook and flipped through a few pages. "Not to be confused with sprites. Faeries are immortal magical beings who utilize bargain magic and are fairly removed from the rest of paranormal society. They prefer to keep to themselves, and rumor is that there aren't many of them left. Sprites are mortal magical beings who utilize nature magic and are literally everywhere." She flipped the book around so I could see the pages and pages of lore she'd written. Then she turned in her seat and jutted her chin toward a group in the corner. "Those ladies in the corner are definitely a shimmer of sprites."

"They sent me a gift basket."

She pointed at me and made a clicking noise with her tongue. "That they did."

"What do I do with it? With any of the gifts? Do I return them? Or . . ."

"Oh!" She waved her hand. "Enjoy them. The factions know that you'll get something from everyone, and they don't expect you to give the gifts back if you don't ally with them. No worries. It's all part of the custom."

"Then why did you tell me not to ride the new bike?"

She grinned. "To see if you would listen to me." She pointed her fork at me. "I needed to know your character before I decided to work with you for real. I know I'm younger than you, but I know things, and you have to trust me."

"You're tricky," I said, narrowing my eyes.

"You have to be as a human obsessed with the paranormal."

Huh. That made an odd kind of sense. "Okay. I'll keep an open mind. That doesn't mean I'll do everything you say, but I will appreciate and consider your input."

Gemma beamed. "That's all I ask." She tapped her fork against her empty pie plate. "That and more pie."

I laughed. She peered at me through her thick glasses.

Oh, she was serious. "Um . . . maybe next time. I need to head out." While our meeting had been very enlightening on so many levels, it was time for me to go home and ruminate on everything Gemma had said. And text Al. I should text Al.

Gemma pushed out her lower lip in a pout. "Fine," she said dramatically, which threw in stark relief that I was hinging a lot of my decisions on information from a freshman. A knowledgeable one, yes, but still a smol teen.

Speaking of. "Hey, did those girls who vandalized your locker get in trouble?"

"Yes. You were right. The hallway camera caught everything. And all three were suspended."

Wait. Hallway cameras. All the hallways had them. Which meant there had to be video of the fight. The fight that triggered my first glimpse. The murderer would be in that video.

Gemma tilted her head to the side. "You look like smoke should be coming out of your ears."

"Um . . . question."

"Answer."

"You're resourceful. How would you go about getting video from one of those cameras?"

Gemma tapped the tines of her fork against her plate. "I have connections in the AV club. They could get it for me. Why?"

"I need to see video of the fight."

"Your first glimpse." She nodded as she stirred the melting whipped cream of her caramel concoction with her straw. "What did you see?"

"None of your business," I snapped. I took a breath. "Sorry. It's not something I want to talk about."

Gemma held up a hand. "Okay. I'm guessing you don't know who triggered it?"

"I don't."

She hummed. "Consider Gem-Jam on the case. I can also search for any videos that may pop up online. I'm sure someone filmed it."

"Thanks. That would be very helpful."

Gemma shot me a finger gun. "No problem, partner."

Oh no. Partner? I mean, I guess we technically were. Maybe Gemma was more my life preserver while I was drowning, and once I was back on land, where everything made sense and I wasn't navigating rules and social norms I didn't understand, we'd go back to being casual acquaintances.

Anyway, it was time for me to go. I grabbed my iced mocha and stood. "Well, this has been fun, but—"

"Gem."

Val's voice, coming from behind me, pinged my already frayed nerves. I jumped and dropped my drink, the remnants of iced mocha splattering across the floor and the hem of my jeans, reminiscent of my first day of school.

"Crap," Val said, stepping into my eyeline. "Ugh. Sorry. I didn't mean to scare you."

"Oh. No. It's fine. I'll just—" I grabbed a handful of napkins and dropped to my knees.

Val followed me to the floor. "No. Wait. I'll get a mop."

She reached out and loosely grasped my hand to stop me from spreading the mess around with the soggy napkins.

I was in a car. The shitty speakers fuzzed and buzzed a summer pop song. The heels of my stacked maroon boots crinkled the fast food wrappers that littered the floorboard. The scenery outside my cracked window blurred by as we drove through a popular commercial area. It was hot, but the wind whistling from the open windows offered a breeze as long as we were moving. And the rush of sound was a steady underlying hum to the music on the radio.

"I hate to admit it," the driver said—a guy no older than twenty with spiked blue hair, who was wearing a muscle shirt—"but this song is a bop." His arm rested on the edge of the car door, and his fingers drummed on the sun-faded plastic. "What do you think, babe?" He glanced over, his mouth pulled into a smirk.

I took a sip of my red slushie. "It's fine. It's no Metal Spike Baby, but it's not bad."

"Well, yeah. It's no MSB. Nothing can top MSB."

He reached over the console between us and grabbed my hand. He brought my fingers to his mouth and pressed a kiss to my knuckles.

I giggled and tightened my grip as our joined hands dropped to rest between our seats.

"You're such a sap, babe—watch out!" I screeched.

He dropped my hand and gripped the steering wheel, his foot ramming down on the brake. Our tires squealed. My seat belt snapped tight and hard across my chest, squeezing all air from my lungs as we thankfully slammed to a stop, barely missing the large dog that was running across the street. A leash trailed behind her, flapping along the asphalt.

My heart banged against my ribs.

And then our car lurched forward with the sound of crunching metal. My body whipped toward the dash, then backward, my head smacking against the head restraint.

Ow.

I squeezed my eyes shut as my boyfriend cursed, unbuckling and throwing open his door to yell at the person who had rear-ended us.

My eyes fluttered open to find Val staring at me with her blue eyes wide and a coffee-stained napkin in her hand.

"What the *hell*?" she asked, her mouth hanging open. "Oh my gods. Are you that clairvoyant?"

I groaned as I pushed myself to my elbows. I was splayed on the floor of the coffee shop. My legs were curled beneath me as if I'd fallen backward from where I'd knelt. My gaze flicked to Gemma, who had her phone aimed at me.

"Really?" I asked.

Gemma shrugged. "For verification. If you want."

"Are you okay?" Val asked. She reached out to help me, but I scrambled away, shoes slipping in my spilled mocha. Val curled her hands against her chest and shot a glare at her younger sister. "Gemma, put the phone down."

"Fine," Gemma said with a roll of her eyes, tapping on her screen.

I pulled myself back to my chair and sat on it heavily. "I'm fine," I said, leaning against the curved spindled back, arms hanging at my sides, legs pushed out, like a rag doll propped clumsily for a little kid's pretend teatime.

"Are you sure?" Val asked. "I didn't mean to scare you. I was just asking Gemma if she wanted a ride, because my shift is over soon, and my boyfriend is coming to pick me up."

"Wear a seat belt," I said.

Val nodded slowly. "I always do. Are you sure you're okay?"

I gave a weak thumbs-up. "Yeah. I'm good."

"I'm going to get a mop and a new coffee for you." She held out her hands awkwardly. "Just don't slide out of your seat. I'll be right back." She all but ran to the counter.

Gemma raised her phone and focused it on me again. "What did you see? For documentation purposes only. I promise I won't share it on social media unless you want me to."

I rubbed my brow. "Your sister's boyfriend slams on his brakes and doesn't hit a dog running across the street. But they get rear-ended."

"Any other details?"

"They're listening to a pop song. And her boyfriend kisses her knuckles like he's Mr. Darcy and she's Lizzy Bennet."

Gemma grinned. "Oh, that is so going to ruin her cred. She's going to owe me so much pie."

I hid my face in my hands. While I was happy for Gemma's future, which would apparently involve copious amounts of pie, I was even more conflicted about my own.

13

THE TEXT CAME THE NEXT MORNING.

You're 2 for 2.

Val is fine. Her boyfriend's car is not.

Let me know when you decide what to do.

I didn't decide on Sunday. I didn't text Al either. Instead I threw myself into my homework and caught up on all the reading and assignments I had missed. I even checked over upcoming coursework and added notes to both the calendar on my phone and the one on my desk, because I was nothing if not great at avoiding the larger issues by focusing on minutiae.

And I didn't want to think about how my last two glimpses had been correct, because that meant the first one probably was too, and I couldn't allow my brain to spiral down that road.

Monday morning dawned, with a slight nip in the air signaling an early fall. Al didn't meet me at our corner, so I couldn't show off my new, sparkly bike. And I couldn't unload everything that had built up in my chest over the weekend. Which was probably a good thing.

When Al didn't sit next to me in lit class, instead choosing a seat at the back of the class next to their witch friend Lex, I received the message loud and clear. I sat hunched over my notes, denim jacket tucked tight around me, gamer gloves on because I didn't have Al's intimidating glare to ward off any unwanted conversations. I half-heartedly listened to the teacher while I did everything in my power not to look over my shoulder.

By second block, my back and neck muscles were stiff from tension.

"Are you okay?" Kaci asked softly.

I turned in my seat. Her hair was braided into two long pigtails that draped over her shoulders, the reddish blond stark against the deep blue of her blouse. Her green eyes were a little hazy and there were circles beneath, as if she'd had a few restless nights, but she smiled gently. And I appreciated it because it was the first time that day someone had regarded me with something other than curiosity, fear, or like I was an exhibit in a zoo.

"Yeah. I'm fine. How are you? You weren't here Friday."

Her hands fluttered over her journal, her long, delicate fingers tapping against the paper. "I'm fine. I had a bad day."

"Ah, well—I hope you're feeling better."

Her smile blossomed like a flower. "I am. Do you like your bike? I helped choose it."

That was strangely sweet. "I love it," I said. "But I don't know if I'm going to become part of the Psychic Guild. That's all up in the air."

"That's fine. We can still be friends."

And wasn't that a knife to the gut. "Thanks. I'd like that."

Kaci grabbed her pen and made a note in her journal, then nodded. "Okay."

By lunch, I didn't know what I was going to do. I could go hide in the lab room and hope Mateo was there, but Kaci was in school, so he probably wouldn't be. The other option was to suck it up, go to the cafeteria, and hash it out with Al. Or maybe I could just skip. Avoiding everything did feel like the safest choice, but I didn't have a chance, because once I was a few feet from the door of the cafeteria, Javi looped his arm through mine.

"Hello there, Cam," he said as he guided me toward the entrance. Well, "guided" was a loose term. He basically dragged me into the senior lunch line. His hand clutched the crook of my elbow hard, with his fingers bunching the fabric of my jacket.

"Um . . . hi?"

"What would you like for lunch?"

"I don't think I'm allowed in this line . . . ," I said, trailing off as Javi grabbed a tray and slapped it down on the metal rail.

"Of course you are. Danny is a senior," he said, jerking his thumb over his shoulder. And oh, Danny was right there. "He usually buys mine and Teo's, so we're just adding you."

"Oh."

Danny sighed but nodded.

Javi grabbed a few items. "Chicken nuggets and fries for Teo. Oh, a salad with extra bacon bits and no cucumbers for Kaci. Pizza for me. Danny?"

"Salad."

"Salad for Danny. And for you, Cam?"

"Uh. Nuggets are fine."

"And nuggets and fries for Cam. Soda?"

This was awkward and bizarre. Was this meant to be a gift from the werewolf family? Was this their way of, for lack of a better word, courting the potential clairvoyant?

"Sure."

Once the tray was laden and paid for, Danny picked it up and trailed after Javi.

"So, look," Javi said, his hands on my shoulder as he pushed me onto a stool at a long table. "We know Al is your best friend, so we're aware that the witches have the upper hand here. So don't feel like you have to abandon a friendship to ally with us werewolves."

Huh. If he only knew.

"But?" I asked, because there sounded like one was needed.

"But we are worried about your safety. Al can only glare so much, and they weren't able to stop Dennis the other day."

Irritation pricked along my spine, and it wasn't from the fabric of Javi's shirt brushing along the back of my neck as he stood behind me.

"So we've decided, as representatives of the local combined werewolf families, to make sure you're not made uncomfortable by unwanted advances."

"Like right now?" I blurted out.

Javi threw back his head and laughed. "Nice. No wonder Teo likes you."

My skin flushed so rapidly that I went lightheaded. Mateo liked me? As how? A friend? Of course, as a friend. He had Kaci. He couldn't like me as anything else. I should just be happy that Mateo had mentioned me to his brothers. That he'd even *noticed* me.

"Javi," Danny said, his voice low, a warning. Danny placed my chicken nuggets in front of him. "Tact. Please."

Javi waved off his brother's concerns. "Anyway, so Teo is going to sit with you at lunch from now on. And where Teo goes, so does Kaci. Their BFF vibe is just like yours and Al's."

My whole body went rigid as my internal panic ramped into hereby uncharted territory. Javi obviously felt it, as he let go of my shoulders immediately.

"Whoa. You okay?"

"Fine," I croaked as Danny set the extra bacon salad at the empty spot across from me. And the other chicken nuggets next to it. "BFFs?"

"Kaci and Teo have been best friends since they were babies. Literally. Like they met in day care and have been inseparable since. Kaci is like the little sister we never had."

Huh. Okay. Worldview significantly altered. But that didn't quite mean that Kaci and Mateo weren't dating. Did it?

"Oh, is it embarrass-Mateo time?" Kaci asked as she joined the group, sliding into the seat across from me.

Mateo grumbled, dropping his backpack at his feet as he sat next to her, pulling his food closer. He was devastating today in his jeans and gray shirt, with a maroon jacket casually hanging off his broad shoulders and his long, loose curls artfully styled. He was the opposite of Javi, who looked like he had rolled out of bed, wild hair and all, and come to school in his T-shirt and flannel pajama pants.

"It's always embarrass-Teo time!" Javi said with a cackle.

Mateo frowned and shot Javi an annoyed look. "Mateo," he corrected.

Javi sighed dramatically. "Oh, right. You're all grown up and now only your favorite cousin is allowed to call you that."

Mateo squinted at his brother. "Do you even have this lunch period?"

"Technically, no. But—"

"Go to class, Javi," Danny said, his tone brooking no argument. "And leave our brother alone."

Javi snagged his slice of pizza, took a huge bite, and chewed obnoxiously. "Yes, big brother. I'm going now. Geez."

Danny rolled his eyes and swore under his breath. I looked to Mateo, who pointed at Danny with a see-I-told-you-so expression.

I hid my mouth behind my hand and chuckled.

"See you after school, Mateo." Danny rubbed his palm over Mateo's hair, sending the soft waves everywhere. Then he grabbed his own salad and headed to a table filled with upperclassmen.

"Wow," I said, stunned. "That was a lot. They are a lot."

Mateo huffed. "My brothers tend to not understand that they overwhelm people. We don't have to sit with you if you would rather we didn't."

And oh, Mateo was so kind. It was unfair that someone so ridiculously attractive was also considerate. "No! It's okay. It's fine. Kaci and I just talked about becoming friends this morning."

She smiled dreamily. "We did. It was nice." Her gaze drifted to the side, where Dennis sat alone, and she frowned. "That ghost again." She shook her head, her pigtails swaying. "I don't like that one."

"Then don't look," Mateo said, settling his hand over hers. "It's okay."

She nodded and looked down at her food. "Oh," she said, brightening. "Extra bacon bits."

And wow. The whiplash was unsettling. It didn't seem to bother Mateo. He merely squeezed her fingers and let go to eat his own lunch.

"Is this where we're sitting?" Gemma slammed her tray on the table and unceremoniously plopped into the seat on my right, across from Mateo. She was a flurry of pink and rainbows and energy. She dropped her massive backpack with a thud and sighed in relief, rolling her shoulders. "Wow, trying to get through the underclassman lunch line sucks." She nodded toward Kaci and Mateo. "Hi, I'm Gemma. I'm Cam's paranormal advisor. You may know me from my wildly popular ClickClack account, Situation Paranormal. I also run a website and offer other services." Gemma reached into the small pocket at the front of her purple-checked flannel shirt and pulled out her card. She thrust her arm across the table at the pair, the glittery cardstock jutting out between her fingers.

Mateo and Kaci shared a glance. Mateo gently took the card.

"Your account is only wildly popular because you posted a video of Cam," Kaci said. She wasn't cruel—I didn't think she had the ability— but her tone was surprisingly stern, bordering on accusatory.

"I know. And I've apologized."

"It's okay," I said. "Gemma and I talked it out."

"It's nice to meet you," Mateo said, tucking the card away.

"You're a werewolf," she said, her large eyes staring at Mateo. "I would love to pick your brain about what it's like to grow up in a werewolf family without the ability to control your shift. It's so interesting. Most werewolves learn to manage their abilities between ages ten and thirteen, but you're fifteen—almost sixteen."

Mateo's mouth dropped open. Pink bled into his cheeks and into his ears, which began to lengthen under Gemma's scrutiny. He ducked his head, grabbed his beanie from his jacket pocket, and tugged it on.

I elbowed Gemma hard in the side. "Gemma," I admonished in a harsh whisper.

"Ow. What?" she asked, rubbing her ribs. "That was unnecessary."

"So was sharing that deeply personal piece of information with everyone."

"How do you even know that about Mateo?" Kaci asked. Her lips were pressed into a thin, annoyed line.

"I have connections. Just like I know you see ghosts but can't interact with them. Most mediums can at least *hear* ghosts, or ghosts can signal to the medium in some way, but you can't breach the dimensional barrier. You can only *see* them. And you can't turn it off, which means you basically see them all the time."

Kaci stiffened. "I'm *working* on it."

"Gemma," I said, voice sharp. "You're being rude."

"I'm just pointing out that the three of you have the same issues. You have no idea how to control your power, and they can't either. It's fine. You're peas in a pod. Birds of a feather. A matching set. And I didn't even mention that Al can't—"

"Al can't what?"

I twisted around in my seat so fast, my preciously balanced nuggets tumbled onto the table. "Al!"

"Is this seat taken?" they asked, gesturing to the one on my left.

"No. It's not. It's all yours."

Al placed their tray down carefully. They eased into the seat, thoughtfully assessing the group of teens gathered together. "I'm Al," they said to the others. "And apparently I can't do something."

Al leveled a glare at Gemma, who shrank in her seat. "Um . . ."

"It's fine. It's nothing. We were all just getting to know one another." I scrambled to gather my wayward nuggets back into their little basket with my sad, limp fries.

"Great. I can't wait to get to know you too."

Another voice. A new person joined our lunch crew, sinking into the seat next to Kaci. He had green eyes, bright red hair, and wore a sweatshirt with the school's cross-country team logo across the front, and . . . wait a minute.

"Reese," Mateo greeted him stiffly.

"Lopez."

My mouth flapped open. I pointed at him. "You're the sprite who started the fight in the hallway."

Reese turned up his nose. "I didn't start anything. It was Nate." His gaze cut to Mateo. "Who is part of Mateo's pack."

Mateo's eyes narrowed. "'Family.' Not 'pack.' We're not animals."

"Fine. *Family.* But don't think I haven't noticed that we have one member of the Psychic Guild, another from the Shady Hallow Coven, and one from the Lopez werewolf family. I am *not* allowing the Sprite Alliance to be excluded from whatever this is."

"Lunch?" I offered.

He scoffed. "Right. Lunch."

"All we're missing is a faery," Gemma breathed, as if all her unicorn dreams had come true. "But no faery children attend this school, since the local grove is located in the East Shady Hallow school district." Her brow furrowed. "Aw, shucks. I could've had a paranormal bingo of friends."

My whole body wilted. I rubbed my brow. This was *great.* "Please don't go befriending a faery," I muttered.

"Oh, I won't. Not yet, anyway. Not until we've solved your problems," she said with a sharp nod. "Which, by the way—still working on that video. But I should have a solution by tonight."

"Great. Thanks."

The rest of the half hour passed in total anxious silence. The ambient noise of the rest of the students in the cafeteria only seemed to enhance the oppressive atmosphere of our table. A raucous laugh behind me, an excited yell somewhere off in a corner, rapid-fire chatter in another direction—all indicating that those around us were having a normal, fun lunch hour, while our vibe was so strained, we were like a stretched rubber band ready to snap back or break.

Mateo wouldn't look at Reese. Kaci frowned, her gaze drifting toward Dennis and the ghost she didn't want to look at, for some reason. Gemma pulled out a small tablet and tapped away at something—probably an article for her website. "The Top Ten Best Ways to Ruin Free Time," or "How to Lose Friends and Annoy People." Al kept their head down and silently ate their lunch. Reese grinned the entire time, chewing obnoxiously, as if the whole situation were *hilarious* and not the most awkward meal in history.

And I . . . well, I tugged off my gamer gloves and methodically ate my chicken nuggets, trying not to imagine what microbes were clinging to the breading since the nuggets had touched the table. But whatever. It was better than vibrating out of my seat because Al was next to me and Mateo sat across from me. And because I was the center of a paranormal gathering that might erupt at any moment.

Finally, after an eternity, the bell rang.

"Well, this was fun!" I said, jumping from the table. "But I have to go back to history and learn about the paranormal revolutions in medieval Europe."

I picked up my garbage and made a beeline for the trash can and then the door.

"Cam. Wait!"

Al jogged to catch up with me. I slowed my walk, and they joined me until we were outside the cafeteria door. Not wanting an audience for this conversation, I turned down a nearby hall, ducking out of the stream of other students heading back to class. Only a few students followed us, heading to their lockers; otherwise the hall was quiet, save for the spinning of locks and the slam of metal doors.

"Hey," I said, hands in my pockets.

"Hi."

"So that was the worst lunch in history."

They smiled, a small upward nudge at the corners of their mouth. "It was pretty awkward. I don't know how you befriended Gemma James."

"Purely accidentally."

"And what was up with Reese and Mateo?"

I rubbed the toe of my shoe against the linoleum. "I have no clue. Definitely some bad feels exist between those two. But I don't know why."

They cleared their throat. "Speaking of bad feels. What is going on with us?"

I looked up from my study of the floor. "I don't know. Why didn't you explain to me about the whole . . ." I flapped my hands uselessly. "The whole needing-to-ally-with-one-of-the-factions thing? I had to learn that from Gemma."

Al grimaced. "You have to understand. I'm in a weird position. My loyalty is to the coven first. And our friendship wasn't really a problem when . . ." They trailed off.

"When I was just human."

They scratched the back of their neck. "Yeah. You were a distraction then, but now you're . . . well . . . Now it's complicated."

"Wow." Hurt surged beneath my ribs, like I'd been stabbed. "Um . . . okay. I don't understand how that's a problem. Kaci is a medium and Mateo is a werewolf, and they're best friends. Why can't we still be?"

Al looked away.

"I don't get it, Al. Wouldn't your coven want you to be close to me to entice me? Or is there some kind of witch rule against it?"

Al's jaw clenched. "It's not that."

"What is it, then?" A new, horrible thought wiggled its way into my brain. That Al was pulling away not because of the whole clairvoyant thing, but because of just . . . me. "Are you ditching me for Lex? Is that it?"

Al's brown eyes flashed. "You ditched me Friday to hang out with Mateo."

"How do you even know that?"

"Lex told me she saw you two in the honors science lab."

My stomach churned, and it wasn't the questionable nuggets. "I didn't ditch you. I was overwhelmed and happened to wander into the lab while Mateo was there. That was not planned."

"Fine. Then what was today?"

"What *was* today? Do you think I had any hand in that?" I swung my arm out to gesture toward the cafeteria. "Mateo showed up because his brothers made him, and Kaci followed. Gemma is a whirlwind of chaos and does what she wants. And Reese was there for the giggles, if you didn't pick that up."

Al crossed their arms over their Hexes hoodie. The one we'd waited hours in line for because we both *had* to have the merch. My first real concert, and Al and I had done it all by ourselves. And it had been the best day, a bright spot in a summer of turmoil and loss and sadness. I can't believe Al was giving up on us . . . on me.

"Look," I said, swallowing my pride and my discomfort, "I'm sorry. I don't know how to balance all this stuff. I am new to this world, and it's confusing. Not to mention that Aiden is gone. I can't even imagine my parents' reaction when they find out. Our friendship is the only constant I have right now. I don't think I can do this without you on my side, Al."

Al bit their lower lip. "And I don't think I can be on your side, Cam. I can't handle all of this with you, not when I need to focus on myself. I'm a witch, and my coven needs me. It's my *family*."

They didn't say "and you're not," but it was heavily implied. My throat went tight with clogged tears. The inevitable end of Cam and Al, of Al and Cam, was happening right then in the pristine hallway of Central Shady Hallow High. I'd thought sharing a new school would bring us closer, but it had only served to break us apart.

"Okay. I get it." I'd wanted it to come out biting, but my voice trembled more than it cut. I wanted to be mad, to yell, but I couldn't.

"I'm so sorry, Cam."

My heart sank. "I'm sorry too."

Al blew out a breath, their cheeks puffing, and they placed their hands on their hips. "The last verified clairvoyant was aligned with a coven. We have access to their records. If you really need help, you could always ally with my coven."

I stiffened. "Seriously?" And there was the ice I couldn't find in the beginning.

"What?"

"You're using our friendship as a bargaining chip? Really?"

And suddenly I was on the wrong end of one of Al's impressive glares. "That's not what I said. But glad to know our friendship isn't special enough to warrant allying with my coven."

Ugh. How dare Al turn things around on me. "That's not what I said either. You know what? Kaci offered to be my friend in spite of the Psychic Guild, not because of it."

Al dropped their crossed arms. "Wow. You're comparing me to Kaci? Kaci, who you've known for two whole weeks?"

"No, I—"

"You just did!"

"Well, of you, Kaci, Mateo, and Reese, you're the only one who had the nerve to even bring up allying with your faction. They haven't even mentioned it."

"Oh, they're thinking it. Why else would they sit with you?"

I clenched my fists at my sides. Anger stoked hot in my middle. It was the truth. And it stung. "Really? You know that after one interaction?"

"You're the one who is suddenly BFFs with them after one lunch period," they shot back. "Why don't you tell me?"

"I can't with this. Where is this all coming from? You've been weird since the first day of school."

"And you've been so clingy since Aiden left. I can't even wave to a friend without you spiraling!"

I took a step back, their words hitting me like a slap. I swallowed. Luckily, the bell rang overhead, signaling we were both late to class. "Okay. Sure. Yeah."

"Cam—"

"I can't promise I'll ally with your coven," I said quickly, cutting off whatever platitude they were about to offer. "I don't even know if I'll ally with anyone. I need help and guidance, and I have to find someone who can provide that. Other than Gemma. You need to do what's best for you. And I'm going to do what's best for me."

Their expression hardened. "Fine. But don't come crying when the others reveal their true colors."

"I won't." I scrubbed the sleeve of my hoodie over my eyes, wiping away the water that had collected in my lashes. "So, what now?"

A tear tracked over Al's cheek. "I don't know."

"So this is us embracing our futures, huh?" I wrapped my arms around my body. "A friendship breakup."

"Yeah. I guess it is."

"Okay. Well. I have to go."

I didn't want to leave. My feet were stuck. It was my second tardy already in the school year. One more and I'd be written up, but I didn't care. Because once I walked away, that was it. Al and I would no longer be friends. I wouldn't be able to hang out at their house and eat all the junk food that I wasn't allowed to at mine. There would be no more lazy days of listening to music together in the wee hours of the morning and secretly buying concert tickets with scraped-together birthday money. There would be no more gossiping about the people we liked at school. Like my crush on Mateo and Al's crush over the summer on the pretty lifeguard at the new pool. There would be no more meetups at the movie theater to watch the newest summer flick, and no more messages via Lenore.

Al had been my whole childhood, and I'd never needed to question whether they would be part of my future. For the first time since the other fight in the hallway, I wanted to use my stupid ability, reach out, and touch Al's warm brown skin to see if this would really break us, or if by some stroke of luck we would still be friends down the line.

But I didn't. I curled my fingers into my palm.

"Reynolds. Wilson. Why aren't you in class?"

It was Mr. Cutshall, the vice principal.

"Cam was helping me find my contact. It fell out."

His stern expression softened. "Well, get to class, then. You're both tardy."

"Going, sir," Al said, brushing past me. "See you around, Cam."

"See you around, Al," I echoed.

Mr. Cutshall huffed and gestured for me to be on my way.

I left the hallway, dragging my feet.

14

C AM! IS THAT YOU?"

My mother's shrill voice hit me in the face as soon as I walked into the house. I groaned, dropping my backpack from my shoulders onto the entryway's cushioned bench. I wrestled out of my hoodie and hung it on the coat hook, jamming the gamer gloves into the front pocket. I toed off my shoes while lamenting the fact that my presence had not gone unnoticed.

"Yes. I'm home. I'm going to my room."

I picked up my bag by the top handle and swung it as far as I could up the stairs. It landed on a step and teetered for a moment, but thankfully it did not topple down.

"No. You need to come here, please. Now."

I tipped my head back, my eyes squeezed shut. I had a throbbing headache from trying to bite back my sorrow at my friend breakup with Al. I just wanted to wallow in my loneliness and listen to a Hexes sad song compilation while drawing gloomy landscapes. And yet that did not seem to be my fate anytime soon.

"Coming."

I rounded the corner from the hallway into the living room and stopped dead.

My dad was also there. He stood slightly taller than my mom and had a slim build. He still wore the suit he'd worn to work, though the tie was undone.

"Oh—hi, Dad."

"Cam," he said with a nod. His voice wasn't overly deep, but the way he said my name, clipped and strained, let me know the gravity of what was about to go down.

My mom sat on the edge of the couch, her back ramrod straight, her briefcase at her feet. She gestured sharply toward the armchair. "Sit."

I did. So did my dad, easing himself beside my mom. He ran his palm over his blond hair, his eyebrows knit together.

"Is there something you want to tell us?" Mom asked.

Oh. They knew.

I gripped the plush arms of my chair. "Not especially."

"Right. Let me try again. Is there something you think we should know about, that you might have neglected to tell us? Maybe something about a viral video?"

Fear roiled in my gut. A cold sweat prickled across the back of my neck. My parents had made it clear that they weren't fans of the paranormal community. They weren't overtly hostile to anyone, but a polite unease tempered their every action and decision when it came to nonhumans. It was a quiet discomfort around the people or things they didn't understand or didn't *want* to understand. They didn't frequent certain restaurants. Or have friends outside their known circles. They had never supported my friendship with Al, leaving that to myself and Aiden and Al's mothers. They hated that I liked paranormal bands. When watching sporting events or scrolling through newsfeeds, they would grumble under their breath when they perceived that something was unfair to humans, despite humans being the majority and having the most powerful voices and the most influence.

Aiden had always pushed back against them. Had always spoken out when he'd thought they were in the wrong.

I hadn't, because it had never affected me. Not really. I was going to be friends with Al no matter what my parents said.

But now that this might all go south, I realized how wrong I'd been to hide in my own complacency. I'd had the fleeting thought months ago that maybe Aiden's clashes with my mom and dad were a reason why he hadn't returned. But would he cut me off too?

"Cam." My mom's voice snapped me out of my thoughts.

Oh. Right. Interrogation.

"Fine. Yes. There's a viral video of me."

"And . . . what happens in this video?"

"I have a psychic interlude in the middle of the cafeteria, and then it cuts to a basketball game where the glimpse I had is proven accurate."

My dad cleared his throat. "A colleague at work showed it to me. Is there a possibility it could be . . . what did he call it? A deepfake? Created with AI or a computer program?"

I blinked. "No, Dad. It's me. That happened."

"So you're a . . ." My mom trailed off.

I leaned forward. "I'm a . . . ," I prompted.

"What that girl said. A seer?"

"I prefer 'clairvoyant.'"

My mom rubbed her eyes. "This isn't a joke, Cam."

"I wasn't joking. I prefer the term 'clairvoyant.' It has a certain je ne sais quoi, don't you think?" I said, parroting Gemma.

My dad's expression was a thundercloud. "Cam, be serious for once."

I straightened. "I am serious. Look, I didn't know I was one until the first day of school. It's not like I planned it. Or that I wanted that video to spread all over social media. But"—I shrugged—"it's out there now. I can't take it back."

"You've confirmed it?" My mother asked, her tone biting. "With whom?"

"What do you mean? I didn't make a declaration or anything."

"Good!" my dad said, snapping his fingers. "We can come out and say it is not you. That it was a fake or a hoax."

"Yes," my mom agreed. "We'll draft a statement, and Cam can read it on video, and we'll have"—she sighed, as if she couldn't believe what she was about to say—"Gem-Jam of Situation Paranormal post it. Hopefully enough of her audience will see it, and all this will die down."

"What? No!"

"It's for the best, Cam." My dad leaned back on the couch. "And then you can put this behind you and never have another . . . interlude again. Matter solved."

"The paranormal community has already seen that," I said, gesturing to where my dad had the video pulled up on his phone. "The fruit basket was from the Sprite Alliance."

My mom's hand flew to her mouth. Her fingers curled in horror. "I ate *several* of those peaches."

"Good for you," I said. "I bet they were delicious."

"They were," she said, appalled.

My dad frowned. He reached and took my mom's hands, their fingers threading together. "It's okay, dear. I ate one of the apples, and I'm fine."

I rolled my eyes.

"Cam," my dad said, addressing me with his steely gaze. "No more. This stops now. The video says there have to be three, right? Well, don't have any more. We won't make a big deal out of this as long as you don't add fuel to the fire. Got it?"

My heart ached. "Yeah. I got it."

He nodded. "Good. We ordered takeout. It's on the way. Why don't you go up to your room and work on your homework? I'll call you when it gets here."

"Sure." I stood like a zombie, my mind reeling, and shuffled to the stairs.

"It's just like what happened with Aiden," I heard my mom say. "How have we failed so badly?"

"I know, honey. But it's okay. We'll steer Cam right."

"We should have never allowed him to be redistricted to that school. It's filled with paranormal students. We should've fought the school board harder."

"It's okay. We'll make sure he doesn't fall into the traps that Aiden did. It'll be fine."

I froze at the bottom of the stairs. What did that mean? What had happened with Aiden? Did they know where he was? Could they have contacted him this whole time? Whenever I asked or brought him up, they shut down. I thought it was out of grief because Aiden had cut us out of his life, but ... was I wrong?

I grasped the banister, my knees suddenly weak. Hauling my body up the stairs, I grabbed my backpack, which sat in the middle of the staircase, and continued to my room. I pushed open the door. I was on autopilot, stunned by how my parents had acted. Like this was something I could just shove back into a box. Granted, I didn't even know if I wanted to be a seer. And I definitely didn't want all this attention.

But I couldn't deny what I was, either.

Two for two, as Gemma had said.

I tugged my phone from my pocket and pulled up my text conversation with Gemma.

Well, I had promised Al a themed school year. I'd promised to embrace my true self. I didn't know what that had meant at the time I had agreed to it, but I knew it now. Aiden's last texts to me had told me to follow my own path and to trust myself.

I could do that.

Maybe. Potentially. In theory.

Spite was a powerful motivator, and well, I wouldn't know unless I tried.

I took a deep breath as my fingers hovered over the keys. I typed a message to Gemma, and without overthinking it, I hit send.

Post the second glimpse.

My phone immediately rang.

"Are you sure?" she asked. She sounded out of breath.

I'd already lost Al. The cat was out of the bag to my parents. And they were pissed. They couldn't really get any madder. I had nothing to lose. "Positive."

"Okay. I have it all ready. I'll only allow comments from registered users at first, and if it gets too weird, I'll freeze them."

"That's fine."

There was a pause. "Are you sure? You sound a little . . . sad."

My cold, dead heart warmed at her concern. "Yeah, I'm sure," I said, trying for enthusiasm. "I'm good. Do it, Gemma. Before I have a chance to change my mind."

"On it, partner."

"Thanks."

"Oh, by the way, I got the video from the AV club."

I sat heavily on my bed. "And?"

"The stupid welcome banner was in the way. Sorry, Cam. I couldn't see anything."

Fuck. Well, par for the course, unfortunately. "It's okay, Gemma."

"I'm still trying to find another video angle. So don't give up yet! We'll find whoever touched you and triggered that first glimpse. Okay. Got to run. Night, Cam!"

Oh, right. The first very terrifying glimpse. *That.* I'd pushed it to the back of my brain in the face of everything that had occurred the last few days.

I checked my weather app. It was supposed to be warm all

next week. Good. I still had time. Because I needed another correct vision. And once I had that, I was sure I would be able to acquire help.

I would need any and all of it to hopefully stop a murder.

15

GEMMA DROPPED INTO A SEAT BESIDE ME IN THE CAFETERIA, pouting at her phone as she did so. Her backpack slid from her shoulders with a thump. Despite her colorful outfit—a mixture of yellows and oranges today—her demeanor screamed disappointment.

I could relate. Except the colorful outfit part. I'd been sticking to my hoodie and gloves for days.

"What's wrong?" I asked when she made a pointed sigh and set her phone down next to her tray.

Kaci and Mateo settled in across from us. My pulse raced when Mateo uttered a quiet "hello" as he slid onto the stool. I still couldn't believe that Mateo now sat with me at lunch. Even if it was under threat from his brothers, I'd take it. I needed all the good at this point.

"The second video hasn't garnered as many views." Gemma opened the tab on her can of soda and took a long gulp. "I don't get it. It's edited cleanly. I used all the same tags so it could be easily found. But it's not gaining traction." Her shoulders slumped. "It's not even close to viral. I wouldn't even classify it as an infection."

Ew. Gross. I did not appreciate that comparison. But Gemma's pouty face wasn't something I wanted to deal with. "Maybe because it's not firsthand video," I said with a shrug. The video was missing

136

that "oh shit" moment of disbelief and awe that the first one had. It was literally a video of me in a clairvoyant state on the floor of a coffee shop, then telling Gemma what I saw, and then an account from Val of the car accident. Her story had matched the vision, and then Gemma had filmed the back of the boyfriend's car.

"But it's eyewitness accounts."

"There's no drama," Reese said, dropping beside Kaci. "The basketball video was suspenseful, you know? There was that knife's-edge moment of whether Cam's prediction was right or not. This second one was kind of dull." He pointed his fork at Gemma. "It lacked spark. No offense, Cam."

"None taken."

"Full offense," Gemma muttered under her breath.

Reese was not wrong, though. The response to the second video was less intense than to the first.

I had made the decision to post the second glimpse knowing it would draw attention my way. That didn't mean I would revel in it. It was mostly just to defy my parents and, well, attempt to lean into this whole psychic thing and embrace my true self. Whatever that was. I was still trying to figure that out.

Also, Gemma had mentioned perks. If I was going to have terrifying glimpses of murder, then I wanted the perks, thank you very much.

"Did you at least ask permission this time?" Kaci asked.

Gemma huffed, then shoved her finger into my arm. "He literally told me to do it."

"I've chosen to go with it," I said with a shrug. "I am welcoming my potential as a member of the paranormal community, as a possible clairvoyant who has glimpses of the future that happen to be accurate."

"That sounds unexpectedly mature." The side of Mateo's mouth lifted in a smile. "For you."

Teasing! I would never get over the fact that Mateo was secretly witty and surprisingly playful. "Well, what can I say? I've grown," I said, straightening from my slouch dramatically.

Mateo snorted in amusement.

"So you just need one more documented correct glimpse?" Reese asked.

I nodded. "Yeah. Just one more."

He took a bite of his salad and chewed thoughtfully as ranch dressing dripped out the side of his mouth. "How are you going to do it?"

And that was a good question. All my glimpses thus far had been accidents. Someone had touched me in the hallway in the middle of the fight. Dennis had shaken my hand. Val had tried to stop me from making an even bigger mess in the coffee shop. If I was going to do this, if I was really going to be a verified clairvoyant, I wanted to be in control. I wanted to be purposeful about it. I wanted to be the one to initiate the process.

"Cam?" Kaci gently prodded me.

"I want another glimpse," I said quietly, my hands shaking in the pocket of my hoodie. "I'm clairvoyant." And wow, that was weird to proclaim with utmost certainty. Thus far I'd only said it in response to probing questions from others. I'd not really said it of my own volition. But I was clairvoyant. I had seen the future at least twice. I licked my lips and raised my head to meet all their probing gazes. "I want to see if I'm for real. If I'm verified."

Gemma's eyes were huge under her glasses. "I'm so excited," she said in an awed voice.

Reese hummed, then stuck out his hand, palm up on the table. "Do me."

I choked on air. "What?"

He wiggled his fingers and his eyebrows. "Come on. Let's do this. Gemma can take a video, and we can get this last one done. Then bam, certified fresh prophet."

"I prefer 'clairvoyant,'" I said as I stared at Reese's pale hand; my brow was furrowed.

"You don't have do it right now, Cam." Mateo frowned at Reese over Kaci's head. "Reese should know that ordering someone to perform on demand is rude."

Reese smirked like he knew he'd touched a nerve. "Of course Cam doesn't *have* to do anything. I'm offering. As a new friend. Unless *you* are up for a little glimpse of your future, Lopez."

Mateo scowled. The tips of elongated canines pressed against his bottom lip. He hid his hands in his lap.

"I thought so," Reese said with a nod. "Kaci?"

Kaci startled out of a daze, her gaze snapping away from where it had drifted toward Dennis, as she focused back on our group. "Oh no," she said with a shake of her head, strands of her hair falling in her face. "Cam would see the ghosts. I don't think he's ready for that."

She was absolutely correct. I might be ready to declare myself a psychic, but I was *not* ready to see ghosts. "Thanks for being considerate."

She smiled brightly. "No problem."

"Fine. Gemma?" Reese prodded.

"Ah, no thank you." She held up her phone. "Not interested. Observer only."

Reese puffed out his chest. "And there you have it. I'm the only one at the table who is ready to help. Unless Al is joining us today?"

A sharp pain twinged my ribs. "No. Al won't be joining us. Today or for the foreseeable future."

Mateo's frown deepened, but he didn't comment.

"'Foreseeable future,' huh? That's an interesting turn of phrase." Gemma cocked her head to the side, her rainbow earrings swinging. "Can Cam see his own future? That's something we'll have to investigate."

Ick. Suddenly I was with Mateo, uninterested in hypothetically witnessing my own future. I held up my gloved hands. "Okay. So this has dipped into not-fun territory. I do want to finish up the magic three that I need, but not in front of half the student body again. And while I appreciate the enthusiasm and consideration on all your parts, give me a second to think."

Kaci tapped her fingertips along the edge of her plastic tray. "Cam, if you don't want to—"

"I want to." I was so close to validating myself. I pulled on the cuffs of my hoodie sleeves and flexed my fingers in my gloves. But what if whatever I glimpsed didn't come true? Would all my new potential friends leave like Al? What if it *did*? Would there be more gifts? More attention? "I guess I should wait until we have a safe place. Away from prying eyes, and where Gemma can get good video."

Mateo heaved a sigh. "We could use the honors science lab." He muttered it under his breath, reluctant but ever helpful. He looked at me, and I flushed, thinking about our private lunch the previous week.

Reese raised an eyebrow. "You can get us into the swanky lab?"

"Don't you know?" Kaci said, squaring her shoulders and lifting her chin. "Mateo is in all honors classes."

Reese huffed. "Nerd."

"Anyway," Gemma said, leaning forward in excitement, "like, now?"

They all looked to me. I swallowed. "Yeah. Now."

"Sweet!" Gemma pumped a fist. "Let's go." She jumped to her feet, opened the top of her backpack, and dumped her entire lunch inside. Luckily it was all packaged, because otherwise the inside of her unicorn bedazzled bag would've actually looked like the theoretical inside of a unicorn.

I stuffed my still-wrapped cheeseburger into my hoodie pocket, along with a bag of chips. "Let's go."

We made a weird duckling line of students as we headed out of the cafeteria. Luckily, no one challenged us, and I was one-hundred-percent sure it was because Mateo was the head of our procession. He was an honors student and not known for causing trouble or even being in the wrong place at the wrong time, unlike his older brothers.

He led us to the lab. It was locked, but Mateo fished around in his own bag and pulled out a set of keys.

"I'm the only student with keys. If we make a mess . . ." He trailed off.

"We won't. I promise." I nodded toward Reese. "Right?"

"Yeah. Right." A flush worked up the column of his throat and into his face. "I promise."

Mateo let us in. We spread out in the large space. I sat at the same table as Reese and Gemma. Mateo and Kaci sat a few tables over. I quickly shoved my cheeseburger in my mouth, because as previous interludes had shown me, I was usually squeamish after a glimpse. So I ate my burger and a few chips, took one long swig of my soda, and then rolled my shoulders.

"Okay."

Reese held out his hand over the tabletop.

"Ask Cam a question about your next class, Reese," Gemma said as she swiveled her phone at the pair of us. "Maybe Cam will get a glimpse of the end of the school day."

I didn't know if that was how it all worked. But it couldn't hurt. And I wanted to find out. I did want to know the rules of this ability, because maybe it would help me find the girl or find her murderer.

"Okay. Is Ms. Shachti going to collect the homework that I didn't do?"

"Really?" Mateo asked, unimpressed.

Reese shrugged. "What? I didn't have time for homework because of cross-country practice. And some of us aren't honors students."

Mateo huffed from his table.

"You know what—I usually fall when I do this. Can we?" I gestured to the floor.

After a small readjustment, where Reese and I sat cross-legged on the cool tile, I took a breath, removed a glove, and then grasped Reese's hand. His skin was unusually cool against mine.

And that was all I registered before the lights around me winked out. I was in the dark. I was hunched over, my cheek pressed into my outstretched arm. Oh! I was asleep. Or Reese was. He was snoozing, but he was definitely in a class, because his feet were tangled in the basket beneath his desk.

"Reese!"

A sharp prod to my shoulder blade followed.

I roused slightly, my eyes still firmly closed. "What?" I said, the word jumbled in my mouth.

"Wake up! We have a pop quiz."

I groaned and sat up. The flutter of papers being passed down the row was the only sound in the otherwise silent room. I took the stack from the girl in front of me, anxiety making my stomach swoop, and took a page. I turned to hand it off to the person who'd poked me.

I looked down at the sheet and grumbled as I jiggled my leg under my desk with nervous energy. At least I could write my name. I wished for a spiritual or paranormal intervention, because looking through the questions, I could honestly say I knew the answer to only two of them. I circled the correct letter choices for those two, and then I flipped the page. My heart sank as the questions continued.

The high-pitched squeal of the fire alarm pierced through the room. I jumped in surprise, my pen scratching across the page and leaving a long mark. Looking up from the quiz, I saw the light above the door flashing in bursts of bright white. Saved by the literal bell! I checked the clock on the wall. Two fifteen. I inwardly cheered that the alarm would probably take the rest of the school day.

"Leave your belongings," Ms. Shachti yelled as my classmates and I stood. Most of us didn't listen, and we grabbed our bags as we shuffled out of the room, and—whoa, there was actual smoke in the hallway. This wasn't a drill.

Panic slammed through me as I saw the source. A fire in the chemistry lab right next door. The teacher wielded a fire extinguisher while students rushed out. A few fellow sprites ran in to help, including my friend Faye, who was a lake sprite. Another was a girl who could manipulate fire. I desperately hoped they wouldn't ask me to use my powers. I quickly turned away and joined the line of fleeing students. And then I was surrounded on all sides by a squeezing darkness.

I'd learned that coming to from a psychic interlude was never going to be a dignified experience. When I blinked and found myself in the honors lab, I was once again lying on the floor.

"Cam? You there?" Mateo asked from my side.

I squinted into the bright light overhead. "Yeah." I pushed my fingers into my hair and brushed my bangs from my forehead. I was a little woozy, but at least I didn't feel like I had to vomit. "What happened?"

"You glimpsed," Gemma said, her phone trained on me. "And when it was done, you slumped over. Good thing Mateo caught you before you brained yourself on the leg of the lab table."

Mateo had caught me? And oh, that was his hand cradling the back of my head. Embarrassing. I quickly pushed to my elbows, and Mateo continued to support me, his firm touch moving to between my shoulder blades until I was in a sitting position. But once I was upright, he didn't move away from my side.

"What did you see?" Reese asked.

I knew I was unusually wan and bleary-eyed after interludes. I'd seen the video. But Reese was unnaturally sallow as well.

"Wait! Don't say anything!" Gemma swiveled the phone to

Reese. "We don't want anyone to think you're influenced by what Cam says. So leave the room."

"What?" Reese said, crossing his arms. "I don't get to know my own future?"

"No!" Gemma shooed Reese away with her non-phone hand. "Kaci, can you go with him and confirm that he doesn't hear anything?"

Kaci gathered her things and stood from her stool. "Okay."

Reese frowned but picked up his trash from his lunch and followed Kaci out, looking over his shoulder as he closed the door behind him.

Gemma focused her camera back on me. "Okay, Cam, what did you see?"

I rubbed the back of my neck. "A fire alarm will sound at two fifteen because of a fire in the chemistry lab. Reese isn't involved. He does have a pop quiz in his class that's interrupted because the school evacuates."

"That's amazing!"

I cast a withering glare at Gemma, who amended quickly, "I mean, I hope everyone is okay."

"I don't think anyone was injured. I didn't see anything that would indicate otherwise."

"Then I stick with my original sentiment. That's amazing!" Gemma ended the video and shoved her phone into her pocket. "Do you know where the chemistry lab is? I'll use my yearbook staff privileges to get out of my own fourth block so I can be there when it happens."

"Uh . . . it's next to Reese's last block class."

"Great! I'll get it all on video and edit it tonight. And it'll be ready to post on your command."

"If the fire happens," I said. "It might not."

Gemma snorted. "If? Cam, be serious. You're already verified two for two. That's better than any other would-be clairvoyant has done in fifty years. If you ask me, it's a lock."

I gulped. "Fifty years?"

"Oh yeah. I'd be surprised if minutes after it posts, you don't have more gifts and the faction leaders breathing down your neck for meet and greets. It's going to be *awesome*," she said, making jazz hands. Her glittery fingernail polish gave the action quite the effect, as did her excited giggles.

"Yay," I replied, deadpan. "Awesome."

"Okay. I'm going now. Talk to you later!"

Gemma left in a tornado of orange and yellow, leaving me on the floor with Mateo right by my side. He wasn't touching me, but he was warm and solid, and if I wasn't already lightheaded, I totally would be just from his presence alone.

"You okay?" he asked, his voice low.

I sighed. "Yeah. It's just"—I waved my hand helplessly—"all overwhelming."

"I get that."

"You do? How? You grew up a werewolf. You're basically entrenched in paranormal society. You *are* the paranormal. None of this is new to you."

Mateo bowed his head, but his lips twitched into a grin. "Just because I'm a werewolf doesn't mean I don't understand what it's like to be under pressure from family and friends and other outside forces."

"Really? I find that difficult to believe."

"Try being the youngest in an extended family of werewolves, with two exceptional older brothers and several older cousins. And well, I have a hard time with . . ." He trailed off. "I know you've noticed." He vaguely waved at his ears.

"I have noticed," I said. I took a breath. "It's endearing."

His grin softened into a smile. Then he cleared his throat. "My parents are supportive, but . . . they can be overbearing with wanting certain achievements."

"Yeah, well, at least they're attentive. My parents would rather have me hide the one thing that might make me special." At the thought of our conversation the previous day, anger and hurt welled inside me, burning into my throat and behind my eyes. "I get being cautious and timid around all this stuff. But they could've at least made sure I was *okay*. That I had what I needed. But instead they looked at me like I was a stranger. Like a faery had come into the house and switched out their human kid for a psychic one. At least your parents can't be as awful as that."

"It's not a contest, Cam."

I winced. Yikes. "You're right! I'm sorry! You were commiserating and trying to be helpful, and I made it weird. Sorry."

"No, it's okay. I'm sorry that happened with your parents."

I rolled my shoulders and stood from my awkward sprawl on the floor. "It's . . . well, it's not okay. But I will learn to deal. Or they will. Something will happen."

Mateo stood as well. He fiddled with the strap of his backpack, which was on the lab table. "I talk with Kaci about our respective powers a lot. Gemma was right, you know. We're all in the same situation."

"I believe Gemma called us a murder of crows."

Mateo chuckled, a low sound that made my middle flutter like a hundred butterflies.

I cleared my throat. "But yeah. We are. Birds of a feather and all that."

"Your parents . . . ," Mateo started hesitantly. "They're not pleased you're a seer?"

I let out a loud burst of obnoxious laughter. "The opposite. The very much opposite. Like, so much the opposite, it's the difference between the Mariana Trench and Mount Everest."

"Do you have anyone to talk to about it?"

I shoved my hands into the front pocket of my hoodie. "Ah. No. My older brother, Aiden . . . left. And Al and I, we're not really talking right now. I'm honestly not quite sure why."

"Well, if you ever need to talk, you can reach out."

"I don't have your number."

Mateo took his phone from his bag, his fingers sliding over the screen. Then my phone pinged in my pocket.

"Now you do."

"Wait, how did you have mine?"

A blush seeped into Mateo's cheeks. "Kaci gave it to me."

"Oh. Right." I took my phone from my pocket. Sure enough, there was a text from an unsaved number. "Thanks. I'll be sure to use it."

"You're welcome. And please do. If you need to."

This was awkward. But it was sweet. And having Mateo's number and permission to use it was almost worth all the other things going on. Almost. "Wait, is this a ploy to entice me to ally with the werewolves?"

"Maybe," Mateo said with a playful grin. "Or maybe it's a genuine overture of friendship."

"I like that second option better."

"Then that's what it is."

I ducked my head as I felt my own blush burn my cheeks. The bell rang, interrupting us, which was probably for the best since I couldn't stop smiling.

At exactly two fifteen, the fire alarm blared through the school.

I exchanged a glance with Mateo, then packed up my sketchbook and the rest of my belongings and headed outside with the student body. My palms were slick with sweat as I tugged on my gloves. I was three for three. If I'd had any doubt before, it was sufficiently erased.

I was a *verified* seer. A true clairvoyant. An oracle. A prophet. A . . . soothsayer, if I wanted to go vintage. All those things. Holy shit.

I was stunned. I could actually see glimpses of the future. For real. Like, how amazing was that? Though that meant there was no way to avoid the fact that I wasn't just part of the paranormal community, I *was* the paranormal. And a small shiver of fear worked its way down my spine. Not only because of my parents, but because of the apparent importance of my role.

And that meant my very first glimpse was *real*. And I still had yet to find the girl or her murderer. And I had no leads, and no help.

I took a shuddering breath.

The blaring sirens of the incoming fire trucks were loud enough to make me wince. I noticed Mateo tugging on his earlobe, his expression tight, until the trucks were parked and silent.

"Three for three," I said, once the alarms shut off.

Mateo's grimace eased, and he placed a comforting hand on my shoulder. The weight of his touch was welcome and grounding over the thick fabric of my jacket. "It'll be okay."

"I hope."

Kaci bounded over to us. She'd located us quickly in the crowd that was hanging out in the bus loop. We'd managed to find a small clump of shade under a spindly tree.

"Mateo texted me what would happen," she said, leaning in conspiratorially, "so I wouldn't be surprised."

"Ah. Did he tell you it wasn't a drill?"

She nodded. "Yes."

I squinted toward the exit, where students continued to walk out. "I hope Gemma left and didn't hang around to gather more video evidence."

"She seems smart," Kaci said. "I'm sure she evacuated."

I arched an eyebrow. "She is smart, but I've noticed she has a tendency to hyperfixate on certain things."

I spied Reese with a shimmer of sprites who were encouraging a row of small shrubs to grow. He looked over to us, his green eyes glowing in the sun, and offered a quick wave but didn't come to join us.

"What's the deal between you and Reese?" I asked Mateo. It seemed a safe question, since Kaci was basically a Lopez in everything but name and Gemma was nowhere to be seen.

Mateo huffed. "It's not a me-and-him thing."

"It's a sprite-and-werewolf thing?"

"Sort of."

"Mateo's beautiful cousin Juana used to live in New Amsterdam with her family," Kaci said, bouncing on the balls of her feet. "And while she was there, she fell in love with a gorgeous garden sprite named Mia."

"And?"

Mateo sighed. "And Mia requested permission to propose to Juana. The werewolves said yes, but the sprites refused. And gave Mia an ultimatum."

My mouth went dry. "Let me guess—leave Juana or leave the Alliance?"

"Yes," Mateo confirmed.

My eyes went wide. "That's the beef between the Lopez family and the local chapter of the Sprite Alliance? A star-crossed-lovers story?"

"It's not just a story. Juana was crushed," Mateo said, hands clenched in the straps of his backpack, the blunt nails of his fingers sharpening into claws. "She even left to study abroad. And she's only just come home."

"Like when Jane left for London after Mr. Bingley's rejection."

Mateo shot me a dark look.

I held up my hands. "I'm just trying to make it relatable. But I get it. I'm sorry."

"Juana is Mateo's favorite cousin." Kaci leaned close to me as if imparting a secret. "He loves her. Probably more than he loves Danny and Javi, but don't tell them I said that."

I would never tire of seeing Mateo blush. "I missed her. A lot," he said. "I'm happy she's come to stay with us now that she's finished traveling."

"Well, okay, but what does that have to do with Reese?"

"Oh, his dad is second-in-command of the New Amsterdam Suburb chapter of the Sprite Alliance," Kaci said. "He made the decision to turn Mia's proposal down."

"Ah. Okay. Family tensions. Got it."

Kaci glanced toward the crowd, then quickly turned away. I followed her line of sight and caught Dennis glaring at us.

I nudged Kaci with my elbow. "Are you okay?"

She nodded. "Ghost." Leaning in, she dropped her voice. "She follows him, and she always looks so angry." She brushed her long hair over her shoulder. "And so does he."

"Aren't most ghosts angry?" I waved my hand. "You know—at, like, being dead."

Kaci shook her head. "No. That's a harmful stereotype."

"Ah. Okay. I stand corrected."

She smiled slightly. "Good."

I glanced back at Dennis. He met my gaze, then turned abruptly and pushed his way through the growing crowd.

Mateo stood on his tiptoes and surveyed the area. The number of students leaving the building had dwindled, and teachers walked through the groups, counting their students and checking off names on the rolls.

"Do you see Gemma?" I asked.

Mateo frowned. "No. I don't."

"Okay. Well. I don't feel great about this. So let's split up and find her. I want to make sure she's okay."

"Kaci and I will search the bus loop," Mateo said.

"I'll go check the other exits. Maybe she went out another way. Text me if you see her."

Kaci nodded as she and Mateo went in opposite directions into the crowd.

As much as I didn't want to go looking for trouble, I'd feel horrible if Gemma were somehow hurt trying to film my recent correct glimpse. Yes, she was annoying and loud and colorful and the opposite of everything I would have chosen in a friend, but as much as it pained me to think so, she *was* my partner in crime . . . er . . . clairvoyance. And if Mateo and Kaci could extend their friendship to me, I could do the same to Gemma.

Besides, she was my anchor in the world of the paranormal.

And if I was going to fulfill the role of verified clairvoyant, I needed her.

I rolled my shoulders, tucked my gloved hands into my pockets, and, discreetly as possible, broke off from the main group of chatting students and ducked around the side of the school.

16

THE BUS LOOP WAS ON THE OPPOSITE SIDE OF THE BUILDING from the grand entrance of the school. There were three other potential exits—the gym via the enclosed middle courtyard and the two side exits. I headed for the one that dumped out from the small theater.

The area was empty, save for a handful of lit and drama students vaping and gossiping about the fire they'd seen in the chemistry lab. They mentioned a teacher using a fire extinguisher, and that there had been a fire sprite and a few water sprites who'd assisted as well to contain the fire. I remembered that from my glimpse. And I also remembered Reese's anxiety about being asked to step in to help. As if Reese hadn't wanted to use his own sprite powers.

Huh. I wondered why.

"Can we help you?" one of the group said, arms crossed over their torso.

"Oh, hey," I said. "Have any of you seen Gemma James? Tiny freshman with bubblegum-pink hair?"

They scoffed. "No."

"Okay. Thanks."

I left before they asked me any follow-up questions and continued around the side of the building. The large front entrance was next, but there were only a few office staff milling around. Seeing no sign of Gemma, I kept walking. I turned a corner that led me to the back of the cafeteria, where several dumpsters lined the alleyway.

As I approached, I heard an unmistakable voice.

"I'm sorry, but I can't help you with that," Gemma said. "It's not in my purview."

I picked up my pace. On the other side of the dumpsters, Gemma was standing with her phone clenched in her hand and Dennis looming over her. The hell? Dennis had been in the bus loop with the rest of us. Had this been where he went when he'd stormed away?

"So what? He only uses his powers for the paranormal kids now? Do the Lopez assholes have the monopoly?"

"No." Gemma stubbornly lifted her chin. "Cam has not allied with a particular faction yet. He's not even verified."

Dennis scoffed. "Yeah, right. Look, you little gatekeeper—" He took a step forward, and despite her strong stance and firm tone, Gemma flinched. "I need my future read. And you're going to help me get it done."

"Hey!" I yelled.

Dennis rounded on me. His eyes narrowed as he looked over my shoulder. "Where's your bodyguard?"

"Bodyguard? You watch too many crime dramas, my friend."

With Gemma forgotten, Dennis moved toward me in a way I could only describe as menacing. "I need to know the basketball game score for tonight. I have to know if we win." His voice cracked with desperation. His expression switched from one of intimidation to one of downright pleading. I understood pressure, but I also knew that I couldn't allow a precedent of giving in to the demands of people wanting to use my ability for their own. And while I maybe had an inkling of how the whole psychic thing worked, he didn't need to know that.

"Uh . . . so last time was a fluke. I don't really know how to control glimpsing, and I might not even see the basketball game. I might not see anything, because I'm still not quite sure how to activate my abilities, and—"

Dennis's jaw tightened, his eyes turning hard, and then he lunged. He grabbed me by the front of my hoodie, his hands twisted in the fabric. He threw me bodily against the wall of the school. The air was knocked out of my lungs as my back smacked against the brick.

"Stop making excuses," he said while pinning me to the wall like a butterfly under glass, his large hands on my shoulders. "You don't understand. I *need* to know."

I grabbed his wrist to try and ease his grip, thankful that I'd slipped my gloves back on during the evacuation. But this was bad. Being physically assaulted was not at the top of my to-do list for the day. "You know, all I have to do is yell, and my werewolf bodyguard will come running. He has great hearing." I wasn't sure if that was true or not, but I was not above bluffing.

Dennis sneered. "And I know that a little bit a silver is all it takes to render a werewolf harmless."

"Oh? That sounds threatening. But you do also know that I have more than a werewolf in my new group of friends, right?"

Dennis scoffed. "The ghost girl? She's not an issue. The only other danger is Al, and everyone knows that they've abandoned you."

My stomach twisted with grief. Everyone knew?

"Well, I feel left out."

I craned my neck, the back of my head scraping along the brick.

Reese stood there, pouting. His eyes glowed a vibrant green. Tendrils of sprite magic crawled beneath his skin, illuminating the muscles of his arms with the colors of verdure and spring. "Did you forget about me?" Reese tapped his chin, and small glimmers of water and foliage flicked from the tip of his finger.

"Are you really his friend?" Dennis sneered. "I thought you only joined their little lunch group for the perks."

Reese shrugged. "You willing to find out?" He cracked his knuckles. Reese was tall but slight. He was athletic from being on the cross-country team, but he didn't have near the bulk or heft of Dennis. Even with his powers, I didn't know if he had a chance in a physical altercation. But I was grateful for his posturing.

"He *did* fight Javi Lopez in the hallway," Gemma piped up from where she'd slowly edged to Reese's side. "I wouldn't try him."

"She's not wrong." Reese cocked his head. He narrowed his sparkling eyes. "Now, release him."

"Or what?"

Reese flexed his fingers and thrust his hand toward a small strip of grass in a landscaped bed. It quivered in the breezeless atmosphere, then shot upward, thickening and spilling over the concrete barrier and slithering in thick, vibrant tendrils toward us. Reese's body glowed with power, a golden-green halo surrounding him.

"Do you really want to fight a sprite?" Reese said through gritted teeth. "Or do you want to let Cam go?"

Dennis released me instantly. I slid down the wall in a heap, landing on my butt.

"Whatever," Dennis muttered. He gave me one last glare, then turned and walked away.

Once he was gone, I sighed and slumped over, my cheek on my knee. Reese dropped his arm, and the grass and vines shrank back within the confines of the greenery bed, though it remained a little wilder than the manicured space it had been a few moments ago.

"Are you okay, Cam?" Gemma asked, rushing over. "I didn't mean for that to happen. I was just filming the lab, and when they forced me to evacuate, I came out the side door, and he cornered me. I didn't know what to say or do, and—"

"You did fine, Gemma," I said from my place on the ground. "We were worried when we couldn't find you, so we split up to make sure you were okay."

Reese offered his hand to me, and I checked to make sure my gloves were firmly on. They were, so I took it, and he helped me to my feet.

"Thanks," I said, for both the help up and the intervention.

Gemma blinked. "You were worried about me?"

"Well, yeah. It was an actual fire. We all wanted to make sure you were okay."

I wasn't prepared for Gemma to launch into my middle. She *hugged* me, her skinny arms wrapping around me like Reese's vines and squeezing tight like I was a stress ball or her favorite teddy bear. Her face smacked into my sternum, and if it weren't for Reese grabbing my upper arm, I would've been back on the ground.

"Thank you," she said.

Then she released me and barreled into Reese as well. She embraced him hard, and he awkwardly patted her back. "Uh . . ."

"Thank you," she said again once she'd disengaged from him. She held up a finger. "I am going to the bus loop right now and hugging both Mateo and Kaci too. And then I'm going to edit this video. Once it's done, I'll text you, and you will be a verified seer!" She clapped her hands, then waved and ran off, disappearing in flurry of ribbons and rainbows.

"Wow," Reese said from beside me. "She's intense."

"For real." I pushed my hands into my pockets. "Thanks for that, by the way. I don't know what would've happened if you hadn't come along." I massaged my shoulder. "I didn't think Dennis had it in him to be aggressive. But apparently he can be."

"Desperate people do desperate things," Reese said with a shrug.

"Yeah. I guess. So anyway, thanks for threatening him with your powers. That was pretty awesome."

"That?" Reese said, jerking his thumb over his shoulder. "That was toddler-sprite level. I didn't even tap into my real powers."

Oh. Well, that was amazing and a little frightening. "Um . . . I'm sorry to ask, but I don't know much about sprites. You're a leaf guy, right? I don't really know the designations."

Reese snorted. "'Leaf guy'? Seriously?"

"Um . . . yeah? Is that offensive?"

He laughed, his mouth splitting into a grin. "No, it's not. And no worries. I get you're still new to this stuff. But anyway, sprites have a deep and special connection to the goddess of nature. We receive our magic from her, and each of us has a specialty stemming from either one of the elements or from a particular ecosystem. Mine is a little rarer than the others."

"What is it?"

Reese ducked his head and scratched the back of his neck. "Uh . . . well . . . have you ever visited a swamp, Cam?"

I squinted. "Can't say that I have."

Reese smirked. "Consider yourself lucky. They're hot and humid, and they are fragrant in not great ways."

"Is that what you are? A swamp sprite?"

Reese's shoulders rose and fell with a sigh. "Yeah. Because of all the potential sprite domains I could have, I was gifted with the great and wonderful powers of a swamp."

"You didn't use your specialty powers during that fight." I furrowed my brow. "I remember water and leaves, but I definitely would've remembered a swamp, I think. I don't know—my brain was pretty addled."

Reese huffed a laugh. "No, you definitely would have remembered."

"I mean, swamps are pretty cool ecosystems."

"Right. They're damp and gross, and they smell. I try to use my swampiness as little as possible. Because it's just not pleasant for me or for anyone around me."

"Okay. Well, still, thanks for threatening to use your powers." I elbowed Reese in the arm.

"What are friends for?" he said with a grin. "And you're welcome. Just, next time, warn me about the pop quiz?"

I laughed, the tension easing from my body. "Yeah. I will."

17

GEMMA AND I AGREED TO WAIT UNTIL THE END OF THE WEEK before posting the third and final video. I wanted a few days of rest before the big reveal and the inevitable change to my life it would bring. She wanted to heighten the anticipation so that the video would become another viral sensation.

So I enjoyed the rest of the week eating lunch with my new, eclectic group of friends. Even if I missed Al desperately, and Reese and Mateo sat stiffly on either side of Kaci, and Kaci watched Dennis warily, and Gemma rambled incessantly about anything and everything that popped into her mind. At least Mateo's calm steadiness was a comfort. So was Reese's physical presence. And Kaci's dreamy observations. And yes, even Gemma's constant commentary, which provided a background buzz to my own wayward thoughts and feelings about *everything*.

At the end of the day, I couldn't help but appreciate them all. They'd stepped in when Al had . . . cut me out. And though I hadn't texted Mateo to talk about paranormal abilities or parents or anything else, the idea that I *could* offered a semblance of reassurance that I'd been missing.

Gemma posted the final video on Friday during lunchtime. Comments were limited to registered users. And as Reese had noted, the dramatic video of the actual fire and fire alarm gave it a little more flair and urgency that skyrocketed the views. It went viral almost immediately.

"My email is clogged with requests from anyone and everyone to meet you," Gemma said as we lounged on the stairs outside of school, waiting for Val to pick her up. "And my website crashed. Holy crap, Cam. You're a sensation."

Embarrassment burned my cheeks. "It's nothing."

"Don't be modest. You're a verified clairvoyant." She scrolled through her phone. "Oh, the Psychic Guild wants to talk as soon as possible. That is definitely the one you should go to first."

One thing I hadn't really considered was what the different factions would actually *want* from a verified clairvoyant. Yeah, seeing the future could be a great benefit, but to what end?

"Uh . . . what exactly would the Psychic Guild get out of me joining them?" I asked, stretching out along several of the gleaming steps.

Gemma refreshed her ClickClack account, eyes sparkling at her increasing numbers of followers. "The prestige, of course. A verified seer in the ranks of the Psychic Guild would give them the status, notoriety, and renown that, to be honest, the local branch is sorely missing."

"Huh."

"Yeah. I can imagine they'd have you show up to a meeting a few times a year, see a future for someone, and look pretty. And I hear they offer college scholarships and business courses, but we'll work all that out in a contract if you decide to join them."

College scholarship? I might need that, depending on how my parents reacted to this third video.

"Okay. Book it for next week."

Gemma snapped her head around, her blue eyes wide. "What?"

"I trust you," I said with a shrug. "If you say it's important, then that's what I should do, right?"

Gemma beamed. "Yes! Okay. I will respond to them first."

My own phone pinged in my pocket. I fished it out and smiled at a text from Mateo.

My family is having a cookout tomorrow afternoon. Can you come?

My blush deepened. Mateo inviting me to a cookout? That was freshman Cam's dream come true. I felt a little giddy when I texted back.

Am I attending as Cam your friend? Or Cam the Clairvoyant?

The response came quickly.

Are they two different people?

I frowned. Surely Mateo understood that they were. They had to be. Yes?

Both, then. My family wants to meet you.

But I would like to hang out together.

Kaci will be there too.

Ah. Okay.

Gemma leaned in. "Huh," she said, reading over the texts.

I jerked my phone away. "Hey!"

"Sorry. But . . . uh . . . that sounds like an invitation to meet the Lopez werewolf family."

I sighed, my heart sinking. "It does. Doesn't it?"

"Not that I think Mateo isn't our friend. It's just . . . he was probably pressured by his family after the third video released."

"What would a werewolf family want from a clairvoyant?" I asked, my throat tight.

Gemma cocked her head to the side. "Protection, most likely. They've had a rough time over the centuries, as you're probably learning about in World History right now, so having a verified clairvoyant on their side could help them with upcoming conflicts between their own families, or with the other paranormal factions, or the most likely culprit for conflict—humans."

Protection. That was a much heavier ask than prestige. Scary, even.

My heart raced as my fingers hovered over my phone screen. When I took too long to respond, another text came.

It's a celebration. For Juana coming home.

I took a breath. Can Gemma come too?

Of course. I've already texted her.

Gemma's attention jerked back to her phone. "Oh," she said, fingers tapping quickly on the screen, "he did. It was just lost in all the other notifications."

I didn't know how to feel about that. Did he invite her because she was his friend too? Or my human advisor? Ugh.

No Reese. He's not invited.

That part I understood. Okay. We'll be there! Thank you.

Great. See you at 3 at my house.

"Well, I have a lot of work to do," Gemma said, heaving to her feet. I had no idea how her spine was not curved from the sheer weight of her pink unicorn backpack. She wrapped her hands around the straps. "I'll come to your house tomorrow, and then we'll go over together. Val can drive us."

"Okay."

"Cool. I'll text you tonight with your homework."

I furrowed my brow. "Homework?"

"Well, yeah," she said, like it was obvious. "You're in the next stage, my friend. You're going to be swamped with learning everything about the factions you're meeting with and the paranormal beings that make up each one." She clicked her tongue and made a finger gun. "The more you know and all that. It'll help you make a good choice about your allies."

"Oh. Right." And this just further drove home the fact that this fun cookout wasn't about Mateo being my friend, but about who my allies were going to be now that I was "verified."

Gemma shook her head. "It's a good thing you have me, or you'd be totally screwed."

She flounced down the steps to where Val's car had pulled in and rumbled to a stop. I watched in awe as she swung her bag into the back seat with little effort, then hopped in the front. She waved out the window as Val pulled away.

I mustered a half-hearted wave in return and then stood to get my bike from the rack.

Thankfully, my ride home was uneventful. My parents weren't there yet, and I sighed in relief as I trudged to my bedroom. I tossed my bag in my desk chair, then dropped onto the bed and fell asleep.

A tap-tap-tapping at my bedroom window woke me from my nap. I rolled over and blinked sleepily. Night had fallen; my room was completely dark, and I had no idea what time it was. Another rap sounded, and I jolted fully awake as soon as I realized what, or who, it was.

"Lenore!" I said, shooting upright with a gasp.

She peered at me with her black, beady eyes and ruffled her dark feathers. Then she tapped her beak again on the pane of glass.

I scrambled toward her and flung the window up. She stuck out her leg.

"I've missed you," I said, ignoring the message for a moment and running my finger over the crown of her head and down her back. "Thanks for coming to visit."

She nibbled my finger in a sign of affection, then shook her leg again.

"Fine," I said, and took the message.

Since our friend breakup, I hadn't talked to Al, and I had a guess what this message could be about. Since the third video had gone viral just a few hours before, I imagined it had something to do with that.

I took the note to my desk and turned on the lamp. I unrolled the parchment and held it under the light.

The coven saw the third glimpse. They're concerned. Be vigilant. Don't respond. Don't text. Destroy after reading. I'll talk to you at school on Monday if needed.

I read the message again. Al had reached out to warn me? I flipped the scroll over and found nothing else. I blinked. That was it? No *miss you*? Or *I hate that we fought*? Or *we both made a mistake; can we be friends again*?

I pinched my eyes shut. Okay. Fine. They could reach out to me, but I couldn't contact them. Great. Just great.

I opened my eyes and turned to the window, but Lenore had already flown away.

"Cam?" I startled at my mom's voice in the hallway, which was followed by a soft knock at my door. "Cam?"

"Yeah?" I called, shoving the note into my pocket.

"Dinner is ready."

"I'll be down in a minute."

I closed my window, then wiped the remaining sleep from my eyes and steeled myself to have an awkward family dinner with my parents.

--

I should've been more prepared for the inevitable dinner-table discussion, but that nap had left me bleary and sleepier than when I'd fallen into my bed a few hours ago.

"So," my dad said as he cut his pork chop, "there was another video from this Gem-Jam account. Posted today."

My throat went dry. I grabbed my glass of water and took a long drink. There was no denying it. "Yeah. There was."

"I thought we agreed you would not post another of these . . ." He gestured with his fork. "Psychic visions."

"They're called glimpses."

"Right. But we agreed—"

"*You* agreed," I muttered.

"But what does this mean going forward?" he demanded. "Are you part of their community now? Are you going to run away and join some traveling spectacle, telling fortunes for money?"

"Wow, Dad. There was nothing about that sentence that wasn't horrible or filled with vaguely racist and/or prejudiced views about an array of people."

"Dear, Cam has done what he has done for whatever reason," my mom said, her voice light but with an underlying false sincerity that grated on my nerves. "And now he must endure the consequences." She swirled her wineglass. "Cam, since you have disobeyed your father and me regarding this clairvoyant matter and gone forward with no regard for our wishes, you have put us in a position where we will now have to acknowledge that we have a son who is . . ." She paused, as if searching for a word, and finally settled on, "Different."

Tears stung behind my eyes. "Seriously? That's what you're worried about? You can say 'clairvoyant' or 'psychic' or even 'paranormal.' They're not bad words."

She pursed her lips. "Fine. Psychic. Your father and I will work to educate ourselves. Does this mean you'll receive more . . . gifts?"

"Probably. If you actually watched the videos, then you'd know that what I can do is a highly valued skill. All the local factions will want to talk to me."

My dad frowned. My mother shivered and took another gulp of her wine.

"We can deal with this," she said, locking gazes with my father over the fake flowers in the center of the table. "We will."

My father nodded. "Fine."

He pointed his fork at me. "If there are going to be any more videos, could you at least warn us before they post? I hate that my coworkers know more about you than I do."

I bit back the retort on the tip of my tongue about how he could simply ask me about my life instead of relying on his coworkers, but I didn't want to stir the pot more. Especially since my mom seemed weirdly okay about things. Not happy, by any means, but not ready to kick me out of the house yet.

Silence descended around the dinner table, and after I'd cleared my plate, I asked to be excused.

They acquiesced, and I disappeared upstairs.

I grabbed my phone and stared down at the screen. I had a message from Gemma that I ignored for the moment. Without conscious thought, I opened my contacts and flicked to Aiden and the last messages he'd sent me.

My last text to him had been undeliverable, but that didn't stop me from trying again.

Have you seen the videos? Pretty cool, right?

I hit send, not expecting anything, and switched to the message from Gemma. It was a series of links about werewolves and their family structures and everything I would need to know to not make a jerk of myself at the Lopez house the following day.

I tossed my phone on my bed and then changed into my pajamas. After washing my face, I crawled into the sheets and settled in, propped on my pillows, ready for a long night of learning.

18

THE NEXT MORNING I HAD A PACKAGE.

There was no return address on the nondescript box, only my name in neat cursive across the front. I opened it, and nested inside among copious amounts of bubble wrap was a brand-new phone with an uncracked screen. I fished a card out from the bottom of the package, flipped it over, and then froze.

From the Shady Hallow Coven of Witches & Warlocks.

I gulped. The phone was a few models newer than mine, and it certainly wasn't damaged from a fight in the hall between a were-wolf and a sprite, and I really had wanted and needed an upgrade. But Al had warned me the night before about their coven. And that meant something after our breakup, that they would risk reaching out. It was unnerving. I put the phone back in the box and left it on the table in the entryway. I'd deal with it later.

The morning crawled by. I spent the early afternoon trying on different outfits and jewelry and trying to style my hair. My brown roots were beginning to grow back in, offering a contrast to the honey blond of my hair.

I settled on a simple pair of ripped jeans, a plain white T-shirt underneath my denim jacket and a plain leather bracelet. And despite the warm late-summer day, I tucked my gloves in my pocket. Just in case.

A car honked impatiently outside, and I thundered down the stairs. I slipped into my sneakers and was out the door in record time.

Val's car, a small, old, but pristine hatchback, idled by the sidewalk. It gleamed bright red in the afternoon sunlight.

Gemma rolled down the front passenger window and waved enthusiastically.

"Val said she'd drive us."

I walked toward the car. "That's nice of Val."

Gemma hopped out of the car and hit a button to slide the front seat forward.

"Get in," Gemma said. "We don't want to be late."

Gemma held a glass casserole dish in her hands, and a delicious smell wafted from it. My stomach rumbled.

"What is that?"

"Tangy glazed meatballs. Family recipe from our grandma."

Val rolled her eyes and leaned over. "Who literally found it on the back of a bottle of Worcestershire sauce. Can we please go? We're wasting gas."

I climbed into the back seat, scrunching my knees to my chest when Gemma flipped the front seat into position. I struggled with my seat belt until it clicked. Somehow there were two other seat belts in the back, as if three humans could fit in this cramped area.

"So," I said as Val shifted into drive, "are the meatballs some kind of offering?"

Gemma shrugged. "This is your first meet and greet with a paranormal faction. I thought it would be polite to bring something to share to this cookout."

"Um . . . oh. Should I run back inside and steal a bottle of my parents' wine from the cellar? Because I do not have anything to bring, other than my awkward self and anxious demeanor."

"Ah. We'll just say it's from both of us."

"Cool."

"Did you watch the videos I sent?" Gemma said over Val's music.

"Yeah," I said, leaning forward. "I did."

"Excellent! Then I don't need to brief you on anything."

"Great," Val said. "Then stop talking." She glanced over her shoulder at me. "And quit breathing down my neck." Then she immediately turned the music louder, the rock song blaring in my ears.

I slumped into the seat. Despite having watched all the videos the night before, I was nervous. Werewolves were considered children of the moon goddess, and even in their human forms they had increased hearing ability as well as strength. We were about to be in the midst of at least a dozen of them. Not that I was scared they'd *hurt* me in any way, but I worried that they'd be able to tell that I was completely out of my depth. Or worse, I might commit some irreparable social faux pas and Mateo wouldn't want to be friends anymore.

That was a horrible thought. I liked Mateo and didn't want to lose him the way I'd lost Al. Okay. I needed to focus on the other things I'd learned. One was that most werewolves could only shift into their full wolf forms on or close to a full moon. Though there were some shifts they could make on command, like claws, which I imagined would be handy for opening mail and cans. Like other paranormal folk, they had a few specific weaknesses, like being susceptible to silver, but otherwise they were hardier than humans and healed faster. I wondered if that meant they couldn't contract the common cold. Did that mean Mateo and his brothers had perfect attendance? Huh.

Anyway, the Shady Hallow and Sunny Peak Combined Werewolf Family was a conglomeration of several different local families. Mateo's aunt was their current elected leader.

Val slowed down as she entered a neighborhood and then stopped in front of a modest brick house. Gemma hopped out, a bundle of excitement in yellow overalls, rainbow sneakers, and spiked bright pink hair. She clutched her casserole in her hands.

"Thanks, Val," I said as I squeezed out.

"No problem, clairvoyant guy. Text me when you two are ready to leave."

"Will do."

I closed the door, and Gemma and I briskly walked down the path and up a few steps to the front door.

Okay. I had nothing to be worried about. Mateo had invited me. I had Gemma with me. It wasn't like this was a date. It was a party for a friend's cousin and a potential paranormal meet and greet. And I was used to the paranormal. I'd been friends with a witch for years and had been around their family all the time. And I ate lunch with a sprite and a medium. There was *nothing* to worry about. At all. Nothing.

Gemma rang the doorbell.

The door opened almost immediately.

I'd expected Mateo or Javi or Danny, or maybe even one of their parents.

It was none of the above.

"Welcome! Oh, you must be Gemma. And Cam! Teo has told me so much about you."

Every molecule in my body locked down. I couldn't move. I couldn't *breathe*.

"I'm Juana. Teo's cousin," she said as she pushed open the outer screen door. "I'm very excited to meet both of you."

"Nice to meet you, too," I managed to whisper.

Because standing in front of me was the girl from the clearing. The girl I'd been searching for.

The girl who had been murdered in my first glimpse was Mateo's cousin.

She smiled wide. "Don't be shy. We're all out on the back patio. Come in, follow me." She waved her hand, her painted nails catching the light, and when she turned, her long golden-brown hair swayed behind her, falling in styled waves to the middle of her back.

"Wow," Gemma said in an awed voice while handing off the casserole dish and stepping over the threshold. "I've never been in a werewolf family's house before. It's beautiful. I love the mahogany banister on the stairs. And what is that delicious smell? Is that carne asada?"

I followed. The screen door swung shut behind me, and I froze in the hallway. Gemma rambled. Juana indulged her with an airy laugh. She half turned, saw that I had stalled in place, and gestured for me to continue.

But I couldn't; I was stuck. Because every time I looked at her, I could only see vision-Juana dead in a field, her light brown skin splattered with blood.

"Cam?"

Mateo's voice startled me. He had come from another door nearby and stood in front of me. Kaci was just over his shoulder.

"Hi," I said, my voice barely a breath.

Mateo's brow furrowed in worry. He reached out to touch me, but I flinched violently away, my elbow knocking into the doorknob, a flare of nerve pain shooting down my arm into my fingers. Mateo's mouth pinched. "Are you okay?"

"You look like you've seen a ghost," Kaci said lightly. "I would know."

"I . . ." I licked my lips. "I have to go."

I spun on my heel, pushed the screen door open, and tumbled onto the front porch.

"Cam!"

"I'm sorry!" I scrambled to my feet and held up my hands. "Sorry."

Mateo followed. "What's wrong?"

"Nothing. I'm sorry. I just . . . have to go. Sorry."

Then I ran. I didn't know why I ran, but my brain just screamed at me to go, to run, to get away from the girl flashing across my mind's eye. So I turned and bolted, my shoes slapping against the pavement of the driveway and then the asphalt of the street. A collective of voices yelled something behind me, but I didn't hear them over my pulse thudding in my ears and my own jagged breath.

My legs pumped. My heart threatened to burst from behind my ribs. My chest heaved as I tried to suck in air, but it was like trying to breathe through a straw.

Holy shit. Mateo's favorite cousin was the girl I'd seen murdered.

My jacket flared behind me. My eyes blurred with tears, but I kept going until I'd made it a few blocks away in the quiet neighborhood.

Then I allowed my body to slow, and I stumbled to a stop at a corner with a large tree shading the area. I staggered to it, my legs giving out now that I had stopped. Falling to my knees in the grass, I felt the giant, snaking tree roots knocking hard against my kneecaps and the heels of my hands. I sank my fingers into the soil, trying to ground myself, but the images of that glimpse flashed behind my eyelids, across the canvas of my thoughts, like a grotesque painting in the blues and grays of the night and the red, red, red of her blood. My ears reverberated with her pained pleas, and the smell of the rain mixed with sulfur burned in my nose.

Without thinking, I reached into my pocket and yanked out my phone.

I hit the first saved contact of my list, the only person who I could think of while in the middle of this crisis, the only person I wanted to hear from.

"Cam?" Al's voice came over the speaker. "I'm kind of in the middle of—"

"I found her," I said in a tone bordering on hysterical, my words thick with tears and terror. "I found her, Al. I found the girl."

"Cam? Are you okay? What's going on?"

"The girl from the glimpse. I know who she is. I met her. And I can't—" Tears spilled down my cheeks. "I can't—" I choked on air. I couldn't catch my breath. Every inhale was a struggle, and every exhale was a sputtered wet mess. Against my ear I could hear the notifications of texts piling up, probably from Mateo and Kaci and Gemma, but I ignored them.

"You're scaring me, Cam. Okay? I need you to take a breath. Can you do that?"

I tried, but my lungs hitched, the air stuttering through them. "Al," I said, my fingers clenched in the earth, the knees of my jeans torn and dirty where I'd all but fallen. "I can't. I need . . ." *Help*, but I couldn't finish the sentence.

"Where are you? Can you tell me where you are?"

I opened my eyes, not realizing I'd closed them, the sunlight still blinding despite the shade of the tree, the rays piercing through the canopy of red and orange leaves above me.

"I'm in a neighborhood. Mateo's neighborhood."

"Okay. What street?"

I swiveled my head and found a sign marking the cross street.

"Moon View Lane and Howl Road."

Al muttered under their breath. "Okay. Got it. Stay right there. I am on my way."

I nodded, then realized they couldn't see me. "Okay," I said.

"Good. Stay on the phone. You don't need to say anything, but don't hang up. I'm coming to you."

"Thank you," I wheezed.

My hand dropped to the ground, but I kept my phone gripped in my fingers. I managed to hit the speaker button so I could hear Al's stream of conversation as they readied and left the house. The familiar sound of a chain and spokes and tires on asphalt filled my head, replacing the sounds of the glimpse that had been looping in my brain.

"Okay. I've left. I'm not as good at biking as you are. So ten more minutes. How are you doing, Cam?"

I swallowed. My throat was dry. My face was smeared with tears and dirt from my fingers. But at least I could take a breath, though everything was still tight. "Okay," I rasped.

"Good. Just relax. I'll be right there."

I leaned my head back against the tree and closed my eyes again. My hair caught on the scratchy bark. There was a soft breeze, which cooled the sweat at my temples and the back of my neck. I shivered. The air had turned slightly colder as the calendar tumbled toward autumn. Tear tracks lined my face. I had dirt on the knees of my jeans, but I couldn't muster the energy to care about anything beyond Juana falling, lifeless, in the field.

As my adrenaline crashed, I floated in a blank space, my body not feeling like my own, my bones too big and too small all at once, my frame unable to contain all the things tumbling inside me, too delicate to carry it all.

The rumble of an engine and the squeal of brakes broke through my haze.

"Cam!" That was Gemma.

A door opened, then slammed. Multiple pairs of shoes smacked against the sidewalk.

"Cam!" And that was Kaci.

"Don't touch him," Mateo said as Kaci dropped to my side.

"Cam," Kaci said again, her voice soft and low. "Are you hurt?"

I pried my eyes open. There was an unfamiliar car stopped at the intersection, and the smell of exhaust billowed toward us, turning my stomach. Juana stood at the door on the driver's side. The windows were rolled all the way down, and a '90s pop song vibrated out the open doors.

"I'm fine," I said, which was such an apparent lie that all four of them frowned at me in unison. I licked my lips and tried again. "Okay. I'm not fine, but"—I glanced at Juana—"I don't want an audience."

Mateo understood. Of course he did. He was as kind and perceptive as he was handsome. He turned. "Juana, can you go to the house and let them know we're okay? We'll be along in a bit."

Juana hesitated. "Are you sure?"

"Yeah. He's fine."

"Okay," she said, hesitating.

Gemma, who had been staring wide-eyed, quickly went to the car and shut the open doors. "All set. Thanks for the ride, Juana."

"You're welcome," Juana said before sliding into the car. She made a U-turn in the middle of the road and drove back down the street.

"Cam!"

I whipped my head around. Al slid to a halt and jumped off their bike. It rattled when it hit the ground, and they tripped as it caught their trouser leg, but they righted quickly. I pushed off the tree, my knees trembling as I stood.

Al didn't stop. They rammed into me, wrapping their arms around me in a tight embrace. I squeezed back, not caring if accidentally touching their skin launched me into a glimpse right then and there; I just needed them. I buried my face in their shoulder and shook.

"It's okay. I'm here."

They held on as I fell to pieces.

We sank to the ground in a heap of arms and legs. And I sobbed. I couldn't help it. In the beginning I'd clung to the hope that the glimpse had been a hallucination, and then I'd shifted to hoping it was a false future. Then, when I'd gone three for three, I'd pushed it to the recesses of my mind because I'd had other things to address. But I couldn't run away from it anymore. Confronted with the actual person involved, knowing she was indeed *real* and alive and part of Mateo's family, broke something inside me.

The floodgates opened, and all the stress from the past few weeks came gushing out. I didn't want it. I didn't want this power. I didn't want this knowledge. And I had pushed toward the verification to spite my parents, to spite Al, to spite anyone who'd thought I was nothing but a fake. And it had been for the *wrong* reasons. But I couldn't back down now. I couldn't take it all back. I was stuck. Stuck with an image of a dead girl in my head. Stuck wearing gloves because I couldn't touch anyone's bare skin without my ability activating. Stuck with always being wary of people who might want to use my glimpses for their own gain. And I couldn't handle it.

Al didn't offer any placating words, because they knew there were none. They merely held on, and that was what I needed.

After what felt like a lifetime, I managed to calm down.

A delicate clearing of the throat followed.

"Um . . . ," Gemma said. "What was that?"

"I think what Gemma means to say," Kaci said, with an elbow to Gemma's arm, "is, are you okay, Cam?"

Gemma made an *O* with her mouth. "Yes. Are you okay? What was that?"

Kaci rolled her eyes.

But it drew a chuckle from me, and I pulled away from Al's shoulder and swiped at my wet cheeks. "I . . . uh . . . I . . ."

"You don't have to tell us." Mateo stood off to the side, his arms crossed, concern radiating from him as his gaze flickered between me and where Al sat at my side. "If you don't want to."

And oh, my heart *ached*. I had to tell him. I had to tell all of them. But not yet. I didn't want to ruin Juana's day.

I stood and brushed the dirt and bracken from my clothes, then wiped my face with my sleeve. I'm sure I looked like a complete mess. "I'll tell you. Just not right now. Let's go enjoy the party."

"Are you sure?" Mateo dropped his arms. "If you're uncomfortable around my family, then—"

Wait. What? "No!" I shouted, my stomach sinking at the thought that Mateo believed I was afraid. Of his family. Of him. "No. That's not it. At all. Sorry if I gave you that impression."

Gemma cocked her head to the side. "You ran away and cried. What else should we think?"

"Not *that*!"

Al stood beside me. They had a stain on their shirt. And dirt on their pants. I winced as they attempted in vain to wipe it all off. They must not have mastered the stain removal spell yet.

"Then what?" Gemma demanded. "I don't understand."

Al raised an eyebrow and tossed their curly hair over their shoulder. "You don't need to. Not right now."

Gemma nodded. "Right. Fine. I'm glad you're okay, Cam."

"Thanks."

"Well," Al said, hands on their hips. "I'm going to go home."

"No," I said it so quickly, so desperately, that I hadn't realized I *had* said it until Al turned toward me. I looked to Mateo. "Can Al come to the party?"

"Of course."

Al raised an eyebrow. "Are you sure? I'm a witch. Isn't this your"—they gestured toward me—"attempt to, like, woo him to your side?"

My middle fluttered at the term "woo" despite completely knowing that was not the connotation Al meant, but I was a teenage boy with a crush who'd just had a breakdown. I could focus on the silly things if I wanted to.

Mateo shook his head. "It's a party for my cousin. Besides, Kaci is a psychic."

Kaci's hand shot in the air. "I *am* a psychic. I'm a medium. Not all psychics are mediums, but all mediums are psychics." She smiled. "And I'm always welcome at Mateo's house. Even though I picked out Cam's gift from the Psychic Guild."

Al and I shared an amused glance.

"Okay, then," they said with a sigh. "As long as Mateo doesn't mind. Let's go."

Al picked up their bike, and the group of us walked back to the Lopez home.

I forced a smile throughout the whole affair.

Danny and Javi were, well, Danny and Javi, roughhousing, making loud jokes, and devouring everything in sight, which made Juana and Kaci laugh and their parents admonish them. They even took turns showing off their werewolf powers. Danny grew large furry ears that twitched on the top of his head, and Javi used sharp claws to open a soda can. Mateo stiffened at their teasing as they dared him to try to grow a tail, but Juana stepped in quickly to defuse the situation.

She was so sweet and kind, ensuring that I was okay amid the chaos of the community of werewolves. I white-knuckled my way through each interaction with her. Even though her makeup was perfect, and she was dressed in trendy clothes, and her smile was genuine, I couldn't help but see her as I had in my vision—her brown skin covered in blood, her clothes ripped and dirty, and her expression contorted in pain and fear. Mateo's parents were equally nice, though I could tell they were sizing me up along with Al and Gemma during the party. They asked a few questions about my ability, the glimpses I'd had to that point—I carefully omitted the first one—and if I'd met any of the other factions yet. Gemma took the lead for most of the conversation, speaking confidently and professionally. Thankfully, they didn't ask me to *prove* it. Which was nice.

Mateo didn't hover, per se, but he didn't stray far from my elbow, and whenever he did, he would come back within a few minutes, asking me if I was okay.

It was endearing.

By the time the party wrapped up, I was exhausted. Gemma texted Val, and the group of us wandered to the front steps by the street.

"Thanks for inviting us," I said to Mateo as Gemma, Al, and Kaci walked farther along the driveway to where Al had parked their bike. "Sorry about earlier. Juana is really nice. I see why she's your favorite."

Mateo smiled softly. "Don't tell Javi and Danny. I'll never hear the end of it."

"No worries." I nudged his shoulder with my own, which was like hitting a warm brick. "Your secret is safe with me."

The soda can Mateo held in his hand burst open as his fingernails suddenly grew into claws.

Mateo squeaked in embarrassment. The can crumpled in his hand. "Sorry!" he said as soda sprayed across my jeans.

I smiled widely and shrugged. "No worries, Mateo. The soda really just adds to the aesthetic of my already grungy look."

He laughed in surprise, a burst of sound that was not at all like the usually reserved Mateo. I beamed in response.

"Glad to be of help, then," he said evenly as he gently retracted his claws from the crumpled can.

"I hate to be that person," Gemma yelled, interrupting our shared moment of levity. She pushed her glasses up the bridge of her nose. "But our ride is almost here, and we need to talk before we go."

I sighed. Mateo and I left the porch and joined the others at the edge of the pavement.

"Are you going to reveal what that was earlier?" Gemma asked.

Al and I exchanged a glance.

"Tomorrow," I said after checking the weather app on my phone, just in case. "At Drip. At ten."

Kaci clasped her hands. "Are you sure, Cam? You don't have to tell us."

"I do, actually. But tomorrow."

Val roared to a stop just in time to cut off any further questions. Gemma and I climbed into her car, and while Gemma leaned out of the window, yelling and waving to the others as Val pulled away, I basked in the fondness of Mateo's expression. Because I was sure he would hate me once I told him that his favorite cousin was going to die.

19

SECURED A TABLE IN THE BACK CORNER, AWAY FROM THE DOOR and the watchful eyes of everyone else in Drip. The fact that it was after the breakfast rush and too early for the lunch crowd meant there weren't many people. The lull was perfect for my upcoming revelation to my friends. Luckily, my parents had left for their own engagement this morning, a previous appointment of sorts that I didn't ask questions about, which allowed me to sneak out without the passive-aggressive conversations that were the norm these days.

Al was the first to arrive.

They ordered a latte and slid in the seat across from mine. "Hey," they greeted me.

"Hey."

"I thought I'd be late," they said, looking around the shop and not meeting my gaze, the awkwardness between us as thick as the fog this morning on the mountains in the distance. "Our coven had a meeting today that involved only the elders of the council, so I was able to come."

"I'm glad you did."

Al kept their head bowed. They traced a scuff on the table. "Yeah. Me too."

"Your coven sent me a phone."

Al's lips twitched. "I told my moms you needed one since your screen was cracked. They must have told the head elder witch."

"Thanks. Is it . . ." I hesitated. "Safe to use?"

Al shrugged. "I don't see why not. The coven isn't going to listen to your phone calls, if that's what you're scared of. And if they wanted to, they'd use a spell instead of a phone."

Well, that wasn't comforting. "Ah. Why are they interested in me, anyway? Isn't divination something a witch can learn?"

Al's shoulders sagged. They wilted against the high back of their chair. "Seeing the future is one of the most difficult abilities for a witch to master. Even if they did, none of them could grow as powerful as a natural clairvoyant like you. And having your gift in our ranks would make us a powerful coven for a small town, even as powerful as some of the larger covens from the big cities."

Al leaned forward, their forearms on the table, as if imparting a secret. Their voice dropped below the scattered chatter of the shop. "Can you imagine how awesome it would be to accurately predict the weather and use that to increase the growth of ingredients for potions? Selling potions is one of the main ways our coven makes money. And a verified seer might be able to help our own diviners be more accurate by sharing glimpses." The more excited they became about the possibilities, the faster they spoke. "The clairvoyant could know how an important meeting would go, which would help us with political maneuvering among the covens. Tensions are high between the eastern covens right now. The New Amsterdam Coven has been trying to absorb the smaller ones, including ours, for years, claiming that it would be best to aggregate power. But if we had a verified seer, that would make us as powerful as them," they said, tapping the table for emphasis, "if not *more*, because they aren't allied with any psychics. We would know how to fight back and keep our coven's autonomy."

I gulped. "That sounds like a lot of pressure and responsibility for a teenager."

Al huffed and flopped back in their seat. "So now you understand," they muttered.

"I'm sorry. It's just . . . a lot to take in."

Al took a sip of their drink. "Well, be prepared. The last clairvoyant of this area did become part of the local coven, and the elders want to 'keep the tradition,' as they said."

"Oh."

"Yeah. My moms are super stressed, and there are all these meetings." Al blew out a breath. "It's been hectic."

I gripped my iced mocha. "And it's okay that you're here?"

"I'm not telling them that I am in contact with you, if that's what you're asking."

"Oh. Yeah." I frowned. "Look, are we going to address the weirdness between us or—"

"Hi!" Gemma yelled from the counter, waving, the sparkles in her hair shimmering in the light. "Be there after I get my pie."

Behind the counter, Val grumbled as she slid open the rack of pie slices.

"Later," Al said.

"Okay."

Kaci and Mateo arrived next. Kaci gushed about Val's hair at the counter while she paid for her and Mateo's coffees. And Mateo smiled in amusement, then guided Kaci over to the table. Okay, that was four of five.

The last to arrive was Reese. He made a face when he entered and skipped the counter, sauntering to our table and dropping into the seat between me and Gemma. Reese nodded toward Al and Kaci and grunted in Mateo's direction. Mateo jerked his chin in response.

I rolled my eyes. "Okay. Great. Now everyone is here."

"Not going to order anything, Reese?" Gemma asked around a mouthful of pie. "I'll get it for you. As a thank-you for the other day."

Reese shook his head. "Cross-country season." He held up a water bottle. "I have to choose my caffeine and sugar carefully." He sniffed as he looked around. "And nothing that this place serves is worth the extra laps."

"Good to know," Val said with a snort as she walked to the table. "Other than the jerk, the rest of you guys okay?"

A chorus of yeses followed.

"Good." She wiggled her fingers at the group of us. "As long as you buy something, I'm not going to break up whatever weird paranormal D&D party this is, but don't make too much noise. I don't want to get in trouble with my boss for letting you stay here."

"Got it, sis!"

Val sighed and turned away, muttering a derisive, "Teenagers," as she did.

"So why did you gather us all here today?" Reese asked with an arch of his red eyebrow. "No offense—I did intervene with Dennis, but I'm not on board to act like a member of a superhero team where we have to assemble whenever you feel like it."

I rubbed my hands on my thighs, scrubbing my palms against the denim. My insides were a jumble of nerves. "Right. I get it. I just . . . Okay. Here's the thing." My leg bounced under the table. "You know I have . . . glimpses."

"Yes?" Kaci said. "We've been there."

"Right," I said again. I took a sip of my iced mocha. "It's a new thing for me. I didn't know I had the ability. And honestly, if I could go back in time, I'd choose not to have them at all. But I do. And if I'm going to be clairvoyant, then I want to be able to help people if I can. And . . . um . . . well . . . the day of the fight in the hallway, that was my first glimpse ever."

Reese stiffened at the mention of the fight. Mateo made a low noise in his throat. Ugh. I couldn't deal with them if they were going to make vaguely aggressive sounds at each other the whole time. But I pressed on.

"And that glimpse hasn't come true yet."

Gemma's eyebrows shot up. She reached for her phone. "Do you want me to record—"

"No!" I squeaked.

Al reached over and yanked the phone from Gemma's hands. Then they set it on the table out of her reach. "Not the time, Gemma."

"I was just asking," Gemma said, crossing her arms and sticking her bottom lip out in a petulant pout. "And since when were *you* invited? You stopped eating lunch with us over a week ago, after your friend breakup with Cam."

I really had missed Al's impressive glares.

"Because Al knows. Okay? They know the details, and look, this is hard. What I saw . . . it was frightening. And I . . . I don't even know if I should tell you. But you should know." I met Mateo's gaze. "You should know."

Mateo's frown deepened. His fingers gripped the edge of the table. "What did you see?"

Under his intense scrutiny, my mouth went dry. I reached for my drink and took a large gulp as the images of the glimpse tumbled through my brain like clothes in a laundromat dryer. Okay. I could do this. Just say it. Tell them. Because as I had found out the day before, I couldn't carry this burden alone.

"I saw Juana." My voice cracked. "Through the eyes of someone . . ." I trailed off. I couldn't continue. I couldn't form the words in my mouth, couldn't push the air out of my throat. Al grasped my gloved hand under the table and squeezed, nodding for me to continue. I squeezed back. "Through the eyes of someone who hurt her. Who . . . killed her."

Mateo sucked in a harsh breath. The table splintered beneath his grip, dust blooming in the air from the strength of his fingers. Kaci grabbed his forearm.

Gemma's mouth dropped open. Reese froze, stunned.

But my eyes were locked on Mateo. All the blood drained from his face; his lips were pale and his brown eyes so wide, they reflected the midmorning sun.

"What?" he whispered.

"I'm sorry," I said. "I didn't know it was her. It was my first glimpse. I didn't even know that was what had happened, that it was a real psychic interlude. Not until the school nurse said it was and Al confirmed. And then I didn't know if what I saw was even *real*, that it could come true. Al and I tried to find out who the girl was, and we couldn't find her in the yearbooks, and she wasn't a student, and I had no idea why she would be in my glimpse anyway. And when the other glimpses started coming true, were being proven accurate, I knew I had to help her. I knew I had to find the girl, but it wasn't until yesterday that I *did*."

"Whoa," Gemma said quietly.

Kaci rubbed Mateo's shoulders as he quaked silently in his seat.

"Is that why you ran?" Kaci asked, voice soft and sympathetic.

I nodded. "When she opened the door, it completely caught me off guard. I had no idea. Please, Mateo. If I could take it all back, I would. I would never see that glimpse. I wouldn't—"

"No," he said, voice raspy but firm. "No."

I didn't know what he meant. Did he not believe me? My heart pounded. I scrambled for my backpack and yanked out my sketchbook. I flipped it to the drawing I'd done that first night and slammed it down on the table in the middle. Everyone leaned in.

The sketch was unmistakably Juana. "Look at the date," I said, pointing to the bottom.

Reese's throat bobbed. "The day after the fight."

"I drew that when I couldn't sleep. But it's been seared in here,"

I said, jamming my fingertip to my temple, "since that day. I see it *all* the time. When I sleep. When I daydream. When I think about glimpses, this is the video that plays on loop." I swallowed. "Juana, in a field, covered in blood."

Mateo's whole body was a taut line. He looked like he was about to flee or flip the table or punch me. He was a bundle of potential energy ready to release.

"Mateo, please. I am so sorry."

"No," he said again, shaking his head. "Don't be sorry." His chest heaved. "If you didn't see it, then we wouldn't know. And we wouldn't be able to stop it."

My stomach was in my throat. "I don't know if stopping it is possible." My hands shook. "All the other glimpses have come true. I don't know if we can prevent the future."

Judging by the perplexed expressions on everyone's faces, no one knew the answer to that.

"We have to try," Kaci said with a firm nod. "We can test your power in some way. Figure out if a glimpse can be changed if the subject is told."

That surprised me. I was certain it would be Gemma who would be eager to make me a test subject, but Kaci obviously loved Juana almost as much as Mateo did.

"I still don't know how these powers work, other than I touch someone and then I see the future."

Gemma gasped. "That's why you asked me about the video from the fight. To see who touched you to trigger that glimpse. Because they would be the person responsible for hurting Juana."

"Yeah." I took another sip of coffee to wet my anxiety-parched throat. "At first I thought the girl must have been in the hallway with us, but when I had the second vision, I saw the basketball court through Dennis's point of view. So I knew it was the murderer who'd touched me."

"Well, that's our list of suspects," Gemma said. "Whoever was in the hallway at the time of the fight, who could've touched Cam."

"And these are our clues," Al said, tapping my sketchbook. "Cam wrote down everything he remembered from the glimpse."

The words were right there in charcoal—the bright moon obscured by clouds, the wet grass, the breeze, the gleaming knife, and the smell of blood and sulfur.

Gemma stood and angled her phone, taking a picture.

"No sharing on social media," I said quickly.

She nodded. "Yeah. Of course. No sharing."

"Wait," Reese said, shaking his head. "Wait. Wait. Wait. I didn't sign up to be in some kind of teenage detective gang. Real life isn't a *Scooby-Doo* episode. Okay? We should tell an adult. Any adult. And let them handle it." He pointed at the picture. "I mean, look at what you drew. That's a lot of blood. That's . . . terrifying."

"Okay," I said. "Which adults should we tell? My parents can't even look at me right now because they're freaked out over my new-found abilities. This situation would not help at all." I pointed at Reese. "Your parents?"

He scoffed. "As you know, the tension between the Sprite Alliance and the Lopez family doesn't make my parents the best candidates."

"Great. Then we tell the witches who are preoccupied with try-ing to get me to ally with them instead of anyone else at this table. Or how about we go to Mateo's parents, or Juana herself?"

Mateo winced. The tension in his body had eased slightly, but his jaw remained clenched. "No. My parents would automati-cally blame the sprites. We could tell Juana, but . . . she's only just returned and she's still fragile emotionally. I wouldn't want her to leave and be out of reach for us to help her if we can. We should find more information first."

"Shouldn't we warn her, though?" I asked.

"I'll tell her," Mateo said. "If it comes to that, I'll do it."

"Okay," I agreed. "That's fine. Kaci? Gemma? Any input?"

Gemma held up her hands. "My mother already thinks I'm too enmeshed in the paranormal for a human. She'd flip."

Kaci swallowed. "My aunt and grandparents only dabble. They wouldn't know how to help. And I wouldn't tell anyone else in the Psychic Guild. It's hard to know who to trust."

Reese rubbed his hand over his face. "Right. Great. Okay. Scooby gang it is, then."

Gemma pulled out a notebook from her massive backpack. She clicked a glittery purple unicorn pen and wrote at the top "Project Fix the Future" in a looping script.

"Okay. What should we do first?"

I hugged myself, gripping my elbows with tense, gloved fingers. "Kaci is right. We should see if we can sidestep one of my glimpses."

Gemma nodded and wrote the first step in a flowing purple script. "Step one: see if one of us can avert a glimpse."

"And I need more information," I said, "about how all this works."

"Adding that as part A of step one. Cam needs more knowledge about the nuances of his powers. Next?"

"We find out who was in the hallway," Al said, their expression grim.

Gemma nodded. "Adding that as step two. We need to make a list of the people who could've touched Cam. And of course that leads right into step three, which is: we need to establish motive and use the clues that Cam provided to narrow down our suspects and the time frame in which this could happen."

"Step four: we need to protect Juana," Mateo said. His clawed fingers curled over the edge of the glossy wood table, his sharp fingernails leaving deep furrows with every anxious flex of his hands.

Gemma nodded. "Step five: we need to keep an eye on the factions for anything suspicious."

"And we need to keep this between ourselves," Kaci said pointedly.

Gemma sighed but added the addendum. After writing each step, she flipped the page and wrote "Suspects" at the top.

Al smirked. "Well, we know one." They smiled at Reese. "You were there."

Reese scowled. "So was Nate. So were Danny and Javi. And Mateo."

I whipped my head to stare at Mateo as Gemma hastily scribbled names. "I didn't know you were in the hallway."

"I sensed Javi was in trouble."

"You can do that?"

"It's a werewolf thing."

Huh. So Mateo had seen me get slammed into the lockers. Great. Nice. Awesome. Not embarrassing at all.

"We can't accomplish this all today," Gemma said, setting down her pen. "So we need to break into groups."

I licked my lips. "I want to accomplish step one as soon as possible. It'll guide us with the other steps."

"I'll help Cam with that," Kaci said. "Since we're both psychics. And I'm a member of the Guild. I can arrange for Cam to meet with the members there, who might be able to help provide answers."

Gemma nodded. "Fine. I had reached out but hadn't received an answer from them yet. So I'll leave that to you, but no meetings unless I'm present."

"Noted."

"I assume that you all can each keep an eye on your own factions and report back if anything is suspicious? And I have my own network of . . ." Gemma trailed off; her nose scrunched. "Informants," she settled on saying.

"You have a spy ring?" Reese asked. "Like, for real?"

"How do you think I know everything?"

He crossed his arms and laughed uncomfortably. "You don't know *everything*."

Gemma cocked her head to the side. "For instance, your *real* first name is—"

"Fine!" Reese said, panicked. "Fine. Okay. The little freshman with the rainbows has a spy ring." He ran a hand through his hair. "Unreal."

"No more unreal than a guy who can control how grass grows," she shot back.

He huffed. "Point taken."

"Anyway," Gemma said, checking her phone for the time, "it'll be the full-on lunch rush soon. Let's hash this out."

Despite the inherent stress of a future-murder investigation, it was freeing, allowing Gemma to take control and organize. She was going to try and find another video of the fight. Reese agreed to write down the names of everyone he'd remembered seeing. Al couldn't commit to much more than keeping in touch, but at least they weren't going back to radio silence. Mateo would keep an eye on Juana after school. Since the glimpse had happened at night, we knew she'd be safe during the day. And we all set alerts for weather matching the glimpse on our phones.

We had a plan.

Relief from sharing the burden washed over me. The sting of tears gathered behind my eyes, but thankfully they didn't fall. Maybe this whole clairvoyant thing wouldn't be so bad, as long as I had this group around me. But I only *had* this group because of the glimpses. If I weren't psychic, would they still want to be friends?

"Cam," Gemma said, her voice bringing me back. She had the strap of her backpack over one shoulder. "Val's shift is over, so I'm heading out. See you tomorrow, but text me if you need me. Okay?"

I nodded.

Reese left shortly after Gemma. Then Al, when their moms called. Kaci excused herself, stating her grandmother wanted help in her garden that afternoon.

Which left me and Mateo.

We exited Drip together and stood on the sidewalk next to the bike and broom racks.

"I'm sorry," I said once again as I spun my lock and unhooked my bike.

Mateo sighed. "It's not your fault, Cam. Blame the person who is going to do it, not yourself."

"Yeah." I ducked my head. "True." I took a breath. "But I'm also sorry I kind of freaked, then zoned out at Juana's party. I know I wasn't the best company."

Mateo smiled. "It's understandable. You've had a lot going on."

"Okay, well. I just didn't want you to think that it was anything you or your family had said or done. It was all"—I made jazz hands—"this." Then I mentally berated myself for *making jazz hands*. "Anyway, what little time we've hung out, I've enjoyed it."

"Me too." He knocked a pinecone off the sidewalk with his shoe. "I think we should do it again. Hang out. Just us two."

My heart stopped. "Uh . . ." *Think, Cam. Answer. Form words. Don't leave him hanging! Give him something.* "Yes!" I coughed. "I agree. We should hang out. More. Again. Just us."

"Maybe Saturday?"

Was this a date? Had Mateo just asked me on a date? "Yeah. That would be great."

Mateo beamed. A blush bloomed across his cheekbones. He ran a hand through his thick, dark hair. "Great."

"Yes. Awesome."

"Good."

"Yep." I laughed. "I should go. I have homework, and despite the chaos, my parents still expect at least decent grades."

"You can always ask me for help. If you need to."

I made a finger gun and then rolled my eyes at myself. "Right. Honors student."

"Right."

"Okay."

Wow, we were a couple of dorks. But birds of a feather and all that.

I gripped my handlebars. "See you tomorrow at school." And to prevent even more awkwardness, I hopped on my bicycle and pedaled off toward my neighborhood. At the first cross street, I paused and glanced over my shoulder. Mateo was standing where I'd left him. He waved. I waved back, laughing, then pushed off and biked home.

20

KACI AND I SAT ACROSS FROM EACH OTHER ON THE FRONT steps of the school, right under the "No Everything" signs. We were both cross-legged, my denim-covered knees brushing her bare ones, the concrete unforgiving beneath my tailbone. She had her reddish-blond hair styled in long pigtails today, and she wore a cute blouse and a pair of shorts. School had not started yet, but the day had dawned hot. I was glad for the continuing warm weather despite the calendar showing that the first day of autumn was within the next two weeks. It meant that we still had time to save Juana, if we could.

Kaci had her palms up on her knees, and she allowed her head to drop backward, tilting her face to the sun. Her apple cheeks were pink, and her freckles were bright. She took a deep breath and let it out slowly.

"Okay. I'm ready." She opened her eyes and squared her shoulders.

I wasn't, but this was what I had to do. "Great. Ask away." It was still only a theory that having the person ask a question about what they wanted to see would help me focus, but it had worked with Reese.

"Cam," Kaci said, staring into my eyes, "what will happen at school today?"

I inhaled. I reached out and lightly touched Kaci's slim fingers.

I blinked, and the discomfort of the steps and the warmth of the day melted away, my senses overwhelmed by a bright, blinding light. Then I squinted, and the world flickered into blankness, a moment of existing in a complete void: no sound, no feeling, no sight, save for an all-encompassing white.

I blinked again, and the universe crashed in, an earsplitting cacophony, followed by pressure on all sides like I was being squeezed. Then a *pop*.

I was in the school theater. Instead of the concrete beneath me, it was the plush seats of the front row as I stared up at the stage. The area was dark, save for the stage lights and the large glowing exit sign above the emergency door, which led out of the school. I tossed a pigtail over my shoulder as I patiently waited for the argument onstage to end, so class could begin.

A water sprite—a girl named Faye—and her friend, who was a green sprite, argued with the drama teacher, Ms. Adams, over the use of sprite magic in their monologues for the next assignment.

"The answer is, not unless it is approved by the administration and the school board," Ms. Adams said as she tapped her pen in agitation on the clipboard in her hand. "I'd love to say yes, but my hands are tied, thanks to the new rules."

"But a rain cloud would make so much sense for my character, who is *standing in the rain*," Faye said, stamping her foot. "We were allowed to do it last year."

"And look, I can make vines wind into an arch for the scene that takes place in a garden."

Ms. Adams gave them a sympathetic smile. "Like I said, you have to take the request to the admin and the board."

"But it's not fair!" Faye said, throwing up her arms. Droplets of water spritzed the stage.

Ms. Adams sighed heavily. "And who is going to clean up the rain, Faye? And the leaves, Gayle? I wouldn't be able to award extra points, anyway. It's not fair to the kids who don't have sprite magic."

"Ugh," Faye said. "Just let me show you! It's basic sprite magic. It's not even difficult." Faye made a complicated motion with her hands, and a small globe of water formed in front of her.

"No, me first!" Gayle yelled, thrusting her hand toward the exit door, brow furrowed as if willing the plants outside to respond to her.

"Gayle, stop!" Faye said, shouldering her out of the way. Her ball of water rippled with the impact. "This was my idea first. You're copying me."

"*You* stop!" Gayle elbowed her back. "I have every right to try it too!"

The demonstration devolved into a shouting match, while Ms. Adams tried to calm them both. Uninterested in the argument, my gaze drifted away to the side of the room where Dennis sat in a darkened corner at the end of a row. He wasn't paying attention to the stage at all; instead his head was bowed as he scribbled in a notebook.

Hovering over his shoulder was a young woman. A young woman I didn't recognize at all, in a sweater and jeans, her brown hair hanging in her face. She touched Dennis's arm, but her hand didn't make contact. It . . . disappeared into him?

What? That couldn't happen unless . . .

And that's when I realized I was seeing a festive poster about homecoming *through* her torso. The edges of her body blurred into the background. The colors of her clothes were muted, the yellow of her shirt grayed out, the blue of her jeans faded. She placed her hands on her hips, tossed her hair, and opened her mouth in a soundless scream. She balled her fists and stamped her feet and shouted again and again, right into Dennis's ear, but he couldn't hear her. No one could. Not even me.

I made a distressed noise in my throat.

She paused, then whipped around toward me. And that's when I saw the head wound—how her hair on one side was matted with blood. Deep, bloody slashes crisscrossed her torso and ran over her cheeks, her neck, her clavicle. She stared at me with wide, unblinking eyes, a knowing gaze that pierced into the heart of me. She *knew* I could see her. And she dared me to look, to catalog the wounds: the awkward twist of one leg, the blood that stained her clothes and her skin.

My heart lodged in my throat when her angry stare met mine.

She narrowed her eyes. Then she rushed toward me, speeding through the air, her hair whipping back, her mouth open in a terrifying silent scream.

Before she reached me, a yell yanked my attention back to the stage. Faye had tripped over a small vine that had slithered through the crack in the door. She wheeled her arms as she attempted to stay upright, but her wavering sphere of water suddenly became a projectile. It flew and smacked me right in the face, the cold liquid soaking my hair and blouse.

I jolted out of the glimpse.

My chest heaved from where I was sprawled on the concrete. I ripped my hand out of Kaci's and hastily shoved on my glove, blinking away the sight of the ghost. I stared into the bright blue of the morning sky.

"Cam?"

My body jerked in fear. I pushed to a sitting position and stared at Kaci.

Her lips turned down. "You saw a ghost, didn't you?"

"Yes," I breathed.

"Which one?" she asked, resting her chin on her fist.

I rubbed my chest. My heart beat a mile a minute under my palm. My hands were clammy. How did Kaci survive seeing ghosts every day? Especially if they all looked like that one? Oh my gods, I had seen a *ghost*. A person's spirit. The remnants of a soul. I shivered. New nightmare unlocked for sure.

"The one that follows Dennis," I finally said. I wrapped my arms around my body and squeezed, like I was giving myself a hug. Or like I was holding myself together and trying to find comfort in the corporeal.

Kaci frowned. "Oh, she's angry. All the time." She tugged on her braid and added in a softer voice, "She scares me."

"Does she always yell at him?"

Kaci nodded.

"Well, she's terrifying." I rubbed my arms, chilled despite the heat. "I'm sorry you have to see her."

Kaci shrugged. "It's not all the time. She's not always there. It's fine." She smiled. "So I see her in drama class. I will try to use my psychic blocks. What else happens? Anything interesting?"

Oh. Right. Step one on the project checklist. "Um . . . yes? The front row where you sit becomes a splash zone."

Kaci made a face. "A splash zone?"

"Water sprite magic. An argument onstage ends in you being soaked."

She nodded and gave me a bright grin. "Okay. Then I won't sit there."

I offered a wan smile in return, because I hoped beyond hope that being assaulted by sprite magic was not in her future. Because surely now that Kaci knew what third block would entail, she could change what I saw. Because she had to be able to. She had to.

And as we gathered our things to go inside, Kaci chatted away about math class. I didn't respond. I didn't want to upset her, but I couldn't help but note how the ghost I'd seen through her eyes had been covered in slashes, just like my vision of Juana.

--

"I tried," Kaci said as she sat down at the lunch table, her hair damp, her upper body encased in a large hoodie. She nonchalantly set her tray down while all the breath left my body in one panicked whoosh.

Mateo's concerned gaze darted between us. "What happened?" he asked.

Kaci frowned and shook her head. "The blocks didn't work. I saw her."

"Saw who?" Mateo asked again. "What is going on? Why are you wet?"

I couldn't answer Mateo around the lump lodged in my throat. Kaci couldn't prevent herself from seeing the ghost. And the evidence that my glimpses weren't only *real*, but set in proverbial stone, was the wet ends of Kaci's braids.

Gemma plopped down beside me in a flurry of papers and rainbows, her shoulder knocking into my stunned frame, and slapped a paperback onto the table. My flatware rattled with the force of it. "What's up, partner and friends?"

Reese joined less than a minute later. And then, surprising us all, Al sat down as well. I looked over Gemma's head and met Al's gaze. "Is this okay?" they asked.

"Yeah," I said immediately, my voice choked. "It's great."

They raised an eyebrow. "It doesn't sound great."

"No," I said with a creak. "It is."

They glanced over their shoulder, where Lex conversed with a handful of other witches at a table a few rows down, then leaned in close to our group. "I told them we have an assignment to work on together." They smirked. "Which we kind of do."

Yes. We did. The literal worst group project ever.

Kaci cleared her throat. "Cam saw me in theater class in his glimpse this morning. I sat in the front row, and I got splashed because of an argument between a water sprite and the drama teacher."

I gulped. "And?"

"I moved to the other side of the theater, three rows back." She pulled at the fabric of the hoodie. "Still experienced a spring shower. I had to get this from the lost and found to cover my ruined blouse."

Any hope I'd had that Kaci had gotten wet a different way was dashed. "Oh."

Gemma's mouth opened in a perfect O. Reese grimaced.

Because there you had it. Try as she might, Kaci hadn't been able to avoid what I'd seen in the glimpse.

Mateo's brow furrowed. "Are you sure?"

"Yes," Kaci said evenly. "Cam said I would get wet and see a ghost—"

"You always see ghosts," Gemma said, but her voice was low and awed.

"I tried to use my psychic blocks to not see the ghost, but they didn't work. And I tried not to get wet."

"Okay. Well, that was just one attempt at subverting a glimpse," I said, trying to inject some kind of hope into the situation. I couldn't bear the expression on Mateo's face as the realization dawned on him. "And we know that Kaci's not the greatest with her psychic ability—no offense."

"None taken."

"And I don't know how powerful Faye is. Maybe the whole theater got wet, and there was no way to avoid it."

Gemma huffed in disbelief. Reese quickly shook his head.

Kaci reached over the table and took my gloved hand in her manicured ones. "My attempts to subvert the glimpse didn't work, Cam. It's okay."

Mateo frowned. "Does that mean—"

"We can try again," I hastily offered, cutting him off. "Shouldn't we have a larger dataset?"

"Sure," Gemma said, though skepticism dripped from her voice. "Anyway. Does anyone else have something to share with the class?"

Reese dug around in the pocket of his jeans and pulled out a piece of wadded paper. He opened it and spread it on the table between us, smoothing out the creases. "A list of all the people in the hallway during the fight."

It wasn't a small list. In fact, it was two columns that took up an entire page. "There's more on the back," Reese supplied helpfully.

At the top, in Reese's succinct print, were the names "Danny," "Javi," and "Mateo," along with his own.

Mateo raised an eyebrow. "You don't honestly think that Danny, Javi, or I would want to hurt our cousin."

The corner of Reese's mouth ticked up. "We said *everyone* in the hall. And you were there, and so were your brothers."

"How do you know this is everyone?" Gemma asked.

"I have ways, just like you."

Her nose scrunched as her skepticism elevated.

Reese sighed. "I asked around, okay? I'm an upperclassman. I know a lot of people. Besides, it's the best any of us are going to do, unless we can get video." He tapped his fingers along the table. "You can trust me."

He wasn't wrong. And despite the history between Mateo's family and Reese's, I felt like I *could* trust him. He had stepped in with Dennis, and he had offered to be the subject for the third glimpse. And he didn't have to, but he *had* joined the whatever-we-called-this-group to help. I refused to reference our group with a cartoon starring a dog, even if only in my head.

Gemma acquiesced with a nod. "Okay. Yes. Great."

"Thanks, Reese," I said. "This is really useful."

I scanned the list on the front, then flipped the paper over. And there on the back was the name I'd been looking for. Kaci stiffened and dropped a chip on her tray, and I knew she'd noticed it too.

"Well, I have news." Gemma pushed the paperback she'd been carrying to the center of the table. She flipped it open. "This is the Psychic Guild's weather almanac for this year. Using the clues that Cam gave us about the conditions that night, I've been able to pinpoint a range of dates for the attack." Mateo made a low noise that almost sounded like a growl. Gemma paused, closed her eyes, and shook her head. "Sorry. A range of dates for the glimpse." She pointed to the page. "Cam said that it was bright out, despite it being at night and taking place in some kind of meadow where there would be no artificial light, so that means that it has to be close to a full moon. And it had rained and was cool but not cold. According to this, not only is the harvest moon the brightest moon, but also the weather the week around that moon will be damp."

I sucked in a breath. "When is the harvest moon?"

"In ten days."

Mateo shook his head. "That doesn't make sense. Werewolves gain strength leading up to the full moon and are strongest the night of. No one familiar with the paranormal would make a mistake to . . . assault"—he stumbled over the word—"Juana when she'd be at her physical peak."

"I took that into account too," Gemma said, pointing at the page. "The knife must have been silver." Gemma pointed to the clue of the gleaming blade. "It would have to be, for it to do enough damage to significantly hurt her."

Based on Mateo's deepening frown, Gemma's logic was sound.

"So I bet they know about the moon cycles too," she continued. "Which means the attack will happen *after* the harvest moon, when the moon is waning and when a werewolf's strength would be decreasing. And for two to three nights after the moon, we'll have cloudy and damp weather."

I couldn't help but be impressed.

Al took the book from Gemma's hand and peered at the page. "Is this thing even accurate?"

"Well, not as accurate as Cam, but the publisher boasts an

eighty-seven-percent accuracy rate on their website." Gemma took it back and flipped it open. "The Psychic Guild stamp is right there." She pointed at Kaci. "What do you think?"

Kaci delicately took a bite of her sandwich and chewed. After she swallowed, she rested her hands in her lap. "I think," she began in her quiet, airy voice, "that Dennis is our top suspect."

Gemma dropped the book. "What?"

"Yeah, what?" Reese asked.

Al raised their hand. "Thirding the *what*."

"Cam saw the ghost."

Everyone except Kaci turned toward me. I shrank in my seat and flicked a kernel of cafeteria corn across my tray. "In my glimpses, I see what the person sees. I saw the ghost that follows Dennis."

Al's jaw dropped. "You saw a ghost."

I nodded. "Yeah. And it was *disturbing*. Like one of those jump-scare horror movies in real time."

"Wow, that's so *cool*." Gemma pulled out a notebook and started scribbling across the page. "Tell me everything."

"Like how you think it's Dennis, for starters," Reese said. "Does he even know Juana?"

Reese's gaze darted to Mateo.

Mateo, who had remained mostly stoic, merely shrugged. "I don't know." He hadn't even touched his food. And by the clench of his jaw and the way he was gripping the edge of the table, this whole conversation was upsetting him. His hair had grown shaggier just in the time we'd talked, and he had tucked his probably clawed fingers into the sleeves of his shirt. Maybe he shouldn't be part of the cartoon-reference gang if the information was going to cause him this much turmoil.

"Mateo, if this is too much—" I began.

"I want to know," he said, his teeth gritted, and oh, his canines had definitely lengthened too. "I need to know."

"Okay." I took a breath. "We know he was in the hallway, according to Reese's list. He assaulted me and Gemma outside the school the day of the third glimpse, so we know he can be aggressive. And he mentioned using silver against my werewolf bodyguard, so he knows how to *hurt* a werewolf. Furthermore, the ghost . . ."

"She's angry," Kaci said. "At him. She yells at him all the time."

"And she has slashes all over her." I hunched further. "Like Juana did."

Our entire table except Kaci turned to stare at Dennis where he sat at his usual lunch table. He scrolled on his phone as he ate alone, like he always did.

He must've felt our energy, because he looked up at us and glared.

I whipped back around and took a long gulp of my soda.

Gemma ducked her head and immediately scribbled down information.

"Okay," Al said, drawing out the vowel. "Do we have any other leads? We shouldn't put all our eggs in one basket, especially if there is no connection between Dennis and Juana. There is no motive."

"Other than to get to Cam," Mateo said.

My whole body went taut. "What?"

"He's tried to use you for your power three times now and was only successful once. Maybe he tries again, and Juana gets in the way."

"Why would Juana get in the way?" I asked. "She barely knows me."

The tips of Mateo's ears turned red and then began to lengthen. Mateo scrambled for his beanie, yanking it out of his jacket pocket, but he fumbled with it due to his claws.

Kaci smiled. "Because Mateo likes you."

Oh. Well. My cheeks heated so quickly, I knew they were bright pink. I probably matched Gemma's hair.

"Anyway, I do have another lead," Gemma said. "Remember the girls who destroyed my locker?"

"Yeah," I said.

"Well, they received in-school suspension for a few days. And since then they've been leaving not-so-nice comments on my videos."

"Um . . ." I scratched the back of my head. "That's not really a reason to suspect—"

Gemma held up her phone. The ClickClack app was open to her page.

You'll get yours.

Well, that wasn't too bad.

So will Cam and Al.

Okay.

And all your new friends.

And this was slowly getting worse.

Herbicide for your sprite. Silver for your werewolf. Fire for your witch.

I gulped. "I guess we shouldn't rule them out."

Reese picked up the paper. "Were they in the hallway?"

Gemma pursed her lips and then sighed. "It doesn't look like it."

"We'll still keep an eye on them," Mateo said. "They shouldn't be harassing you or making threats."

Gemma straightened immediately, a smile stretching across her face. If she were an anime character, she'd have heart eyes. "Thank you."

"Okay," I said, rubbing my hands along my thighs. Ten days. We had ten days to get our shit in order. "We have the potential when and a possible who; now we just need a where."

"Maybe it's in these other clues," Gemma said, opening the picture of my sketch she had taken on her phone. "A meadow that smells like metal and sulfur? Where would that be?"

"Near a factory?" Al guessed. "Or the landfill?"

Reese abruptly stood. "I just remembered—I need to meet with a teacher. I'll see you tomorrow." He grabbed the trash from his lunch, tossed an awkward wave over his shoulder, and then he was gone.

Weird.

A notification went off on Gemma's phone. She grabbed it and let out a squeak.

"Cam," she squealed. She grabbed my sleeve, her small fingers wrapped around my covered forearm in a death grip. Her expression almost manic.

"Yeah?" I asked.

"The Coalition of Faeries wants to meet with you."

"The what of what?"

"The Coalition?" Al asked, dropping a chicken nugget. "The faeries want to meet with Cam?"

Gemma vibrated in her seat. "Yes," she said. "This is my chance for a paranormal bingo!"

"I thought faeries didn't take interest in the drama of the other factions?" I asked, looking between Mateo's deep frown and Al's wide eyes.

"They do now. This is amazing. I have to do research!" She gathered her things and darted out of her seat, ribbons flying behind her. "I'll send you study materials!" she yelled as she disappeared out the door.

I rubbed my hand over my face, hoping the entirety of the cafeteria would chalk up the theatrics to Gemma being Gemma. I'd already seen a ghost that day, and I couldn't wrap my mind around faeries at the moment; from the expressions on my friends' faces, I didn't think I wanted to yet, so having an awkward social encounter was not high on my list. I sighed, took a bite of my chicken sandwich, and hoped I could make it through the rest of the day without another mishap.

21

HEY."

I startled and dropped my bike lock. I quickly reached down to grab it, then stood with my fingers wrapped around the handlebars of my bike.

Al stood in front of me. Their hands were looped through the straps of their bag.

"Hey," I said.

"Can I walk home with you?"

I blinked. "Sure."

"Not all the way," they said, crinkling their nose. "But to the corner."

"Yeah, that's fine."

I pulled my bike from the rack and maneuvered it onto the sidewalk. They fell in step beside me.

"Mateo likes you, huh," they said without preamble.

I grinned. My face heating with a blush. "We have a date."

"Get out! Seriously?"

"This Saturday. I have no idea what we're doing, but yeah. He asked me out after our meeting at Drip."

They smiled and smacked my covered upper arm with their open palm. "That's great. Congrats." The happiness in their smile dimmed. "Just be careful."

My shoulders slumped. "Yeah, I know. I don't think Mateo would ask me out just for my powers, but Danny and Javi basically made him sit with me at lunch. And he did. If they asked him to take me to the movies, then he probably would."

"I hope that's not it."

"Me too."

"That said," they said as we took a left, heading toward the corner where we'd met the first day of school, "I wanted you to know why we . . . why I . . ." They huffed. "Why I've been a jerk."

I stopped. "You haven't been a jerk."

They leveled a glare at me.

"Okay, fine. A little bit of one. But you were right—I've been clingy. I freaked out when you waved at Lex, thinking you were going to ditch me, because my mom had crawled into my head and placed that awful thought there. And I'd basically pinned all my hopes and happiness for the school year on you. That was unfair and not cool friend behavior. I'm sorry."

"But I should've understood what you've been going through. Your brother basically disappeared, and he was the one normal person in your family. No offense."

"None taken." I scuffed the toe of my shoe on the sidewalk. "You set a healthy boundary. You tried to do it gently, and I didn't take it well. I understand, Al. Not going to lie—some of the things you said in the hallway really hurt, but I get it."

Al tipped their head back and blew out a breath. "Ugh. I hate that you're being so mature about this."

"Why?"

"Because—" They winced. "I maybe was, you know, a little jealous."

I froze in place. "What? Jealous?"

They paused beside me and kicked a pinecone with their chunky boot. "Yeah. You know, I've been a witch my whole life. And

I've worked really hard to become part of our coven. And my mothers have put a lot of pressure on me, especially since Amy is exceeding all expectations. And they have been all over me about focusing more on spells and potions and improving my control."

"Yeah. I know."

They took a deep breath. "Well, with all that hanging over me, it sucked to see you just . . . luck into your powers."

I almost dropped my bike. My jaw fell open. "Luck into my powers?"

"Yeah. One minute you're normal Cam, and the next you're, like, viral psychic clairvoyant Cam who can predict the future, and suddenly everyone wants to be your friend and invite you into their factions with no training and no work. It was . . . difficult for me."

Al was envious? Of me? For powers I didn't even know I had? Much less know how to *use*? "For real? That's . . . inconceivable."

They crossed their arms. "Well, conceive it, because I was."

And wow. That actually made me angry. "Al," I said, staring at my gloved hands, which were gripping my bike so tightly, my knuckles ached, "I was terrified. I had a glimpse of someone dying. I barely knew what was happening to me."

"I didn't say I was proud of it," they snapped. "I know it was shitty. Okay? I'm sorry. I really am. I was worried about the coven, too, and my place in it. And I did need to concentrate more on my own spells and potions. That wasn't a lie."

I licked my lips. "I didn't say it was."

"Look, it was childish and immature. And I hate that I put you in a weird position, and I hate that now I'm limited in how I can help you. Please believe me when I say that I'm sorry."

I hated it too. But I couldn't blame them. Their mothers expected so much from them, and their younger sister was eclipsing them in magic.

"You came when I called," I said softly. "When I was crying and running from Juana, you came. And, well, that meant the world to me. Thank you for that. And thank you for being honest with me."

Al reached out and grabbed my gloved hand. "I want us to be best friends, Cam. As soon as all this is sorted, I really want us to go back to the way we were."

I shook my head. "No. I don't think we can do that."

"What?"

"You were right, Al. I was too dependent on you. I still want us to be friends, and we will be, just in a better way. But I think you were right that we need a little breathing room."

Al's mouth formed a smile, but it trembled at the corners. "Okay. Yeah. That makes sense."

"When this is all over, we'll figure out a way to be a better us."

"I'd like that."

"Me too."

"Good."

We started walking again. The sun shining through the trees dappled the sidewalk in light and shadow.

"My poor parents," I said with a wry grin. "My mom wanted me to make friends so badly with humans, and not only is my witch best friend back, but I have a date with a werewolf and regularly eat lunch with a sprite and a medium. The only other human in our group is far from normal. And I love her for that."

Al laughed. "Oh, by the way, your parents visited the coven house the other day."

"What?" I shouted, snapping my head up. Absolute shock rocketed through my body. I almost dropped my bike again. "My parents? Are you sure?"

Al nodded. "Yep."

"Bullshit."

Al chuckled as they jumped over a crack in the pavement. "Nope. They were there. They talked with the elders. They wanted a protection spell, I think? Or a charm? It was weird. I couldn't hear the entire discussion, but after your parents got what they wanted, the whole conversation changed direction toward how the elders could entice you to ally with the coven."

Huh. My parents had never reached out to Al's family before. Throughout my friendship with Al, I think my mom had talked to Al's mothers only a handful of times. And only when she absolutely had to. "I can't believe they did that. What the hell?"

"I know, right? My mothers were beside themselves. And your mom was so uptight the whole time. She sat right on the edge of her seat."

That sounded like my mom. "You saw them?"

"I watched through a crack in the door. I heard part of the conversation before I was shooed away."

"Great." I groaned. "I hope they behaved themselves. And didn't utterly offend your coven."

Al shrugged. "I didn't hear otherwise."

"A protection spell? From what? And what if your coven was able to sway them to convince me to ally with them? That's going to be an awful dinner conversation."

"I can find out more if you want."

I waved away the offer. "I don't really want to know. Whatever they're up to doesn't need to concern me. If they think they need protection from me, or from the gifts that are showing up to the house, that's their problem." My heart sank, though, at the thought that my parents might believe they needed to be protected from my ability. Did they think I was going to try and see their futures? And use what I saw against them? That . . . really hurt.

"Your face says differently."

"Okay, well, maybe ask your moms if it comes up in conversation."

"I'll see what I can do."

"Thanks," I said with a sigh. "Hey, maybe we can procure a protection spell for Juana. Do you think that would work?"

Al hummed. "Possibly? Two thoughts, though—one is, didn't you prove today that your glimpses can't be avoided? And two—a protection charm isn't strong enough to ward off a werewolf's greatest weakness."

"The silver blade of the knife," I murmured.

"Exactly."

We made it to the corner, and Al paused. They took out their phone and tapped out a text to their ma. "Speaking of alliances, any thoughts on who you'll pick?"

I sighed. "None. I have no idea. I've only met with the werewolves, and well, you know how that went. And now the faeries are next."

Al narrowed their brown eyes. "Be careful. The faeries are notoriously aloof. They don't usually concern themselves with the affairs of the rest of the factions. It's kind of a big deal that they contacted Gemma."

So not only did I have a murder mystery to solve, but my parents were also acting weirder than normal, and a coalition of powerful immortal magical faeries wanted to meet with me. "Great," I said with no enthusiasm. "Just great."

"Cheer up, buttercup." Al replied, slinging their arm over my shoulders and giving me a squeeze. "At least you have a date with Mateo on Saturday. You only have to make it through the rest of the week!"

Yeah. I only had to survive classes, a potentially murderous classmate, and whatever else the paranormal world wanted to throw my way. "Thanks for the pep talk," I muttered.

Al grinned. "What are friends for?"

--

Dinner that night was hilariously awkward.

My dad scrolled through his phone as he chased peas around on his plate. My mom glared at him and didn't even look my way.

I cleared my throat. "I talked with Al today," I said, because I had decided to be an agent of chaos. My mom's fork clattered against her plate. My dad pulled his gaze away from his screen.

"And what did they have to say?" my mom said primly.

"Only that you two went to the coven house the other day."

They exchanged nervous glances. My dad coughed. "Well, son—"

"Yes?" I asked, raising an eyebrow. "Any particular reason you went to converse with witches? When you've basically snubbed Al's moms for the entire time we've known them?"

My mom's lips twisted into a frown. "We're human, Cam."

I didn't respond, because that classification didn't really fit me anymore. "And?"

"And we went there to . . . talk to Al's mothers about . . . how to raise a gifted teenager," she said, then took a large sip of her wine.

"We don't have any experience with this," my dad continued. "It's new to us, and we thought the Wilsons could help."

Oh. That was not what I was expecting at all. It made a strange kind of sense.

"Wow. Okay. Thanks."

My mom gave me a tight smile. "We're trying, Cam. We don't want this to place any more strain on our household. So your dad and I decided to take a few steps and make an effort."

"We want to know about your life," my dad said, setting his phone down. "This . . . new ability is important to you, so it's important to us."

Wait. What was happening? Were these really my parents? Or had someone replaced them when I wasn't looking? "For real?" I asked.

My dad chuckled under his breath. "For real."

Was this . . . an olive branch? Were they actually trying to accept my clairvoyant ability? Or better, trying to accept *me*? A small tendril of hope bloomed in my chest. "And you met with the coven elders? What did they say?"

My mom huffed. "They gave us a sales pitch. But it wasn't very convincing."

"They did mention that they sent you a new phone," my dad said, nodding to my cracked screen on the table. "Why aren't you using it?"

"Oh." I squashed a bit of meatloaf with my fork. "Because I haven't transferred my data over yet. That's all."

"Well, it was a thoughtful gift."

I couldn't believe my dad had said that. This coming from a man who recently had been wary of fruit from the Sprite Alliance. But it seemed like he *was* trying. "It was thoughtful," I agreed.

My mom reached over to the empty seat next to her that was usually Aiden's. She picked up the box that I'd left in the hallway and set it on the table next to my plate. The brand-new phone was nestled inside. "Have you thought about which faction you are going to choose?"

That fledgling hope shined a little brighter. They had done research. I straightened from my slouch. If this was an olive branch, a path toward a peaceful family life, a way to repair the rift between us, I didn't want to ruin it by being clandestine. I could offer my own gesture of goodwill by answering their questions. "I don't know yet." And that was one-hundred-percent honest. "I'm meeting with the different factions with Gemma from Situation Paranormal to ask questions and gather information. Gemma is my human advocate."

My mom pursed her lips. "The girl from the video app?"

"Yeah. That's the one. She's knowledgeable about the paranormal."

"Is this interrupting your school day?" my dad asked.

I shook my head. "No. We meet at lunch, but we've also met after school at Drip, the coffee shop in town."

My mom set her fork down and folded her hands. "Have you met any of the factions?"

"No—well, I went to a party at the Lopez house. They're werewolves," I clarified, because I had no idea if they knew anyone's names. "But it wasn't a formal situation. It was just for fun."

My mom's eyebrows twitched, but her expression remained impassive. "For fun?"

"Mateo is a friend of mine." I omitted the part about having a date with him. That was for a different conversation, and I didn't want to snuff out this little spark of hope just yet. "It wasn't just me. Gemma, Al, and my other friend Kaci were there."

"Kaci? You haven't mentioned her before."

"She's a psychic. A medium, to be more specific. She sees ghosts."

My dad paled. My mom took another gulp of wine.

My dad cleared his throat again. "Any other new friends?"

"Reese. He's a sprite."

"Uh-huh." He shoved a large forkful of meatloaf into his mouth and chewed.

"You wanted me to make new friends. And I have. One of them is human. The others are from different paranormal factions."

"Just be careful," she said.

"We love you, son," Dad said with a wink. "I know we're not the greatest at showing it now that you've grown into an opinionated teenager. And we've been a little stressed this year. But we don't want to lose you."

Just like we lost Aiden, was left unsaid.

"Okay. Yeah. I'll be careful. I promise."

My mom smiled, and it was warm and genuine. "Good." She reached over and gently squeezed my shoulder.

I couldn't remember the last time she'd touched me. Not since

Aiden had left, I knew that for sure. And I couldn't help but melt into it.

It was a dream come true. They were being supportive, which was more than I'd hoped for.

"Thank you," I said to them both.

"Well," my dad said, dropping his napkin on the plate, "what do you say to a movie? I know the perfect one."

Movie night? It wasn't even Thursday. He must be as happy as I was about us clearing the air.

"Yeah. Okay."

He jumped from his seat. "Great. I'll make popcorn."

Mom nudged the box toward me. "It would make me happy if you used the new phone. Then I'd know that you were able to contact anyone if you needed. And I wouldn't have to worry about your cracked phone malfunctioning."

"Yeah," I said, taking the cell phone from the package. "I'll transfer the data during Dad's movie."

She smiled again, and I felt warm all over.

"Good." She petted my hair with a soft giggle. "Does this mean we can talk about your hair color?"

"Ack. No!" I said as I ducked away, laughing.

For the first time in months, I didn't feel like I had to be on the defensive around my parents. The relief was palpable. This was a step in the right direction. This felt like a good omen, that the tides were turning, that my parents were on my side.

And for the first time in a long while, I felt like everything might turn out okay.

22

"WHY ON A WEDNESDAY AFTER SCHOOL?" I ASKED AS I squirmed on the front steps of Central Shady Hallow High. Gemma was standing next to me, squinting down at her phone.

"Don't the faeries know we have important stuff to do?" I pitched my voice low. "We have eight days, Gemma."

"Until the harvest moon. The attack happens after." She stood on her toes and craned her neck, trying to peek down the road. "And today worked well for them."

"Did they ask if it worked well for me?" I crossed my arms. "I don't understand why we are doing this when we have leads to follow and—"

"Because it's the Coalition of Faeries. No one turns down an invitation from them. *No one.*"

"Okay. Whatever. I just feel like it's a waste of time right now with everything else going on. Shouldn't I be meeting with the Psychic Guild to figure things out?"

Gemma sighed loudly, tipping her head back in frustration. "You are meeting with the Guild later this week. Look, I know you're antsy, so listen. The girls who vandalized my locker weren't in the hallway, so despite their creepy comments on my videos, we can rule them out as suspects. Kaci and Mateo are out looking for the 'where' it will happen, based on the sketch and the clues. Reese has a lead on a video from the hallway. And Al is working on a tracking spell for Dennis." She ran a hand through her hair. "So all you have to worry about right now is meeting with the faeries."

My mouth dropped open in awe. "You organized all this?"

"Of course I did. It's what I do."

Okay. Wow. I felt wrong-footed and a little out of the loop. "Well," I blustered, "maybe I had other plans."

"What else would you have going on?" A slow smirk stole over her features. "Unless you have plans with Mateo?"

I glared. "No. For your information, that's not until Saturday."

She snorted. "Gross."

"What? It's just a date. Besides, I'm sure you have had crushes before."

"Nah," she said, twirling one of the ribbons on her backpack. "Dating is overrated. I'm not interested in that at all right now. But maybe in the future, in a romantic sort of way."

"Ah, okay. Cool."

Gemma bounced on her heels, her unrelenting energy on clear display. "Anyway, Val should be here by now. I wonder where she is. I don't want to be late."

"We'll be fine, Gemma. They're immortal. They have all the time in the world."

Gemma gave me a very unimpressed look. "Well, at least I know you read the materials I sent you."

"Of course I did," I said, affronted. "I didn't even read for lit class because I was deep in faery lore."

The materials Gemma referenced were a fifty-page document written in an impossibly small font. I guess the faeries would have a lot of history, being immortal and all. But from what I gathered, they lived outside the bounds of our reality somehow. And they were experts on bargain magic and on the manipulation of space and time. While the witches received their powers from a goddess of magic, the werewolves from a goddess of the moon, and the sprites from a goddess of nature, the faeries obtained their abilities from a god of time.

"Good," she said with a sharp nod. "Because this is *the* meeting. Like, huge. Beyond what I had expected. I mean, the Coalition of Faeries makes the Psychic Guild look like a bunch of middle schoolers in a bad Model UN."

Okay, well, Gemma needed to stop because I was beginning to sweat. I kind of knew this was a big deal based on the reactions of my friends, but all of this was a big deal to me. I didn't need any more pressure.

Thankfully, Val pulled into the parking lot. Gemma hurtled down the stairs, while I followed at a more sedate pace.

Except Val wasn't alone.

Juana stepped out of the passenger side, holding two to-go cups. Her long golden-brown hair was pulled up into a ponytail, and she wore a cute dress with leggings and soft ankle boots.

"Iced mocha for you," she said, offering me the drink. "Val told me you've ordered it twice."

I gulped. With a shaking hand, I took the coffee. "Yeah," I said, my voice a squeak. "I have."

"And extra caramel drizzle for you."

Gemma's heart eyes were a sight to behold as she took the drink from Juana. "Thank you," she said with reverence. "I now understand why you are Mateo's favorite cousin."

Juana giggled.

"I told her you didn't need the caffeine." Val's voice drifted from the driver's side. "But she wanted to get your favorite. She's a nicer person than I am."

"I agree." Gemma flung her backpack with one hand into the

back seat, then climbed in. "Come on, Cam," she yelled, when I stalled. "The faeries are waiting."

Juana laughed again. "Sorry," she said, leaning in. "I hope it's okay that I crashed the party. Val and I were hanging out when she said she had to come pick you up. I wanted to tag along."

My mouth was dry. I took a sip of the drink through the straw. "I didn't know you knew Val," I said.

Juana smiled. "Teo mentioned Drip in a conversation the other day. I went to check it out, and Val and I hit it off immediately. She's so cool."

"She is." I stood there awkwardly, unsure of what to do or say, because here Juana was so vibrant and beautiful and *alive*, and I knew for a fact that was going to change in about eight days. "Thanks for the coffee."

"You're welcome. Anything for Teo's friend." She winked.

Oh, he'd totally told her about our date on Saturday.

"Cam!" Gemma said with a whine to her voice. "We need to *go*."

Juana gestured toward the back seat. "After you."

"Thanks." I set my backpack on the floorboard, then crawled into the car, balancing my coffee as I clicked on my seat belt. The back seat was so small that Gemma and I were pressed together uncomfortably, and my knees no doubt were poking Juana in the back as Val drove away from the curb.

I wasn't sure where we were going, other than it was out of the central school district. Val followed the directions from Gemma's phone, and thirty minutes later, after hitting a blip of traffic, we pulled in front of a cottage set on a verdant square of property. I could feel the waves of magic surrounding the scene; a tingling sensation scraped over my skin as I slid from the car.

Val stepped out and crossed her arms over the hood of her car, eyeing the cottage with a raised eyebrow and a wary expression. "Um . . . okay. No. You're not going in there."

Gemma frowned. "Why not?"

"Because it's unsettling. I mean, look at it."

Val was correct. On the property sat a cottage—a very small, very fairy-tale-esque house, with wooden slats on the outside, a small porch, and vines and flowers crawling over the façade. The roof was moss-covered, and the walkway from the concrete sidewalk to the front door was cobblestoned. A little wishing well with a pulley and a bucket sat on the side of the house. The porch had a lattice of roses on one end and a swing on the other that was painted a weathered white. It was as if every person's vision of what a house from a folktale would look like had been transplanted from our collective unconsciousness into this very spot. Compared with the rest of the neighborhood, which was populated with sprawling McMansions, the little cottage exuded a strangeness that was unparalleled.

It *was* unsettling.

Because I wasn't sure if it was *real* or *unreal*, a mirage made of magic. It was so perfect. Creepily so. Not a blade of grass from the lush lawn out of place. No sounds of traffic from the neighborhood, only the babble of a nearby brook and the songs of birds that were perched on the rafters of the well. Combined with the crawling feeling of being watched by someone unseen, the whole vibe of the property was "cottagecore meets the uncanny."

"We're going," Gemma said firmly. "They invited us. It would be uncouth of them to do something weird to us."

Val rolled her eyes. "Yeah. That's a great excuse." She pressed a hand to her chest and, in a high, mocking tone, said, "'Sorry, Mom, Gemma said she would be safe because it would be rude of the faeries to harm her.'"

"First," Gemma said, ticking a list off her fingers, "Mom doesn't sound like that. And second—"

"It's fine," I said, waving them away. "I can go alone."

Juana's lips pursed in concern, but she didn't say anything. I shouldered my backpack and gripped the straps. "It's me they want to talk to, anyway."

"Cam," Gemma said, bolting from my side to stand in front of me. "Remember what you read?"

I nodded. "Yeah. Faeries are immortal. They use bargain magic. They also can stretch time and create mirages, but other than that, not much is known about their powers. They keep to themselves and stay out of faction politics. They're powerful but really just want to be left alone."

"Okay. Good. So you understand why it's so strange they contacted you, right? I have no idea what they want with you."

A cold prickle of fear made the hair on the back of my neck stand on end. "Yeah."

"We'll stay," Juana said, arms crossed. "Until you come back out."

"You don't have to."

But Val's and Juana's expressions said otherwise. "You left your bike at the school," Juana said evenly. "You don't have a ride home. So we'll stay."

I couldn't argue with that. "Okay. Thanks."

I stepped around Gemma and headed for the walkway. At the edge of the concrete, where the cobblestone met the sidewalk, I paused and stared at the cottage. It was like looking through a thin sheet of glass, which added to the eerie image, the picture of the cottage itself wavering with the sunlight. I took a breath and stepped onto the stones.

A wave of magic scrubbed over my skin, cold and seeking, as if making sure I wasn't a threat. As soon as my sneaker hit the stone, the door of the house opened of its own accord.

I looked over my shoulder. The three girls were still there but blurred, as if they were on the other side of whatever encased the house. Juana's teeth were bared in a snarl. Gemma's eyes were wide, and despite Val's attempt to appear unaffected, even her face was pale.

Great. Well, too late to turn back now.

With a stride that looked far more confident than how I actually felt, I walked down the path, crossed the porch, and entered the house.

Another wave of magic washed over me, but this time it wasn't prying like the other one. It was welcoming, like a warm hug or a hot cup of tea or a fuzzy sweater. While everything on the outside of the cottage had screamed danger, the magic inside felt . . . safe in a way. Still powerful and peculiar as fuck, but without the sinister undertones.

I was in the entryway of a massive house. The floor was a gleaming black, and the walls were white, leading to a huge, vaulted ceiling and a massive golden chandelier. My mouth hung agape as I took in the magnificence of the interior—the glossy cherry half-moon table on my right, the gilded mirror above it, the wide staircase with shiny metal banisters leading to another level that certainly did not exist on the outside, and the emerald-green plush carpet that ran from the door to the base of the stairs. Wait, was that carpet or . . . grass with little white flowers sprouting from it? Heavy curtains hung over the windows. The eerie, disembodied sound of distant piano music emanated from somewhere within.

I took a hesitant step forward, craning my neck to take it all in. The unnerving feeling from before tickled the back of my brain again when I spied the closed doors that lined the room, and the paths of the grand staircase that wound around each side and led farther into the structure.

The sound of approaching footsteps reached me, and I stiffened, composing myself as best as possible in the face of powerful magic. I'd visited Al's home and the coven house, and I'd been to a werewolf picnic, but all of them were *nothing* compared to this.

"Hello. You must be Cam."

A woman appeared from around the corner, and despite hearing her approach, I still jumped, my hands white-knuckled on my bag.

"Hi. Yes. I am."

She smiled. She was tall, with light brown hair. And while I had expected to meet someone in a power suit or an evening gown, she was dressed in yoga pants and a flowy white shirt, and she was barefoot. She had white skin and red eyes and sparkling gossamer wings that fluttered behind her. Her pink lips pulled into a wide smile.

"I'm sorry. This must all be overwhelming."

I wanted to lie, but I felt like I *couldn't*. Like if I tried, I wouldn't be able to. Instead I nodded.

"Yes. I have no idea what I'm doing."

She laughed, and it was like tinkling bells. "I can't imagine how difficult it has been for you since the first glimpse. My understanding is that you had very few interactions with the paranormal until that event."

I found myself smiling too.

"You're right."

Her eyes crinkled when her grin grew, but I couldn't guess her age at all. She could've been twenty or a thousand. I wouldn't have known, and I didn't dare ask.

"My name is Ileana. I'm the leader of this grove. But I'm not the one who invited you here."

My blood ran cold. "You're not?"

I followed her to the sitting room, and she beckoned me to sit on the couch. I sank into it, placing my bag at my feet, while she sat opposite me in a high-backed armchair. The cushions of the sofa seemed to mold to me instantly, rearranging themselves for my comfort. They were so cozy, I was scared I'd fall asleep, so I straightened my back and sat up the best I could.

Ileana watched me with an amused expression.

"Faeries don't have much need for a clairvoyant. We tend to keep to our own. We're working on integrating more with the world, but that movement is led by our grandchildren."

"Grandchildren," I sputtered.

She laughed. "Yes."

"Then why am I—"

Ileana stood. "Oh, here he is. I'm sure you'll have much to talk about together."

I swiveled to look at the person who approached and shot to a standing position when I realized who it was. "Aiden?"

He raised his hand and waved. "Hey, Cam. Thanks for coming."

I didn't care if it was a trick or a mirage. I launched myself at my brother, falling into his body and wrapping my arms around him in a tight embrace. If it was a trick, it was a good one, because they had his height perfect—several inches taller than me. And when he hugged me back, it was just like all the hugs we'd had over the years. Overwhelmed, I buried my face into his shoulder, and tears leaked from the corners of my eyes. I didn't care that I might have a glimpse. All I cared about was hugging my brother.

"Hey," he said, rubbing his hand between my shoulders. "It's okay." Even his voice was perfect.

"I have so many questions," I choked out into the flannel shirt he wore.

"I know. I have answers." Aiden pulled away, prying off my claw-like grip, and held me at arm's length. "You look good," he said with a crooked smile. "I love the hair."

I self-consciously tugged on a strand. "I was bored."

He laughed. "Sounds like you. Come on—let's go into the garden. You'll like it. It's beautiful."

Aiden picked up my bag and took my gloved hand. He led me out of the sitting room and down the hallway. The door in front of us glowed as he approached, then swung open before he even touched it.

The garden was as beautiful as the house. We walked down an earthen path to a gazebo in the middle. A cool breeze ruffled the plants hanging from pots and carried the fragrant smell of flowers. We were surrounded by buzzing bees, singing birds, and colorful plants that were vibrant and heavy with fruit. It was like we were in a picture book, on a page depicting an ideal spring day.

"It's amazing, isn't it?" Aiden asked as he sat on a bench. He beckoned me to join him, and I weakly sank down next to him. Because it was Aiden. His brown hair was a little longer than the last time I'd seen him, and he had added to his ear piercings, but it was him. It was my brother.

"It is," I finally answered after taking him all in, and then reality slammed into me. My brother was *here*. "What the hell, Aiden? Is this where you've been? Why haven't you called me? Do Mom and Dad know?" I dropped my voice and whispered, "Are you trapped? Kidnapped? If so, I have several friends who might be able to help you get out of here."

Aiden held up his hands. "Slow down, Cam. First, no. I'm not trapped. I can leave anytime I want. In fact, I do leave to go to class."

"You're still in college?"

He smiled and rubbed my shoulder, his touch comforting and firm. "Yes. I'm still at the university in New Amsterdam. But when I saw the videos of Shady Hallow's new clairvoyant, I took a quick break to come down and check in on you."

I fiddled with my uneven nails. "You saw those, huh?"

"Oh yeah." He ruffled my hair. "You went viral, Cam. It was all the buzz, even at school. Three correct glimpses. That's amazing."

"Thanks."

"Any thoughts about what you're going to do with your clairvoyant abilities?"

I narrowed my eyes. "Is this you asking, or the Coalition of Faeries?"

Aiden raised his hands. "Just me." He crossed his heart. "Promise."

Beyond saving Juana, I hadn't really thought about my future, other than knowing I would have to ally with a faction. "I think . . . I want to be able to help people. However best I could do that."

"That sounds awesome. I'll support you in whatever you do."

"That's great, but none of this explains why you're in a faery grove and why you went missing for months."

Cam sighed. "I'm not missing. Mom and Dad know exactly where I am."

"Oh." I frowned. "Why . . . why did you cut us off? Was it something they said? Or I did? Did I do something, Aiden?"

"What? No!" He recoiled, horrified. "I didn't cut you off. Mom and Dad cut *me* out. They stopped paying my tuition. They cut off my phone. They forbade me from trying to contact you."

My whole body went cold. "What?"

"I didn't reach out to you at first. That's true, and I'm sorry. But when I saw the videos, I gathered the courage to comment and maybe get to you via Gem-Jam, but she had comments limited to verified users. And so I thought I'd email her, but I was terrified it would get back to Mom and Dad. I had no idea how they were reacting to everything. I was scared they'd do something drastic to you."

I flinched. That sounded like our parents from weeks ago. But not now. Not with their current mindset. They were different. Weren't they?

"You could've tried harder," I said, tears clogging my throat.

"Cam, they said they'd file harassment charges if I tried to talk to you, when they first cut me off."

"They did?"

"Yeah."

"Why?"

Aiden shook his head and ignored my question. "I wanted to make sure you were okay. That they hadn't done the same to you. That they hadn't kicked you out."

I blinked. "They weren't happy," I said, staring at the wooden floorboards of the gazebo. "But they've kind of come around. They're trying. There have been olive branches."

"You can't trust them, Cam."

I snapped my head up. "Aiden—"

"Cam, I'm serious. I know they're our parents. But you can't. They're unyielding when it comes to certain things, and the paranormal is one of them."

"And I'm supposed to trust you?" I asked. I gestured to everything around us. "We're in a faery grove. Magic is all around us. This could all be a ploy to get access to my glimpses. I'm not even sure that it's the real you I'm talking to. And . . . and . . . I haven't seen you in months. You disappeared. You sent me cryptic messages and then didn't answer my texts. And you still haven't told me *why* we are meeting in a faery grove!"

"When you were three, I grabbed the back of your shirt. When you pulled away, I let go, and you nailed your head on the toy box. You had to get a butterfly bandage on your forehead."

I absently touched the thin scar next to my hairline. "And?"

"And you sucked your thumb until you were six. Mom put that nasty-tasting deterrent on your nail, but it didn't make you stop. You only stopped when you met Al and were afraid you'd be teased."

I gulped. No one outside our family knew that. I hoped. Because it was a little embarrassing. "Is this you proving that it's actually you?"

Aiden shrugged. "Maybe." He clasped his hands. "As for us meeting in a faery grove, uh . . . there's someone I'd like you to meet."

"Huh?"

A rustle in the flowers caught my attention. I turned to see a girl emerge from a deeper path in the garden.

Aiden stood. He held out his hand to her, and she slid her slim fingers into his. She was beautiful. As she stepped out from beneath the shade of a tree, the sunlight illuminated her white skin, her long black hair and her bright blue eyes. She was also barefoot like Ileana.

But instead of yoga pants, she wore a long dress, and she didn't have wings.

"Cam," Aiden said, pulling the girl toward him, "this is Astra. My girlfriend."

She leaned into Aiden's side, wrapping her arms around him as a smile bloomed across her face. Aiden pushed a strand of her hair behind her ear. And ugh. It was obvious he was utterly smitten. But she looked like she was too.

I crossed my arms, annoyed.

"Hi, Cam," Astra said, beaming. "I've heard so much about you. I'm so glad to meet you."

"Are you a faery?" Oops. That wasn't quite the question I'd wanted to lead with.

"I'm half faery. One of my parents is a faery, and the other is not."

"Ah."

My gaze flitted between the two of them. "And she's why . . ."

"Mom and Dad didn't approve of me dating Astra."

And okay, maybe I just didn't understand. Because a girl, even as beautiful as she was, wasn't a reason to leave your whole family. And I had needed Aiden for the past several months, and he was with *her*. And I couldn't stop the jealousy that flared to life within me.

Aiden must've noticed my incredulous expression, and he sighed. "Cam, if it wasn't Astra that led to Mom and Dad cutting me off, it would've been something else. They didn't like the classes I took. They didn't appreciate it when I called them out on their prejudices. If I wasn't going to be the perfect son and meet all their standards, then it was only a matter of time. So even if Astra and I don't work out," he said, squeezing her waist, "it will have been worth it. And I'm not sorry for it."

I narrowed my eyes. "Okay. Fine. But did you ever think that *I* might have needed you?"

"That's why I'm here now. That's why I invited you. Getting the chance to introduce you to Astra was just a bonus. But I really wanted to see how you were doing. To offer help. To be here for you."

"A little late," I said. "I have friends who are helping me." Yes, I was being petulant, but it was bizarre. Here was my brother, standing in front of me and telling me that our parents were bad people, and then *leaving* me with them. Like, the hell? I stood, because I didn't like that he was standing over me, and even though he was taller, at least it didn't feel like he was talking down to me.

Astra moved out of Aiden's embrace. She stood on tiptoes and kissed his cheek, murmuring something, and then left the gazebo.

He watched her walk away with an awed expression, then turned to me. "Okay, fine. What do you want me to do?" He matched my stance and my tone. And oh, he was mad at me now. Well, great.

I took a breath. "Nothing."

He blinked, taken aback. "What?"

"You can do nothing. I have a support system of friends now, and just because you couldn't work it out with Mom and Dad doesn't mean I can't."

"Trusting them is a mistake, Cam. I'm warning you."

I shrugged. "Then it's a mistake. But I get to make that choice." I gestured to the garden around us. "You've made yours."

I grabbed my bag, then tromped down the wooden gazebo steps onto the garden path and headed back toward the cottage.

"Can't you just be happy for me?" Aiden called.

I paused. "Yeah," I said, turning on my heel, waving at the magic surrounding us, and forcing a smile. "I'm happy for you. See you around."

"Wait! At least take my new number. You can text me if you need help." He pulled a scrap of paper from his pocket and held it out. "Please, Cam. If you ever need to text me, you can. I'll come. I promise."

I swallowed down my tears and my hurt and nodded. The paper

trembled in Aiden's grasp, then flew upward. It floated toward me, and once it was near enough, I grabbed it out of the sky. I shoved it in my own pocket.

"Thank you," he said. "It was good to see you."

"It was good to see you, too." I took one last long look at my brother, because I didn't know when I'd see him again, and then I left.

I entered the back door and ran right into Ileana.

She frowned at me.

"That didn't appear to go the way Aiden had planned," she said softly.

"Thank you for the invitation and the hospitality, Ileana," I said, ignoring her statement. "If at a later time you do have an interest in clairvoyance, please contact my human advisor, Gemma James."

"Of course."

"Thank you."

She guided me to the exit. The door opened of its own accord, and I stepped outside.

Dusk had fallen. The cool air and crisp breeze were a far cry from the bright sun and humid atmosphere of the garden. I hurried down the cobblestones toward the sidewalk. The door of the cottage shut behind me with a creak, but I didn't look back. And as I stepped through the barrier onto the sidewalk, magic prickled across my skin.

Val's car was gone, but Juana sat on the sidewalk, reading a battered paperback. Great.

"Um . . ."

She looked up and smiled. "There you are! Val had to take Gemma home, but I told them I'd wait for you. Danny is on his way with the car."

"How long was I . . ."

"A few hours."

I scrunched my nose. "But—"

"Time displacement," she said. "It happens with faeries."

"Thanks for waiting."

"No problem." She beamed.

I sat next to her on the sidewalk and took out my new phone. The battery was completely dead. "Crap."

Juana hummed. "Faery magic," she said by way of explanation. "It's brutal on electronics."

"Huh. You know a lot about this stuff."

She shrugged. "I don't know what Teo told you, but I've done some traveling this past year. I've met different people and been to different places. And I learned a bunch of new things."

"That sounds nice."

"Yeah. It was." She nodded toward the cottage. "Did everything go okay in there?"

"Not really." The dejection and the jealousy the whole encounter had elicited bubbled right underneath the surface of my skin, as if I were a volcano of negative emotions on the verge of exploding. "I mean, it could've gone worse."

She gave me a side-eye. "That doesn't sound promising."

"It is what it is."

"Do you want to talk about it?"

"Not really." Especially not with the cousin of the guy I had a date with in a few days.

"Okay. I'll accept that."

We sat in silence on the curb. I stared at the darkening sky and wondered what I'd done in a previous life to land me in an emotional blender since the beginning of the school year.

"Okay, I'm going to ask," Juana said, breaking the silence and closing her novel with a snap. "Why don't you like me?"

"What?"

"You ran away at the cookout. You try not to look at me, and when you do, you become jittery and pale. Like Kaci used to do when she saw a ghost. Teo has even become a little weird around me, and I can't help but think it might be your influence."

That stung. Mateo acting weird made sense from my end, but she wouldn't know why. I didn't want to be blamed for putting a strain on Mateo and Juana's relationship. She continued before I could find a plausible excuse.

"And I know Teo looks up to me, so I don't want him to see me in a bad light, you know? If he thinks we don't get along, I don't want him to think I'm the problem. And I'm sure you don't want him to think you're the problem, since I kind of get the feeling that you want to be closer than you already are. I want to try and be friends. So what am I doing wrong?"

I froze. I couldn't tell her the real reason. Or maybe it would be easier if I did. No, Mateo would kill me, and he'd already said he would handle that. He'd be upset if I overstepped. So I went with a half-truth.

"You're intimidating," I said. "Your whole family is, really, but especially you."

"Me?"

"Mateo loves you. You're his favorite person. And I don't want to mess up in front of you." And that piece wasn't a lie at all.

"Oh," she said on a breath.

"Yeah."

She laughed then. "Wow. All this time I thought it was the scandal with the sprites. I know you're also friends with Reese."

I raised my eyebrows. "You think I didn't like you because you got your heart broken by the Sprite Alliance?" I grasped my shins and tucked my chin on my bent knees. "Do I really exude jerk vibes?"

"You are difficult to read," she said with a grin.

"Years of hard work perfecting my resting bitch face." I picked up a stray pebble from the sidewalk and rolled it between my fingers.

She laughed. "Wow. That's amazing."

I smiled.

"Anyway," she continued, "while I was pretty upset, I wouldn't say I was heartbroken."

"You weren't?"

"Not really. I mean, I was the one who called it all off."

"Huh?"

"I broke up with Mia."

I dropped the pebble. "You did?"

"She was willing to leave the Alliance and planned for us to run away together, but I just couldn't abandon my family." She shrugged. "I broke it off. She was upset and kept trying to reach out, blowing up my phone, showing up at my classes. It was a mess. I took a vacation to get away."

Wait. What? That was *not* the story Mateo had told me. He'd made it seem like Juana was the jilted party. But I was shocked to find out that *she* was the person who'd broken a heart. And who'd recalled the whole situation rather callously. Why would he lie?

"Anyway, now that we've cleared the air—I know you want to romance my cousin."

I shuddered at the term "romance" but hesitantly nodded. There was no use in lying. We did have a date planned.

"Okay, great. I'm going to help you out. I'm on your side, Cam. I think Teo needs a little romance. Maybe it will help him with his ... problem."

"Problem?"

She waved a hand toward her ears. "Spontaneous shifting. He's so bent out of shape over it, which only makes it worse. And don't get me started about the full moon. He has such a problem shifting out of the full wolf form; it sometimes takes days. Poor guy."

I was slightly mortified that Juana was telling me all this. Wasn't this considered personal? Would Mateo even want me to know this?

Juana continued, "Maybe some romance will help ease the

frustration." She clapped her hands on her knees. "I'm going to help you."

"You don't really have—"

"Here, read this." She thrust the paperback into my hands. "It's an extremely popular book series, especially among us werewolves. I love this author because they get all the lore correct."

I turned the book over, and my eyes widened at the steamy cover. It was a werewolf romance novel. "Um . . ."

"Go on, it's yours. I've already read it twice." She winked. "It's really good."

"Thanks," I said, shoving the book into my bag, quietly discomforted.

"You're welcome!" she said, beaming. "Oh, Danny's here." She stood and brushed off her jeans as the Lopez family van drove into view. "I enjoyed our talk, Cam," she said, tossing the end of her ponytail over her shoulder. "I hope we can get to know each other better."

"Yeah," I said slowly, my thoughts running a mile a minute. "Me too."

When Danny dropped me off at home, it was much later than I had expected to stay out, especially on a school night. I waved goodbye to Danny and Juana as I walked up the brick steps to the front door, nervousness and uncertainty swirling in my gut. I hoped to creep in unnoticed by my parents, because I wasn't quite sure what to say to them. My missing brother had just told me not to trust them. That they had cut *him* off, not the other way around. And I didn't know how to process that. I knew my parents could be dismissive and absent and even harsh on occasion, but I didn't know them to be cruel.

In the foyer, I dropped my backpack on the bench and worked

on wrestling my jacket off. It caught at my wrist on the material of the glove, and as I flailed, I knocked into my precariously perched backpack. It fell with a loud smack, splitting the zipper open and sending books and pens tumbling from the top, including the romance novel. It flopped against the hardwood a foot away, face up, its incriminating cover on full display. What's more, the scrap of paper with Aiden's number fell out and fluttered to join the rest of the mess on the floor.

"Cam?" my mom called. "Are you home?"

Crap! Would she recognize Aiden's number if she saw it? Would she know I'd seen him? I couldn't take that chance.

Her footsteps on the hardwood became louder as she moved toward me.

Still twisted in my jacket and utterly panicked, I kicked the novel underneath the padded bench. Then I dropped to my knees as I managed to wrangle out of my denim prison and snatched the paper. I shoved the slip of paper into my jeans pocket just as she rounded the corner from the kitchen.

"Cam?"

I grabbed a handful of pens and pencils. "Hi, Mom," I said, a little breathless.

She raised an eyebrow and crossed her arms. She was in her pajamas, and I could hear the sound of the TV coming from the family room—some political news show.

"You're a little late coming in."

Oh no. I couldn't tell her I'd been with the faeries. "I was with Gemma," I said, unceremoniously cramming books, papers, and highlighters into my backpack. "I have a meeting with the Psychic Guild coming up, so we were learning things about . . . things."

Smooth.

"You couldn't have texted us?"

"My phone died. I forgot to charge it last night, and then I didn't bring a charger with me to school, and we were really deep in the stuff we were researching. So sorry." I finally managed to clean up my mess. I picked up my jacket from where it was draped across the bench and hung it on a hook, then hoisted my bag.

Her expression didn't change, but I knew she wasn't pleased. "We wanted you to use the phone from the coven so that you'd be able to stay in touch, now that . . ." She paused, her jaw working as she found the right words. "Now that you're special."

Ouch.

"I know. I'm sorry."

She nodded. "Okay. Try not to stay out so late on a school night again."

I scratched the back of my neck. "Yeah. We lost track of time. It won't happen again. I promise."

"Fine. Now I think it's time you got ready for bed."

"I agree."

My mom didn't move. She stayed, leaning one shoulder on the wall, waiting. There was no way I was going to be able to grab the book. I'd have to fish it out later.

I edged past her and headed up the stairs, her disapproving gaze a physical presence on my back until I reached the landing. Once inside my room, I closed the door and collapsed on the edge of my bed, allowing my bag to thump to the floor. That had been close.

I took the paper with Aiden's number from my pocket and stared at it. A deep well of resentment rose in me at the thought of him hanging out in a faery grove with some girl this entire time while I'd been floundering. When I'd *needed* him.

But he had contacted me in the way he thought best. He was still my brother. And I missed him terribly. And maybe, even though I was still mad, he could offer some advice on this whole clairvoyant deal. He obviously knew way more about the paranormal than I did. He could be a good resource if my friends and I needed help.

I tapped his number into my contacts, putting it under the name "Faery Pizza Delivery" for a later time when I wasn't pissed off. I flopped back on my bed with a dramatic sigh, my head hitting the pillow, my arms spread out over the bedding, and closed my eyes. I hoped beyond hope that tomorrow wouldn't be as strange as today, but if the last few weeks had taught me anything, it would be even weirder.

23

THE SHADY HALLOW BRANCH OF THE PSYCHIC GUILD HELD meetings in the community building on Main Street in the center of town. Which was a far cry from the coven house, the faery grove, or the Lopez home. And granted, I wasn't expecting much when Kaci dragged me into the meeting room, but I'd thought there might be a little more grandeur than folding chairs, a few plastic tables, and two grandmas playing checkers.

Thankfully, one of the tables had snacks. I was starving. I hadn't eaten much—not since the day before, when I'd met with my missing brother in a faery grove and found out that my crush had lied about a few details regarding his cousin. It was all a confusing mess.

At least Gemma was on top of things, if a little annoyed that she hadn't been able to join me in the faery grove and had a conflict that didn't allow her to be present for this meeting.

Anyway, this was step one, part A, of the things I had to accomplish. We'd already determined that my glimpses couldn't be avoided even with prior knowledge of the event. The second aspect of step one was figuring out why I saw what I did when people touched me. And that might lead us to the killer.

"Is this everyone?" I whispered to Kaci.

"Yes." She looked around, then pointed to the corner. "Can you see the person over there?"

"No."

"Then you are the single new member." She smiled brightly.

The meeting was only a handful of people: the two older ladies, a man with a handlebar mustache, a young couple who had been holding hands since they'd entered, and the middle-aged supposed leader lady. She held a clipboard and stood by the snack table.

"If everyone could take their seats," she said, tapping her pen against the papers in her hand, "we'll get started."

Kaci led me to a pair of folding chairs, and we sat together.

"Thank you." The leader looked at the grandmas. "Alma and Edith, are you going to join us?"

One of the ladies considered the board in front of her, narrowed her deep brown eyes, and drummed her fingers on the table. She didn't pick up a piece or move at all, other than the rhythmic tapping of her fingertips, but then she suddenly straightened. "I win."

The other member, a white woman with light blue eyes, huffed. "You read my mind," she grumbled.

The rest of the members chuckled.

"Game over, Edith," the winner, presumably Alma, said, holding out her palm. "Pay up."

Edith cursed under her breath and handed over a single coin.

"Yes," Alma said, swiveling her chair. "We are now paying attention, dear."

The leader smiled. "Welcome, fellow spirited. Thank you all for attending this month's meeting. We are very excited to have a potential new member with us today."

I cringed internally but raised my hand in an awkward wave.

"Cam is a sophomore at Central Shady Hallow High. He is a verified clairvoyant, and we hope that he chooses to join the Guild. Please, everyone offer him a warm welcome."

A smattering of applause followed. "Thanks for the bike," I said. "I really appreciate it."

"Oh, we're so glad," the leader lady said, one hand pressed to her chest in faux humility. "Thank you. And now, on to other important matters." She droned about "old business" and "new business," and within twenty minutes, the meeting was adjourned.

Most everyone descended on the snacks at the side of the room, including Kaci, but I stayed rooted to my seat. I didn't quite know what to do. And I certainly didn't want to engage in small talk with the couple or the handlebar-mustache guy, who were all three standing around the punch bowl like it was a watering hole in the desert.

"Psst—Cam."

I perked up at the sound of my name. Alma and Edith beckoned me over to their little table. Edith used her foot and pushed out a chair.

"Come join us," Alma said, patting the seat.

I glanced at Kaci for help, but she was busy munching on a mini donut while glaring at the empty corner.

Edith waved her hand. "We don't bite, darling."

I stood, walked the few steps over to their table, and sank into the seat.

Alma sat in a wheelchair. Her dark brown eyes glinted with mischief and warmth. She was hunched over the table, but her movements were sharp as she rearranged the checkers back into formation. Edith sat a little taller, and had curly white hair and an air of no nonsense. She peered at me over the rim of her glasses.

Alma reached over and smacked Edith's hand. "Now, don't do that," she grumbled. "Let him be."

Edith sniffed primly. "I was merely reading his aura."

"Yeah, and I read your thoughts. He's a good boy and certainly not faking."

I bristled at the insinuation but kept my mouth shut.

Alma smirked at me, and then I had the realization that she could *hear* my thoughts.

"Not all of them," she said softly. "Now, tell us about your power."

My mouth went suddenly dry. My stomach rumbled.

Edith snapped her fingers. "Jason," she called to the man with the handlebar mustache, "bring Cam some snacks and a cup of punch, if you please."

Alma chuckled at my expression, then poked me in the bicep. "Tell us, young man."

"I touch people, and I see a glimpse of their future."

"Touch telepathy," Edith said as Jason set down a cup of punch and a plate of crackers, cheese, and cookies. "Not uncommon with clairvoyants."

"I didn't know it had a name."

"Of course it does. Do you only see the future, or do you see the past and the present as well?"

"Uh . . . just the future so far."

Edith stole a cookie from the plate. "What about emotions? Thoughts? Auras? Do you see any of those when you touch someone?"

"Um . . . I don't know. I just mostly feel scared." Strangely, I didn't mind admitting that to Edith and Alma. And honestly, since I'd sat down with them, I had been calm. Calmer than I'd been in ages. All the worries I'd had were softened somehow, as if I were in one of those soap commercials where the person eases into a bathtub and all their stress melts away, and . . . wait a minute.

Alma snickered. "He figured it out, Edith."

Edith ate another cookie. "Smart one, then."

"What is happening?"

"Edith can project emotions as well as read auras. She thought you looked like a skittish woodland creature about to dart away. And I agreed."

I swallowed. "That's a great skill."

"So is seeing the future," Edith countered. "But I sense you don't see it that way."

"I don't know. It's only brought stress thus far."

Alma nodded. "You have a strong mind and a strong psyche," she said, tapping a checker against the table. "You'll settle into yourself. But it will take time. Just like with all of us spirited."

Spirited. Kaci had called me that. "What does that mean? 'Spirited'?"

Edith hummed. "It's an old term, one not used much now, except among our own circles." She took another cookie. "Many psychics believe our powers originate from the strength and vigor of our souls. You, darling, have a strong spirit. You would have to, to have accurate glimpses."

I gulped. "But how?" I asked. "What happened to me to make me this way?" The question came out so soft, so meek, that I was surprised at the vehemence of Edith's and Alma's responses. Edith's gaze cut sharply from the pile of cookies, and Alma's sweet expression went suddenly stern.

"It didn't *happen* to you," Alma said, smacking her checker down on the table. "It's what you *are*." She wagged her finger at me. "Do not diminish yourself for others. You are a psychic, a seer, spirited, whatever you want to call it."

"I prefer 'clairvoyant.'"

"Whatever," Alma said. "And you are wonderful."

"Now, sit up straight," Edith added. "Head up. Make eye contact. Be confident."

I immediately sat up like my spine was a solid rod and nodded quickly. "Yes. Okay."

"Good," Alma said. "As to your next question"—at my surprised face, she chuckled—"how to control it. That was your question, wasn't it?"

"Yes."

"Take off your gloves," Edith said.

I didn't hesitate and yanked my gloves off by the fingers.

Alma took my hands in her own, her touch warm against mine.

I inwardly braced for the glimpse that was sure to come, but nothing happened. "I have my psychic blocks in place," she said nonchalantly, turning my palm over and running her wrinkled brown fingers over my skin.

"You can do that?" I breathed. It was the first time in almost a month that someone had touched me and I hadn't fallen into the future. Tears sprang into my eyes. I relaxed in Alma's comforting hold.

"Yes." She nodded to Kaci. "It's a skill you will need to learn in order not to experience a glimpse anytime someone touches you. And it's one that Kaci still struggles with. Since her powers manifested a few years ago, she hasn't been able to go a day without seeing into the beyond, and one day I'm afraid it will overwhelm her. Managing how and when to use your power is the first skill any spirited person should learn."

I took a gulp of my punch. "How do I create a block?"

"Imagine it," Edith said, touching her fingertip to her temple. "Use your mind to visualize a barrier, and implement it."

"It takes focus," Alma said. "And training. But you'll master it."

"And how . . . ?" I trailed off.

Alma nodded encouragingly.

I took a breath. "How do I influence what I see?"

"We're not clairvoyants," Edith said, munching on the last cookie. "I sense auras. Alma reads thoughts."

Alma grinned. "I use blocks to only read the thoughts I want to, so don't worry."

"But I imagine," Edith continued, "that it is also a matter of focus. And sometimes you must open the portal first in order to close it."

That didn't make any sense to me. The proverbial portal was already opened. Way opened.

Alma hummed. "There was a girl who read tea leaves, who was a member about twenty years ago. She was good at it. Not as accurate as yourself, but passable. And she said it always helped during the reading if the person concentrated on what they wanted to know. Asked a question or thought about a specific scenario."

That made sense. That had worked for me so far with Dennis, Reese, and Kaci. "My first glimpse was random. I saw something . . . horrible."

Edith frowned. "That happens sometimes."

"An unfortunate side effect," Alma said. She squeezed my hand.

"What should I do? I can't stop it. Kaci and I tried to stop a different glimpse, and it didn't work, and—"

"You can't stop the future," Alma said gently. "No one can. But you can be prepared for it."

Edith narrowed her eyes. "And it might not always be what it seems. You see a piece of what's to come, not the whole pie."

Alma released my hand. "I believe that's called 'missing the forest for the trees.'"

Huh.

Kaci wandered away from the corner and flopped in the empty chair at the table, across from me. Alma smiled, and Edith tilted her head as she regarded Kaci.

"No luck?" Edith asked.

Kaci sighed, tendrils of her hair fluttering with her breath. "No. I tried to block him out, but I still see him. Well, until he drifted away."

Alma patted Kaci's hand. "It's okay, dear. You'll get it. Don't give up."

"Just continue to develop your barriers. It will click for you. Do we need to remind you how long it took Alma to be able to filter the thoughts she heard and not just be overwhelmed?"

Alma kicked Edith under the table. "And may I remind you," Alma said, voice sharp, "how long it took Edith to realize that she was actually seeing auras, and it wasn't just her astigmatism?"

Kaci giggled behind her hand. I swallowed a laugh that turned into a cough.

Edith pointed at the plate of snacks that was only now crackers and cubes of cheese. "Eat, Cam. Before Jason asks you to perform a party trick."

I shoved a cracker in my mouth.

After observing a game of checkers between Edith and Alma, where Alma won again and Edith grumbled while handing over another coin, Jason did indeed approach me to use my power and see if he would adopt a puppy or a kitten from the local shelter. It was the easiest glimpse I'd done, and when I came to, sprawled on the floor as usual, I could confidently say, "Both."

24

I WAS MISSING SOMETHING. I COULDN'T FIGURE OUT *WHAT*, BUT I had a nagging feeling in the back of my brain that there was an important detail that I just wasn't putting into place.

I voiced this to Kaci and Gemma on the front steps of the school before the bell. It was another hot morning, and I'd bunched up the sleeves of my shirt to take advantage of the slight breeze.

Gemma frowned. "What do you mean? Like something that was in the glimpse?"

I tugged on my hair, frustrated. "I don't know." It came out sounding like a whine. "Like there's something there, just right outside my grasp." I shoved my hands in my pockets and tapped my foot. "We have a possible *when*, but our *who* is tenuous at best. And we have no *where* to speak of. There are only five days left until the harvest moon. We're running out of time, and I am a little stressed." "A little stressed" was a comparative term, because in the grand scheme of things, I was a lot stressed. I looked down at my hands. "What is the point of having glimpses if I can't do anything about them?"

"Okay, take a breath, partner," Gemma said.

I did. But it didn't make me any calmer.

Gemma pressed her small hand against my shoulder. "Cam, do

you think you should read Juana's future? We could totally plan it, and she'd be none the wiser. Juana and Val have been hanging out at Drip, and we could arrange an accidental touch."

I shuddered. "I mean, if we have to? I'd rather *not* see that again, but if it would help us with more clues . . ."

Kaci pressed her lips into a thin line. "I'm going to talk to the ghost."

Gemma turned wide eyes to Kaci. "I thought—"

"I've been working on it," she said in response, in as close to a harsh tone as I'd ever heard from her. "She'll be able to tell us what happened. And then we can be certain if Dennis is or isn't involved."

"Kaci," I said, "you don't have to do this."

"I do. And I am." She tossed her hair over her shoulder. "I'd rather talk to the ghost than force you to see that glimpse again."

"That's really thoughtful of you." I bit my bottom lip. "But don't do something you don't want to on my behalf."

"I want to," she said with a firm nod. "Like you said—what is the use of having these powers if I can't use them to help my friend? So I'm going to."

"You have fun with that." Gemma dropped her hand from my arm and heaved her backpack onto her shoulders. "I have research to do. You know what they say about real estate—location, location, location."

"I don't even know what you mean," I said, shaking my head.

"I'm going to try and find our *where*." Gemma smiled, then hopped down the stairs and disappeared around the corner into the side entrance.

"Are you sure?" I asked Kaci again.

Kaci threw the strap of her messenger bag over her shoulder. "Yes. I can't promise I will be able to do anything. As you saw last night, I'm not that good. The first skill a medium is supposed to learn is how to implement psychic blocks, how to stop seeing *them*, and I haven't mastered it." She took a fortifying breath. "But I will try."

A thought struck me then, of something that Edith and Alma had said the night before. "I don't know how all this works, but Edith and Alma mentioned opening and closing portals. You've spent so much time trying to close the portal. . . . Have you ever tried opening it?"

Kaci blushed. "The portal is open. It's always open, which is why I see them all the time."

"Well, maybe you can try to open it wider?"

"Okay," she said, nodding. "Yes. Okay. Let's find her."

She marched into the building, her messenger bag banging against her hip. I followed, tripping over my feet to keep up. We walked through the cafeteria, where students were eating breakfast, and then through the courtyard and into the gym.

Kaci stepped over the threshold of the entrance, her shoes squeaking on the freshly mopped surface.

The parquet flooring gleamed in the sunlight pouring in from the high windows, the logo of the Central Shady Hallow High Saints standing out in stark blue and gold at half-court.

The smack of a basketball against the floor reverberated throughout the space. I peeked over Kaci's shoulder to spy Dennis shooting hoops alone. He had a rack of balls next to him, and he stood on the foul line, taking shots.

"She's here," Kaci whispered.

"Where?" I asked.

Kaci's gaze zeroed in on the stands. "Right there."

With renewed determination, she strode across the floor in a series of squeaks.

Dennis whipped his head around.

"What are you doing here, seer?" he demanded, ball on his hip, a sneer on his face. "Come to tell my future?"

"No and I prefer 'clairvoyant.'"

Kaci strode across the floor without pausing. "I've come to talk to your ghost."

Dennis dropped the ball. His face paled so suddenly, I thought he was going to pass out. "What ghost?" he said weakly.

"The one that follows you around." Kaci stopped at the bleachers and crossed her arms, staring at a space about a third of the way up the steps. "The one who is *right here*."

"You can't be serious," he said, though he'd scuttled backward to where his bag lay on the end line. "I'm supposed to believe you can see ghosts?"

"She can." I stood at half-court, shoulders back, straightened to my full not-impressive height. "And there is a girl covered in bloody cuts who haunts you. I've seen her too."

Dennis scooped up his bag. "Stay away from me," he snarled. "Both of you. Or I'll report you for harassment." And then he ran out the back door.

That was weird and not at all incriminating.

"Is she still here?"

"Yes." Kaci set her jaw. "What are you trying to tell me?" she whispered. She clenched her fists at her side, then squeezed her eyes shut and leaned forward.

I couldn't see what was happening. I had no idea what Kaci was doing. If it was even working. And I couldn't deny that it all looked a little comical with her willowy figure and her scrunched face.

"Louder," she said again, turning to press her ear against the air. "Please. I want to hear you."

There was a pause, followed by a gasp and a flinch, then suddenly Kaci screamed. It wasn't a kids-playing-outside kind of screech, but a horror-movie-jump-scare shriek.

I abandoned my place at the half-court line and sprinted across the court just as Kaci yelled "stop," then crumpled to the ground.

"Kaci!"

I slid to her side on my knees, my ripped jeans providing my skin little protection. I'd surely have friction burns, but that was the least of my worries.

Kaci's eyes were closed. She was breathing, which was good, but she didn't appear to be conscious.

I tapped her shoulder, which garnered no response. Then her cheek. "Kaci," I said again. "Come on. Don't do this to me. I'm stressed enough as it is. I'm going to have a heart attack."

No response.

Fuck.

Shit.

I grabbed my phone from my pocket and hit call on the topmost contact.

Al's voice came over the line. "Hey, where are you? I thought we were supposed to meet on the steps, like, ten minutes ago."

"In the gym! Kaci tried to talk to the ghost, and I don't know what happened, but she passed out and we need help!"

"We're coming right now!"

I set the phone on the ground, hitting the button for the speaker. A jumble of panicked voices and words erupted from my cell as Mateo's, Al's, and Reese's voices overlapped.

All I managed to hear was that I needed to make sure she was breathing.

I scooted closer just to make sure, and the bare skin of my wrist brushed her fingertips.

I sucked in a breath. Oh no. I tried to imagine every metaphor to stop this from happening—slamming a door, raising a castle draw-bridge, shutting a window—but it was too late. I fell down a dark tunnel.

And woke up outside the local hospital.

Ambulance sirens echoed around me. The flash of red and blue lights swept across the entrance to the emergency department. The asphalt glittered with raindrops from the glow of the illuminated signs, and the cool air nipped at my exposed skin. I whirled around, my damp hair whipping across my skin, looking for someone in the darkness of the night, my heart beating fast. But they weren't there on the sidewalk in front of the automatic sliding glass doors, and they weren't in the parking lot, either. My stomach sank.

"Where is he?" Mateo demanded.

"I don't know," I answered in Kaci's voice. "We left him right here. He was only going to make a call."

"But he's not here now!"

"He's not inside, either." That was Gemma. She sounded tired and upset.

Mateo stalked forward, coming to stand beside me. "Something has happened. I know it."

I took a deep breath. Fear and anxiety swept through me, making my hands tremble. I knew what I had to do, even if I had only just mastered controlling my access to the beyond. "I have to open the portal." I squeezed my eyes shut, steeled myself, and imagined grasping the handle of a door and yanking it open. Then I opened my eyes.

Where originally there were three others with me, there were now *dozens*.

Rows upon rows of ghosts stood around us. They were everywhere—some dressed in hospital gowns, others in clothing from across the spectrum of history. Some were bloodied with skin torn, while others were pristine. In a horrifying visual, they all swiveled around to stare at me, as if they sensed I could see them and interact with them. I bit back a scream as their voices penetrated my head, garbled sounds tumbling over one another in a torrent.

I smacked my hands over my ears and imagined closing the door slightly, narrowing the gap until the voices decreased to merely a few.

I met the gaze of a girl in front of me. She had blood smeared across her face, some dripping from her mouth, and a slow ghostly smile stole over her features.

"Ask me," she said, her voice low and distorted, her teeth stained crimson. "I'll tell you."

I jerked awake.

I was on the basketball court. Al, Mateo, and Reese stood over me. "Kaci?" I said, my voice bordering on hysterical. I'd just seen her at the hospital. Was she okay? What was going on? "Kaci!"

"Right here," she said from where she sagged against the bleachers. She limply waved.

"Are you okay?"

"I'm fine. I opened the portal too wide."

Oh. Oops. I winced.

"The rest of us don't know what that means," Al said, gesturing to the two of us. "Care to explain?"

"Yeah. Now that you're both awake," Reese said, his hands on his hips. "What the hell was that? What happened?"

Kaci groaned and pressed the heel of her hand to her temple. "I tried to talk to a ghost."

I struggled to a sitting position, opting not to take the hand that Al had offered and giving a quick shake of my head. They apparently understood and didn't take offense.

Once sitting, I leaned forward, elbows on my knees, head dropped lower than my shoulders, eyes closed. "How did it go?" I asked.

Kaci shrugged. "She screamed at me."

"She screams at everyone," I muttered.

"But I *heard* it this time."

I opened my eyes and turned my head. Kaci beamed, her eyes shining with pride. "I couldn't ask her anything, and I didn't even make out what she said. But I *heard* her scream."

"Congrats."

"Wait, that's a good thing?" Reese asked, his eyebrows raised.

"It's progress," Mateo answered. "Kaci is gaining control of her powers."

And based on my glimpse, as well as the rattle of voices in my head and the fact that Kaci had interacted with one of the ghosts milling outside the hospital, she would have great command of them in the future. At some point. But thank goodness it wasn't today. I couldn't handle an emergency department visit along with everything else.

"But you didn't get any information about who she is, and why she follows Dennis, and if we should worry that he's some kind of aggressive, knife-wielding maniac?"

Al elbowed Reese hard in the side.

"Ow! What? I was just making sure."

"No," Kaci said softly. "I failed at that part. I'm sorry."

"It's fine, Kaci." I heaved myself to my feet. "I'm sure we'll figure it out." I gave her an encouraging smile, despite not being sure at all.

"What about you?" she asked. "What did you see?"

The entire group looked my way. They were all tense and stressed and . . . I couldn't heap more on them. I couldn't add another thing to their already full plates. And besides, it looked like they had all been fine in the glimpse, just frantic about something. I could let them know later if needed. But for now I decided to keep this one to myself.

I shrugged. "We were all hanging out."

Kaci brightened. "Oh. Outside of school?"

"Yeah," I said, which was not a lie. "We were."

"That's nice," she said with a smile. "I'd like that."

Reese looked skeptical, but for once he didn't voice it. "Yeah, whatever," he said, his hoodie askew, as if he had run just as fast as Mateo and Al. "But can we do it *after* we have this current dilemma wrapped up?"

"Of course!" Kaci said, eyes crinkling with a big smile.

I wholeheartedly agreed with Reese. We needed to figure things out. And fast. Time was running out, and we were no closer despite all our hard work.

--

At lunch, Gemma slammed a yearbook onto the table and flipped it open to a page. She pointed with her pink, glitter-tipped finger. "Is that your ghost?"

Kaci and I both leaned in. It was a senior portrait from five years ago. She looked different, but there was no denying that it was the girl who followed Dennis around.

"How?" I asked.

"Dennis's older stepsister died in a car accident right after her graduation. She had a different last name, and their parents weren't married long, so when I did my background check on him, she didn't show up. But if that's your ghost, then Dennis didn't have any hand in her death."

I set my cheeseburger on my tray. The group of us were at our regular table, all gathered around, in various states of thought. "Oh wow, that's great," I said.

"Great that our prime suspect is cleared?" Al asked. "It sends us right back to the beginning. What are we going to do?"

"I think . . . ," I said, rubbing my brow, "I need to glimpse Juana's future."

Mateo straightened. "Cam—"

"No, look. I've thought about it all morning. We've been spinning our wheels since that day in the coffee shop, and we've gotten nowhere."

Gemma scoffed.

"No offense," I said. "I'm not discounting your work."

"Offense taken, though," she muttered.

"But we're running out of time." I ticked off the points on my fingers. "First, our prime suspect is no longer a suspect. And second, trial and error has shown that it really is easier to glimpse a future when the subject is focusing on it. And yes, that first glimpse was random, and we don't know who touched me, but Dennis would actively have to be thinking about Juana or, in the case of Mateo's scenario, thinking about me. But he has no connection to Juana, and he never interacted with me until *after* my powers were revealed. It's not him."

The rest of the group stared at me with a variety of expressions, but no one spoke, so I plowed on.

"Third, we know we can't stop the glimpse from happening, but we can be prepared for it. We need more information, and we should get it from the source."

"But she'll know." Mateo's voice was soft.

"She won't have to," I said, drumming my fingers on the table. "It can be an accidental touch. And I'll try to focus on the event and get more clues. And then we can decide if we want to tell her and let her prepare for it herself."

Gemma hummed and shoved the yearbook back in her bag. "We can do it at Drip. Juana has been hanging out there with Val."

"That's a little too public for me," I said, twisting my fingers into a knot. "I was a mess after that first glimpse, and if I have to see it again, I want to see it somewhere I can freak out afterward. Quietly. On my own."

"Our date," Mateo said, eyes fixed on the table. "I'll ask Juana to drive us, and I'll plan for something quiet."

"Whoa, wait a minute. This is juicy. You two are dating?" Reese asked. "When did that happen?" He narrowed his eyes and wagged a soggy fry in our direction, little splashes of ketchup littering the table. "Wait, is this for an alliance? I know the sprites have only sent the fruit basket, but we can do better if we need to."

Mateo growled.

Kaci shook her head. "That's not nice, Reese."

"It was a joke."

Joke or not, that small seed of doubt I'd had when Mateo had originally asked me out sprouted into a tiny plant. Any excitement I'd had for Saturday absolutely evaporated. I'd kept the promise of the date tucked away in my thoughts like a fragile secret. Since Mateo had asked me out, so much weirdness had happened, but the assurance of something good had still been there, a silent motivation to get me through the week. And I didn't want it ruined.

Thanks to both Mateo and Reese, it was well on its way. Yet the glimpse had to be done. I couldn't ignore that fact. I couldn't run away from it.

"Great," I said, feigning excitement. "That works."

Al frowned and tapped their fingernails against the table. "The rest of us should be nearby."

I balked at that. It was bad enough that Juana was tagging along on our date. I didn't need the rest of our weird friend group there as well.

Al leveled a glare at me. "We should be there to hear all the specifics again fresh. It may spark a clue. And as you said, you were a mess after the first time. You might need moral support. Especially if you break down again."

Ugh. I hated that Al was right. *"Fine."*

"Okay." Gemma leaned in. "Meet after school at the car pickup loop, and we'll hash out details so we'll all be prepared for Saturday."

The bell rang, and we all parted ways. I trudged back to my third block, disappointment seeping from every pore.

25

THE PICKUP LOOP WAS UNUSUALLY CROWDED.

When I'd met Gemma out there after school for our faery meeting, it had only been us and a few other kids. Today was wall-to-wall high schoolers.

I shouldered my way through the pack, sleeves pulled down into my gloves. Gemma stood on the very edge of the crowd, her short frame difficult to see over the much taller people around her. There were a few students using levitation spells to peer over the others. There was more than one conjured cloud providing shade. Two girls zipped by on brooms, their hair whipping behind them from beneath their helmets. Everyone else was on their phones, looking down at their screens instead of where they were walking, sometimes stopping abruptly right in front of others. I'd already rammed into one person's backpack.

"This is dangerous," I said as I joined Gemma. "It's like a mosh pit without the music." And right as I said it, the new Hexes single blasted out from magicked speakers to the roar of the crowd.

Gemma sighed. "Ugh. I hate teenagers."

"You are a teenager."

"And?"

I shrugged. We managed to find a spot of real estate right next to the place where cars turned off the main road into the pickup loop. It was a blind turn and stupidly dangerous in design.

"It's not usually like this," Gemma whined. "Why is it so loud?"

"At least we're in the shade."

The branches of the old oak loomed above us and forked out in a thick fingerlike growth. The foliage had begun to turn, the commencement of autumn evident in the rust orange and yellow of the leaves. Another reminder that we were running out of time.

"Why are all these kids out here?" Al asked as they joined us.

Reese jogged over a moment later, dressed in his cross-country uniform, his wind pants and light jacket zipped up.

"One of the buses isn't running." He towered over the rest of us as he took in the scene. "Lopez had better hurry up. I have a meet today and can't be late for stretches."

Kaci joined us quietly.

"You okay?" I asked.

Her brow furrowed. "Yes," she said. She twirled a strand of her hair around her finger. "I think . . . I closed the portal this morning." She stood on her tiptoes. "I haven't seen any of the regulars all day."

"Isn't that good?"

A slow smile eased across her face. "Yes. I think so."

Gemma huffed and tapped her foot. "Where is Mateo? He is literally the most important part of this mission—other than you, Cam, of course. He needs to be here, or we'll have to resort to text messages."

Al raised their hand. "I don't mind text messages."

Come to think of it, I didn't either.

We waited a little while longer, the crowd thinning out as students hopped into their rides home.

I blew out a breath. Maybe Mateo had changed his mind, and he didn't want to take me on a date on Saturday. Or maybe he didn't want me to read Juana's future, which would be weird. No, it definitely had to be the date aspect. Or he needed to talk to Danny and Javi before making any decisions, because this really was an attempt to bribe me over to ally with the werewolves and—

The screech of tires broke my train of thought.

A car barreled into the loop. The driver, distracted by his phone, didn't see the cars parked ahead until it was too late. He hit the brakes, the sound of squealing tires rending the air. He jerked his wheel to avoid rear-ending another car and, in doing so, hopped the curb.

And headed directly to where Kaci, Gemma, and Al had drifted.

"Watch out!" I yelled.

It was a split second, a miniscule slice of time, and they could do nothing. There was no way they could scatter out of the way to avoid being hurt.

Someone pushed me to the side, and I stumbled to my knees, my gaze locked on my three friends.

A mesh of thick vines suddenly erupted from the ground right in front of them. Kaci fell backward with a yelp. Al dodged to the side, and Gemma managed to skitter away. The car struck the tangled net of vegetation, stopping on a dime, the metal crinkling and popping, steam billowing from beneath the hood on impact.

Beside me, Reese glowed.

His eyes were the green of spring. Beneath his skin, veins of bright energy traced along his bones and muscles, illuminating him from within as his body trembled with the strain of manipulating the flora.

The vines engulfed the car.

I stood, amazed, mouth open in awe. Then I noted how it wasn't just the vegetation that had caught the car. The back wheels of the vehicle had sunk into deep, rich mud.

A mud that smelled . . . *awful.*

Like rotten eggs.

I wrinkled my nose and froze. I knew this stench. That was the piece that had been missing. The clue that I hadn't been able to puzzle together.

Slowly Reese's power ebbed away, the green glow of his eyes and skin receding. Gemma and Al helped Kaci to her feet as the driver exited the car, yelling about the damage.

And all I could do was stare at my friend.

"Reese?" I asked, betrayal and hurt thudding beneath my ribs. "What . . . ?"

His shoulders sagged, and his lips turned down. He appeared utterly defeated. His eyes dimmed as he gave me a sad smile. "Sorry, Cam."

"I don't understand."

He ran a hand through his sweat-soaked hair. "I've wanted to tell you—"

"Reese!"

Mateo had emerged from the school in time to witness the accident, and his voice cut through the chaos with a roar. He must have put the clues together as well, because he was charging toward us. His expression was murderous. And his hands were . . . claws.

I didn't know what Reese was going to say. I didn't know if there was a good explanation. But I knew I wasn't going to get it if this turned into a physical fight. I made a split-second decision, just as Reese had, and hoped I didn't regret it later.

"Run," I said softly.

Reese's eyebrows drew together. "What?"

"Run!"

He didn't need to be told again. He took off, tossing a spark of sprite magic behind him. A wall of thick grass burst upward, concealing his path of escape and blocking anyone from following him.

I made a show of tripping over an obstacle of roots myself and fell to the ground, crying out in fake pain, holding my ankle.

As I expected, Mateo slid to a stop beside me.

"Cam! Are you okay?"

I waved away his help and sat up, my jeans and gloves covered in dirt and bracken. "I'm fine. How are the others?"

Mateo bit down on his bottom lip. He glanced over his shoulder, then back in the direction that Reese had run. His claws stretched and curled as his chest heaved. I didn't think he even realized.

"I don't—"

"You should check on them," I said, quickly cutting him off.

"Yeah." He swallowed, his throat bobbing. "Yeah."

He stalked away from me, toward the others.

I sat in my spot in the shade, marveling at the vines wrapped around the car and at the swamp that had emerged from the concrete.

I didn't know how to feel. I was angry, of course. The glimpse had plagued me for over a month, and one of my new friends had *known* since the day in the coffee shop that he was somehow involved. And he hadn't said anything. He'd watched us toil and struggle to make plans and accuse someone else. He hadn't spoken up.

But he'd saved Gemma from Dennis. He'd just saved Al and Kaci too, when he'd known that it would reveal himself. And he hadn't *hidden* he was a swamp sprite. He just hadn't pointed out how the clues connected.

And if he had, how would we have reacted? He knew he was the one with the most fragile connection to the group. He wasn't anyone's BFF or human advisor.

But I just didn't get it.

I added "sad and confused" to my growing list of emotions.

Gemma came over and plopped down next to me. "It was Reese?" she asked tentatively, tears gathering behind her glasses. "He's responsible for the smell in the meadow? He knew this whole time?"

"I guess," I said with a shrug. "He was in the hallway. His powers smell like a swamp and match the smell I had in the glimpse. And he has a motive, since I learned it was Juana who actually broke up with Mia, and apparently Mia didn't take it well."

"Wow," Gemma said. She swiped the sleeve of her pink hoodie over her cheeks. "Our friend is a potential murderer."

My stomach sank at the thought. "Yeah."

"Wait. Juana broke up with Mia? Does that mean Mateo lied too?"

"Yeah. Maybe."

Gemma sniffed. She wiped away another tear and smeared swamp mud across her face. "I don't believe it," she said, her jaw clenched. "There has to be another reason for him being there. He wouldn't hurt anyone."

"Gemma," I said wearily, rubbing my fingers over my brow.

"What? He could've been protecting her, for all we know. He could've been trying to stop what happened. Maybe he was in the wrong place at the wrong time. Maybe—"

"Okay!" I said, dropping my arms and staring at her. "Maybe, but try explaining that to Mateo."

Gemma wilted. She kicked out her foot. "This all sucks."

"Tell me about it."

"What do we do now?" she asked. "Should we tell the Lopez family?"

"Not yet," I said, watching as Mateo hugged Kaci, his hands back to human, and made sure Al was okay a few feet away. "I still want to have my date."

26

I FIDDLED WITH THE BUTTONS ON MY SHIRT.

I'd done my best to dress nicely—a pair of jeans and a button-up shirt with my denim jacket tossed over it. I styled my hair and added hints of makeup and some nice jewelry. My teeth brushed, my gloves and wallet in my jacket pockets, and my phone in my hand, I sat in my desk chair and waited. I jiggled my leg in anxious energy, and my stomach was a ball of anxiety. All my prep hadn't done anything to quell my nerves.

This wasn't my first date. I'd had exactly one other, and it had been to a middle school dance in eighth grade. I'd met the girl there, given her a few flowers, and then she'd promptly abandoned me for her friends. I'd spent a lonely night drinking punch and texting Al from the gym bleachers.

Things could only go up from there.

Well, it certainly couldn't get any worse. I mean, it *could*. Maybe I shouldn't tempt fate. I needed to think positively. Mateo had asked me out, but he'd also lied to me. And so had one of my friends. And my brother was living in a faery grove, and I wasn't quite sure I could trust him. I didn't think I could trust my parents, either. Maybe. And a girl was going to die if I didn't figure out who had touched me in the fight in the hallway.

Speaking of, said girl was going to crash my date. Every time I thought of her, I couldn't help but see the image of her in the field, which didn't really add to the romantic nature of the affair.

I froze. Romance.

Oh, *shit!*

I flung myself out of my room and down the stairs. Once in the foyer, I dropped to my hands and knees and ducked to peer under the bench, pleading to any deity that would listen for it to miraculously still be there. It had been *days* since I'd dropped it and frankly forgotten about it. I stuck my arm underneath, squirming until my whole shoulder was firmly wedged beneath the bench, my fingers scrambling blindly along the hardwood. But aside from finding a lone sock and a bunch of dust bunnies that my mom would inevitably yell at the cleaning service about, there was nothing.

Maybe it had slid somewhere else, or maybe kicking it under the bench had been a fever dream, or maybe . . .

"Looking for something?" my mom asked.

I jolted, my shoulder slamming into the bench. I lurched to my feet, frantically brushing off the dust all over my arm.

My mom leaned against the frame of the archway that led to the dining room. She had a glass of wine in her hand and was dressed down in a T-shirt and yoga pants, her usual Saturday night, going-to-bed-early attire.

She held up the book.

I died a little inside. My hopes of avoiding this exact scenario shriveled up like a raisin.

I cleared my throat and shoved my clammy hands into my pockets. I didn't have my gloves on because I'd been practicing my psychic blocks, like Alma and Edith had advised. "Yes?" I hedged.

She raised her perfectly sculpted eyebrow.

"Yes," I said, reaching for the book.

She snatched it away, dangling it between two of her fingers like it was a used tissue instead of a popular book series. "Really, Cam?"

"It's research!"

Her eyes climbed into her hairline.

"No!" I raised my hands. "Not that kind of research."

"I read it. How is this research?"

"You read it? Really?"

"Not the point, Cam."

"It's for the lore!" I blurted. "The author is really accurate. I haven't even read it yet. I dropped it the other day, and I'm meeting with the werewolves again soon, and—"

"Accurate?" she asked, cutting me off. Flipping the book over in her hand, she eyed the cover. "This book is accurate?"

"According to the werewolf who gave it to me."

She hummed, then tucked the book under her arm. Her gaze cut to me. "And what are you all dressed up for?"

"I have a date."

She arched an eyebrow. "A date?"

"Yeah. A date. Not clairvoyant-related."

Which was a lie, but ever since I'd met with my long-lost-brother at the faery grove, I'd been a little reticent to share everything with my mom and dad. Not like I was open with them to begin with, but Aiden's warning rang in my head despite the general atmosphere of acceptance that my parents had been giving off around me lately.

"Well," she said, "you look nice."

"I do?"

"Of course. As best you can with dyed hair."

I rolled my eyes. "Mom."

She raised her hands, the contents in her glass sloshing. "What? I like your natural color. But at least the styling suits you."

Well, that was the best I was probably going to get. I'd take it. "Thanks."

She swirled the dark wine in her glass, the wave perilously close to spilling over. "I hope you have a nice time."

"Thanks. Me too." I rocked back on my heels. "So," I said, wincing, then trailing off.

My mom sighed loudly. "When did it get so hard to talk to me, Cam?" She took a gulp. "Was it when Aiden left for college? No," she said softly, answering her own question. "It was before that."

And honestly, I didn't know the answer. Maybe it had happened because I'd defaulted to going to Aiden instead. He was the person I'd told everything to and the person I'd sought for advice or for comfort. And that had been since I was small. He was approachable, and he gave great hugs, and he didn't mind if I climbed into bed with him when I was upset. And I never felt any judgment from him about any of my life choices, like loving art or being best friends with a witch.

There was a lot to repair in the relationship with my parents if it was worth salvaging at all. According to Aiden it wasn't, but I wasn't sure. Right then my mom looked so vulnerable, so *sad*, and I didn't feel great about it. I sighed. "What . . . what do you want to talk about?" I asked. I ground my toe into the hardwood of the floor, my sneaker squeaking.

"Oh," she said, and then finished off her wine, setting the glass on the side table. "How . . . how are things going at school?"

I took a breath. "Ah, well, you know how high school is. Classes and studying and making new friends." The last bit was my not-so-subtle reminder of what my parents had wanted for me at the beginning of the year and how I'd followed their advice . . . just not in the way they'd wanted.

"Well, I hope these new friends of yours like you for you and not for what you can do for them."

Ah. I should've known my mom would turn it around on me. How was she so adept at knowing the things I worried about and then managing to expertly poke at them? I nervously fiddled with a button on my shirt. "I think my friendships are pretty solid."

"Oh, good. Though I'd imagine you can never be too careful."

My mom tilted her head to the side as if in thought. She ran her fingers along a slim chain around her neck, a necklace I hadn't noticed before. She pulled the charm from beneath her shirt and absently ran it back and forth, causing a soft susurration as she slid it along the silver.

Then she smiled. "But don't worry, Cam. I'm certain you'll make good decisions and trust in yourself and your feelings."

That caught me off guard. "You think?"

"Of course." She took a step toward me, and I braced myself, imagining a thick barrier in my mind, as she cupped my cheek in her cool palm. "And it shouldn't be something to worry about right now, anyway, because things might change."

I didn't glimpse. I could feel a tug, the smallest shivery call of my ability, but I blocked it out. And all that was left was the press of my mom's touch against my cheek. And that was *all*. In my elation, I missed most of what my mom said, but I didn't care. I hadn't *glimpsed*.

"Cam," she said, dropping her hand to my shoulder. "Did you hear me?"

"Yes! I did. But could you repeat it again for emphasis?"

"You're only in high school," she said, squeezing my upper arm. "You're young. Things change. Relationships change. So you shouldn't worry too much about it right now."

The doorbell rang.

I jerked out of her grip and hurled myself at the door, wrenching it open. Mateo stood on the other side. He clutched a small bouquet of flowers in his hand. His leather jacket sat askew on his shoulders, and a small blush painted his cheeks, but otherwise he looked just as he did every day at school.

"Hi, Cam!"

"Hey, Mateo."

"Ready to go?"

My mom padded forward. "Cam, aren't you going to introduce me?"

"Uh. Sure. Mom, this is Mateo Lopez. And the girl idling by the curb in the car is his cousin Juana. She's going to drive us."

Mateo fidgeted on the doorstep. He awkwardly thrust out his free hand for my mom to shake. "Very pleased to meet you, Mrs. Reynolds."

"Nice to meet you," she said, gingerly taking his hand. "And where will you be going?"

"We're heading to Drip first for coffee." I cleared my throat. "It's where I hang out with Gemma," I said at the same time that Mateo blurted, "We go all the time."

If a hole could've swallowed me at that moment, I wouldn't have been mad.

"And after?" my mom prompted.

"A walk in the park," Mateo said stiffly.

My mom threaded her fingers together. "That sounds like a nice time."

"Well!" I said, clapping my hands and rubbing them together. "We should head out. Don't you think? Yep, let's go. I won't be out late. I promise. I have my phone!"

I pushed by Mateo on the stoop and slammed the door behind me.

Mateo exhaled shakily and followed me down the steps.

Juana greeted me when Mateo opened the back door. "Hey, Cam," she said with a grin. She had perfect makeup, and her long hair was tied up in an intricate knot. "That looked a little awkward."

I winced. "My mom can be a little ... well ... intense sometimes."

"Ah, most parents are. Did you have a chance to read the book I lent you yet?"

"Oh, no, not yet." I climbed in and, once seated, gave Juana a weak grin. "I've had a lot going on."

She nodded. "Well, I'd *love* to hear your thoughts when you do."

Mateo settled in beside me, his brows drawn together in question. I just shook my head, not wanting to explain.

We sat in the back of the car together while Juana drove. She had her music on low but left us to our own devices.

"You're not wearing gloves," Mateo said, noticing where my hands grasped my knees.

"Oh yeah. I'm practicing my psychic blocks. Kaci inspired me. I know she's been exercising her psychic powers way longer than I have, but seeing her succeed really helped."

Mateo cleared his throat. "Does that mean I can try holding your hand?"

My mouth went dry. My fingers twitched. "Uh, not now. The blocks just worked on my mom, but I don't know how strong they are. Best not to test them right away. I don't want to accidentally glimpse in your cousin's back seat."

Mateo frowned in disappointment.

I drummed my fingers against my knee. "But we can try later? Before I . . ." I glanced to where Juana sang softly to the music as she ran through a yellow light.

"I'd like that."

"Me too."

After a few minutes, Juana pulled into the small parking lot next to Drip. She bounced inside, calling out to Val as soon as she crossed the threshold. Mateo and I followed at a more sedate pace. He paid for my large iced-coffee-and-sugar concoction, and we settled at a table while Juana talked Val's ear off behind the counter.

I checked my phone. I had one text from Al, another from Gemma, and a third from Kaci, all stating they had made it to the old pool park. And then another one from Al with a selfie of the three of them, taken from a park bench with the view of the playground, pickleball courts, and the little kids' soccer field behind them.

I sipped my coffee. "The others are already in the park," I said, my voice low. "Al has sent picture evidence."

Mateo snorted. "So much for our quiet date."

My shoulders rose and fell in a shrug. "We'll go on another one later. After this is all settled." I squirmed in my seat. "I mean, if you want to."

Mateo ducked his head. "I want to. I just . . . don't know why this isn't one. You don't need to do this, Cam. We know who the perpetrator is now."

I took another slurp, the cold coffee sliding down my tight throat. "We don't have all the information," I said diplomatically. It still hurt to think that Reese could be a person who would commit such a violent act. Even with Gemma's denial and hope for another reason that Reese could have been there, I couldn't pretend that the clues didn't stack against him perfectly. Yet I couldn't help but bristle a little that Mateo so readily accepted that Reese was the villain of this story. It bothered me that he didn't seem to be as conflicted about it as I was. "We need the location, Mateo. We can't stop the glimpse, but we can give your family all the information they need to intervene if they can."

He grumbled. "Fine." He took a breath as he spun his own coffee in his hands. "I really like you, Cam."

The corners of my lips ticked up in a helpless smile. "You do?"

Mateo nodded.

And for some reason that probably could be chalked up to bad self-preservation skills, I had to push. "Can I ask why?"

He raised an eyebrow.

"I just—" I said, my plastic cup dimpling under my grip, "you're popular. You could choose anyone from school."

"You're cute," he said quickly. "And you care about people, and you accept people as they are without conditions."

Warmth bloomed beneath my skin and spread into my cheeks. "Thank you. I like you too, for the record."

"Can *I* ask why?"

"You're thoughtful," I said, my brow furrowed as I glared at the table. "And you listen, and I like that you're quiet. It's nice to be around you when my thoughts are loud." I took a sip of my drink. "And you're hot."

"Thanks," Mateo said, muffling a chuckle with his hand. "I want to take you on a real date. Not one where our friends are waiting for us, and not one where my cousin has to drive us around."

My middle fluttered. "I'd like that. But the driving-around part might have to wait a while. I don't have a license."

Mateo grinned. "I will soon. I turn sixteen in a few months."

"Well, I look forward to that." I held out my cup, and with a fond shake of his head, Mateo knocked his drink into mine with a plastic *thunk*.

"Ready to go, lovebirds?" Juana asked, bounding over and wiggling her eyebrows.

Mateo blushed. My face burned hotter than it already had, and I knew my cheeks were fire-engine red. It helped that Mateo's ears had flushed and pointed as well, so at least I wasn't alone in my mortification.

"Yeah." I stood, my drink clutched in one hand, and followed Juana and Mateo back to the car. Mateo and I slid into the back seat, our knees knocking.

Juana pulled out of the parking lot and turned onto the main road.

Silence descended between us, the only sounds being the soft strains of a pop song on the radio and the road beneath Juana's tires. While it could've been awkward, especially since we'd just admitted our mutual affection, it was more comfortable. An understanding had passed between us. We would date once this whole mess was behind us. Any niggling feeling that Mateo might only have been doing all this so that I would ally with the werewolf faction melted away in the face of his warm brown eyes and the sincerity in his expression.

I leaned against the car window as the day faded slowly into dusk. Juana paused at a stop sign and turned right. Wait.

"Um," I said. "The old pool park is to the left."

"Oh, we're not going there," she said, winking at me over her shoulder. "The sun is about to set, and where better to see it than the river park?" She took another turn.

I swallowed. "Well, I just thought—"

"Trust me, Cam. The river park is beautiful at this time of day. And they do have the best benches." At a red light, she twisted toward the back seat. "I said I'd help you, remember? The river park is *romantic.*" Oh no. This was not part of the plan. Discomfort squeezed in my chest.

Mateo gripped my knee, the weight of his hand heavy on my joint. "It's okay," he said, his voice low. "We'll recalibrate."

I nodded, but unease prickled through me. Especially when we turned into the parking lot and passed a huge sign by the entrance.

THIS PARK IS MAINTAINED BY THE NEW AMSTERDAM SUBURB CHAPTER OF THE SPRITE ALLIANCE.

"Is this Sprite Alliance territory?" I asked.

Juana shrugged. "Not any more than our neighborhood is Lopez werewolf territory. They don't own the park. They just manage the upkeep."

The lot held a smattering of cars. Juana parked in a space beneath a towering tree with thick branches, then turned to look at me. "It's sweet that you're worried about me, Cam. But it's okay. You and Mateo will be able to have a nice walk, and I'll be in your eyeline the entire time."

Ha! Juana had read my apprehension as worry for her and not

for myself. Which was great for the plan. But not so great for me.

Mateo and Juana exited the car, and I followed. I wasn't as familiar with this park as I was with the one toward the center of town. I didn't come here often. A cool breeze floated off the water, and the sun dipped toward the horizon, highlighting the sky and the ripples of the river with every shade of pink, orange, and gold. The flora in the parking lot alone were breathtaking, the air fragrant with the smell of flowers and the foliage a collage of vibrant colors.

I pulled out my phone to fire off a text to Al and inwardly groaned when I saw that I had absolutely no bars.

"Do you have a signal?" I asked Mateo as we followed Juana to the paved walking path.

He pulled his phone from his jacket pocket. "No. But I'm sure we'll get one somewhere."

"Yeah. Sure." I typed a message anyway and hit send, hoping that once I did get a signal, the text would go through. Then I shoved my hands in my jacket pockets and meandered after Juana and Mateo.

Juana found a bench on a sandy part of the river shore and plopped down on the sun-bleached wood. She had brought a canvas bag that contained a bottle of water, a book, and a large hoodie.

"Okay. This smutty werewolf romance is calling my name." She shooed us away with her hands. "Off you go. Have fun. But not too much fun. And just yell if you need me. I'll be able to hear."

"Thanks," I said with false cheer. But Juana didn't pick up on my insincerity, judging by the large, toothy smile she cast my way.

I briskly marched down the paved path that curved around the river and toward the footbridge that spanned over it. The greenery on either side of the path was thick and verdant and tall, so much that I doubted Juana would be able to see us. Mateo jogged to keep up, then matched my pace, but neither of us said a word.

"I'm not okay with this," I finally said through gritted teeth after we were halfway over the sparkling river. I paused at the apex and stared out over the park, taking in the setting sun. "We're in sprite territory, and if Reese *is* the culprit, we could be in danger. And I'm not comfortable with glimpsing without Al, Gemma, and Kaci nearby. That was not the plan."

Mateo held up his hands. "I'm sorry. I didn't know she was going to change our location."

"Why didn't you say anything?" I hissed. Annoyance and anxiety swirled in my middle.

"Juana does what Juana wants. She's a free spirit."

"Yeah, well, being a free spirit doesn't give her a pass to be a jerk." I rubbed my hands over my arms.

"She's not a jerk, Cam."

I blinked but didn't say anything. I didn't want to pick a fight, and Juana was Mateo's favorite person in the world, even if I thought the sentiment was misplaced. "Well, what are we going to do?" I yanked my phone from my pocket. The text to Al hadn't sent.

Mateo shrugged. "We could enjoy the date?"

"Really?" I asked, sarcasm dripping from my tone. I tugged on the hem of my jacket. "Do you think that enjoying anything is even a remote possibility for me right now?"

"Yeah. Really. We can walk around the lake until we get a signal to alert the others, and once we do, we can decide if it makes sense for them to come over here."

I took a deep, centering breath. "Okay." I gripped the glossy railing of the footbridge and peered over the edge. The crystal water swirled in small eddies beneath us as fat, golden fish darted in schools along the edges, probably hoping for some breadcrumbs from us. The lights along the path flickered to life as the sun sank below the horizon. Mateo joined me, his shoulder brushing mine. This should've been romantic—standing on a quaint bridge over a babbling river while the sun set, the perfume of flowers thick and intoxicating. But despite the atmosphere and Mateo's presence, an eerie gloom settled around us, and the incongruence of the setting versus why we were really there cast a pall on the whole misplaced concept of our date. The situation felt jumbled like a dropped puzzle, like nothing fit, and it unnerved me down to my core.

"Come on," I said, jerking my head toward the other side of the path. "Let's go and see if we can find a signal."

"Wait," Mateo said softly. His hand hovered over mine where my bare fingers were gripping the bridge railing. "Are your psychic blocks up?"

My eyes fluttered closed. I imagined a large castle drawbridge pulled up and locked tight, the portcullis lowered and the draw-bar pulled across the back of a heavy inner door. That was the most secure barrier I could imagine.

"Yeah," I said, my throat dry.

Mateo's touch was hesitant at first, but as his fingertips slid along the back of my hand and I managed to ignore the tug of a glimpse, he became emboldened. His fingers were warm against mine, a little rough and calloused, his knuckles large bumps, one of them slightly crooked. His palm was clammy when he pressed it into mine and interlocked our fingers.

"Are you okay?"

I licked my lips. "It's nice."

"It is."

He squeezed my hand and then, without warning, leaned in and kissed my cheek.

My psychic barriers were strong enough to survive his touch, but they crumbled under the warm, wet press of his lips.

The world pitched beneath my feet.

And I fell.

27

I **STOOD IN A FIELD.**

A chilly wind blew across my skin, blades of grass tickling my ankles in its wake.

Moonlight illuminated the scene. Trees lined the perimeter in the far distance, and a low-rolling fog obscured the edges of my sight. Clouds swept in front of the moon, bathing the scene in blue gray, muting the colors of the landscape into grayscale.

I took a step, my bare feet sinking into the wet soil, and I shivered in the damp cold. The air smelled like a mixture of rain and fresh mud, with a hint of sulfur and metal.

Oh no.

Fear shuddered through me as I looked up and saw the figure of a girl lying in the meadow.

No.

I didn't want to see this.

I shuffled forward anyway, unable to stop.

Juana raised her head. Her golden-brown hair fell around her in wild tangles. Her eyes were wide and scared. The scant light from the moon illuminated the blood spattered across her face. Her blouse was stained dark red. Her jeans were soaked. Crimson seeped from deep wounds in her torso and slashes across her arms.

"Please," she said, her voice weak. She pushed herself up. Her arms trembled.

"Please," she begged again, raising her hand. Her palm was streaked with bright white and blood red. She hoisted herself to her knees but flopped sideways with a gasp after only a moment.

Familiar voices shouted in the distance. A bush rustled off to the side. Twigs snapped in the forest.

My gut wrenched. I hesitantly stepped closer, despite everything screaming inside me to look away. To stop.

"Please," she whimpered again, but it was barely a whisper.

I couldn't reassure her. I couldn't do anything, impotent with fear.

Juana stilled. Her body lost all tension, and her eyes slid half closed, staring unblinkingly through the grass . . . at me.

My heart lodged in my throat. I wanted to scream. I wanted to run, but my feet were stuck fast, sinking into the viscous swamp mud. I wanted to do anything, but all I could do was stare as her breath stuttered to a halt.

Just as before, my gaze dropped to the object I held at my side. My fingers curled around the handle of the weapon. Not my fingers—fingers that had been holding my hand only moments before. Mateo's fingers were wrapped around the ornate handle of a silver knife.

The blade gleamed in the scant moonlight; the sharp edge was tinged red with Juana's blood.

28

LURCHED AWAKE.

Night had fallen completely while I was out, the only light coming from the streetlamps overhead. My back hurt from where I'd fallen onto the bridge planks, and my stomach bubbled with nausea.

Mateo stood over me, his head haloed by the artificial lights, his features obscured in shadow.

"Cam?" he said hesitantly. "I'm so sorry. I didn't think, and—" He continued to speak, but my hearing fuzzed out, and my muscles seized in terror. He reached down and I flinched, spurring myself into motion, scrambling away on my elbows, my feet kicking out to propel myself backward. He paused. "Cam?" he said again. "What's wrong?"

"Don't come near me," I said, my voice a rasp.

Mateo had been the one who'd touched me in the hallway during the fight. Mateo had triggered my first glimpse. Mateo had held the knife as his cousin had cried in the meadow, blood-smeared and dying.

I heaved to my feet, staggered to the other side of the footbridge, and promptly threw up over the side. My back arched and my stomach cramped as the images of the glimpse assaulted my mind's eye in a gruesome loop, along with the fact that it was Mateo. *Mateo.*

"Cam?"

My mouth tasted like bile and coffee. My heart thundered in my temples. I was alone with two werewolves in an unfamiliar park. My phone had no signal, and the sun had set.

I trembled as I gripped the bridge railing.

"Cam," Mateo said again, his tone hard. "What did you see?"

He sounded almost sinister, and for the first time since I'd bumped into Mateo in the hallway freshman year, I felt something other than infatuation. I was afraid.

I didn't answer. He had to know, right? What I'd seen? What I had planned to see from Juana's point of view that night but unwittingly saw again from his? There was no way he didn't know.

I spat out the lingering taste of vomit into the river, then dragged my sleeve over my mouth. My body trembled with fatigue and fear.

But I had only one choice.

Pushing myself away from the edge, I turned and ran across to the other side of the river. It was a dumb move, running from a werewolf. Mateo could easily catch me if he wanted, but maybe he'd be too stunned to follow quickly. Maybe my phone would pick up a signal, and maybe Al and the others would come to my rescue.

The lights overhead illuminated the paved walking path as I ran as fast as I could. Mateo shouted behind me, his voice echoing from the bridge. I was unsure if he followed me, because I couldn't hear his footsteps over the pounding of my shoes against the asphalt and the thump of my pulse in my ears.

One thing was certain, though—I needed to get off this path. The river was on my left, but to my right was a wooded area, a dense growth of trees.

I took a sharp turn and pushed through a small gap between two spindly saplings. Branches whipped and stung my skin as I stumbled into the bracken, but I didn't stop plowing ahead, snapping twigs with each step, panting as sweat dampened every inch of my skin. Maybe I should've stayed on the path because plunging into a forest was noisy, but I'd made the choice, and I couldn't turn back now. I kept going, cursing the sprites as lush bushes and sharp thorns snagged my jeans, biting into the skin beneath. Breathing harshly, I bumped into trees, disturbed nests of small woodland creatures, and ran through spiderwebs, which was a horror I didn't need to add to my already lengthy list of things that had gone wrong that evening.

Note to self: I was not made for fleeing.

The farther I ran, the darker it became underneath the canopy of leaves. Every noise, every rustle, every step brought with it a potential new danger. My heart thudded so fast, I thought I might pass out. But I kept going, spurred on by pure panic. Without the lights from the paved path, my way was dark, and I ran blindly until I took one misstep. My foot twisted on a loose branch, and I fell to my hands and knees.

A pinecone bit into my palm. My ankle throbbed as I lay sprawled on the forest floor. It hurt, but it made me take a moment to pause, to reassess. I strained to hear evidence of a pursuer, but for the moment I heard nothing other than my own stuttered breathing.

I scurried to the base of a large tree, pushed my back against it, and pulled out my phone. I drew my knees to my chest and cupped my hands around it, huddled over it, just in case the light might give me away.

I slid my thumb over the screen and, oh thank fuck, I had a bar.

My text to Al had gone through, and I had responses from the rest of the group, wondering where we were, what was happening, and if I was okay.

I was far from okay.

My hands shook as I pressed the button to call Al.

They picked up on the first ring.

"Where the hell are you?" The connection popped and crackled, but it went through, and there was no mistaking their annoyance.

"I don't know," I said, whispering, my voice shaky with adrenaline and panic. "In a forest, somewhere, by a river park in sprite territory."

"What? I can barely hear you. Can you speak up?"

"No," I answered. "Something has happened."

There was a murmur of voices on the other end, and then Al responded. "Cam, you're scaring me. What is going on?"

"Mateo kissed my cheek," I blurted out, whisper-harsh. "And I glimpsed. And it was him! It was Mateo!" I pressed my forehead to my knees. A tear slipped down my flushed cheek, following the line of my jaw, mixing with the sweat already on my skin.

There was a beat of silence. "It was Mateo what? Who kissed you?"

I shook my head, then realized they couldn't see it. I ran my hand through my hair, smearing blood and mud into the sweat-damp strands. "No. I mean, yes. Mateo kissed me, and I saw . . ." I swallowed around the lump in my throat. "I saw the glimpse again. It was him the whole time, Al."

Al sucked in a sharp breath. *"Where are you?"*

"I don't know." I turned my head to look behind me, and all I could see were trees. "I ran from the path. Juana took us to the river park managed by the Sprite Alliance instead of taking us to the old pool park. I glimpsed, and then I ran." I clutched the phone in my trembling fingers. "I don't know what to do."

There was a rustle of cloth and a flurry of movement on the other line. I heard a car door slam and then another voice, though I couldn't make out what they said.

"Stay where you are," Al said firmly. "Send me a pin of your location." It took me a few tries because of how hard my hands shook, but I managed to hit the right buttons. It didn't go through; the connection was too shoddy.

"Al," I said, my voice cracking. "It won't—"

"It's okay. I have a spell for this. I'm sending help, and then I'll be there, okay? We're on our way."

I hunched down, curled my shoulders, and made myself as small as possible. "Thank you," I breathed.

"No worries. But look, Mateo has been blowing up Kaci's phone, saying he's worried."

My body tensed in fear. "Don't tell him where I am."

"I'm not. It's okay, Cam. Kaci is handling Mateo."

I flinched. "Kaci needs to stay safe," I said, a breathy whisper into the phone.

"She is. Don't worry."

I hoped she was, because if Mateo could do that to Juana . . . could he do that to Kaci too? His best friend? What about the others?

"Gemma, Val, and I are on our way to you. We'll figure it out. Just trust me."

I wanted to say that I did. But I had trusted Mateo. And he was . . . he was . . . Another wave of lightheadedness washed over me, and I screwed my eyes shut. My thoughts ran rampant as remnants of the horrifying glimpse replayed on a loop in my head.

I don't know how long I stayed there, huddled on the forest floor, shaking. My screen dimmed as the battery ran low, but I didn't want to cut the call with Al. The road sounds and the low radio from Val's speakers offered surprising comfort with their familiarity. My fingers ached from the grip I had on my phone, and my head hurt from how tightly my teeth were clenched, but slowly—as I waited in the dark and the quiet, and the only sounds came from my phone—I allowed my body to relax.

I was lulled into a false sense of security, because at some indeterminable point later, there was movement above me.

I jerked my head up as my breath caught in a harsh wheeze. I quickly raised my phone, the light barely cutting a swath in the darkened wood, but a flash of purple-black feathers streaked across my vision, followed by an assuasive and recognizable caw.

"Lenore?" I whispered. "Is that you?"

The large raven floated down from the trees and landed at eye level with me on top of a shrub. She ruffled her feathers, hopped down, and approached. Once in reach, she nipped my fingers affectionately.

"Did Lenore make it?" Al's voice came from my phone.

I jumped, forgetting the call was still connected.

"Yeah," I said, my voice cracking with gratitude and relief. "She's here."

"Great. She's going to lead you to the road. Follow her."

Lenore croaked, then flew upward to a branch a few feet away. Using the tree trunk behind me, I creaked to my feet, my knees and back complaining from being huddled for so long. But once I had feeling in my legs, and my head didn't feel like a balloon ready to float away from my shoulders, I took a tentative step, and then another, until I was under Lenore's perch.

She flew to another tree, and I followed.

Dried sweat made the back of my neck itchy. My nice clothes were stiff with perspiration and torn from thorns and branches. My ankle was hot and swollen under my sock, and I felt awful, fatigued from stress and from the burden of the glimpse.

Despite Lenore offering a modicum of reassurance and having Al on the phone with me the whole time, I felt uneasy, like I was being watched. There was no sound in the forest other than my own trudging footsteps, and while I had taken that as a good sign when I had first run in and hadn't heard anyone following, it now felt ominous. Shouldn't there be animals scurrying about? Owls hooting? At the very least, frogs and bugs chirping? But there was nothing, as if the woodland itself had frozen in fear.

My head was muddled, a headache twisting right behind my eyes and in my temples, and I felt woozy, but I kept going, my gaze locked on Lenore.

It felt like I'd walked forever when there was finally a break in the trees, and a short distance farther I spied a road. A car idled to the side, and I hobbled faster until I broke through the tree line.

"Cam!"

Al hurried toward me and caught me as I stumbled into their arms. I was too tired for psychic blocks, but they didn't touch my skin, merely gripped my waist and tugged me close.

"Wow, dude," Val said from the other side of the vehicle. "You look rough."

"Understatement of the year," Gemma said, leaning forward from the back seat. "Are you okay, Cam?"

I shook my head. "No. Can we go, please?" I was proud to hear only a slight tremble in my voice.

"Yeah. Where are we going?" Val asked, spinning her keychain on her finger. "To the hospital?"

"No." The suggestion wasn't unwarranted—my ankle did feel like it was sprained in some way—but everything else probably looked worse than it was, so I declined.

"Our house," Gemma said. "Mom won't mind."

Al tossed a treat to Lenore and brushed their fingers down her back. They whispered something to her, and she took off with a squawk and an impressive display of her wingspan.

Al slid into the back seat next to Gemma and pulled the front seat into position. I gratefully sank into it and closed the door behind me. I peered into the woods but didn't spy anyone or anything.

Val threw the car into drive, and we moved away from the curb. I checked my phone for the time and couldn't believe how late it was. I'd been in the forest for hours.

But at least now I was relatively safe, and I slumped into the seat and shut my eyes.

29

GEMMA'S MOM WAS A SHORT, MIDDLE-AGED LADY WITH graying hair, deep laugh lines, and wrinkles that I imagined came from raising two very different children. She took one look at me and immediately went into care mode, wanting to dab every cut with peroxide, ice every bruise, and wrap me in a blanket and feed me soup. Gemma stepped between us before I could flinch and cause offense.

"He's a touch telepath, Mom," she said, hands raised. "You can't just poke and prod him. But we'll take the first aid kit and some snacks."

Gemma convinced her mom to allow Al and me to stay the night, for which I was grateful. I didn't want to show back up at home covered in scratches and try to explain to my parents how badly my date with a werewolf had gone. I revived my phone with a borrowed charger and sent my mom a text that I was staying at Al's—something she was used to seeing. She only responded with a short "okay," and that was that.

After a shower and some first aid, I sat in Gemma's family room in a T-shirt and pajama bottoms I'd borrowed from Val (pink with skulls).

Al and Gemma blew up an air mattress on the floor while I

sprawled on the couch, my ankle propped with an ice pack and a blanket covering me.

"Hey, want to hear something hilarious?" Al said as they poked at the mattress they were filling with air.

"Sure. I wouldn't mind a moment of lightheartedness."

They snorted. "It involves your parents."

"I'm intrigued. Do continue."

"They went to the coven house again tonight."

I perked up from my drowsy state. When I'd left, my mom had been in her wine-mom attire. She wasn't dressed to go out.

"What? When?"

"Tonight. And I don't know how, but they ticked off the coven elders. And were asked to *leave*."

I sat up and gasped. "Get out!"

Al giggled and pointed. "Yes! Exactly like that."

"What did they do? Did they offend the coven or something?"

Al shook their head. "I have no idea. My moms didn't tell me—just that your parents had said something that led to the coven kicking them out."

I groaned, smacking my hand over my face. "They're so embarrassing. I don't even want to know what they said or did."

Gemma spread out a sheet on the air mattress, then tossed a pillow and two fluffy blankets onto it. She disappeared into her room and came back with two more pillows.

"Unicorn?" she asked, holding them up. "Or regular?"

"Regular is fine."

She shrugged. "Your loss." She tossed me the regular pillow, and I shoved it behind my back.

Al settled cross-legged into a large recliner and stared at me. They too had changed into a pair of borrowed pajamas from Val. They were decorated with cartoon bats with candy-corn fangs.

"All right, tell us what happened with Mateo."

I sighed, scrunched down onto the couch cushion, and pulled the blanket up to my neck. I recounted the whole date, from the conversation with my mom, to Juana taking us to the wrong park, to Mateo kissing me on the cheek, which had led to the glimpse of Juana's attack. Then my running into the forest instead of confronting the problem.

Gemma's frown deepened with each detail. "Does that mean Reese is exonerated?"

"I don't know." I twisted my hands into the blanket. "The swamp smell was there, and what I thought was mud from rain could've been Reese's doing, but Mateo was definitely the person holding the knife."

Al and Gemma exchanged a glance. "We should get some rest," Al said, "and approach it in the morning."

I agreed.

Gemma and Al shared the inflatable mattress, and I took up the couch. I didn't think I would be able to fall asleep, not with my tumultuous thoughts bouncing around in my brain, but after a few minutes of listening to Gemma and Al murmur to each other quietly, I drifted off.

My cheek was buzzing.

Wait. No. That wasn't right. Something *under* my cheek was buzzing.

I pried my eyes open, wiped away the sleep, and gingerly sat up from Gemma's surprisingly comfy couch. I reached beneath my pillow and pulled out my phone.

The screen read two thirty a.m. and buzzed again and again as several texts came through. I had a dozen missed calls from Kaci and Mateo. And I had a ton of texts. It appeared as if my phone, now fully charged and with full bars, was catching up from the night.

And a flood of messages from everyone was now coming through. I sighed heavily and pushed my hair away from my face.

I swiped my thumb over my screen and opened my messenger app. Other than the older messages from my forest ordeal, there was a newer cluster of messages from around midnight. All from Mateo.

I can't sleep until I know you're okay.

Are you okay?

Cam, are you there?

Can you answer?

I didn't mean to make you glimpse.

I should've asked before kissing you.

I just really wanted to. I know that's not an excuse.

I would like to talk to you.

I understand if you would rather text Kaci just to let us know you're okay.

I squinted at the text. My brain was foggy with sleep, and I didn't know how to deal with this. But I couldn't help but feel bad that Mateo was upset, despite the fact that he could be the attacker. And then there were the more recent texts.

Still can't sleep.

I'm really sorry.

I'm heading to your house.

What the fuck?

I quickly texted back, my fingers fumbling over the screen. I'm not there. The last thing I wanted was for Mateo to wake my parents. That would surely end in a shit show. And I don't know why I did it, but I added, I'm at Gemma's.

Okay, that was probably stupid.

I'll be there in a few minutes.

Oops. That was not quite what I had wanted to happen. But I couldn't take it back now. How did he even know Gemma's address? Did Kaci tell him? Wait, it didn't matter. What mattered was that he was on his way, and I was half-asleep, kind of gross, and my hair was standing on end. Ugh. I'd just add all of those to my growing list of embarrassing things that had happened the last few days.

I leaned over the edge of the couch. On the other side of the ottoman, Al and Gemma were fast asleep. Gemma was propped on her unicorn pillow and curled into an impossibly small ball, and Al was splayed out as they usually did in sleep, half on the mattress and half off. As quietly as possible, I untangled from the blanket and stood. I bit back a gasp of pain when I put my weight on my ankle, and hobbled toward the front door. I twisted the lock, wincing at the sound, and did my best to open the door slowly, hoping the creaks wouldn't wake the others. I squeezed through the small opening I'd made and gently shut the door behind me.

Gemma's house had a screened-in front porch with wicker furniture. So I took a seat on a springy cushion and waited.

I didn't have to wait long. I had no idea if Mateo had run the entire way to Gemma's, but that was the only explanation for how he arrived a rumpled, panting mess with no car.

"Cam," he whispered.

I heaved myself up from the chair and faced him through the screen door. He stood on the path that led from the driveway to the front stoop.

He took a step toward the house. "Stay there," I said, my voice trembling with fear and fatigue.

Mateo paused. The moon was waxing, the harvest moon only a few days away, and the light illuminated Mateo enough for me to make out his features. He was tired, his posture wilted, his hair a sweat-soaked tangle.

"Are you okay?" he asked. He bit his lower lip, and his body vibrated in place, like he was holding back from ripping the door off the hinges to ensure I was all right.

"Not my best day," I said. "But I'm okay."

"I'm sorry," he said again. "I'm so sorry. I should've asked before I kissed you. I didn't mean to make you glimpse. I never wanted to make you uncomfortable."

I narrowed my eyes and crossed my arms over my chest, hiding the big pink skull that was printed there. "Yeah, well, Juana taking us to a different location than we planned made me really uneasy."

He turned his head, staring at the grass, the sharp line of his clenched jaw apparent in the moonlight. "I didn't know she would do that. I'm sorry."

I rolled my shoulders, trying to ease the tension that had gathered in my body. "Why did you lie to me?" I blurted out. That wasn't quite the question I'd meant to ask, but it was the one in the forefront of my mind. "You lied about Juana breaking up with Mia."

"Because that was what Juana told me!" he said, pushing his finger into his chest. "And that's what I told Kaci, so don't be mad at her."

"I'm not mad at Kaci."

He nodded. "Good," he said softly.

"Okay. If I accept that you didn't lie about Juana, you still lied about touching me during the fight in the hallway."

He snapped his head up. "What? I touched you in the hallway?"

"Yes!" I snapped. "*You* triggered my first glimpse!"

Mateo's mouth flapped open. "I did?"

Annoyance swept over me. "What the fuck? You didn't know?"

"No, I didn't know. I was in the hallway, and I was trying to stop Javi from making things worse, and I grabbed you once off the floor, but that was by the shirt. And then we all fell down, and Danny lifted you and took you to the nurse, and I picked up your phone from where it fell." He ran a hand through his hair, causing it to stick up wildly. "I didn't know." His shoulders hunched. "Is . . . is that what you saw when I kissed you?"

"Yeah," I croaked. "I saw it all over again."

"No wonder you ran," he said with a huff. "But I promise you, I didn't know that it was me."

I dropped my arms. Mateo didn't know? I licked my dry lips. "Were you thinking about Juana during the fight?"

Mateo wrinkled his nose. "Probably. It was a conflict with the sprites, and she was returning the next day."

Exhaustion built behind my eyes. I was tired, emotionally fatigued, and so confused. "Mateo, why would you have a silver knife and be standing over your favorite cousin who had just been attacked? Is there any explanation for why she would be pleading for help, and you would just not move?" I shuffled forward and pressed one hand to the screen over the door, resting my head on the wooden frame. "Any explanation at all?"

He swallowed. "No." He shoved his hands in his pockets. "I have no idea."

"How can I trust you?"

Mateo sighed. "Do you honestly think I could hurt Juana? That I could hurt you? That I could hurt anyone?"

And that was the question, wasn't it. Was Mateo capable? Was

Reese capable? The stereotype was that werewolves were aggressive. But the other stereotypes were that sprites were mean-spirited, and psychics were detached, and witches were immoral, and humans were afraid of them all. And hadn't my friends proved all those were wrong?

I took a shuddering breath. "No. I don't."

Mateo tipped his head back, his features bathed in the moonlight. "Good."

"I still don't understand, though."

"Because we're missing something."

I was startled at the sound of Gemma's voice and turned quickly to find her and Al standing in the doorway. Al had their phone, and from the screen I saw that Kaci was connected via video chat.

Kaci's arms were crossed. Her hair was a bird's nest, and she glared at me with sleep-heavy eyes. "I'm really annoyed with all of you right now," she said, then yawned widely.

"I'm annoyed with myself," I replied.

She huffed.

"Cam, think," Al said, slumping against the door. "Did you see anyone use the knife? Or hurt Juana?"

I shook my head. "No."

"Then it's possible that Mateo was just there," Gemma said.

"If I was there, I would've intervened and stopped whatever was happening," Mateo said from the pathway. "I wouldn't have held the knife, for sure."

"Cam?" Kaci asked, eyes closed, head propped up on her palm. "Did Edith or Alma say anything about your glimpses that could help?"

"We talked about psychic blocks and their powers and—" I froze. Edith had said that my visions might not always be what they seemed. That I only saw a piece of the whole pie. "I've missed the forest for the trees," I whispered.

"What?" Al said, voice flat.

I sank back into the wicker chair. "Mateo would never hurt Juana."

"I agree," Kaci said from the phone.

"I think the vision is Mateo arriving after the fact. My guess is that he finds the knife and picks it up and approaches Juana." I rubbed my breastbone. "And all the fear I felt wasn't just mine. It was Mateo's too. Like how I felt Dennis's excitement at the basketball game and Reese's anxiety about the pop quiz."

A tear slid from the corner of my eye and rolled down my cheek.

"Cam?" Al asked softly. "Are you okay?"

"I'm sorry," I breathed. Mateo had moved closer to the house and now stood right outside the screen door. "I'm sorry. I'm so sorry, Mateo. I shouldn't have run. I should've thought it through."

"I wish you had," Mateo said. "But you were frightened. And already off balance. I understand why you did."

Al moved behind me and rubbed my back, their touch comforting. Gemma put her hands on her hips, frown on her face.

"I hate to say this," she said, "but I do think it's time we told an adult. We still don't know who the culprit is, and we're running out of time."

Mateo snorted at that, and I realized he was still firm in his belief that it was Reese. But if that night had taught me anything, it was that I had glimpsed only a small piece of the puzzle, and a little knowledge could be a lot dangerous.

Gemma twisted her hands in the mane of her unicorn pillow. "We know for sure that it happens, and we have a potential *when*, if not the where."

"I'll tell Mateo's parents tomorrow," I said. At Mateo's wide-eyed glance, I shrugged my shoulders. "It's what I should do. Probably what I should've done as soon as I realized it was Juana in the field. And if they need more convincing, I can show them the drawing." I winced, then groaned. "Which I'll have to go home to retrieve."

"Hey, losers." Val appeared in the doorway, opening the door wider and bodily shoving Gemma to the side. "You're loud."

Gemma paled. "Um . . . we'll be quieter. Sorry, my big sister, whom I love."

Val crossed her arms and rolled her eyes. "I'm not going to snitch to Mom, because I don't care. But go to sleep. You and your weird friends can plan shit in the morning."

"But—"

"Now!" She tugged Gemma's unicorn pillow from her arms and tossed it into the house.

"Hey!"

"Also," Val said as Gemma trudged past, grumbling, "consider us even. No more pie."

Val was right. "We need to rest," I said. Al agreed with a nod and followed Gemma into the house. I turned to Mateo. "I'll come over to yours as soon as I can get home and deal with my parents. Will you be okay to get home?"

Mateo nodded. "Yeah. Javi is at a party nearby. I'm meeting him there."

"Okay." My fingertips curled on the porch screen. "See you tomorrow."

"Yeah." Mateo cleared his throat and bounced in place. "Um . . . for the record, I was having a nice time until . . . you know."

Despite my exhaustion and guilt and fear, my cheeks heated. "Yeah, me too."

"Good night."

I went back inside and flopped on the couch, burying my head in the soft pillow and tugging the blanket over my body. Al opted for the recliner, and Gemma curled onto the air mattress.

I was not looking forward to the next day and the awkward conversation I'd be having with Mateo's parents, but at least we'd have the help of mature adults, and maybe that would finally release us all from the burden we'd been carrying. I wouldn't mind passing off the responsibility of the whole situation to someone else, and I hoped there would be an accompanying bit of relief that might come with it. With that hopeful thought, I fell asleep.

30

ILEANED BACK IN THE FRONT SEAT OF VAL'S CAR.

"Thanks for driving me home," I said, looking out the window as she slowed at a stoplight. "And for picking me up last night. I'm sure you're tired of carting Gemma's weird friends around."

Val shrugged and fiddled with the buttons on her heating, trying to get warm air circulating. "I don't mind."

"That's a lie."

We'd already dropped Al off at their house and were now headed to mine. It had been an interesting morning, to say the least. I had woken to a text from Mateo saying he was with Javi and had made it home. The time stamp was around four a.m., and I hoped Mateo hadn't gotten in trouble for being out so late. I had texted back that I was glad he was safe and that I would see him later, then had gone to change into my clothes from the night before.

After a homemade pancake breakfast, Gemma had volunteered Val to drive Al and me home.

"No, really." She drummed her fingers on the steering wheel. "Gemma has never really had friends. She's been bullied, and she never had anyone sleep over or come to birthday parties or that sort of thing. Her interests are a little rigid and hyperfocused, and sometimes she's not the greatest with her social skills." When the light flashed green, Val turned the wheel and took the left onto my street. "I was worried for her at high school. But I'm glad she has a group. Even if it's all psychics and witches."

"A werewolf and a sprite, too."

Val smirked. "Yeah. She talked my ear off about Reese when he stood up for her. It was all I heard about for, like, a week." She eased close to the curb in front of my house. "I'm glad she found you guys. Even if it means that I am the chauffeur until one of you gets a license."

"I'm glad we found her too," I said, my heart twisting at the potential of losing any of my friends. "And bright side, Mateo gets a license soon. And I know Al will as well."

"Great. But until then, I'm okay with driving you all around. As long as it doesn't interfere with my job or social life," she said, pointing a finger in my face. "I'm cool to be the big sister if you need one."

"Thanks. I really appreciate it."

"Good. Now get out. It's my day off, and I don't want to spend it idling here."

I hastily unbuckled my seat belt and hopped out of the car. I slammed the door and waved as she drove away. Then I quickly headed to the front door to escape the wet, chilly conditions. Fall-like weather had finally arrived to Shady Hallow.

I hobbled up the front stoop, took a breath, and braced myself for whatever conversation was about to happen with my parents when I pushed open the door. But when I walked in and called out my usual greeting, there was no answer. And huh. Well, it was Sunday. They always went to brunch on Sundays.

Yay. The house was empty. I'd totally dodged a bullet.

I headed to the kitchen and found a note on the table in my mom's handwriting.

Out for the day. Be home tonight. We need to check in.

Okay. That didn't sound too bad, as long as she didn't bring up the werewolf romance novel again. I could do that. It might be nice after whatever happened at the Lopezes'. With that thought, I climbed the stairs and collapsed on my bed.

It was close to dinner by the time Mateo texted me that his parents were on their way home from their Sunday excursion. I grabbed my keys, phone, and wallet and slung on my jacket before calling a ride via a car service. It was too far to bike, and hopefully Danny or Javi would be willing to give me a ride home after—if me telling their whole family about my gruesome glimpse didn't destroy the tenuous relationship I had with them.

The car dropped me off at the edge of the driveway, and I hopped out, tapping my phone to add a tip, before limping to the front porch, my ankle still tender from the night before.

"Hey," Mateo said, opening the door. He was dressed in jeans and a T-shirt, and his feet were bare. His long hair was wet, the ends leaving damp spots on his shoulders, as if he had just stepped out of the shower. "Come on in."

"Thanks."

The cold had deepened the past few hours, and I clutched my denim jacket closer around me as I stood in the foyer of his home.

"My parents were out with Juana all day. They're on their way back now."

"Cool."

"Do you want anything?"

A way out of this mess. "Um . . . a glass of water?"

"Sure."

I followed Mateo to the kitchen and propped myself on a stool near the center island while he retrieved a glass from the cupboard and filled it with filtered water.

"So," I said, my feet wedged into the bars of the stool. "Sorry again for last night. And for, like, everything."

Mateo gave me a tight smile. "Me too."

And I was, especially now that I'd had time to think about things from Mateo's perspective. The more I replayed my actions after the glimpse, the more I wished I'd taken a second and just *thought* before taking off. "I didn't mean to hurt you, but I'm aware that running away probably did. And so did ever entertaining the thought that you could hurt your cousin. I'm sorry. I know that words probably aren't enough, but I really am sorry."

Mateo heaved a sigh. "It did hurt," he admitted, his voice low, his gaze focused on the countertop. "Especially right after. But I talked with Kaci, and she gave me a psychic's point of view."

"Yeah? What was that?"

He set the glass in front of me. "That your panic was the result of experiencing the glimpse again unexpectedly. Adding the fact that you thought I lied—I get why you ran."

Thank gods for Kaci. "I'm still sorry, but yeah, seeing that again was not fun. Zero out of ten. Would not recommend."

A smile ticked at the edge of Mateo's mouth.

"So we're good?" I asked.

"Yeah. We're good." He finally met my gaze. "Well, I mean, we still have that first date to go on."

I leaned my elbows on the island. "Yeah?"

He hummed in response.

"I'd better work on my psychic blocks, just in case you get the urge to kiss me again."

Mateo laughed. "Yeah. Good idea."

I beamed. "I'm looking forward to it."

We chatted about school and art class while I drank my glass of water and we waited for Mateo's parents. It was obvious we were both skirting around the elephant in the room, but it was nice just to be teenagers for a minute and complain about teachers and gossip about the other students. Time stretched on, and when I glanced out the window over the sink, I noticed the sun would set soon. I checked my phone for the time and winced when I saw I had several missed calls from Gemma.

"Ugh," I said. "I think I need to—"

Mateo's phone buzzed on the table. His brow furrowed. "It's my parents." He scooped up the phone and answered the call. "Oh," he said, glancing toward me. "Um . . . yeah. That's okay. I guess. I just need to talk to you guys. At home. But we can wait a little longer?" He posed the second part as a question and looked at me.

I nodded in confirmation. My mom hadn't given me a firm time to return home. I could wait another hour. Maybe.

"Okay. Love you too. Bye." Mateo hung up. "My parents went to dinner, but they'll be home in an hour. Is that okay?"

"Sure." I held up my cell. "Let me see what Gemma wants."

I slid off the stool and left the kitchen to stand in the darkened entryway. Gemma picked up immediately when I dialed.

"Cam!" she screeched in my ear.

That wasn't her usual scream of enthusiasm. It didn't sound like an excited Gemma. It was a panicked one.

"I made a mistake! I think. No, I'm sure I did. I'm sorry!"

Uh-oh. My stomach clenched. "Hey, whoa, slow down," I said. "It's okay. Take a breath."

"I'm sorry. I didn't *think*."

Alarm bells rang in my head. Gemma had been trying very hard to be conscientious since I'd scolded her for posting the first glimpse. And for being a little too direct with the members of our group. And she took that in stride. An upset Gemma was a bad sign.

"I'm sure we can fix whatever it is." I walked back to the kitchen and put Gemma on speaker. Mateo raised his eyebrows, and I brought a finger to my lips in a "be quiet" gesture, then pointed to the phone. "Gemma, calm down and tell me what you did. You're on speaker with Mateo too. We're both here to help."

"Okay. Okay. Okay," Gemma said in succession, more frantic

than before. "I told Reese." Then she made a noise as if she'd clapped her hand over her mouth.

All the air seemed to get sucked out of the room. I winced. Mateo frowned. "Told him what, exactly?" I asked, in a soft and measured tone.

"About last night! That it was Mateo in the glimpse. I thought it could help him, you know? To hear that it wasn't him. That maybe he could come back to the group as our friend. Because he is our friend. And I wanted to help him, but I think I messed it all up."

Ah. "Um . . . well . . . I think that's okay."

Mateo huffed.

She made a high-pitched squeaking noise that alerted me that there was probably more to this story coming. "He reached out to Juana."

Fuck. Okay. *That* wasn't good. I grabbed the kitchen stool to steady myself, my knees suddenly weak. Mateo's expression was thunderous. His own hands gripped the kitchen island, and his fingernails elongated, claws dragging furrows into the tile. "He what?"

"He said he wanted to clear his name. He wanted to meet Juana in person. So she could then tell Mateo that Reese wasn't involved with everything that happened before."

"*What?*" Mateo yelled. "When? Where?"

"I don't know!" Gemma wailed.

Mateo's gaze snapped to mine, his brown eyes flashing silver. "My parents dropped Juana off to meet with a friend before they went to dinner."

Oh no. Oh no. "You don't think . . . ?" My throat tightened. "Text your parents. Find out where."

Mateo fumbled with his phone, frustrated, claws scratching the case, until he took a breath and his fingers shifted back to human. Then he tapped in a furious blur on the screen.

Gemma sniffled in my ear. "It's not after the harvest moon," she said, voice small. "Was I wrong about that too?"

"It's okay." I didn't quite believe that, but I couldn't have Gemma spiral, especially since we needed her. "We'll think it through."

Mateo's phone buzzed. "They dropped her off at Drip."

"Okay! See. That's fine. That's a public place, right? Are Javi and Danny around? Can they give us a ride there in the van?"

Mateo shook his head. "I'm the only one home."

Yikes. Okay, we could figure it out. "Gemma, is Val at the coffee shop? She could keep an eye on them for us."

"She's off today."

Right. Shit. Okay. We needed to find a way there and see for ourselves, just to make sure that Juana was okay.

I polished off my glass of tepid water. "Do you know how to drive?" I asked.

Mateo's throat bobbed. "I have my learner's permit. My dad's car is here."

"Okay. Let's go."

"Cam!" Gemma's voice blared from my phone. "What should I do?"

"Gemma," I said seriously, "do what you do best. Communicate with the others, and tell them what's happening. We'll keep you posted."

There was a slight pause, followed by a confident, "Okay! On it!"

"Keep in touch."

"Got it, partner."

I hung up and was surprised to find that Mateo had left the kitchen. I scrambled after him, and he was already halfway out the side door that led to the garage, keys in hand. He didn't even stop for a jacket or shoes before he slid into the front seat of the car. I had to jog to catch up or risk being left behind. The garage door opened before I was fully buckled. Once settled, I pulled my gloves from my jacket pocket and tugged them on.

"Are you okay with this? You might get in trouble."

He shrugged. "No more than Javi does on a regular basis."

The engine revved, and as soon as the door opened, we lurched forward. I grabbed the handle that hung from the car ceiling and gripped it tight as Mateo bottomed out leaving the driveway, and a splash of sparks lit up the rearview mirror. When the first curve had my shoulder slamming into the passenger side door, I realized that this might not have been the best idea.

But I didn't want to tell Mateo to slow down. Not when the sun had set and the moon was visible, waxing full and bright, and cloudy skies drifted in the distance, slowly migrating to hover over us. Small sprinkles of rain dotted the windshield as we moved closer to town. My whole body tensed, and it wasn't just because of Mateo's bad driving. *This* was the weather in the glimpse.

It was happening.

31

I BRACED MYSELF WHEN MATEO SLAMMED ON THE BRAKES IN front of Drip. He was barely in between the lines, but I wasn't about to critique his parking, especially since his hands were claws again. I scrambled out of the car and hopped up onto the curb.

Mateo joined me. His eyes were silver instead of their usual warm brown, and in his haste, he hadn't slipped on shoes. Which was probably good, since his feet now had claws as well. And come to think of it, his shirt barely contained his broadening shoulders; his thighs appeared thicker too.

"I'll go in," I said, grabbing Mateo's forearm and giving it a comforting squeeze. "Maybe go find a good spot for the car in the parking lot, okay?"

Mateo glared.

"Look, I don't know exactly what's going on with you, but you look like you're about five seconds from ripping out of your clothing. And normally I might not mind, because we've talked about how I think you're hot, but I don't know if the people in the coffee shop will think the same. Okay?"

Mateo's fists clenched, but he nodded.

I let out my breath and left Mateo on the sidewalk, pushing into Drip with a purpose.

I scanned the tables and didn't spy a shock of red hair or hear Juana's twitter of a laugh.

Tripping my way to the counter, I addressed Val's coworker. "Hey," I said, cutting in line to the general grumble of the customers who were waiting. "Sorry. But have you seen a tall guy with red hair and a really pretty girl with him? She has brown skin and golden-brown hair."

The guy raised an eyebrow. "Yeah. They were here."

I didn't know whether to curse or be relieved.

"He had a water, and she had a maple latte."

"When?"

"About ten minutes ago."

I left without saying thanks, slamming out the door. Mateo was not on the sidewalk where I'd left him, so I headed for the side parking lot. I found the car in a space and Mateo leaning against it.

"They were here ten minutes ago," I said. "But they left."

"Where would they go?" Mateo's voice was guttural.

"I don't know." I squeezed my eyes shut. "The glimpse was a meadow or a clearing, I think. Is there anything around here like that? In the middle of town?"

Mateo shook his head. "I don't—" His voice cut out as he doubled over, clutching his stomach.

"Whoa! What? What's happening?" I ran to his side, my hands hovering over his trembling form. "Mateo?"

"She's in trouble," he gritted out.

"Can you tell where?"

He shook. "Nearby."

Where the fuck was there a grassy open space nearby surrounded by trees? That had to be some kind of meadow, right? Or a clearing. Maybe a field.

A field. Oh shit, a *field*!

"The old pool playground," I breathed. "The little kids' soccer field. That's why Juana's palm had white on it in the vision. From the lines on the field. It's not in a forest, but there is a tree barrier."

I had barely finished my sentence when Mateo was off like a shot. He ran with an inhuman burst of speed, and there was no way I would ever catch up, but I took off after him. While running, grunting with each step on my painful ankle, I pulled my phone from my pocket and hit redial without looking.

"Cam?"

"Gemma! The glimpse is happening now!"

"Now! But it's not—"

"I know. But it's happening. The weather. The moon. Mateo's bare feet."

"What?"

I shook my head. My jacket flapped behind me. A chill breeze blew across the back of my neck, and my hair stood on end. "The old pool park. Meet us there. Tell the others."

"On my way, partner."

I hung up, trusting in Gemma.

The park was not that far from the coffee shop, but I was not in the best physical shape, as I had determined the other night. And Mateo had paranormal abilities. I was never going to catch up to him, but I pushed myself, my shoes slapping against the sidewalk. Despite how hard I ran, in the back of my mind I knew I would arrive too late to stop whatever had happened to Juana.

Mateo would find her first; his bare feet would sink in the mud, the wet grass would tickle his ankles, and he'd find the weapon. He'd pick it up and approach an already attacked Juana as she begged for help, covered in blood, her hand slipping in the paint used to line the soccer field, while the moon broke through the scattered clouds to bathe everything in watery light.

I wasn't prepared for this. Alma had said to prepare for the future, and I *hadn't*. Ugh. I had spent so much time worrying over who and where, I hadn't thought about what to do once it actually happened.

The park lights were out when I approached, which was why the glimpse had been dark—one of the reasons I had believed it had taken place somewhere out of town, and more evidence of how I'd only seen a small piece of the puzzle. I hopped over the low closed gate that blocked the parking lot after dusk, and ran down the winding path that led to the playground and covered pool. The last time I'd been there had been with Al, tucked away by the old clubhouse, crying and clutching my knees because of what I was about to witness.

My pulse pounded. My skin was slick with sweat and drizzle. My clothes were damp and cold, and despite my physical exertion, I shivered down to my toes as I spied the outline of a figure in the distance standing in the field.

Mateo.

He took a slow step, and my heart stopped when I saw movement in the grass. Oh no. It was happening. I kept running until I skidded to a halt right behind Mateo.

The smells of copper and sulfur were dense in the air. And when I stepped forward, it was right into a puddle of swamp mud.

"Please," Juana whispered as she crawled backward.

Then she fell, her body limp and unmoving.

Mateo was frozen in fear, but I rushed toward her despite nausea crawling up my gullet and every part of my brain screaming at me to run. I fell to my knees beside her. Just as in the glimpse, she was covered in blood, her blouse and jeans slashed. She was on her side, and I rolled her body to her back, careful not to worsen her wounds or accidentally brush her skin with mine, not wanting to risk the stress on my psychic blocks. I tried to remember the first aid we'd learned in freshman PE. I needed to help in some way—in any way— but I was completely overwhelmed with panic.

Her eyes were open. There were wounds across her body, and an especially deep gash across her palm. And her chest was still. . . . No, wait. . . . I leaned in, tilted my head to the side, my cheek by her mouth. The faintest flutter of breath caressed my skin, and I could've sobbed.

She wasn't dead. Yet.

"Mateo," I yelled. "Tell me what to do. Tell me how to help her!"

But he didn't respond. I turned back to Juana. She was still breathing. Okay. What should I do? Call for help. Yes. I needed to call for help.

"Cam!"

I jumped. That wasn't Mateo's voice.

"Gemma?"

Gemma ran over from between the trees, followed by Kaci. Gemma had a bag looped over her shoulder, and she dropped to Juana's side, ripping open the zipper. She yanked out a package of damp cloths.

"Here! Put these on her wounds."

"What?"

She slapped one down over the gash on Juana's stomach and then stretched another over her leg.

"Do it, Cam!"

Her sharp tone startled me into movement. I wrapped one around Juana's palm and then another over a slash in her shoulder.

"What are we doing?"

"Silver is poison to werewolves," Gemma explained as she worked. "That's why these wounds aren't healing like they should for a werewolf so close to the full moon. These," she said, shaking a cloth, "are soaked in a solution specifically made to draw out the poison. They've also been enchanted with a healing spell developed by Al's coven to help."

Juana gurgled and shuddered as we jostled her body.

"Gemma," I said, my throat tight. "She's barely breathing."

"I know!" she snapped. "But at least she *is* breathing. Okay. And chest compressions would only push the silver around more in her body. We have to draw it out first."

I wrapped the last one around a wound in her leg as Gemma removed a bottle from the bag. She took a breath and sprinkled a dusting of something over Juana's body.

"The last ingredient," she said.

Once the bottle was empty, we didn't have to wait long. The bandages glowed a soothing blue. Juana gasped. I fell backward in surprise and scrambled away, staggering to my feet.

Juana's back arched, and her body jerked painfully, but at least she was breathing easier.

Sirens pierced the night air. Peering through the tree barrier, I could see flashes on the other side of the road and heard paramedics trudging through the small copse of trees, Kaci leading them with the flashlight on her phone.

I stumbled out of their way as the paramedics loaded Juana onto the stretcher, taking her vitals and talking to each other in medical jargon. Gemma hovered close by, spouting facts about werewolf healing abilities and following them as they took Juana to the ambulance.

"Mateo!" Gemma called from the tree line. "Come on! You need to ride in the ambulance!"

That seemed to shake Mateo from his fear-induced stupor. He glanced at me and Kaci.

"Go. We'll be fine," Kaci assured us.

He clutched the knife in his clawed hand, then ran to catch up. Gemma wrapped the knife in a plastic bag and handed it off to the paramedics as they climbed into the ambulance together.

As soon as it peeled off into the night, I collapsed into a heap on the field. I buried my face in my gloved hands as Kaci folded down beside me.

"Cam?" she asked. "Are you okay?"

I scrubbed my palms over my face. "I don't know."

She wrapped her fingers around my forearm and squeezed gently. "It's over. You did it."

"I didn't do anything," I said into my cupped hands. My breath warmed the small space, bringing feeling back to my nose and cheeks, which were numb from the rain and the chill.

"You did. You brought us all together. And between us all, we were able to help. If Mateo had been here by himself, it would've been a different outcome."

"Why didn't he—"

"You know 'fight, flight, or freeze'?" Kaci asked. "He's a freeze. He always has been."

I dropped my hands. The sky spat cold drops of water onto my shoulders and hair. The clouds obscured the moon, and I stared at the spot where Mateo had been frozen, unable to proceed, only to watch. If he had been alone . . .

"We couldn't alter the glimpse, but we could be prepared for it," I said, paraphrasing what Alma had told me.

"And we were."

I wiped a mixture of rain and tears from my face with my sleeves. "I made a lot of mistakes."

"Yes," she said. "But it was your first time dealing with an ability you didn't even know you had. All our first times, actually. So yes, we messed up. But we'll do better next time."

I raised an eyebrow. "Next time?" Oh crap. I couldn't even fathom the next time, but Kaci was already looking to the future. She was right, though. I couldn't deny that I would use my clairvoyance again, and that there might be another glimpse to prepare for. And the thing was, I didn't mind that thought at all, especially if it meant my friends would tag along with me. I would just be more prepared.

"I can't believe I'm going to say this, but I don't think I would mind a next time. As long as it involves, like, kittens and not, you know, attempted murder."

Kaci laughed. "I'll be there. So will Mateo and Gemma and Al."

I straightened from my slump. "Where is Al, anyway?"

"They said they were researching. They didn't say what, but they said it was important and that they would check in."

What was more important than the glimpse? That didn't make sense. But I trusted Al.

Kaci hummed. "Come on, let's go to the hospital and see how Juana is." She pulled out her phone. "I'll call us a ride."

The chill had set in, and I was cold down to my bones, especially my legs, which were damp from the grass. I heaved to my feet, stretched my hands above my head, and groaned as my muscles strained and my joints popped.

There was a moan in response.

Gulping, I dropped my arms. "Did you hear that?" I whispered to Kaci.

Another groan, followed by a rustling in the bushes.

What the hell? I motioned for Kaci to follow me, and together we crept toward the sound. A grunt, followed by a curse, came from a clump of bushes on the tree line. Whatever it was, I hoped it wasn't more traumatic than what had just occurred.

Cautiously I peered into the bracken. My breath caught. There was a body sprawled on the ground beneath the branches and leaves. A leg twitched, and the person rolled and sat up, his bright red hair unmistakable.

I couldn't believe it. "Reese?"

32

TRIED TO STOP THEM," HE SAID, LOOKING UP AT KACI AND ME with wide eyes. He had a cut on his forehead near his temple that trickled blood and a large bruise forming on the right side of his face. "You have to believe me."

I reached down and took Reese's hand in my gloved one and helped him to his feet. I steadied him as he stepped out of the bush. Once he was clear, more evidence of a fight was revealed—his tattered shirt; twigs, leaves, and mud clinging to his clothes; and scratches over his hands and arms.

He spun around, his gaze fetching about in the darkness. "Where's Juana?"

"The hospital," Kaci said gently.

Reese raised the heel of his hand to his head. He staggered, and Kaci and I caught him on either side.

"And that's where we're taking you. You probably have a concussion."

Reese squeezed his eyes shut. A tear cut a track through the dirt and blood on his face. "I tried to stop them."

"We believe you," I said. "But stop who? Who did this?"

He shook his head, wincing as he did so. "I don't know. But they weren't sprites, and I don't think they were wolves or witches or faeries. They were human."

Kaci gasped. "Are you sure?"

"No. I don't know." His voice was thick with tears and stress. The gash on his head leaked sluggishly. We needed to get him somewhere safe, especially if those people might come back again. That was a notion I'd not even considered.

"Can you tell us what happened?" I asked as Kaci and I supported Reese to the road, walking through the line of trees to the curb on the other side.

He licked his lips. "I wanted to talk with Juana. I wanted her to know that I didn't have anything to do with Mia, and maybe she'd be able to tell Mateo and you, so I could . . ." He swallowed. "Come back."

Guilt pressed heavily on my shoulders, and it felt a lot like Reese's limp arm.

"I know I wasn't the greatest to be around, but I really liked you guys."

"We like you, too," Kaci said.

Reese smiled, but it was unfocused and hazy. "When Gemma told me that you had figured out it was Mateo who'd triggered the glimpse, I took my chances and reached out to Juana."

We took a wrong step, and Reese's knees buckled. I grunted, holding him up the best I could until he could gain his footing. He was deceptively heavy for someone so tall and slim. But finally we made it to the side of the road. Between Kaci and me, we eased Reese down to the curb as we waited for the car.

"And you met at the coffee shop," I said, prodding Reese to continue.

"Yeah. We talked for a while. When we left, there were people waiting outside for us."

I sat down heavily next to Reese, and he leaned on my shoulder. "People? Who?"

"I don't know. But when Juana and I started walking to our cars, they followed. So we ran, and they ran after us."

Kaci's brow furrowed. "What did they want?"

"I have no idea." He sighed. "We tried to stop them with our powers, but they bounced right off them, like they were impervious to both sprite gifts and Juana's werewolf abilities. Which they shouldn't have been, because they were human. I know they were."

"How is that possible?" I asked.

Kaci cocked her head to the side. "The only thing I can think of is a spell, maybe. But that would mean they were witches."

"No, they weren't."

"How do you know?" I asked, wringing my hands. I wouldn't believe Al's coven could do such a thing, but that didn't mean there weren't other witches who would. But why attack Juana? And for what purpose?

Reese gestured with his hands, his movements uncoordinated. "Because they acted surprised when our powers didn't affect them, like they weren't sure that whatever they had was going to work. But they knew Juana was a werewolf. They said it several times."

"Who would attack a werewolf when her powers would be increasing," I muttered, remembering Gemma's reasoning for why the attack would happen *after* the harvest moon, "other than someone who didn't know all the lore?"

Reese rubbed a hand across his face, smearing blood. "Right. I don't think they were after me, because once they realized I was a sprite, they focused their attention on Juana. They were after *her.*" His throat bobbed. "I tried to stop them, but they knocked me out." He bent his head and stifled a sob with his hand, his shoulders shaking.

Kaci held up her phone, the screen bright in the dark. "The car is almost here."

Together we all stood, Reese hanging between us.

"Hey, Reese," I said.

He turned to look at me, his green eyes watery and unfocused. "Yeah?"

"This wasn't your fault, okay? You did what you could to protect yourself and Juana. And I never got a chance to thank you. Thanks for saving Al and Gemma and Kaci that day. You knew that as soon as you did, your swamp powers would be revealed and we would think you were the perpetrator in the glimpse. But you did it anyway. And I'm sorry that any of us ever thought it was you."

Reese smiled. He jostled me with his arm. "You're welcome. And maybe it's the head wound, but you're forgiven."

"I'm glad you're on our side," Kaci said. "Even if you provoke Mateo."

"I'm glad to be here, Kaci. Especially if it means I get to provoke Mateo."

She laughed, bright and airy, a stark contrast to the heavy and damp night.

The driver of the car service almost didn't let us in, since we were all soaked and Reese was covered in mud and blood, but we promised a hefty tip and he allowed us inside. He blasted the heat, for which we were grateful, and within a few minutes we were in front of the emergency department.

During the ride, Kaci texted Gemma and Mateo to let them know we were on our way. Once we arrived, the two of us managed to extract Reese from the car onto the sidewalk.

"Whoa," Gemma said, meeting us and instantly wrapping her arms around Reese's waist. "What happened?"

"A lot. Come on, let's get him inside. He needs to be seen."

We walked toward the entrance, and I shivered, remembering how Kaci would see this place if she didn't have her psychic blocks engaged. I glanced at her, but she appeared unbothered, more concerned for Reese than anything.

"Juana is going to be okay," Gemma said, talking quickly. "Her wounds are already healing. She hasn't woken up yet, but Mateo's parents are here, and they're with her."

Palpable relief washed through me. "That's great. Now all we have to do is get Reese checked out, and I'll call this night a win. I mean, kind of, but—"

Before we could enter the automatic doors, a large black bird dove down in front of us and perched on the lid of a trash receptacle. She released a loud caw, followed by an annoyed croak.

"What the hell is that?" Reese staggered backward, and it took all three of us to keep him from falling to the asphalt.

"It's Lenore. She's Al's familiar. It's okay."

Reese clutched a hand to his chest. "She's massive."

"She's beautiful," Gemma said. "A real raven."

I untangled my hand from the remnants of Reese's shirt and walked toward Lenore. "She's harmless, but I don't know what she's doing here." I ran my fingers over her head and down her back. She stuck out her leg, a small scroll curled inside the messenger tube. I fished out the note and unfurled it between my fingers.

ANSWER YOUR PHONE!

Oh.

I pulled my phone out from my back pocket and winced. Al had called me several times. Not even "several"; it was more like "a fuck ton." Nine missed calls and fifteen messages.

"Did anyone call Al and update them?" I asked the group.

They exchanged guilty glances, then shook their heads.

"Yikes. Okay. Um, you guys go inside. I'm going to stay out here and call them. I'll be in shortly."

I petted Lenore one more time, and she flew off.

The others shuffled through the emergency department doors, and I stepped to the side, under the awning but far enough that I wouldn't block anyone coming in or out.

I called Al and pressed the phone to my ear.

It rang once.

"Cam!"

"Hey, so sorry. Lots going on, but I must say, you are getting really great at that location spell, for Lenore to find me when—"

"Shut up!" they yelled. "Shut up, Cam, and *listen*."

Al had a history of being mercurial, but hearing them freaked out made me pause. Goosebumps rose on my arms, and a shudder worked itself down my spine.

"Okay," I said, my voice hoarse and soft.

"I found out why your parents were forced to leave the coven house last night."

My throat was tight. "Didn't they just embarrass themselves? Like, offend the coven in some way?"

"No. They were thrown out because they approached our elders with a spell. A very illegal and very cruel spell."

That didn't make sense. My parents were wary of all things paranormal. They wouldn't have a spell, much less one that was dangerous. "What? Are you sure?"

People streamed in and out of the emergency room entrance, casting me wary glances as they did so. I looked down, saw the smatters of Juana's and Reese's blood on my shirt, and winced. Yikes.

I moved away from the hospital doors and walked toward the parking lot.

Al still talked in my ear. "I'm certain! We didn't give them the spell. I have no idea where they found it, but it's awful! And they have a copy of it in their possession."

"Okay." The asphalt glittered with raindrops under the blue and red flashing lights of an incoming ambulance, the siren drowning out all noise, making Al difficult to hear. "What?" I said as I strode quickly away from the noise. "I can't hear you."

"Cam, are you there?"

"Yes. There's an ambulance, and . . ." I trailed off, frustrated. I jogged farther into the lot and paused under a towering streetlight. "What was that?"

"... can't believe ... main ingredient ..."

"What?" I asked, plugging my other ear with my finger. "What did you say?"

"I said the main ingredient is werewolf blood!"

I stumbled in shock over a concrete barrier, almost tripping, but managed to right myself. "What?" The word came out as a breathy whisper, which was all I could muster. "I don't understand. What are you implying?"

"Cam, it's very possible that your parents were behind the attack on Juana to obtain her blood for that spell."

What? They wouldn't. It was unreal to even think they could. That didn't even make sense. My parents hated magic, and they'd never resort to using it. They were wary of the paranormal, but they weren't killers.

"Cam?" Al said. "Did you hear me?"

"Yeah, I did. But that can't be true."

"It *can*. With those ingredients and with the nature of that spell, I think you may be in danger. Are you with the others?"

I gulped. "Yeah, we're at the hospital."

"Okay. Stay there. I'm on my way."

I hung up the phone. My pulse pounded in my ears. My thoughts were muddled from ebbing adrenaline and total disbelief. Could my parents have done this? Was this because I'd wanted to date Mateo? Was it because of *me*? What had Al meant by "the nature of that spell"? What did it even do? I should've asked before I hung up, but I wasn't going to call Al back. I wasn't going to involve them in what I had to do, because I couldn't risk Al or the rest of the group if my parents really were that dangerous.

I shivered in the cold, rubbing my arms to quell the goosebumps. I needed answers. I needed to confront them. I needed to know *why*.

I didn't hesitate when I brought up the contact for Faery Pizza Delivery. I dialed the number. It went to voicemail after a few rings.

"Hey, it's me. Look. Mom and Dad have done something awful. Maybe. I'm not sure. But I'm going to confront them. I just wanted you to know. Okay. Bye."

I took a steadying breath, cast one last glance at the hospital, and then walked out of the parking lot.

33

THE RIDE I'D ORDERED DROPPED ME OFF IN FRONT OF THE house, and I didn't hesitate to run up the steps and burst through the door. During the drive over, I'd worked myself up into a righteous anger over the events of the night. I'd been plagued by that vision for *weeks*, and it was possibly all because of my parents?

I stomped from the foyer into the family room to find my mom and dad lounging on the couch, watching a movie.

"Cam," my mom said, and stood, her eyes wide. "You're home earlier than I expected." She was in her wine-mom outfit, her hair pulled back, yoga pants and T-shirt on, bare feet on the plush carpet of the living room. She didn't look like someone who had assaulted a werewolf.

My dad stood as well, and he too was dressed down in a sweatshirt and sweatpants. Not a speck of swamp on him.

I paused. Maybe Al had been wrong. Maybe it was someone else who had needed a spell.

"What's going on? What are you two doing?"

My mom cocked her head to the side, then gestured toward the television. "We're watching a movie before bed. Why?"

I licked my dry lips. "Is that all?"

"Should we be doing something else?" she asked.

"Popcorn," my dad said, wagging his finger at me. "You're right, Cam. I forgot the popcorn."

I rocked back on my heels, squinting at them both. "No. I wasn't thinking about popcorn."

"Oh. Then I have no idea what you mean."

Except that I was covered in blood and sweat and swamp mud, my shirt crusty from the combination. And any normal parent would've noticed that first, would've made sure I was okay. Unless they knew where the blood had come from. Unless they already knew what I had been up to that night. I tugged on my shirt hem with my mud-encrusted fingers, and I saw the realization of her mistake spread over my mom's face.

My blood went cold. "What have you two done?" I rasped.

"Us?" my mom said, feigning surprise. "We haven't done any-thing, Cam."

We both knew it was a lie.

My dad pulled out his phone and tapped away on the screen, a frown on his face, but didn't respond.

"Don't lie to me." My hands balled into fists at my sides. I was grimy from my hair to my feet. I was mentally and physically exhausted. I had seen two of my friends hurt. I was not going to be played with. "I know about the spell and the werewolf blood."

My mom's confused expression morphed into knowing disdain right before my eyes, confirming every fear that had percolated in my brain since Al's phone call. Her shoulders and back straight-ened, and she immediately transformed from comfy Sunday-night mom into her hardened, no-nonsense self.

"That's not your concern."

I remembered Edith's words. *Head up. Make eye contact. Be confident.* "It *is* my concern! What have you done? Have you lost your minds?"

My dad's gaze snapped up from his phone. "Watch your tone."

"I don't believe this!" I threw up my hands. My heart thundered in terror, but I was more aghast than anything. "Whatever you're planning, you can't do it."

"Oh, Cam. I wish that were true." My mom steepled her fingers. "But we've been left with little choice."

My throat tightened. My whole body ached. The burning sting of tears gathered behind my eyes. "Is this about me? About being clairvoyant?"

My mom hummed but didn't answer.

"I know you didn't want me to post the second and third glimpses, but I chose to do it. I chose to lean into this ability, because for once I was special. I could help people. And I made friends. That's what you wanted me to do, right? Make friends this year? I did, and they've helped me understand myself. I'm not giving them up. I'm not giving up on me." Al's insistence on a themed school year, about embracing our authentic selves, came true in that moment. "I'm a psychic. I'm a clairvoyant. And I'm not scared of being one. I'm not ashamed of it either."

My dad heaved a sigh. My mom put her hands on her hips and rolled her eyes toward the ceiling.

"Well, you've made our choice for us, then," she said, her gaze sad. "The spell was originally for Aiden."

I flinched. "Aiden?"

"To cure him of the love-magic that faery obviously cast on him," my dad said, pocketing his phone. "We know you've talked to him."

I took a step back and awkwardly crossed my arms. "I haven't—"

"We've been tracking your new phone." My dad left his post by the couch and joined my mom. "We know you went to the cottage."

Oh shit. I had to warn Aiden. I had to text him. Oh no. What if I had accidentally lured him here and—?

"But now," my mom said, looping her arms through my dad's, "you've left us no choice but to start with you."

My blood ran cold.

The front door opened, and I whipped my head around, terrified it was Aiden walking into a trap, but it wasn't. Two people stepped in. One was covered in blood and held a vial.

I skittered backward, toward the kitchen and the side door, but it opened as well, and more people spilled in.

"It will be easier if you don't fight," my mom said.

I couldn't believe this was happening. But I was not going to go easily. I ran for the stairs.

The people by the front door lunged.

I danced out of the way of the first pair of hands, silently congratulated myself, then promptly slipped on the carpet runner. My left foot slid completely out from under me, and I fell to my knees. My whole body jarred, and my phone skittered out of my hand. Any chance of escape evaporated as multiple people grabbed me and pinned me to the ground. I immediately concentrated on my psychic barriers, locking them in place, not wanting to accidentally glimpse.

I fought. I squirmed. I yelled for help, but no one could hear me. My shoulders were pushed down, my face smooshed into the floor. My feet were bound. A gag was shoved in my mouth, and a hood yanked over my head, as my arms were secured behind me.

"Quit struggling," one of them grunted. "It'll be fine."

Fine? This was the furthest from fine I'd ever been. I wanted to laugh. I was already crying, tears streaming from the corners of my eyes. I was going to be sick.

"Hold him still," said another voice. "I have something to help."

I did the best I could to struggle, but I was truly stuck. I felt a sharp pinprick, followed by a cool wash of liquid into my arm, and a few seconds later I went limp.

34

I WOKE UP IN A CHAIR.

I blinked in the darkness, and it took a moment for my sluggish brain to realize that the hood was still over my head. My hands were bound behind my back, and my ankles were tied to the chair legs. The gag was also still in my mouth; my lips were dry and cracked around the saliva-soaked fabric.

I had no idea how long I'd been out. I only knew what my body told me, which was that I had an awful headache, and that my limbs and torso were bruised and aching from the events of the night.

I groaned as I moved, spikes of pain driving into my temples as I tilted my head backward and rested it on the high slats of the chair.

"He's coming to."

"Take off the blindfold."

Suddenly I could see light as the hood was ripped from my head; the area was bathed in the soft glow of candles. They were lit everywhere, casting flickering shadows.

Everything around me was fuzzy and blurred, but I was able to determine that I was somewhere with a vaulted ceiling. The space was rectangular, built from brick and about the size of a dining room. There was a small table in the center, and a runner led from the door to the foot of the chair I was positioned in, close to the opposite wall. A large barrel sat off to the side, and shelves were built into the walls on the longer sides. Wait, not shelves. Wine racks. I was beneath our house in the wine cellar.

"Remove the gag."

I flinched as a person stepped forward and tugged the gross rag from my mouth.

"Mom?" I rasped, looking around.

She stepped out of the shadows into the ring of candlelight. When she met my gaze, her expression was soft and affectionate, not the stern and judgmental one I was accustomed to.

"Mom," I said, brow furrowed. "I don't know what you're planning, but please don't do it." I struggled against the restraints as I pleaded with her, the chair rocking dangerously as I tried to yank free. "It's not too late to help me get out of here. I think these other people want to hurt me." My voice cracked at the end.

"Oh no, baby," she said, shaking her head. "We don't want to hurt you. I promise."

She padded carefully forward, approaching me until she was only a few feet away. "Your father and I only want to help you."

A cold sweat broke over my body.

My dad moved into the light. "Your mother is right, son. We only want what's best for you."

"Please don't!"

Panic clogged in my throat. I twisted my wrists against the binding, the rope cutting into my skin, and a whimper spilled through my clenched teeth.

"Don't hurt yourself now," my dad said. "You'll be released soon."

"When?"

"When the spell is completed." My mom laced her fingers together. "We're just waiting on one more ingredient."

The spell. I hadn't given Al the chance to tell me exactly what the spell was, other than that it was dangerous.

"We weren't planning on doing this tonight, but"—she shrugged—"you've given us little choice. I mean, dating a werewolf. Proclaiming you're a clairvoyant." She shook her head in amused disbelief.

"What will it do?" I asked, my voice a low, trembling croak.

"It will remove the curse," my mom said proudly. "We've been researching for months and months. The larger covens refused to help us, but we finally found the correct spell through an exiled witch." She clucked her tongue and placed her hands on her hips. "A few of the ingredients have been very difficult to obtain. But no matter—we have what we need, and we'll perform it to cleanse the curse from you, and everything will go back to normal."

My head spun. My stomach revolted, and I was going to be sick all over the expensive tile. "Months?"

"Well before you and this seer mess happened," my dad said.

"I prefer 'clairvoyant,'" I said, rote, but my dad continued speaking over me.

"You've given us no choice but to try and expunge your affliction first, and then we'll rescue Aiden from that faery's love curse."

My mom gazed lovingly at my dad and looped her arm with his. "And we can go back to being a normal, happy family."

Normal? Happy? Stripping me of my ability? And then "rescuing" Aiden? As if he were a captive? "What the fuck?"

"Language, Cam."

"My clairvoyance isn't a curse! You can't just cut it out of me." The conversation with Edith and Alma about where my ability originated rang in my ears. "That would be like removing my spirit! My soul!"

My mom frowned. "It's what needs to be done."

The coldness of her tone matched the stark and frigid atmosphere of the room, and real fear seeped into my bones. "How are you going to cast this spell, anyway? You're not witches; you can't perform magic. You—"

My dad sighed. "Cam, we've been members of an organization

for a long time now that works to combat the dangers of witches and werewolves and every kind of paranormal faction, and their influence on our children. We were only peripheral members, but when Aiden became ensnared and then you followed, we decided to become more involved. We have worked tirelessly to find this cure and its ingredients, and learn how to implement it."

Organization? Meetings? When? How? *What?* "Your farmer's market runs were anti-paranormal club meetings?"

"Oh, no, dear. We love farmer's markets. The meetings were after."

I reeled. "It's not a *cure*. Al found out about the spell, and they said it's highly illegal."

My mom scoffed. "I don't care what those witches told you. They refused to assist us. They refused to provide us with the ingredients we needed through their ethically sourced avenues. We had to procure them on our own."

My heart sank. "Werewolf's blood."

"It was one of the last elements we needed. It was a stroke of luck that you dropped that werewolf romance book, which confirmed the lore. And you and Mateo told us about the coffee shop your group of friends frequents. All we had to do was wait. We didn't expect the sprite to be there with a werewolf, as I know the Lopez family and the Sprite Alliance are in a tiff, but with the protection charms Al's family did provide"—my mom looped her thumb around the silver chain on her neck and lifted the pendant—"our group was able to acquire the blood."

"You nearly killed her!"

My mom shrugged. "Small price to pay to reunite our family."

The door to the cellar opened, and a person scurried in, a package in his hands. "I have it!" he said, bustling about the space. "I have the rowanberries."

"Excellent." My mom took the package from him and flipped open the lid. "Were they ethically sourced?" she asked with a giggle.

The man laughed. "Of course not."

"No matter. This should do nicely," she said, holding up the cluster of red berries. "Are we all ready to begin?"

Movement beyond the circle of light where my mom and dad stood indicated there were more people in the wine cellar—obviously members of their group. About a dozen figures shuffled forward and watched in rapt awe as my mother began preparations.

"Lock the door, and hang the protection charm on the handle," my dad said, addressing the man who had just come in. "That way we won't be interrupted."

"Wait," I said, still struggling in my seat. "Stop, please. *Think*. I have the ability to see the future. I could glimpse right now for each of you. I could tell you what's coming next, maybe even sports scores and lottery numbers. Isn't that a gift worth keeping? Especially if I ally with you? Just with humans?"

I was not above bribery. I wasn't above anything at this point.

I didn't want to lose my friends or the community I had discovered. I didn't want to lose Aiden again now that I had found him. I couldn't lose the people who had accepted me, especially not when confronted with the reality of my parents' beliefs.

My mom sighed. "Remember how I said you could never know if your new friends liked you for you or for what you could do for them? Once we remove the curse, then you'll know for certain. And that question won't plague you for the rest of your life."

"Shouldn't I have a choice?" I demanded. I hadn't been completely on board with being a clairvoyant from the beginning because I hadn't been certain if it was worth the amount of grief I'd gone through since the first glimpse. But I had made my choice. I chose to be me. To be clairvoyant. That was who I was. That was the community I was part of, the one that had accepted me. "I don't want this."

"You can choose to be a willing participant," my dad said as my mom started laying out the ingredients for the spell on the table. "Or you can be forced."

"The parchment says it's easier if you cooperate." My mom unrolled a scroll and positioned candles at the edges, then ran her finger over the writing. She hummed as she dumped ingredients into a mixing bowl from the kitchen—a measuring cup of red liquid that was probably Juana's blood, the rowanberries, a handful of a pungent herb, and two vials of mystery liquids, one purple and one green. She combined them with a wire whisk, the metallic swish the only sound in the room.

"Please," I said, straining against the bonds holding me to the chair. "Please. Let me go. I'm scared. I don't want to do this." I racked my brain for any other angle I could use. "I'll run away. You'll never have to see me again. You can forget I ever existed."

My mom spun from where she'd been bent over the bowl, her features twisted. "We don't want you to leave."

"No, you have it all wrong, Cam. We love you," my dad said from where he was observing on the sidelines.

My mom went back to the parchment. "We just want you to be normal."

Fresh tears sprang into my eyes. Her words hurt more than the rope biting into my skin, more than any slap or punch could ever have. I hunched down in the seat, trying to shield myself from her and from my dad, from their wrong ideas and convictions, from the stabbing pain etching itself into my skin and my soul.

I wasn't escaping. Nothing I said would change their minds. And I was not strong enough to break free. An errant thought entered my mind, of how it would be easier not to have to worry about glimpses, or which faction to ally with, or if I'd see another almost-murder when I touched someone's skin. But it was gone as soon as I thought about my friends.

I liked who I was, who I was becoming. I liked trying to be a good friend. Despite its trials, I liked being a clairvoyant, and I wanted to learn more, to do more, to master this skill and help people.

"Okay, all set. We need to draw this symbol on his skin with this mixture. Then we'll pour the rest around him in a ring on the floor and chant these words." My mom approached me, then frowned when she looked down at the liquid in the bowl, her nose scrunching in distaste. "I'm not touching this with my hands."

The group scrambled to find something, and after a few minutes, one of them handed my mom a mushroom-shaped cork.

"Oh! This will do." She dipped the small end into the mixture, her fingernails biting into the bulb at the top. The potion smelled like copper and dirt and vinegar. My dad pinched the fabric of my T-shirt and yanked it down, exposing my collarbones and the hollow of my throat.

I tried to wiggle away, but my dad grabbed me by the hair and wrenched my head back.

"Thank you, dear," my mom said, and then she painted the symbol on my skin, the champagne cork her paintbrush.

The mixture was frigid when splashed on my chest, and I shivered.

"Don't do this," I said one last time. "Please. Stop."

They ignored me. With a finishing dot in the center of my throat, she stepped back and admired her work. "There," she said, satisfied.

My dad assisted in pouring the remaining liquid in a ring around my chair. When the circle was completed, the concoction flashed an alarming red, as if activated.

My mom set the bowl down and clapped her hands. "It's working already. Come." She gestured to the others. "It's time to hold hands and start the chant."

I tilted my head back and closed my eyes. Breathing through my nose, I attempted to calm myself, but it didn't work. My chest heaved, my limbs trembled, and despite the ropes not budging an inch, I still strained against them. My tears hadn't stopped, and they rolled into my ears.

The chant began.

The words were unfamiliar, but as the group's voices swelled together in unison, the mixture on my body *burned*.

I yelped, my back arching, as the potion seeped into my skin and the sensation turned molten, traveling down into my core. It *hurt*.

A scream tore from my throat as the worst pain I'd ever felt crashed over me.

I thrashed in my bonds, desperate to get away, to find relief. Every nerve and synapse was alight with agony. It was as if I was being torn apart, as if a crucial essence of self was being excised from me in slow strips, a never-ending torture. The spell was taking the source of my psychic ability. My spirit, my *soul*.

My joints creaked; my muscles spasmed. Blood ran from my nose, sliding in thick rivulets over my lips and from my ears.

The chanting increased, became louder, stronger.

Sparks went off behind my eyes, and I pleaded for them to stop, for a reprieve, but they didn't listen, they didn't pause, not when blood gurgled in my throat, not when my bones seemed to snap, not when I cried out with grief and loss and anguish. Seconds bled into minutes, and I knew I would not be able to hold out for much longer, that I would give in and pass out.

With my teeth gritted and eyes squeezed shut, the back of my head dug into the slats of the chair as my spine bowed with pain.

I didn't know how I heard it over the sound of the voices and the grunts and screams from my own throat, but I did—a gentle rapping on the glass above me.

I forced my eyes open with a gasp. At the ground-level window several feet overhead stood a raven.

35

DON'T PASS OUT. *FIGHT IT. FIGHT THE SPELL. FIGHT THEM.*
Those phrases became an internal mantra. I recited them over and over in my head, hoping they'd give me the strength to survive for a while longer. I held on to the image of my psychic blocks—the drawbridge pulled up, the portcullis lowered—and I added as many other things as I could in my mind. Huge padlocks, chains, a drawbar—whatever I could imagine to protect my power. But the vision wavered and trembled the longer the chanting continued. I gritted my teeth against the pain and squeezed my eyes shut grimly, determined to keep my spirit. Because it *was* me. I wouldn't allow myself to be diminished for the comfort of others.

Amid the chanting of voices came a rhythmic pounding at the door. Yells of my name followed, and the wood popped and crackled under an assault from the outside. The rapping of Lenore's beak increased from above as well, along with her disgruntled squawks and croaks.

The voices around me faltered, their concentration slipping, as the noise from both ends of the room intensified, and with another fissure appearing in the door, the spell broke.

The stabbing pain suddenly ceased, and I collapsed inward, my body a rag doll of relief. The only things holding me up were the ropes still around my torso. And even those had begun to give from the force of my struggles, the knots around my wrists loosened from the twisting of my limbs.

"What is going on?" one of the group members yelled.

My dad held up his hand. "There is a protection charm on the door. Whoever it is shouldn't be able to get through."

"Focus, people," my mom yelled. "We have to finish the spell."

The door fractured inward, a sliver opening wide enough for dim light to shine through. The protection charm that hung on the latch fell to the tile. It was a small round ornament about the size of a marble, and it rolled to the middle of the room, coming to rest on the tile.

A bloody laugh bubbled from between my lips.

Another thwack sounded against the door, and the hinges pulled away from the frame. The group tensed. They scuttled toward the back wall, my parents holding on to each other. Some of the other members grabbed wine bottles and implements from an old fire poker set stashed in the corner, brandishing them like weapons.

"We're fine," my mom said. "We all have our protection charms. Now get it together and chant!"

As soon as the words left her mouth, the glass above them shattered. Shards rained down as Lenore broke through. Screams erupted as she squeezed through the window, flew into the room in a magnificent display of her midnight plumage, and settled high on one of the wine racks, her long talons wrapping around the apex. She cawed, loud and long and terrifying.

"It's an omen," a member of the group murmured.

My mom scoffed. She crossed her arms. "It's Al Wilson's familiar. That raven won't hurt us."

"But whoever is on the other side of that door might," someone muttered.

Lenore opened her impressive wingspan and flapped twice.

A whoosh of magic flooded the room, and every candle was extinguished.

In the dark, the door finally gave way.

Screams rent the air, followed by a low growl and the sound of a scuffle, claws raking across tile, bottles and barrels crashing to the ground. The room erupted into chaos. I couldn't see a thing between the darkness, my waning consciousness, and the bodies in front of me. But with all attention directed elsewhere, I twisted my right wrist and managed to pull my hand free from the loosened ropes. I quickly worked on the binding around my other arm and was able to wriggle free. I went for the ones around my ankles but made poor progress with my clumsy fingers.

But the overhead light flashed on, and I winced, lurching upright in a way that made my stomach churn.

Everyone froze.

The first thing I noticed was the very large, brown shaggy wolf that prowled back and forth in the center of the room. His ears were laid flat, his teeth bared, and he let out a rumbling, menacing snarl that caused the hair on my arms to stand on end. The members of the club pressed themselves against the wine racks, while my dad retreated to stand behind my right shoulder, his gaze fixed on the wolf as it slowly stalked the room. Lazily swiping his massive paw, the wolf knocked the center table over with a thud, the mixing bowl and all the other ingredients smashing to the floor.

The next thing I noticed was that my mom standing behind the door, one hand on the light switch, the other gripping a steel fire poker, her knuckles white from the force.

The wolf didn't see her, his steely silver eyes focused on me.

"Mateo Lopez, stop where you are," my mom said, stepping out from behind the door, her weapon leveled at him. "This may not be silver, but I'm certain it will hurt."

"Maybe stop where *you* are, Mrs. Reynolds," Al said as they walked through the splintered wood, followed by Reese, both of them coming to stand behind Mateo. Their gazes flickered toward me. I had no idea how bad I looked, but seeing Al's mouth pinch and all the color leach from Reese's already pale face made me think it was bad.

"This doesn't have to get any more violent or messy than it already has," Al said. "We're just here for Cam, and then we'll leave."

"You're not taking my son."

Al wrinkled their nose. "We are."

My mom laughed. "How? We have protection charms your coven provided to us, so no matter what powers your wolf and sprite have, you can't hurt us."

Al sighed and shook their head. "You're right. My coven gave them to you. Which means my coven can take them back."

"You can't. You have no power. Everyone knows."

Al smiled. "Which is why I brought my sister, Amy, to help."

Amy peeked around the door frame and waved. "Hi, Cam!"

Al's smile dropped away, their eyebrows drew together, and the siblings both raised their hands and spoke a single word. It reverberated along the brick, several wine bottles bursting from the intensity of the magic. My ears rang. The charms lifted in the air, pulling free from their chains and clasps, until they all hovered in the center of the room, including the one from the floor, and with a twist of Al's wrist and a flick of their fingers, each charm bent and crumpled into dust. They fell to the tile in a series of pings, particles from their demise wafting in the air like smoke.

The whole room paused, took a breath, and then my mom launched herself from the corner and ran toward me. She took a swing at Mateo with the poker as she passed, Mateo letting out a yelp as he only partially dodged the blow.

"Reese!" Al yelled.

Reese's eyes glowed. Vegetation poured into the cellar from the broken window in a large green swath of vines and roots. Puddles of swamp water bubbled up from under the tile beneath the feet of the group members, ensnaring them in mud as they sank up to their ankles, the smell of sulfur permeating the room. The flora ensnared arms and legs, entwining people despite their attempts to run. If someone managed a few steps, Mateo snapped at them with his jaws and forced them back until everyone was either tangled in greenery or stuck knee-deep in muddy pockets of the floor.

The only ones left unscathed were my parents. My dad grabbed my upper arm and yanked me upward. My vision swam. Bile rose in my throat. My knees were weak and my legs uncoordinated, since my ankles were still tied to the chair.

"Cam," he grunted as I staggered. "Stand up."

I didn't even have the energy to tell him I couldn't. My mom grabbed my other side, and I hung limply between them.

"What have you done?" Al demanded.

"What your coven refused to do!"

"You used the spell?" Al's eyes widened. "Where did you find the werewolf blood?"

My mom sneered. "From a werewolf. Where else?"

"The use of that spell is *banned* in all covens. It's dangerous." They gestured to me. "You could have killed him."

"Ha! We didn't. We've removed the curse."

"It wasn't a curse!" Al yelled. "It's a gift. Cam is a gift!"

I lifted my head, my eyes watery with heartfelt gratitude as I looked toward my friends—all my friends. When had Kaci and Gemma gotten there? They stood in the doorway, shoulder to shoulder, Amy squeezed behind them. Kaci glared like a fierce kitten, and Gemma had her arms crossed over her torso and her feet spread wide as if daring anyone to try to flee.

Not that they could, with Reese's vegetation still growing and the swamp water bubbling and Mateo pacing the length of the room in his large wolf form.

My mother pointed at him. "I should've never allowed him to be friends with you," she spat, pointing at Al. "This is your fault. This is all your fault."

"It's not!" I said, gathering myself as best I could, my voice shaky but strong. "It's not them. It's me. I chose to post the second glimpse to Gemma's channel. I chose to verify the third glimpse. I wanted to, and I'm not sorry for it. I'm clairvoyant. And no spell can take that from me."

Gemma smirked. "Good job, partner." She lifted her chin. "Let him go."

"Or what?" my mom said, her fingernails digging into the flesh of my bicep through my shirt. "You'll post another video? Villainize us for trying to save our son from your wicked ways? You've already ruined our lives with three—what's another to add on top of that?"

"As if anyone would believe you, anyway," my dad added. "You have no proof that we've done anything wrong."

Gemma's eyebrows raised. "Oh!" she said with a wide smile. "You've been live this whole time."

My mom's mouth flapped open. "What?"

Gemma pointed to Lenore, still perched on top of the wine rack. "Bluetooth camera in Lenore's message tube." Then she held up her phone. "It's captured everything. And it's all live. I'm streaming as we speak."

"Everything you've said about the *illegal* spell and your unethical procurement of ingredients is on camera," Al said, crossing their arms. "Thanks for the evidence."

"And Cam's declaration of not wanting this done to him was icing on the assault cake." Gemma smiled.

"And I am an eyewitness to the attack on the werewolf you took the blood from. I can easily pick anyone out of a lineup." Reese's arms trembled, and sweat beaded along his forehead, soaking into the bloody butterfly bandage near his temple. "I think I hear the police sirens now," he said with a laugh.

Al's eyebrows rose in challenge.

My dad sighed, and my mom's shoulders slumped in defeat. They let me go. I flopped to the tile on my side. I couldn't move, as I was absolutely drained of energy and still somewhat attached to the chair. But I shouldn't have worried—a blast of magic from Al, and some vine work from Reese, and I was in Kaci's and Al's arms.

"How'd you find me?" I asked, voice weak, eyelids fluttering.

"I asked a ghost at the hospital," Kaci whispered. "I opened the portal just enough to talk and then closed it again."

Huh. That was what I'd witnessed in the glimpse.

"And between Mateo's heightened senses in his wolf form and the location spell I cast on Lenore, we figured out where you were," Al said, gripping the back of my shirt tightly.

"That's amazing," I slurred. "You're all amazing."

"We're just glad we got here," Al said, their brown eyes shining. "You're safe now."

Safe. I was safe. Reese and Al and Mateo and Kaci and Gemma wouldn't allow anything to happen to me. I was finally safe.

"I'm going to pass out," I told them, as if imparting a secret.

"It's okay, Cam," Reese said. "We've got this."

I nodded, then let go.

36

I **WOKE UP ON A COUCH.**

It was a far cry from the wine cellar doorway I had passed out in, and I was grateful. But I couldn't help but wonder how I'd gotten there.

Because this wasn't the couch in my home. Or former home. Huh. How was that going to work? Because I for sure was not going back. Not after what my parents had tried to do, and what they'd said, and what they believed. I shivered just thinking about it and clutched the quilt draped over my shoulders tightly in my hands.

This couch wasn't unfamiliar, though. It was the one in the coven house lounge. I'd recognize the crinkly sound of the leather, the weirdly patterned ceiling, and that fireplace on my right with the wooden mantelpiece filled with knickknacks anywhere.

I stretched my legs, then very much decided that was a bad idea when my muscles spasmed and my ankle twinged. A low groaning noise escaped my throat, and suddenly there was someone hovering over me, taking up the entirety of my vision.

"Cam!"

I squinted. "Aiden?"

"Holy shit. You're awake. How do you feel? Are you okay?"

"I'm tired," I said as I pushed myself up on my elbows. Aiden assisted me to a sitting position and propped pillows around me. I sank into the curve of the couch, the blanket tucked around my chest, and closed my eyes. I furrowed my brow. "How are you here?"

"I got your message and got here as quick as I could. Holy shit, Cam. I can't believe you confronted them."

"Well, it didn't really work in my favor."

"It was brave. I'm so proud of you."

"Did you see?"

He nodded. "I watched Gemma's stream. All of it. From the second Lenore arrived at the window and you were writhing in the chair. I saw what they did to you, and I'm so sorry." With my eyes closed, I couldn't read Aiden's expression, but I could hear the distress in his voice. "The grove has been keeping tabs on you, but I should've been here."

I cracked one eye open. "It's okay," I said. "I had my friends."

Aiden grasped my shoulder. "Yes. You did. And they'll be mad that I haven't told them you're awake, but let's get you cleaned up first."

"Wait." I licked my dry lips. "What happened to Mom and Dad?"

Aiden paused. His head dropped, and he released a gusty sigh. "They won't be coming home for a while. They're not only in trouble with law enforcement but also with the association of covens, the werewolf families, the entire Sprite Alliance, and the Psychic Guild."

I swallowed. Tears burned behind my eyes. "What's going to happen to me?"

"I don't know yet. But we'll figure it out. I promise."

I guess that was the best answer I was going to get at the moment, so I didn't press. With Aiden's help, I shambled to the nearby bathroom. A change of clothes was already laid out for me, as was a towel. The amount of blood I washed out of my hair and face and body in the shower was gruesome.

I shuddered at the sight.

Clutching the sink, I changed into a soft long-sleeved shirt and sweats, then brushed my teeth. Feeling slightly refreshed and smelling of flowery soap, I shuffled back to the lounge.

"You're awake!" Gemma yelled, jumping to her feet.

I flinched at the noise, to which Gemma looked immediately contrite.

They all waited for me. Gemma vibrated in place, bouncing on her heels. Reese sat on the arm of the couch, his bandage looking freshly changed and his complexion better than it had been when he was in the wine cellar. Kaci sat next to him on the cushions, her hands twisted in her lap. Mateo stood off to the side, back in human form, looking as if he too had showered and was wearing borrowed clothes.

Al was on the other side of the couch, gripping the back of it like their life depended on it.

"Hey," I said, my voice a croak.

That was all the permission Al needed. They ran around the furniture and wrapped their arms around me in a bruising hug. They buried their face in my shoulder and clutched me tight. Their shoulders were wracked with sobs, and I grabbed them back, pressing close.

"It's okay," I said. "I'm okay."

Al didn't have a chance to pull away before Gemma launched herself at my side and joined in crushing me. Kaci and Reese were next, both unabashedly swarming me and joining the group hug. I peered over Al's pile of curls to where Mateo held himself stiffly off to the side. I cocked my head and raised an eyebrow.

He read it as the invitation it was. He shyly joined until the group of us were a tangle of limbs.

"Okay," I said, after basking in their hugs for an indeterminable amount of time. "As awesome as this is, I need to sit down."

They all immediately broke apart, and Aiden pushed through

the crowd. He grabbed my hand and guided me to my jumble of pillows, his touch warm and comforting. I collapsed and looked up at
the others around me, all staring with wide, startled eyes.

"What?"

Gemma gulped. "He touched you."

"You didn't glimpse," Al said, frowning, clearly troubled.

"Are your barriers in place?" Kaci asked.

No, they were not. And when Aiden touched me, I didn't feel the
tug I'd always felt when falling into a glimpse. I felt nothing psychic
at all. The sorrow that suddenly engulfed me was crushing. I'd just
embraced my true self, and it was . . . gone.

I gulped. "No."

"Did . . . did the spell work?" Mateo asked. "Did they—"

"I don't know." I cut him off, frowning down at my hands. "But
I . . . I don't want to talk about it right now." I didn't think I could.
Especially if it meant losing them. All of them. I met each of their
gazes. "Okay?"

"Of course," Al murmured.

"Thanks. Um . . . tell me about you guys."

They erupted in commentary, Gemma giving most of the play-
by-play, but the others chiming in to offer insight, their voices
clamoring over one another. I leaned back and allowed the conversation to wash over me.

"Kaci talked to a ghost, and the ghost told us she overheard you
on your phone. And that you'd left the parking lot to confront your
parents."

"Mateo shifted into a full wolf. It was awesome. And then when
all was said and done, he shifted back. Like it was no problem at all."

"Well, I wanted to make sure Cam was okay, so it was easy with
that motivation. But anyway, Al's locating spell for Lenore is spec-
tacular. And did you see how those protection charms burst into
dust?"

"Me? Reese made swamp mud out of floor tile. Like, how?"

"Yeah, but Gemma came up with the idea of having Lenore wear a camera. It was genius."

"Al was so good in leading them to admit about the werewolf blood."

"Juana is recovering well, by the way, thanks to Gemma's quick thinking."

"Well, Reese fought them off. His presence definitely ensured that Juana's wounds weren't worse!"

"Cam admitting on camera that he didn't want the spell performed really helped too. And Cam, the fact that you were still coherent after what that spell did to you was amazing. I have no idea how you held on."

"Just stubborn, I guess," I said.

At some point, my eyes slid closed as they recounted the night.

"Cam?" Al asked after a few minutes.

"I'm listening," I said. "Keep talking."

So they did, and I drifted to sleep to the comforting noise of their combined voices.

37

I T WAS A STRUGGLE TO GET ANY PRIVATE TIME FOR THE NEXT few days. To say my brother and my group of friends hovered was an understatement. But it was nice to be enveloped in their care, which I definitely needed in order to cope with the aftermath. I was just terrified my friends would go away when they realized that I wasn't clairvoyant anymore. That I had been transformed back into normal Cam.

My parents had succeeded. At least I thought they had.

When I finally had a moment alone, I texted Kaci.

She came over right away.

We sat across from each other on the carpet of the coven house lounge. Fall had come and settled in. A small, cheery fire flickered in the fireplace, casting warmth and light into the room. Electric candles floated around the ceiling above us, while Lenore watched from a mounted bust above the entryway. Kaci's hair was in a ponytail, and she wore a flannel shirt and jeans. She pressed her knees into mine.

"I haven't glimpsed," I said softly. "Not since . . . that night. I want to try and see if I can."

Kaci held out her hand. "I've lowered my blocks."

I slid my palm into hers and closed my eyes. But there was nothing.

No familiar tug. No tunnel or blackout into another scene. Nothing.

I sighed and opened my eyes. I shook my head. "There's nothing," I said, tears tracking down my cheeks. "It's gone." I angrily dashed them away. "They did it. My parents managed to make me . . . *normal*. Like they wanted."

Kaci smiled sadly. "It'll be okay, Cam."

"How?" I demanded. "How? I have no ability. I have no way to help anyone. I have no reason to—"

She squeezed my hand, cutting me off. "You still have us."

I inhaled sharply. "How did you know I was worried about that?"

"I'm psychic," she said with a giggle. She leaned toward me, her smile wide and bright. "Don't worry. I promise you—your friends are here for you. And we're not leaving. Whether you are clairvoyant or not."

"Thank you."

She nodded. "You're welcome." She stood gracefully from the floor. "I brought cookies from Edith. She made them just for you."

"I bet it was only an excuse so she could steal a bunch of them. I didn't even get one at the Guild meeting."

"Alma says Edith is always thinking about cookies—especially chocolate chip ones."

Wait. Edith could see auras. Alma could read thoughts. They might be able to see what was wrong with me. They might have answers. They might be able to help. I scrambled to my feet. "Can we visit them?"

Kaci grinned and looked down at my pajamas. "Yes. But you might want to change first."

Edith and Alma were not surprised by our visit to their assisted living facility. In fact, they were waiting for me, despite both claiming they could not see the future like I used to be able to.

I sat with them in the welcome room around a small table. Kaci left, claiming she wanted to talk to the ghosts there, but I was sure she just wanted to give me privacy. A staff member brought a plate of cookies and three cups of juice.

My hand shook as I took a sip from the paper cup.

"Is it gone?" I asked softly.

Edith stared at me with her piercing blue eyes. She squinted and tilted her head, her puffy silver hair framing her face. "You have no aura," she said, her words breathy and awed.

"Is that bad?"

"*Everyone* has an aura."

My heart sank. That didn't sound good.

"Don't scare him, Edith."

For a quick, hopeful second, I thought Alma had read my mind, but she shook her head. "Your expression gave you away," she clarified. "But let's see. Give me your hand." She took my hand in hers, her forehead crinkling as she focused.

"Cam," she said after a few seconds of tense silence. "When the spell was cast, what did you do?"

I frowned, thinking back on that night. I had fought. That was what I had done. As hard as I could. "I tried to use my blocks. I focused on as many locks and defenses as I could imagine."

"Ah." She pursed her lips in concentration, then patted my hand and released me.

"Oh," Edith echoed.

"Yes. That explains it."

"It certainly does," Edith said with a nod. She grabbed a cookie and took a bite.

"What?" I said, looking between them. "What explains what?"

"You were under great distress, and you protected yourself the best you could."

"Which was by creating immensely strong psychic blocks."

"They must be, if Edith cannot read your aura and I cannot read your thoughts." Alma smiled. "You just need to let go," she said fondly. "Though I understand it might be difficult for you right now."

My mouth dropped open. "Are you saying I did this to myself?"

"She's saying," Edith said, waving her cookie around, "that once you feel safe enough, you'll allow the blocks down, and then you'll have access to your powers again."

"Do you want to try it now?" Alma asked. "You're safe with us, you know. And Kaci is nearby."

I was safe with them. I liked them both. And I did want to try. I nodded.

"Good. Close your eyes."

I closed my eyes. I inhaled and exhaled at Edith's command, and then with Alma's gentle presence on one side, and Edith's strong one at my other, I imagined the portcullis rising and the drawbridge falling. When Alma touched my wrist, there was the slightest pull. Not the strong yanks I'd felt before. But it was there.

"I see your aura, Cam," Edith said.

I snapped my eyes open. "You can?"

"Yes. It's flickering, but it's there."

"That's a good sign," Alma said. "Don't force it."

"And don't overextend yourself."

"Give it time."

My eyes watered. I'd been crying a lot over the last few days while everything around me was a whirlwind, so I wasn't embarrassed when the tears dripped down my cheeks. "I will."

"Good," Edith said, handing me a cookie. I took it without question and bit into it. "I'm a little surprised, to be honest. When you visited us the first time, you were so unsure, but now you're confident. You've grown."

"He has," Alma said, sipping at her cup of juice. "And I imagine that touch telepathy will not be the limit for you. If you can create strong enough blocks to keep that spell out and your spirit intact, I can only imagine the depths of your abilities."

I spun my empty cup in my hands. "Really?"

"Yes."

That was interesting news and something I wanted to explore. Later, though. Much later. "Can I get through sophomore year first?"

"Of course."

Edith tapped her fingers against the table. "Anything else, young man? Or can we get back to our thrilling day of television watching?"

I bit my lower lip and nodded. "Yeah. If you had to choose which faction to ally with, who would you choose?"

"It depends on what I would want to do with my powers." She narrowed her eyes and studied me. "What do you want to do, Cam?"

I knew I couldn't change the future. But Alma was right that I could be prepared for it. I had so much to learn, but at the end of the day, I think what I wanted most was to be unafraid. I wanted to help those who needed it. I wanted to be normal Cam in a paranormal way. "I just want to be myself. I want to be happy. And I want to do good."

"Then be yourself, be happy, and do good," Edith said simply. "It's not always easy, but I think you're capable."

And that was a relief. I looked between both women. "Thank you, really. Thank you so much."

Edith winced at the gratitude, but Alma's expression turned soft. "You're welcome, Cam." She patted my hand. "Now, the serious stuff is out of the way. Can I interest you in a game of checkers?"

My first day back at school, I perched on the steps outside the main entrance and watched as Kaci talked with Dennis, standing beneath the large tree right next to the sign announcing CENTRAL SHADY

HALLOW HIGH SCHOOL, HOME OF THE SAINTS. Reese stood next to her, arms crossed in a menacing way, just in case.

Mateo sat next to me, his knee pressed to the outside of my thigh, his fingers tangled with mine.

"I wonder what they're discussing," I said as Kaci gestured to her side, and Dennis just looked so confused.

"She's explaining that his stepsister has a few things to tell him."

"Wow," I said, swiveling to look at him. Mateo had cut his brown hair recently, and it looked so good on him. I tugged on my own, my roots having grown in while I debated if I was going to dye it again. In the sunlight, Mateo's brown skin glowed, and his eyes reflected a bright amber. "I forget you have great hearing."

He smirked. "I know. A lot of people do. It's handy."

"Yeah, about that. You haven't told me what it was like to be able to shift into and out of a huge wolf form. How cool is that?"

Mateo's ears turned red. "I'm just happy that I was able to help you. I was really worried when we couldn't find you in the parking lot. I shifted without even thinking about whether I was going to be able to shift back."

I nudged him with my shoulder. "Thank you."

"I'm just glad you're okay."

"I'm getting there." I took a breath. "You know," I said, leaning into his side, "we never did get to go on that date. We should plan that."

"I was waiting until you were more settled."

I shrugged. "I think I'm as settled as I can be right now."

Al's moms had offered me a place to stay with them until Aiden finished his semester at the university in New Amsterdam and could transfer to the local college. It was nice staying with them in their spare room and having Al just down the hallway. We were closer than ever, and Amy was now a part of that too. It also helped that Amy had mad magic skills, and chores were a breeze. Al's moms were also really cool. They had always been kind to me, but I think they'd kept their distance because of my parents. Now they doted on me, and it was wonderful to be with a family that hugged one another, listened to one another, spent time together, and basically took care of one another.

Mateo squeezed my hand. "Okay. But no parks this time."

I laughed. "No parks. How about a movie?"

"Sounds great."

"And hey, since my psychic blocks are now literal fortresses, when you kiss my cheek, we don't have to worry about any sudden glimpses."

Mateo's smile widened. "Then I might try to kiss more than just your cheek."

I flushed. "Sounds like a plan."

Before the flirting could escalate any further, Kaci bounced over, followed by Reese. Her hair was in braids today, and her skirt flounced as she walked. She was in high spirits.

"How'd it go?" I asked.

"Great," she said, the apples of her cheeks pink. "Dennis didn't make fun of me, and he listened."

Reese cracked his knuckles. He puffed out his chest, which had CSHH CROSS-COUNTRY emblazoned across it. "Of course he listened. I was right there."

Mateo snorted. I refrained from rolling my eyes.

"What?" Reese asked, his voice cracking. "I totally would've used my swampiness if needed. You know I will now."

I couldn't help but laugh fondly. "Yes. You will. And that's amazing. I just wouldn't make it a practice to use it against other students."

Reese grumbled in acknowledgment and crossed his arms. "Noted," he mumbled.

"But thank you," Kaci said, touching Reese's bicep. "You were very helpful."

His whole face turned red as a tomato. His throat bobbed. "Really? Great. That's cool."

"Anyway," Kaci continued excitedly, "Zoe went on her way at the end."

"Zoe?" I racked my brain but for the life of me couldn't remember a Zoe. "Who is Zoe, exactly?"

Kaci giggled. "The ghost, silly. I helped her." She beamed.

"That's incredible, Kaci," Mateo said, hugging her. "I'm so proud of you."

I grinned. "You're awesome, Kaci."

She twirled in place. "I know!" Then she grabbed my hand and tugged me from my warm spot by Mateo. "Come on, Cam. I want to introduce you to the ghost in our math class."

"Wait!" Reese asked, jogging after us. "There's a ghost in your math class? I want to come!"

Val eyed me over the top of the wobbly tripod she'd set up with her phone positioned in the clip. Gemma sat beside me at a table in Drip, the interior brick wall our backdrop.

"Are we centered?" Gemma asked.

Val gripped the bottom of the phone. "I think so? You know I'm not good at this, Gemma."

Gemma rolled her eyes. "Just make sure we're both in frame. This is important, *Val.*"

Val stuck out her tongue. "Yeah, I think it's good. Ready when you two are."

Gemma poked me with her pink sparkly fingertip. "You good?"

"I guess?"

"What's wrong?"

I ran my finger through the wet ring of condensation my iced pumpkin spiced latte had left behind. "Do I really need to do this right now?"

Gemma blinked. "I guess not. But I thought you wanted to?"

I sighed. "Yeah. I mean, I do. But no?"

"Look, I know we've been around each other a lot the past few weeks, but I'm not fluent in Cam like Al is. Can you explain?"

I fidgeted on the stool. "I just—don't want to let anyone down. And I feel like I will if I don't have anything definitive to say yet."

Gemma's blue eyes were huge behind her glasses. "Cam, you've been through several traumatic events in a row. It's okay that you don't have answers. I think everyone will understand."

"You won't be upset?" I gestured to the camera. "This was all your work. It was your thing."

"Me?" Gemma squeaked. "No. Of course not. You've done so much for me already. I have friends, and I just need one more for—"

"Do not say 'paranormal bingo,'" Val shouted.

"Fine," she said with a whine. "But no worries, Cam. We're good. We can do whatever you want."

I took a breath. "Okay."

"Great. Ready now?"

"Yeah. Let's go."

Gemma pointed at Val. Val touched the phone screen, then gave us a thumbs-up.

"Hello, all. This is Gem-Jam with Situation Paranormal. With me today is Cam Reynolds, Shady Hallow's resident verified clairvoyant, and he has something to say."

"Hello," I said with an awkward wave. "I just want to thank the paranormal community for all their gifts and patience. It's been an overwhelming journey up to this point. And I've been working on getting settled after . . . well . . . after what you all watched on the livestream." I swallowed. "Anyway, I understand it's tradition for a verified clairvoyant to ally with a faction for several different reasons. But I talked with two wise ladies who asked me what I wanted to do with my power. Honestly, I just want to be myself and be happy and do good for the paranormal community. And right now I think the best way to do those things is to ally with myself and my friends.

Be a free agent, if you will. That might change in the future, but yeah, that's it for right now." I fiddled with the hem of my shirt. "Please send any inquiries to my advisor, Gem-Jam. Thanks."

Gemma stepped in and added a few more details. I was glad she was at my side. For a while during the whole mess I was scared of being the main character, when I should've realized I wasn't. I was merely part of an ensemble cast, and I couldn't have done it without them.

"Anything else to say, Cam?" Gemma prompted.

"Yeah. I would like to thank a few people who have helped me immensely over the past few weeks. Especially my best friend, Al, and their sister, Amy; Mateo, Kaci, Reese; and my paranormal guide, Gemma, along with her sister, Val. I owe them my life. And I'll be forever grateful to all of them."

Val made a cutting signal with her fingers. And after a second, Gemma regarded me with huge, brimming eyes. "Thank you," she breathed.

"No—thank *you*, partner."

This time I was prepared when she launched herself at me for a hug.

"You doing okay?" Al asked as they arranged the snacks on the party tray. "The real answer, not the fake one. Embracing our true selves, remember?"

I huffed a laugh. "Yeah. I'm good."

"Okay. Well, it's about to get rowdy. Remember that, when they all get here, you can always step away."

"I know." I swallowed. "Thank you, you know. For being my best friend."

They emptied a plastic container of cherry tomatoes onto the tray, which we both knew would only be eaten by Reese and Kaci.

"Best friend?" they scoffed. "I'm your ride or die."

"Same, you know. Ride or die. Forever."

Al smiled. They playfully smacked my arm. "Okay, enough mushy stuff. Cheer up, buttercup. It's game night, and best friend rules are suspended. I'm destroying you at Trouble."

"Oh, bring it on."

They laughed as they hefted the tray. "Grab the plates, clairvoyant."

We left the kitchen, Al with the tray and me with the plates. The pizza had already been laid out in the lounge on the low dining room table, and sodas were stacked on a folding card table by the wall. The doorbell rang, and Al crossed the lounge and opened the door.

Our friends streamed in happily, Gemma leading the group, followed by Kaci. Mateo and Reese entered next, deep in conversation as they crossed the threshold. They'd talked a lot of things out; Mateo had apologized for his misconceptions about Reese, and Reese had apologized for the fight in the hallway and his own prejudices. And while they weren't best friends, they had grown closer. I was glad that the tension between them had eased as they worked toward better understanding each other.

More people arrived, and the lounge grew livelier. I sat on the couch and drank it all in.

I basked in the noise of Reese and Mateo arguing over their pieces on the game board while Gemma read from the rule book. Kaci and Al compared nail colors, while Aiden and Juana microwaved more popcorn in the kitchen as they discussed the creepiest movies for the upcoming All Hallows season. Javi and Astra took control of the music, playing increasingly weird songs on the speakers while Danny and Val attempted to dance to them.

I relaxed on the couch cushions, a piece of pizza on my plate and a soda in my hand. Mateo flashed me a shy smile and a wink as he moved his piece on the board while Reese wasn't looking. I smothered a laugh.

The party continued well into the night, and it was chaotic and amazing as werewolves, witches, psychics, a sprite, humans, and even a faery mingled. It was more than I could've asked for.

And I didn't need psychic powers to see that my future was bright.

ACKNOWLEDGMENTS

While I was in the process of editing this novel, my beloved papaw passed away. He was ninety-one and was the only grandfather I ever knew. So I am compelled to tell this story about him.

There was a point in time when I was estranged from both my parents, so when I would travel to Virginia, I would stay with my mamaw and papaw. As a kid, visiting their house was a fun event and not one we did often, as they lived about an hour away. The times I did visit were usually special occasions, like the holidays, so the house would be filled with aunts, uncles, cousins, in-laws, and so on and so forth. (Mamaw had seven children, so you can imagine the number of cousins I have.) The house had a set of creaky, carpeted stairs that my cousins and I would slide down. It also sat next to the local funeral home (small town!), so we weren't allowed to play outside if there was a funeral. The house was originally purchased by my great-grandparents (my great-grandfather passed away in the den—he was known to everyone as Granddaddy) and Mamaw inherited it. It had been renovated a few times over the years, and so it was fairly large.

Anyway, it was a treat that when I was an adult, I could stay in one of the bedrooms upstairs and have both Mamaw and Papaw all to myself. I didn't have to share them with anyone else. But it also made staying there a little strange, since it was only three of us in their big house.

And I'll never forget one morning when I came down the stairs and went to the kitchen. Papaw was already up and had made coffee and offered me a cup. I sat across from him at the kitchen table while choking down his jet fuel. Papaw was always a little gruff, rough around the edges, and very down-to-earth. He was blunt, but he was kind.

As we sat there, he said to me, "Darling, I'm not mad. But I know you left this house last night."

I was taken aback because I *hadn't* left the house and I told him as much.

He didn't believe me. "You're an adult. It's okay if you did. Just make sure you lock the door behind you."

I was stunned. "Honestly," I said. "I didn't leave. I was upstairs the whole time."

"I heard the front door open and shut." Which he would hear, as his bedroom was on the first floor.

I knew I hadn't left. My mind rapidly ran through scenarios. Did one of my uncles, aunts, or cousins come and go during the night? Or worse, did someone *else* enter and leave? Was there someone in the house right then?

"Papaw," I said with all seriousness, "I did not leave. I was dead asleep upstairs. It wasn't me."

"Huh," he said, with his brow furrowed. He looked me dead in the eye and said, "Must be the ghosts."

I was *floored*.

He nonchalantly got to his feet as if he hadn't completely rocked my view of him and "went to work," which at that point in his life was driving his truck around town at twenty-five miles per hour and spying on people's lawns and their gardens. (He loved gardening and landscaping.)

I sat at the table after he left and Mamaw came into the kitchen. She asked me if Papaw had gone out, and I said he had. Then I told her the story of him drilling me about leaving the house and then just dropping that it could've been the ghosts.

Mamaw laughed. Then she said, "Darling, the only ghost in this house is Granddaddy, and he just goes up the stairs every morning to shave. He won't bother you."

When I tell this story now, I laugh, but at the time, it was pretty creepy knowing that the creaks on the stairs could've been my great-grandfather going about his daily routine. After that point, every morning when I went down the stairs, I said good morning to Grandaddy, just in case.

This interaction with Papaw in that house that I love spurred me to write a story about a girl who inherits a family home and also a ghost. (This was before the TV shows *Ghosts* UK or US.) The novel was not sold and is currently shelved, but when I was writing it, I spiraled and researched everything I could about ghosts and psychics and mediums. I watched videos of psychic readings. I read all about psychics who could see the future, those who could see the past or present, those who could talk to ghosts, those who could hear others' thoughts, and so on and so forth.

When it came time to brainstorm this novel, I used a lot of the information I'd already gathered to develop the characters of Cam, Kaci, Alma, and Edith.

I want to thank Papaw for talking to me over coffee at his kitchen table one random morning and blaming the ghosts for opening the front door in the night. And I want to thank Mamaw for assuring me that it was only Granddaddy. I want to thank them both for their love and kindness. Even when I was on the outs with other members of my family, I always knew I had a place to go if I needed to and an upstairs bed.

And now, on to the rest of the acknowledgments.

Thank you to my agent, Eva Scalzo, who has put up with me for five years already. I can't quite believe it and I bet neither can she. Also, thanks to Eva for the authenticity read.

Thank you to the team at McElderry Books. Kate Prosswimmer

is a brilliant editor, and I'm so lucky to work with her. Also, thanks to Alex Kelleher, Thad Whittier, Andrenae Jones, and Nicole Tai. A million thank-yous to Sam Schechter for the beautiful cover art and to Rebecca Syracuse for the cover design.

Special thank you to my author friends DL Wainright and October Santerelli for being sounding boards and for offering encouragement and support during the creative process. Also, many thanks to my BFF Kristinn and my bestie Amy Y for their continued friendship and for being there for me this past year. Thank you to my internet family and pocket friends, who have been there for me as I work through both creative challenges and life ones as well. My internet family always comes through, and I can't thank them enough for sticking with me this past decade. And thank you to my tremendous colleagues—Beth Revis, Julian Winters, and Kamilah Cole.

And thank you to my "real life" family, especially my spouse, Keith; my brother, Rob; and my sister-in-law, Chris.

I'd like to thank some wonderful independent bookstores who have been so great and helpful throughout my career, especially Malaprop's bookstore in Asheville, Editions bookstore in Charlotte, and Fable Hollow bookshop in Knoxville.

Lastly, I'd like to thank everyone who reads this book, whether you purchased it or borrowed it from a library. Thank you for allowing me to entertain you for a few hours. I'm very appreciative of your time. I hope you enjoyed reading this story as much as I enjoyed writing it. Until next time, I hope you stay safe and happy.

Thank you,

—F.T.